W9-ABJ-993

blood father

Also by Peter Craig

Hot Plastic
The Martini Shot

blood father

Peter Craig

Jefferson-Madison
Regional Library
Charlottesville, Virginia

HYPERION new york

30231 7894

L

LYDIA, THE TATTOOED LADY, By: Harold Arlen and E. Y. Harburg © 1939
(Renewed) EMI Feist Catalog Inc.
All Rights Reserved   Used by permission
WARNER BROS. PUBLICATIONS, U.S. Inc., Miami, FL 33014

Copyright © 2005 Peter Craig

All rights reserved. No part of this book may be used or reproduced in any
manner whatsoever without the written permission of the Publisher. Printed
in the United States of America. For information address Hyperion, 77 West
66th Street, New York, New York 10023-6298.

Library of Congress Cataloging-in-Publication Data

Craig, Peter
   Blood father: a novel / by Peter Craig.—1st ed.
      p. cm.
   ISBN 1-4013-0045-6
   1. Fathers and daughters—Fiction. 2. Young women—Fiction. 3. California—
Fiction. I. Title.

PS3553.R229B57 2005
813'.54—dc22   2004047381

Hyperion books are available for special promotions and premiums. For details
contact Michael Rentas, Manager, Inventory and Premium Sales, Hyperion, 77
West 66th Street, 11th floor, New York, New York 10023, or call 212-456-0133.

FIRST EDITION

10 9 8 7 6 5 4 3 2 1

For My Father and Daughters

acknowledgments

For their help, the author wishes to thank: Peternelle van Arsdale, Robert Benton, the staff at Calipatria State Prison, Catherine Crawford, Jennifer Defrancisco, Leonard in Slab City, Doug Stevenson, and Nat Sobel.

blood father

Investigation Report (#CS 1617117)

Supplement

Reporting Officer: ~~Detective Malcomb~~

Saturday, December 9, 2000

Shortly after hearing a late local news report on the homicides in Topanga Canyon, Charlotte Villalobos, of Canoga Park, CA, called the West Valley Division to inform detectives of a potentially related event.

On Saturday, December 9, Mrs. Villalobos had been working the day shift as a cashier in a Wal-Mart franchise located at 11334 Sherman Way Boulevard. At approximately 3:30 PM, a teenage girl purchased a dozen packages of White Box 9mm Range Ammunition, along with duct tape, rope, and bubble gum.

Mrs. Villalobos states that the girl was shivering, scratching her neck repeatedly, and appeared to be high on narcotics. She was denied cigarettes when she refused to produce identification. When another shopper commented on her purchase, the girl replied that her boyfriend was teaching her to use a firearm.

Approximately 5'10" to 6'0", the girl wore a black T-shirt with a scarf, low-riding jeans, and flip-flop sandals. She is described as having light-colored blue eyes "like a husky," and long black hair.

After paying in cash, the girl stopped beside a young child sitting in a mechanical flying saucer. She gave the boy her remaining change, then inserted a quarter, setting the device in motion.

Subsequent to the call, shell casings recovered at the site on Old Topanga Road have been identified by forensics to be White Box range ammunition.

From A.R.T, Calipatria, 4/10/01.

Lydia Jane

part one

W aiting at the curb with two loaded shopping bags as her ride approached down Sherman Way, Lydia imagined herself in the shotgun seat of each passing car. Disappearing was so easy. Open a door, plead to a stranger.

She might drop down into a whole new life with some unsuspecting commuter, fall in love on her way out of trouble, lose herself in a whirl-wind of gratitude; tell him stories at night, whisper about the miracle of their sudden meeting; then she'd fold his laundry, have his babies, grow old in a weather-controlled rambler out in a bright and treeless subdivi-sion: Anything was destiny if you worked it long enough.

Maybe she'd just turn up dead in a drifter's suitcase, left in a bus sta-tion locker or a rest stop men's room. Every stranger was his own life-and-death riddle.

"Lydia, oh, Lydia," she sang softly. "Have you seen Lydia?" She was drifting down deeper into that trancelike state, seeing messages on benches and storefront signs, intended only for her: *Injured at home or work?* Another bench showed two blurry pictures of runaways, smiling despite their miserable eyes. The bus carried a placard for an upcoming premiere: *He has the power to hear what women think.* . . . All of it together, jumbled along with windshields flaring brief flashes of sunlight, patterns in the traffic, pedestrians in a suspicious swarm, moving as if choreographed, watching her—it was nearly coming together into a mystical language, a prophecy that she couldn't quite decipher.

No, no, she whispered. Coincidence is just God's sense of humor.

It was the sleep dep, she told herself, the sleep deprivation; keep your eyes open long enough and you'll even see visions in a Wal-Mart parking lot. She couldn't remember the last time she'd slept. The days behind her were as cluttered as this boulevard spanning back through light and shade.

She glanced away and read the smudging ink on her palms, an amnesiac's grocery list—*9 mm, duck tape, twine, s.rounds, Winchester, die!!!*—and it seemed now a message from another lifetime. She understood. Spent as she was, she still knew that she was carrying the evidence: Out of all these magazines, at least a few rounds would pass through skin and bone and wind up in a coroner's office or an investigation file. And one of these bullets, down somewhere in the boxes and bags, was meant for *her.* "Lydia the tattooed lady," she sang, laughing suddenly at the thought—she was carrying the receipt for her own execution.

The car pulled up.

Three men were pressed together with jostling elbows into the small backseat, while in the front her boyfriend, Jonah, patted his lap. She sat down onto his legs while he was midstream in an argument: ". . . and when was the last time I broke a promise to either of you?" He tossed back a few boxes, and the car filled with the sound of loading magazines.

By the shady window, the sweaty white kid complained that he was carsick and might throw up. Jonah told him to be professional. This group hadn't put in much work together, and Lydia worried that if he puked on someone, he might set off a gunfight at close range.

Two of the men, Iván Vasquez and Patricio "Choop" Miramontez, had been jumped into a West Side clique long before they were shaving and now earned mercenary cash as bodyguards. Iván was still as lithe and rubbery as a boy, with his shirt off and "El Salvador" tattooed in block letters across his hairless chest. He had a freckling of pink scars across his arms and collarbone where he'd once been sprayed with buck-shot through a security door. Choop, his counterpart, drove the car—a short, broad-faced, broad-shouldered Chicano who rarely made a sound. He had Aztec symbols on his forearms, the pachuco cross, and the word "Kanpol" on the back of his fist, now gripping the wheel.

Neither of these men had much love for the two Valley dealers who tore open the boxes and parceled out magazines. One was Chase Sullivan, a disheveled kid with a goatee and oily hair in his face. In an oversized hockey jersey and shorts that hung to the bright snarl of tattoos on his calves, he seemed less like a gang member than the head of a gangster's fan club. The other was Cully, the carsick dealer from Canoga Park, a short-breathed, heavyset man who still managed to wear oversized pants. With his shaved head and eggshell complexion, he looked like a gargantuan baby. He whined that his gun didn't take these "cheap-ass nines."

"Cully, I thought you had a nine millimeter," said Jonah.

"Nah, I said it a hundred times already. It's a Ruger P89 and it's got an interchangeable barrel. But I lost the other one."

Iván sighed and shook his head.

"So I need thirty-Luger ammo."

"You ain't going to find Luger ammo at a motherfucking Wal-Mart," said Chase.

"Then I'm useless. I got two rounds."

Shifting his weight beneath Lydia, Jonah dropped the mags from two gray handguns, then handed each back for Iván to reload. Cully was still fretting that the ammo was garbage, some of it looked scratched; and he argued with the others about whether or not brass could rust. When Jonah took back one loaded gun, he hugged his arms around Lydia and placed it into her hands, breathing beside her ear.

She whispered, "I don't know what to do with that."

With his lips against her neck, he said, "There's no safety. You just pull the slide. Got to have your finger right on the trigger—square. Hit it. No more problems."

His breath tickled her ear, and his lowered voice reminded her of that soft-spoken quality that had once been so surprising and attractive. When she'd first met him, his green eyes always fled away, toward the floor; his smile was quick and bashful; he withheld so much energy in public, until suddenly, in a private and heated moment, he could explode with a torrent of words—an urgent, intense speech. But what Lydia now recognized was the terrible stillness he showed when he was making plans.

It amazed Lydia that in a car full of loud and rowdy thugs, Jonah should wind up seeming the most dangerous. He wasn't tough or street-wise like his bodyguards. He came from a rarified, wealthy family, raised on both sides of the border, a mix of old-money Mexican and new-money Anglo. There was something about him like a lost and rumpled prince, wearing his nice clothes badly, a silk shirt untucked and sweat-stained. He paid for this support in the car; but they were loyal, Lydia knew, mostly because of this specific quality—the sense that he could, at any moment, do something far outside what anyone had considered. A ghoulish problem solver, he was meditating now; she could feel his heartbeat against her back.

Cully said, "We got a whole trunk full of rifles and shotguns, and she only gets this fucking range ammo. Your bitch fucked up, Jonah. I'm not even going to fire up there."

"Hey," said Lydia, pushing her tongue through her gum and snapping it.

"So don't fire," Jonah said.

"Hey, *excuse* me," Lydia continued.

"Then I'm just going to conserve my ammo, dog. It's like fifty cents a bullet anyway."

Iván said, "Fifty cents a round, you better be in *love*."

"Excuse me!" Lydia yelled over the chatter.

Cully glanced over at her, frowning. A loose bullet dropped onto the floor.

"Listen," said Lydia, pausing as she blew a small bubble and popped it. "You don't know me very well, so this is just, like, I'm telling you my boundaries. Okay? Please don't call me a bitch."

Cully's mouth hung open. Iván and Chase hunched down and squirmed, like pigs at a trough, trying to find the loose round on the floor.

Cully finally replied, "Who are you all of a sudden?"

"I'm asking you politely."

"What is this star attitude now? Just get the right fucking bullets next time."

While Iván and Chase were combing the floor, Lydia and Cully faced each other across the car. She raised her voice over the din to say, "If I made a mistake, tell me in a businesslike way, all right. Without calling me a bitch."

"Bitch, bitch, bitch," he said, making a puppet with his hand.

"Fine," said Lydia. She turned and crossed her arms over her chest, staring out the window for the rest of the ride, still flinching and whispering her side of the argument.

They drove deep into the canyon, coiling upward beneath mountains of scrub and yellow grass, to the end of Old Topanga, where the house sat in a dark recess beneath a cluster of crooked oaks. With brittle and discolored shingles, blankets nailed over the windows, it was the eyesore in the depths of a hippie enclave. The yard was piled with old doors and fence planks, and a narrow garage seemed built from years of accumulated trash.

As Jonah slid out from under her, he told Lydia to go around the back of the house and make sure that no one tried to slip out. He joined the line of men, swaggering across the street, while Lydia stayed in the car with the gun on the seat beside her. Once the five men reached the ragged front yard, they noticed that Lydia was still waiting. Jonah slapped his hands onto his pants and stormed back.

"What?"

"I'm not going."

"*Lydia*. Somebody's going to see you here."

"Fuck this. I'm not going in there with somebody like that."

"Who?"

"That fucking chemo-case over there. I'm not doing shit unless he apologizes."

"Are you serious?"

"Yes, Jonah. He called me a bitch like ten times. To my face. I don't have to take that kind of shit from people. He can get his own fucking bullets."

Jonah sighed, then stomped back and negotiated for a few minutes with Cully, who went limp, as if a puppeteer had suddenly dropped his strings. Then Jonah dragged him across the street, holding his elbow, and told him, "Just say it and let's go."

Cully rested his gun on the closed canvas roof and leaned through the driver's door into the deeper shade. "I'm sorry I called you a stupid skank *bitch*."

"What am I supposed to do with that?" said Lydia, covering her face.

"Listen," said Jonah. "You two work this out—now. Or I'm going to shoot you both and throw you into a ditch together."

Cully's mouth twisted side to side, until finally he murmured, "Sorry . . . bitch."

"What are you, *four*?" said Lydia.

Jonah shoved Cully away, then leaned into the car. He spoke in his lowered but heated voice. "*Lydia*, he's just here to do a job. Okay? Are you going to throw a temper tantrum for every idiot in the world?"

She folded her arms over her chest, stared out at the empty neighborhood, and said, "I don't see why I should help if nobody fucking respects me. What am I even going to do in there anyway?"

With his face stern, he said, "Lydia, get out of the car. Now. I'm not going to discuss this with you right now. Pick up the gun and do what I tell you, or we're all going to be in worse trouble here."

Listlessly, she put on her leather backpack, picked up her gun, and moved to the side of the house, past trash cans swarming with flies, where Jonah hissed at her and told her to guard the back door, mumbling other directions that she couldn't follow.

There was a hornets' nest under one of the shingles and a confused cricket somewhere in the shadows, and she was distracted by the way the sleek, bluish drones squeezed in and out of the narrow space. She hovered by the trash cans, taking a lipstick case from her back pocket and scooping up powder with her pinky fingernail. After a bump of speed in each nostril, rubbing them as they burned, she crept past an open gate into a narrow backyard.

Five boys were wrestled together on a downhill plot of dirt rimmed with weeds and ivy. She was suddenly terrified to be holding a gun. The boys moved chaotically; there seemed to be only one rule to their game: Whoever picked up the chewed Nerf football had to remain on his feet as long as possible, while the others grabbed, scratched, shoved, tripped, kicked, and finally piled on top of him. They hollered and cursed and drove each other into the ground in a fray of ripped cargo pants and bloody knees. One boy, probably ten years old, lay on his back, exaggerating the pain of a wounded hand, dying in simulated slow motion, until he noticed Lydia and sat up, clearing the dirty locks from his eyes.

Lydia blew a bubble and peeled it off her lips. In the churning dust, one by one the other boys stopped playing.

Slowly Lydia moved into the yard with the gun lowered, speaking in a tone for small children: "Okay, hi, kids—I promise everything is going to be fine. There's some grown-up business going on in the house and everybody is going to be just fine. Everybody's going to keep having fun out here."

Her voice shook, and she worried that she would startle the children. Instead, they reacted as if she were an ineffectual babysitter, fanning out around her, shouting questions and asking to see her "gatt." One boy, while pinching blood from a gash in his elbow, said, "Dang, that gun is *tight*. Where'd you get that?"

"No, no, no. Everybody just be real chill, okay. Sit down. I want everybody to sit here in a *circle*—okay? This is a real gun and it's really dangerous."

The boy with the bleeding elbow continued moving toward her, and another two dashed over to peek through the sliding glass door.

"Wait! *No*. What did I just say? You two—away from the door. I told you to sit down. I'm serious."

A tiny, freckled boy cocked his fingers and made firing noises that blew spit around his lips, and another said, "My mom's boyfriend has four guns. I could go get one right now and kill everybody here."

"I'm not kidding," said Lydia. "This isn't make-believe. I'm seriously sketched out and everybody better sit down. Let's go. On the ground."

"I could get his Smith and Wesson and shoot through a plate of steel."

"You're such a loser, Joey. Your mom wouldn't let you—"

"Like you know, *fag*."

"You're the fag."

"Please, let me see it! *Please*. Please! I just want to hold it, I won't shoot it."

Two of the boys rushed at her, trying to grab the gun, and Lydia backed away, gasping, holding it into the air as they jostled against her. She raised her voice sharply and said, "*No*. Stop it. Don't *test* me. All of you go sit over there in a circle. I'm going to count to three and if you're not all sitting—"

"Then what?"

"—then I'm going to pistol-whip you, you little *brat*. Now—a circle, right here. *One*."

The freckled boy shot more imaginary rounds with his finger, then dove onto the ground and rolled like a commando, rising back up and pelting her with a guttural barrage of make-believe grenades. Lydia grabbed him by the shirt and pushed him down. "Good, you sit there— now the rest of you, right here. Take your fucking meds and sit right here. We're going to get in a circle on the ground, just like we're all back in re- form school. Let's go—we're going to go around the group and talk about our feelings."

"My mom's boyfriend lets me shoot his guns all the time. I killed a coyote."

"Well, that's terrible, kid. Hideous. No one should kill anything. Now—*Simon says* sit down. *Two*. I'm counting now. This is the real thing. If I get to three, I'm not responsible for anything I do."

"Just shoot something!" A towheaded boy with a crew cut leapt up and down with frustration. "Shoot anything!"

Three boys now sat Indian-legged in the diminishing dirt clouds, chattering over each other: "Kill Teddy's dad."—"A-ha-ha-ha-ha."—"Teddy, your dad is a *criminal.*" "At least I have a dad, homo." "Shoot that tree. You're not going to get in trouble for shooting a tree!"

Lydia grabbed the towhead and yanked him across the yard, making him sit with the others. Finally the fifth boy drifted over and joined the circle. "There! Motherfucking nap time!" she shouted with her teeth bared. The stress was in her shoulders and fingertips and there was a jolting motion in her chest. She started to cough violently; the kids waited patiently, suddenly intimidated by the hint of illness. "Everybody put your heads down. Maybe you don't take *me* seriously, but don't make these guys mad."

The freckled boy raised his hand, his body twisted down in the dirt.

"What?" Lydia asked.

"Are we hostages?"

"*No,* you're not hostages. I'm just guarding the door—you're just— we're just all going to sit here and stay out of the way."

"You should definitely kill Teddy's dad. He's a dick."

From inside the house, beyond a dim sliding glass door, Lydia could hear scooting furniture, shouting, and splintering wood. The freckled boy blurted out, "Have you ever shot anybody?"

"No," she said, looking back over her shoulder. Her palms were damp with sweat, and she wiped them on her shirt.

Past a patio of loose bricks, through the glass door covered with reflected trees, she could see movement as if in shallow water. She turned back to the boys all lounging in the dirt. She said, "It's just money. It's always money—it's my boyfriend's business."

"*I'm* your boyfriend," said the one with the gouged elbow. They all laughed as he grabbed the crotch of his loose pants.

Just then, a shot fired, louder than a cherry bomb, and all the boys leapt to their feet. There followed the sound of kicked bottles, breaking glass, a woman's muzzled scream.

When a shot burst through the glass door, the boys dashed for cover, sliding downhill and behind the trees in what seemed to be a planned evacuation route for any broken window.

Lydia headed toward the door. She could see into the dim living room beyond the punctured glass, where a woman was sobbing, a noise so strained that she sounded like a suffering mule. Coming through mounted speakers, a CD was playing an interminable guitar solo with an occasional hailstorm of bongo drums, and it took Lydia a moment to realize that the other, more erratic percussion of banging was coming from the kitchen, where Jonah's men were dumping out drawers and tearing through the floorboards.

On the sharp crust around the glass door there hung syrupy droplets of blood, which expanded into a sprayed trail along the walls, across the floor, and into a saturated arm of the couch. The woman sat just below this bloodstain, with her hands duct-taped together, braying in pain with a strip across her mouth. Lydia slid the door open, dropping more chips of glass, and, once inside, she saw the woman's mangled bare foot: the two smallest toes blown off, and blood welling up and leaking down to the floor. The room smelled like burning skin and hair. Up three steps to a short hallway, a shirtless man lay facedown, his twisted arm blocking the kitchen door. Blood pooled beneath his forehead and spread in the grout between the Spanish tiles.

Lydia was numb.

She wanted to say the woman's name, but she couldn't remember it. Probably in her mid-thirties, the woman already had eroded cheeks and witchlike features from years of glass pipes and needles. She wore only an oversized T-shirt stretching over her lap. Over the patch of duct tape, her eyes were sick and raw, and her nose was straining for air.

Stepping casually over the body between the kitchen and hallway, Jonah appeared with his gun at his side. He had a wet paper towel and was trying to rub a stain off his pants. Quietly he said, "Okay, you're here. Take the tape off her mouth. She needs to remember where this shit is or she's going to lose another little piggy."

Lydia's hands were trembling so badly that she couldn't grab the edge of the tape, so Jonah tore it loose, leaving a streak across the woman's mouth.

"Don't start getting paranoid again," he said to Lydia. "Focus."

Lydia nodded and said, "I swallowed my gum."

The woman shouted, "Teddy! Run! Run away, baby! Get out of here!"

"I didn't know we were doing this at a fucking day care center," said Jonah.

Smashing through shelves in the bathroom, Cully was hollering that he couldn't find anything. Jonah snapped his fingers in front of Lydia's eyes and whispered, "Come on, come on. Wake up. I need you to hold her foot against the couch right there. Hold it still."

"Jonah, I can't," said Lydia, hovering in the center of the room. She barely opened her mouth when she spoke. It seemed as if she were watching the scene unfold from a distance, only half involved; every movement had a slow, underwater quality; even her own voice seemed to come from somewhere else in the room, a few steps behind her, as if a ventriloquist were speaking for her.

The woman leaned back against the couch and said in a bleating, hoarse voice that she didn't know where anything was hidden.

Lydia whispered, "She's trapped. She's just lost."

"Lydia, listen to me here: This is a worthless human being. Deals to twelve-year-old kids. She could've saved her old man over there, trust me. Don't get caught up in the drama here—this woman knows what she's doing. She's got a sick calculator in her head, and she knows exactly how much every finger and toe is worth—right? And it's not going to add up to the cash she's hiding."

He pushed the woman's head down against the sofa cushions, and she stared ahead with bulging eyes. "Stay there," he said. Then he reached over and took Lydia's hand, gently raising her gun and guiding it. "Shhh. Just relax. You're going to learn this."

Lydia stayed rigid as he maneuvered the gun toward the woman's temple. He straightened her arms and locked her elbow, as calmly as if guiding her through a tennis swing, saying, "Now it's a light gun, so it's going to kick. Don't look at me, look at her. She lied to you. Show me you can do this, Lydia. This will change you, baby—this will make everything work again."

Lydia's hands were frothing sweat over the trigger as she closed her eyes. Soon Jonah grew tired of waiting, and he stepped back and angled his head and spoke to her with his lips tensed. "Lydia, you're still *here* today, with this choice—because of me. Because I love you, and I stood up for you. This is our chance, right now. If we stand together on this, all of us—then you need to be a part of it, so there's never any doubt. You're a murderer just for *being* here—you know that, don't you?"

The woman was watching Lydia with wide, yellowish eyes.

"Lydia, you'll never understand my life without this. But I need you, and you didn't *let* me lie to you. From the day I met you, you wanted to know *everything*. Well, here it is. For you. Everything. You'll never be the same kid again. And you cross that line, baby, and I'll be right here on the other side, waiting for you."

The song on the CD player changed and Lydia recognized a drawling '60s ballad. She began to laugh and cry simultaneously, overwhelmed by the absurd and maudlin song.

Jonah stroked Lydia around her cheeks and forehead, clearing the hair from her eyes, then he pressed his own pistol against Lydia's face while massaging her back and shoulders like a coach.

"Jonah?" she called, as if in the dark, refusing to look at him as he brushed hair off her ear with the muzzle.

"It's a marriage, kid," he said as he pulled back the slide on his gun, still held against Lydia's cheek. "I'm down on one knee."

From the kitchen, Iván shouted that he had found the stash, and there were cheers and hollers, and Lydia laughed nervously and looked over at Jonah. "They found it."

"Yes or no?" said Jonah. He pushed his gun harder against her skin, smudging her face. The woman was closing her eyes now, breathing in tremors, lying just below Lydia's outstretched arms. "Right here, right now—in this room. The rest of your life."

Lydia turned and faced him, smiling like a madwoman, breaking into harder tears that warped her face. She said, "Okay, baby, okay. I will. I *will*."

Jonah lowered his gun and tilted his head, an expression she'd never once seen from him, softened and affectionate.

Then Lydia raised her pistol in a fluid motion and shot him— through the base of the neck below his gaping mouth. Blood streaked as far back as the kitchen door. The shot deafened her, and Jonah dropped down to his knees, stunned, staring up for a moment with a viscous chunk torn out from his throat, his eyelashes netted with blood and a flood over his collar and down his shirt. He blinked several times, mechanically, before sagging against the steps.

By the time Lydia had fled past the shattered door, nearly tripping on the loose bricks, she knew that the others had found him; and, though it didn't seem real to her in the muted sounds and altered time, she heard them firing. The toe band broke on her sandal. She kicked off the other and leapt barefoot into the ivy, clambering downhill and falling the last few feet into the undergrowth around the creek.

She splashed through shallow, scummy water, stirring up gnats and cutting her feet as she scampered over the broken glass along homeless encampments. The canyon snaked downhill; the creek was a thin groove of moss and silt, and she couldn't tell which way to go once inside the enclosure of saplings and interlaced shrubs. Sirens came from both directions, and a helicopter crossed the narrow channel of lit sky. She crawled past bottles, crushed reeds, and the exposed roots of oaks, until she heard the hammer click back on a revolver.

She had come to an arrangement of stones in a clearing, each covered with years of tangled graffiti. Several of the boys sat around the rocks. When they saw her, they stood upright and puffed their chests like roosters. One boy waited in a dark shadow, holding the gun sideways. "Now who's my *bitch*?" he said.

The other children were pale and hushed.

Lydia said, "You were right about the guns. *Please,* help me. I'm just a kid, too, and they're going to kill me. Pretend it's a game, get me out of here—show me your hideouts. I'll never tell. I swear to God."

The boy's posture relaxed, and Lydia rose, dusting her pants. As they began traipsing through the undergrowth, away from the sounds above, Lydia added, "And *sweetie,* one more thing, don't call me a *bitch.*"

W hen John Link announced for the umpteenth time that he was only here because of his parole requirements, the room filled with a mixture of groans and laughter. At any of the two, sometimes three meetings he attended daily across the Coachella Valley, he would repeat this like the signature line of a deadpan comic. He didn't smile. In fact, ever since the regulars had started to enjoy his grumpy tirades, Link began focusing on the new-comers, who still found him intimidating. He threatened to break their fingers and toes. He claimed that if he had known any of these twelve-step sissies in his prime, he would have run them down like rattlesnakes on the highway.

He sat in the back of a small, smoky living room on a foldout picnic chair, which seemed too rickety for the weight of his beer belly and enor-mous frame; and, playing up his boxer's flattened nose and his thick arms sleeved with tattoos, he bragged that he had never lifted a barbell in his life but had bulked up on a regimen of hurling yuppies through plate-glass windows.

Yet the more he startled the younger kids, the more obliged he was to give them guidance, since, even among the failed marriages, car wrecks, and damaged livers, he still considered himself the lone ambassador from *rock bottom*. His newfound purpose was to represent the furthest limit of what a body could endure. He tried to dole out pithy advice, but his wiser thoughts never turned easily to words, and he could tell when the more educated types became bored by his downshift into platitudes. He wouldn't wish his life on anyone. Let him be an example.

So he told another story, this time about wrecking his chopper at ninety-plus on the PCH and spilling two pounds of crank across rush-hour traffic. "And it was a windy day," he said. "People were rolling up their windows, putting on their windshield wipers, nobody knew what to do. Of course, I heard this later. I was unconscious at the time. Dead for a few minutes—I think."

He once burned down a room at the Disneyland Hotel; he survived an exploding meth lab only by staggering outside to piss. While jousting with pool-cleaning brushes, he broke his tailbone when he was lanced off his chopper. In fact, in his fifty-one years, Link had been stabbed, clubbed, shot, burned, and dragged a half mile down a county road. "And I been sober now for six years, seven months, and twenty-two miserable days. If I can do it—any of you punks can."

Link didn't appreciate the way the new DUI was smirking at him. Just because his beard was almost completely gray didn't mean he was now some quaint grandfather acting like the bogeyman; so he took off his T-shirt for proof, flexing and showing the pink chisel work of scars around faded prison ink, until Kirby, who was Link's sponsor and today's chair, stopped him midway through the rant.

Link allowed him to diffuse the tension. Only Kirby had Link's total respect. Only Kirby had visited Link's tattoo shop, a trailer in the desert, equipped with autoclaves and sonic cleaners, where a single wall served as a scrapbook for his life. Kirby knew how hard Link fought to stay

afloat, making his sketches and stencils, working on just a few regular
clients, drinking his ritualistic Dr Pepper on the front step at sundown as
he watched downshifting rigs and listened to a CB radio. His parole stip-
ulated that he could not ride—so a man who once flew through traffic on
a rebuilt '56 Harley 74 with a suicide shift, power-jumped with hot-
cams, now puttered down main street in a Chevy Nova. He could not
"fraternize" with any of his old buddies or one-percenters, so he lived in
exile among the last-chance services off the highway where it dropped
downhill toward speckled desert. In this clutter of trailers, scrap tin, and
corrugated titanium awnings, Link had soldered his life back together
with God and cigarettes.

But, most of all, Kirby knew about his daughter, the one story Link
would never tell at a meeting.

Once Link had encouraged the smug DUI "to keep coming back,"
Kirby followed him to his car. Link appreciated the old guy's efforts to be
helpful, even when he sometimes looked so damned pious, as if heaven
would owe him his own cloud. Kirby asked Link if he wanted to have a
cup of coffee someplace.

Link said, "I got a lady coming at two. Lives just down the road."

"Decent work?"

"Nah, she just wants a snake crawling out of her sock," he said, raising his steel-toed boot and slapping the ankle. "First installment. Biblical
thing, you know. Then she's talking about Adam and Eve and that whole
situation."

"But the serpent first," said Kirby.

"Yeah, well—probably saving up for paradise."

Three hours later, Link had been overcome by ambition, and his
subject had allowed him to extend the scope of his project. Working in
his trailer, shading the last scales in the serpent's body where it twisted
around the knee, Link had modeled the tattoo on Leonardo da Vinci's
The Fall, mostly because he loved raiding pictures from old art books.
Maybe in order to escape his dreary feeling after the noon meeting, he
had settled nicely into a groove and did some of the best sweep shading
he'd done in months. Onto her shin he feathered lighter, water-diluted

green between the scales; and, around her calf, he made the snake pass through a simulated shadow.

The woman was a talker, though, and her chatter kept drawing him out of his trance. Lounging back on the lifter bench, a cigarette between her lobster-colored fingernails, she grimaced and confessed about cheating on her husband. Why did people always expect Link to have some ready-made advice for bad situations? Something about the low-grade pain and the long penitent hours—it made too many clients treat him like a therapist or a priest.

He grunted whenever she paused.

He knew he would remember the snake on her leg forever, but probably not a single detail from the woman's depressing life. His memory was a tangle of isolated arms and torsos. Skin and pigments and blemishes. After all the time he'd spent doing blue tats in the joint, first with the Polynesian method of dots from a straight pin, then with a homemade gun (slot-car motor, hollowed-out pen, ink tubes, guitar strings, and a nine-volt battery), the years were a blur of cobwebs, clocks without hands, shamrocks, pentagrams, crying women, and granite walls. He kept his tools clean, he worked on any gang sign or religious conversion—on everything from numbers around an eye socket to crucifixes on the neck. Soon he was collaborating with the subjects, making stencils off the library's single art book, broken at the spine. He carved a Chagall into a Ukrainian car thief, and he still recalled how the veins stood up on his pale arms like on the underside of a leaf, though he couldn't picture a thing about the kid's face.

Of all his projects, it was fitting that the only convict he knew and remembered well was the one whose tat he had never finished. Arturo Rios Tehada—temporary cell mate, shot caller in La Eme—had wanted, beneath the usual snake-eating eagle, a landscape of his "varrio" across his broad back, done epic-style like a Hieronymus Bosch, sinners and saints, demons and angels, vying for space on a hill of tombstones and shanties, rising toward a halo of hazy California sunshine. Rios was a good canvas, a wide stretch of parchment-colored skin, and he was usually silent under the scratching in the institutional hush of maximum-security lockdowns.

During a season of overcrowding, both Rios and Link knew the prison administration had dropped them together like pit bulls. Only one was meant to come out alive. But they were united, at least somewhat, in their common hatred of the COs, and they tolerated each other over the months of work. Link even carved the "in memoriam" to his son; and, likewise, Rios watched and sometimes helped Link write inquiring letters to Missing Persons departments and runaway bulletins, regarding his daughter. They would argue about politics and history—Rios was another prison autodidact, always showing off. But they treated each other with the stoicism of castaways on a deserted island.

Now, since he had been on the outside for over two years, Link missed the ornate work on that one tattoo. He had made the rare leap from scratcher to artist, with his sonic cleaners, his top-of-the-line tattoo machines, which he'd bought after six months of hammering nails. But he had a hard time finding any adventurous clients. When he hustled work around the Coachella amphitheater or the Burning Man festival, he did marijuana leaves and pornographic cartoons. Mickey Mouse took Minnie from behind. Tweety Bird held up his middle finger. There was always some vehement rave party idiot waving a handful of cash, some kid wearing stupid glasses and a tight T-shirt, fucked up on ecstasy or hard lemonade. Link would shrug, take his money, and figure that he was laying down a colorful scar from a fleeting and moronic youth. After all, a tattoo might be the only thing in a punk's life that stayed with him forever.

When he finished the serpent, he waited quietly while the woman regarded it from all angles in a mirror. He took a Polaroid and taped it to his wall. While he wrapped her leg in gauze, giving her the instructions—keep it dry, don't get sunburned—he saw the same flush come into her cheeks that he'd watched develop on her bare legs. He realized that she was embarrassed, maybe wanting some response after her long speech. She wasn't a bad-looking old broad, despite the craggy features of a hard-drinking life; maybe, in his youth, he might have ducked forward and kissed her as suddenly as if bobbing for apples. But now he just wanted to be alone with his instant soup and his Dr Pepper. So he looked away and said, "Good luck with, you know, that shit you were talking about."

Twenty minutes later he was listening to a game of Trivial Pursuit on the CB, coming from the trailers down along the Salton Sea. Some jackass thought it was funny to keep yelling "Sasquatch" to every question, until Link keyed in and told him he'd find him and crush his skull. Then he microwaved a cup of minestrone, perched on his front steps, and watched the sun set beyond the chalk-colored mountains.

At least a half hour from any other services, his neighborhood was just a small cluster of trailers in a plot of gravel and dust, strung together with laundry lines and surrounded by flags and anxious, decorative windmills. The dogs were barking at something in the distance, sounding desperate and trapped.

When his phone rang, he hoped that it was the woman, maybe asking him a question about the ink. He'd ask her to coffee—or whatever it was that grown, sober people were supposed to do. He shuffled into the dim trailer and found the phone.

"Missing Link Tattoos," he said.

"Dad?"

The silence lasted long enough for three cars to wash past. Then Link panicked and began tearing down letters and notes from his wall, assembling information across the table.

She said, "It's me. I'm alive. *Barely.*"

He told her to hold on as he searched for a pen. He thought that he needed to have all the supporting documents in front of him, until it occurred to him that this was his *actual* daughter, not some new lead or twist in an investigation. He stopped in the middle of the room, holding the cordless phone to his ear, hearing the ocean in it like a seashell. He could only think to say, "Holy shit, kid."

"I had a bad fucking day, Dad." Her voice trembled like she was running or jumping, and he heard the crash of waves in the background. "I would never bother you like this in a million years, I swear to God—but you're the only person. It's like I'm in one of those places—in *life,* I mean—one of those surreal moments when everything just starts going all fucking Armageddon on you. And it's like one minute, you're just a regular fuckup, you know, and then all of a sudden it's like: *Oh, no, no,* *no—you—*you're coming with me, bitch. You're going *down.* You know what I mean?"

"No."

She was rambling with hardly a pause or breath between words, her voice quivering, her jaw chattering around syllables, with sudden, shouted words barked louder than the rest.

"My point is—and this is so totally, unbelievably rude, okay, and I'm *sorry,* because normally I'd be all: Let's catch up, talk about old times— fucking *current events* and shit—but, Dad, *seriously,* I just don't have the time to put smiley faces and birthday candles all over this shit—so my point is, I need *cash.* Fuck, I'm so sorry about this!"

Link thought for a moment, but she started talking again before he could formulate his words.

"Not a lot. Just a little money so I can skip town—because I'm not even kidding, Dad: I am so dead. I'm like this little insignificant fly that's just about to splatter on a big windshield, you know, a big eighteen-wheeler. I figure I can get up to Portland by tomorrow."

"Oh, okay, Oregon."

"Look, so it rains a lot—*trust me*—that's like the least of my worries right now, okay? I'll live in a poncho. I mean, you know as well as I do, there's some shit that just, like, transcends weather."

He paced down his steps and onto the gravel outside, staring at the trace of the sunset, savoring the first pause in her ranting. Finally he asked, "How much you need?"

"Can I say something, Dad? Can I just say something? That's *first class,* right there, after all the history between us. *Thank you.* That's character— that's what I'm talking about. I figure I need two g's tops, if I'm going to get settled up there and start working—"

"What kind of job you lookin' for?"

"I don't know. Like some kind of nanny or something."

"Why don't I bring you the money?"

"Well, yeah—but I'm just not really at an address—"

"You can't walk into a Western Union if somebody's looking for you. That's the first place they go."

"Okay, okay. That's what I'm talking about: I need cash, I need an escape plan. I need somebody who knows these things."

"What you got to do, kiddo—you got to find someplace where you can be safe for about two and a half hours. Okay? And you tell me where."

"Serious? Don't just string me along, okay—because I'm a disaster right now."

"You just tell me where you're at."

There was a windy pause on the other end, followed by a choking, hysterical sound that he first thought was an outburst of tears. It turned out to be a laugh, yelping and strange, like the excited sound of coyotes when they got into his trash. She said, "God, you must think I'm such a horrible person. I don't even know how many years, and suddenly I call out of the blue for a handout. How pathetic is that?"

"Just settle down and tell me where to go."

"Do you ever just look at your *life* and go—fuck?"

"Hey, *kid,* listen to me. Listen real close. Tell me *something* you see, something around you. Anything."

She seemed bewildered by his stern tone, as if she had forgotten why she'd called, and, as he listened to the ocean, he worried that she'd passed out on the other end. Finally she sniffled and said, "There's a trash bin, and there's some kind of seafood restaurant. The Screaming Clam."

"Okay. Stay there. Sit someplace where nobody can see you."

He walked back up the steps and faced the far wall of his trailer, where there spanned ten years of correspondences with the girl, each letter with an altered slant in her handwriting, like ripples on a changing sea. Amid pictures, impulsive notes on the backs of homework assignments and torn out from spiral notebooks, one layer replacing the last, clear sentences stood out in the clutter:

To John Link, Prisoner #C-77909, Calipatria.

> *Dear Dad, I hate this class!!!!*
> *Mom is driving me crazy.*

On the line, she waited, and the phone was full of passing traffic, sirens, and collapsing waves, until she sighed and said, "I bet you gave up on me, huh? I bet you thought I fell off the map."

"You just stay safe until I get there. That's your only job right now."

When he hung up, he stood for a stunned moment, gazing at the collage of letters, reassembled to match the arrangement in his prison cell. He was face-to-face with the picture used on most of the flyers and Web sites, a school photo from the year she left home, at fourteen. She sat rigidly with a puffy collar and black wavy hair arranged neatly around her face. The picture was beautiful but awkward, and when he stared at it long enough he could see beyond the girl's basic prettiness and privilege to something desperate in her eyes.

Beside it, among the formal responses Link had received from the LAPD Missing Persons Unit, the National Center for Missing and Exploited Children, the National Runaway Switchboard, and so many other services, there hung an age-enhanced photograph, used also for the Web sites, newsletters, and fliers. Link could never figure out the reasoning behind this simulated picture: The forensic programming seemed to predict, from her bone structure and genes, that her face would lengthen like a horse's, that her hair would straighten, and that her nose would thicken at the bridge. Representing only three rapid years through whatever tumultuous adolescence, the photo was unreal and frightening—pretty, pristine, and idealized in a mechanical way—a computer's memory of a human face.

Stretching west along the wall, backward, hung the timeline of pictures and notes. He knew it so well by now that he could have thrown a dart with his eyes closed and hit any snapshot, form letter, or scribbled complaint in the girl's life; yet he felt now, with his chest tight and his stomach wavering, that not a single thing on this wall had prepared him. Soaring again into some dark and unimagined moment, he feared that he had researched and assembled the wrong girl.

So maybe this peaceful interlude in his life was over.

He took a deep breath, smiled, and patted his hand against the age-enhanced picture. "Okay, *kid*. I'm coming."

Link & Ursula
part two

three

n one of his most weatherworn pictures, John Link sits on a stripped down Harley 74 with his tiny daughter in his lap, sometime during the last unraveling hours of her sixth birthday. They don't look happy. Obscured by ribbons coming undone in her hair, Lydia is turning away from the camera like it's a spoonful of medicine, while, decked out in his black riding goggles and threadbare vest, arms scrawled with tattoos, Link appears ready to attack the pink balloon that's just been tied onto the clutch cable. In the background the other parents have gathered to watch, as if the chopper were a drugged swayback pony hired for the amusement of their shrieking children.

The photo session had been the fitting end to an awful afternoon. Link had gate-crashed the party, pulling up onto the lawn at Ursula's new home, the remodeled Valley ranch house of a new husband. Because of a Saint Patty's Day party a week earlier, Link's beard was streaked with green, and from a brawl he didn't remember, his knuckles were still scuffed. But rather than causing the unsettled reaction he had expected among the suburban parents—this degenerate biological father, a relic of Ursula's "checkered past"—he was instead treated like some fascinating countercultural entertainment, as harmless as a sidewalk Santa, as anachronistic as a Viking.

Lydia's mother, Ursula, was at first horrified by his arrival, the bike tearing up sod, then grumbling as he walked it between cars up the packed driveway. But after a few hours and a glass of wine, she began to enjoy parading around this skeleton from her past. She clearly noticed how the other women grew competitive, hauling out their own stories of depravity: One woman had been a groupie with an obscure rock band, and another had overdosed twice on Quaaludes. Every now and then a parent would shout across the yard at a boy throwing rocks, or rescue a bawling child from an overturned garbage can, but for the most part the kids were left alone—little boys flying like hot popcorn kernels off a distant trampoline, paramilitary gangs of muddy children in the trees, and tea-party clusters of girls around mewling, incontinent dolls—so that the parents could sit back on foldout chairs and reminisce about the crazy days, exchanging stories of bad acid trips and teargassed protests. Even Ursula's new husband, a man on the cusp of a well-tanned and simpering old age, whose shirt seemed to come more unbuttoned with each hour, was newly titillated by the implication that his trophy wife had once been a filthy biker moll. "Was she as bad as she makes out?" he asked under his breath. Link wanted to beat him to death with the piñata stick.

"There's kids around," he told the smirking man, then added in a whisper, "you limp-dick *motherfucker*."

He watched the smile fade.

Ursula had certainly come a long way since her youth, ascending social classes with each opportunistic marriage, always as determined to milk her good looks as any athlete would be to cash in on a vertical leap. She was just a kid when Link knew her, and he could hardly reconcile his memory with this lipsticked mother in white pants, who opened her mouth too wide when she spoke, made lavish hand gestures, and threw her head back laughing at her own jokes. When he knew her, she could hardly take two steps without encouragement. He'd hovered over her, telling her again and again that she was a diamond, until she got tired of him and needed a more convincing appraisal.

The summer they first met, Link was a thirty-two-year-old Hell's Angel, on probation for a fight in a bowling alley, wearing a cast on his wrist that was filling up with signatures as fast as an angry petition. He held a state-required framing job that he was planning to quit; everything he owned in the world was either on his bike or in his pockets. He was handsome in those days, except for his habitually broken nose, and he was known among his brothers for being tough, loyal, and quiet. Tall and broad-shouldered, with a few scattered tattoos, Link was still surprisingly boyish, with a round, cheerful face under the stubble and sideburns.

Almost a generation younger, Ursula had grown up in the same shabby cluster of stucco apartments—The Pink Ghettoes of Lakeside, California, which with each passing year looked more like the lush aftermath of a monsoon. Doors were never fixed after police raids; tattered waitress and machinist uniforms hung forgotten off laundry lines among the sycamore trees. Nestled between horse ranches and an Indian reservation, the neighborhood was a stretch of broken bottles, faded pastel paint, and barred windows down amid the date palms and overgrown weeds. Abandoned houses filled up with sparrows' nests and white power graffiti. Once the mills shut down, there was little work beyond the gravel mines; and whenever Link slept late with a hangover, he'd wake to the distant drone of those tractors chewing up the streambed. The gravel companies had to put back every pound they took out, so they filled up the arroyos with scrap metal and burnt-out cars, until the town was ringed by a moat of rust and steel, and the creek where Link had swum as a boy became a junkyard where kids fought, got high, or got pregnant.

Ursula was not one of those kids, though probably every teenager in the town had tried to lure her down there at one point or another.

The summer of 1982, Link was riding with the San Diego chapter of the Angels and sponsoring a young prospect named Hardy Stillman, whom he'd met in county jail. Both were there on possession charges;

both made their living mostly selling weed and hustling. Hardy was a rangy kid, all Adam's apple and stuffed-up nose. Because he liked to wear Luftwaffe helmets and play with nunchucks, he gave Link the impression of an underweight, underage soldier, allergic to the battlefield. Twitchy as a rabbit, he flinched whenever Link made a fist, until a joke developed in which Link would stand up quickly and Hardy would flee the room. But the kid was a shoo-in for the club, mostly because he was a promising mechanic and his ride was a thing to behold—a completely restored 1946 Indian Chief.

Link and Hardy would stay up late, night after night, and Hardy was awestruck by how well Link could draw. His eyes greasy with smoke, Link would sketch motorcycles, mermaids, and bosomy witches in loose-fitting clothes, hovering over the paper for hours in a trance of fidgeting pencils. One night, Hardy showed up at a party with three girls from his old high school, Ursula Carson among them, looking mortified by the scene. Hardy asked Link to draw her portrait—"the best-looking chick in this fucking shithole town!" Hardy soon lost patience with the time it took, rejoining the party. But Ursula sat primly for almost an hour, hands in her lap, on a wooden chair across from Link.

Link could not help but draw how uncomfortable she was, how her eyes had shrunk with fear and her mouth was curving down faintly at the edges. They were the only motionless people in a rowdy place, sitting at opposing ends of a table littered with bottles and smoldering ashtrays. Finally, Link held up the picture for her, and she gave him a strained and self-conscious smile. Then Link raised his voice over the din and said, "You don't look too fucking happy, do you?"

She shrugged.

Link thought there was something odd about his attraction to the girl: She was so damned beautiful that he didn't want to touch her. She seemed breakable. She was pretty to the point of being sexless. She smelled like those stores that only sold soap. Her skin was so fair and clean, touching her might leave a thumbprint. Her neck was thin and white, her wrists were small under the cuffs of her blouse, her hair was pulled back crisply into a ponytail—something about her was like a bed made up so preciously that he'd feel bad messing it up. Raising her chin to project her voice, she said, "You draw so well. You could probably get a job doing *storyboards*."

"What's that?"

She explained that every shot in a movie had to be drawn before it was filmed. She knew this because she had met a director once and talked to him all night. Chattering idly seemed to make her forget her surroundings, and for a long time she told Link about how she intended to move up to Los Angeles and get into "the industry," as soon as she passed summer school. Then she began telling Link everything that he should do with his life, some elaborate scheme for sending his drawings to various people she knew; and she talked about how lots of bikers made money working as extras in films. Link wasn't in the mood to get career counseling from a high school girl, so he tore off the portrait and gave it to her, then walked away.

It was a little past midnight when Link heard some of the Angels harassing her in the bathroom. Grabbing, joking, laughing—it was basic Neanderthal shit, but Link didn't imagine she would be able to handle it very well. Every now and then there was a woman who just abandoned herself to the collective will of the brothers, like throwing herself into rough seas, and he hated to think of Ursula in this position. So Link pushed his way into the room, where two men had stolen one of her shoes and were playing keep-away with it. Link said, "I'm taking her home."

"Fucking A, Link—who made you Gary Cooper?"

"Give the kid her shoe back *now*, Lenny, or I'm going to kill everybody here with that toilet seat."

Still working her foot into the mule, Ursula raced alongside Link as he promised to take her home. She was giddy and shaking, and, all the way down the steps of the apartment and across the street, she was telling Link that he should get away from these people, that he was better than they were.

"Why? Because I drew your picture?"

Hardy was giving rides around the block to Ursula's two friends, and he looked crestfallen as she climbed onto the back of Link's Harley.

Link began racing along dark and empty streets while she wrapped her arms around his waist. It was frustrating riding with her, because she didn't lean into the turns, and when she did, she leaned *too* hard and he needed to compensate. Only to show her how fast he could go, he turned up onto the winding highway and began swerving through the hills, and soon they were descending foggy mountains on slick roads into the Anzo-Borrego Desert. He became so thrilled at the moonlit stretch past tumbleweed and the shadowy tentacles of ocotillo that he forgot about her, as if she were just a sweatshirt tied around his waist, and he rode all the way to Salton City, pulling finally into the last open gas station under a flickering light. There he saw that Ursula had been terrified for the past hour.

He said, "Fun. Right?"

She started crying under the fluorescent lights.

At first, Link responded as if he'd just dropped something fragile, saying, "Oh shit, no. *No, no*—don't do that." But soon, through her sobbing, she was confessing personal things: She was failing trigonometry and history; she wasn't going to graduate from high school; she couldn't stand her mother and they lived together on tiny disability checks in a shit apartment, three months behind on utilities. Ursula said that she would kill herself if she had to spend another day like this. "I mean, I'm just waiting for all the lights to go out!"

The pump clicked, the tank was filled, and Link screwed back the cap. He got back onto his bike and waited. She just stood there, refusing to climb on behind him, until finally she paced back and started kissing him. Never in his life had Link felt kisses like these, like decisive points in an argument: sharp, urgent, and aggressive. A rhythm of long questions and short demands. Link was half aroused, half scared. When he pulled away from the girl, her eyes were dry and hard, and he wondered if he had misinterpreted everything about her in his sketch. She was not timid: She was too hungry for her washed-up little town. They stared at

each other, and she must have felt his hesitation, because finally she
asked, "Do you hate me?"

"No, I don't hate you, kid. Is that what you were shooting for?"

They were together every day and night after that, in a strange, acciden-
tal love affair that covered the better part of ten months and twenty-three
states. During their first hopeful trips through the desert, or along the
shore and mountains, he would start each morning happier than ever in
his life. By nightfall she had always talked him out of it. He'd had a lot of
old ladies, but never anybody like Ursula. She was *serious*. Defensive
about failing out of high school, she wanted to "educate herself," and she
read books and magazines about psychology, astrology, and the movies.
She'd quote authors to Link, explaining his particular form of social mal-
adjustment, along with whatever steps he needed to improve himself, always believing that there was some hidden talent in him that she could
eventually unleash. Between the sissy bars of his Harley, Ursula rode
across the country with an unhappy face. She endured his lifestyle as if
he would owe her something deep and everlasting for each uncomfortable moment she spent in a campground or a cheap motel. At times, she
seemed more like a missionary than his girlfriend. She needed to talk
about her expectations, the relationship, and the *future* at practically
every stop on the road.

Link didn't see how he'd *ever* be able to live up to the dream this
chick had in the distance. And she looked on Link's brothers as the varying symptoms of his disease, tolerating the bike runs as sudden, virulent
outbreaks. She never much enjoyed the scenery, the emptiness of the
Mojave, the Black Hills, or the canyons through Arizona. She brooded,
mile after mile, carrying on a flinching internal monologue. Everything
was "important to experience and learn from," yet she never liked her experiences. She hated going on runs to Bass Lake or Big Bear; she couldn't
stomach all the drunks. Coast to coast, she could never eat anything on
any menu. Link doggedly tried to please her with presents from roadside
stands, moonlit rides, and clichés that always mortified him as soon as

he uttered them—*You're my queen; you're the best girl in the world;* but the harder he tried, the more she treated him like a child offering a home-made, misspelled valentine.

To most of the brothers, Ursula seemed only like a pretty young woman who never smiled. But conflicts had been brewing over the months among the other mamas, who disliked the way she fluctuated between lectures and pouting. She found it appalling what these women *did,* and she disliked the communal, public aspect of sex within the club. Link never earned his red or brown wings with Ursula. And the other women probably felt her disapproval, as if she were that familiar voice from the straight world. Link knew there were several mamas who downright *hated* her, particularly a chick from Lake Elsinore, Sheila Carter, who had threatened to kill her one night with a broken bottle. Apparently Ursula had called her a "black hole," which Link at first thought was a crude insult, but later learned was some kind of astronomy or psychobabble.

Late during a Memorial Day party on a beach in Northern California, Link left Ursula to sit by himself on the dunes after an argument. Much of the story he later heard secondhand, from Hardy and the others: Ursula never could handle drugs or booze particularly well, and she had gotten drunk too quickly. She had turned on Sheila, who was just out on bond for a battery charge. Apparently Sheila had been facetiously hitting on her, whistling and claiming that she wanted "a little taste of vanilla." Ursula had snapped, throwing sand into her face, breaking into tears, and calling her a "fat, jealous prison skank." Clearing the grit from her eyes, Sheila rose up and popped Ursula in the head. Ursula wasn't hurt, just scratched and humiliated, but she came to Link demanding that he murder the woman and all of her friends. Link told her to calm down—nobody was murdering anybody tonight. He returned to the bonfire to discover that all of the women were fed up with Ursula, who had apparently been lecturing them for weeks about their wasted lives and her destiny of fame and fortune. Link joined the other guys trying to defuse the shouting, not thinking that anything out of the ordinary had happened.

He didn't notice for an hour or so that Ursula had disappeared.

He looked around the shore, but when he couldn't find her in the dunes, on the rocks, or along the cliffs of stranded driftwood, he formed a search party. Hardy wanted to come along, as well as two others—Dagget, a redheaded bike designer covered with tattoos of chain mail and battle-axes, and a wild young guy known as the Count, with long black hair, two missing teeth, and the florid tattoo of a dragon devouring its tail. Count was tripping on a half sheet of blotter acid and seemed ready to volunteer for any adventure.

The search wound up lasting three days, with the police trolling the waters, assembling clues from trucker sightings, and later interviewing gas station attendants, who had reportedly seen her running southbound on the PCH. On the third day, Link called her mother in Lakeside to learn that Ursula had stopped at home, packed her things, and moved to Los Angeles with a girlfriend. Link was in a seaside diner when he made the call, and he joined the other three men as they sat around a picnic table overlooking the crashing tide. She was alive, he told them. They nodded at the sea. He said it was for the best. He wasn't one for "big crying bullshit good-byes," and at least she wasn't drowned or raped by a homeless guy. They each agreed that this was the right attitude.

Then Link said, "Fuck her," and they patted and struck his shoulders from around the table. He asked who was up for a cross-country run—and everyone liked the idea. Count just needed to make a few deliveries, but he could have some cash by that evening. So they packed up what little they had, and at sundown they gathered in the parking lot of a beach motel, agreeing that no one would turn back until they hit the Atlantic. Dagget, Count, Hardy, and Link—a splinter group, they said, the one percent of the one-percenters, the worst of the worst, the *really* bad apples. They followed the coast northward at ninety miles an hour on the straightaways, grabbing the suicide shifts around hairpin turns; then they bled onto I-80 in San Francisco and roared over the Sierras in the rain. Dagget had an old pair of tennis shoes flapping from the back rail, and, somewhere in the Great Basin, they came off and smacked Hardy in the face. His cheek was swollen and purple, and Count gave him a handful of unknown pills with a swig of whisky.

They stopped overnight in Elko, where they took speed in order to stay up and keep drinking; then, somewhere in the middle of a glaring afternoon, they rolled into a small casino town, where Count picked up another load of crystal. They stepped on it with baby laxative and talcum powder, skimming off a pound for themselves, and they rode off through Utah, drinking out of a Jack Daniel's bottle in the roaring wind, passing it between bikes along the highway. They went so long without sleep that life seemed composed of just one endless day, light and darkness like an intermittent blinking in the sky. Link was amazed at how sunsets seemed to follow right after the dawn, and he started to think that the road itself controlled time. They lounged on their bikes, soaring along at ninety-plus. Their legs went numb and they could hardly straighten them again in gas stations, where they pissed, ate candy, drank beer and snorted more speed. I-80 grew more boring by the hour, so they all cut south along a smaller highway, and got lost along mountain roads and mining towns, before coming out somehow in New Mexico, days later.

In the panhandle of Texas, they went looking for more booze in an Amarillo Kmart, and got into a fight in the parking lot with a truckload of cowboys. Link was so high on some PCP-laced roach he'd bought back in Las Cruces that an hour later he couldn't remember who'd won the fight. Dagget didn't seem to be with them any longer.

At dusk, they pulled over at a rest stop and tried to piece together what had happened. Count seemed to think that Dagget had been killed or arrested. They all tried to remember the last time they had actually *seen* Dagget, agreeing that it hadn't been for days. Finally Hardy deduced that they had lost him a week or so earlier when they made the turn off I-80. Count and Link started laughing, pounding their legs and howling.

"He's probably still up there looking for us," said Hardy.

"Ah, he'll be fine," said Link. "He's a big boy."

The three remaining bikers carried on for another twelve hours to a town outside of Mobile, where—sometime during the hot new daylight— Hardy collapsed onto the beach. Link and Count sat on opposite sides of him to make sure he was breathing. In the distance, seagulls were swarming around something dead on the sand. Count began rolling a

joint. They lit up and savored the moment, not noticing the cops standing right behind them. When Link looked back, closing one eye to view
the glaring eclipse around the officer's head, he offered the cop a drag,
and felt a steel cuff go over his wrist. Then, for a long time Link and
Count sat shackled in the sand, watching as the officers tried to wake up
Hardy. They asked if he was dead, and Link said, "Nah, he's just all tuck-
ered out."

Count started laughing hard at this, and soon Link was laughing at
his laughing, and the two couldn't stop. In the back of the squad car, they
were like kids with the giggles in church, snorting, holding their breath,
and bursting out with loud guffaws. At the station, they laughed as they
were all fingerprinted together. Link told Hardy he had something on
his face, then pretended to get it off while smudging ink across his
cheeks. They went into a holding tank, where they terrorized some local
drunk, until finally they all faded out and slept for the better part of two
days on the floor. Tired of waiting for paperwork, the sheriff eventually decided to escort them to the state line.

Outside on the street, while two patrol cars idled, Link, Hardy, and
Count broke into an argument about which direction to go. Hardy
wanted to turn back, and Count had sobered up enough to realize he
had business, while Link called them both pussies for stopping so close
to the end. Hardy had a gigantic waterlogged welt on his head, and Link
couldn't remember where he'd gotten it. Count calmed Link down and
said, "It's just business, brother. Got myself a good cash source, and I
can't let it go dry."

He asked a cop for a pen and paper, and then he started writing on
the hood of the car. When the cop honked his horn, Count yelled, "Fuck
you—arrest me then, pig."

He gave Link the paper: On it was the name and address of a man
named "Preacher" Harris, who lived off a golf course in Palm Springs.
Count said, "There's a job in this for you too, brother. Old guy—Berdoo
chapter, founding fathers. I'm going to tell him to expect you when you
get back. Motherfucker's living like a goddamn senior citizen out there
now, but he's making shitloads of money. I'll put in a word."

They shook on it, punched each other's chest, and Link split off in his own direction, crossing the Florida state line.

Some time later, Link met a woman in a bar in Pensacola, and a week or so beyond that, possibly during a blackout, he seemed to have moved in with her. She was an older lady, maybe in her forties, and she had a seemingly inexhaustible supply of cocaine and booze. He would lie on his back in her messy bedcovers and laundry, and she would fuck him with squirms and grimaces, as if getting comfortable in a movie seat. And then he would wander the apartment naked, searching through a mysterious refrigerator, smoking, drinking, pissing off the porch. He would put on his same clothes from the night before, as stiff as a discarded shell, and he would wander back to the bar, where he'd start drinking again with ghostly dedication.

One day, when the woman's old father came to visit, Link worried that he might have actually married her in a blackout. The man came into the room and found Link with his shirt off on the couch, surrounded by bottles and dusty mirrors. Suntanned and wearing a fruity shirt, the old guy began giving Link a speech about how his daughter was a good woman—all he wanted was the best for her.

Link had only blurry recollections of fights, progressively more routine sex, and bouts of illness, as if those memories were all stored in a different, preverbal part of his brain. The woman was crying, and Link realized that the old man was politely asking him to leave. Link shook his hand. His old lady seemed to be involved in a separate drama, running off to her bedroom. Link got onto his bike and saw her waving from her window. For some reason, he suddenly felt lonely for Ursula. Riding away past the spits of shoreline and the seafood shacks, the air thick with brine, he imagined her holding on behind him. He couldn't understand why he suddenly ached so badly for her, like his bones had been hollowed out, but he needed to pull off the road and sit in the gravel and feel the waves of sadness roll over him.

He expected this feeling to go away, but instead, as he turned north to avoid the state of Alabama completely, an eleven-hour looping segue that made him curse himself for failing geography, every passing mile seemed to intensify the empty feeling. He was somewhere in a cicada-filled stretch of Spanish moss and kudzu when he pulled up to a little gas station surrounded by black kids laughing and pointing at him. Inside he found the phone. Somehow, out of all the soggy chaos in his brain, he remembered his old number in Lakeside. Hardy answered the phone.

"I need to find her," said Link.

Hardy was quiet for a long time. Pissed off. Finally he said, "She's been looking for *you*, man. She's up in L.A. She just had a baby, Link. A girl. Says it's yours, you fucking deadbeat: She was pregnant when she left."

Link shook his head and tried to clear his eyes. He asked how the hell it was even possible that she could have a baby already.

"Link—you been gone four and a half months, man."

The room was churning, and there were purple spots floating in his eyes, and Link was quite certain now that these were the side effects of time travel. He couldn't speak, and Hardy started explaining that the baby was born too early, and probably wasn't going to survive.

Link got the name of the hospital, and learned that the baby hadn't been named yet, except with Ursula's last name: Infant Carson. "Infant," he repeated, as if it were his daughter's name.

"She's too scared to name the kid."

"Hardy, you little shit, you do me a favor. You tell Ursula I'm coming. I'm going to make the ride straight through, even if my legs fall off."

"She ain't too happy with you."

"Tell her I'm going to make it up. Everything. No more bullshit."

By the time Link was on I-40 speeding back toward the West Coast, all he repeated to himself was *Infant Carson*, over and over, keeping him awake without drugs, even when all he could see was a black horizon and streams of dotted lines piercing the cone of his headlight. Had Ursula been expecting him to chase her all this time? He couldn't figure it out, and the situation seemed hopeless to him out on the dark roads. He was racing to see his daughter before she died. This was the first real test of his life, and he found himself talking to a God he'd never believed in, begging forgiveness, pleading with him to extend the life of an unnamed girl.

. . .

When his daughter was seven days old, Link made it to Cedars-Sinai Hospital in Los Angeles and bought a newspaper for a souvenir.

The paper seemed a bad omen—a suicide bomber had killed over two hundred troops in Beirut and, for some reason, the United States had just invaded an island he'd never heard of. Link rolled up the paper, as if hunting mosquitoes, and entered the hospital, first washing his hands in the bathroom. In front of the broad mirror, he noticed that his face was scuffed and bleeding from debris and horseflies along the road; and he was sunburned and filthy except for two raccoon circles where his goggles had been. He scrubbed his face and watched the water turn black and sooty as it went down the drain.

When he reached the semicircular desk, there was a nurse who seemed to know who he was already. "Let me guess," she said. "Miss Carson's baby." She was a tiny, wrinkly Southeast Asian woman—maybe Cambodian or Laotian—with square glasses that took up most of her face. She was stern and abrupt. She studied his license, handed him scrubs, attached an ID bracelet around his wrist, and led him down a long labyrinth of corridors to the NICU, updating him as they walked: Ursula had been sent home to rest; the baby's chances were better than they were a week ago, but still not good.

His baby was the only one in a special room at the far back of newborn intensive care, where she lay under a network of tubes and wires in an incubator that looked like a terrarium. He was afraid to go closer. The nurse moved ahead and waved for him impatiently. When he hung over the plastic bassinet, he couldn't believe that the little girl was alive—she was raw and purple and brittle-boned; her lungs heaved; a respirator nozzle wedged into a tiny mouth. There were strange twitches on her chicken legs, and her eyes were closed and crusted over, like a bird recovered from a fallen shell. Link wanted to smash everything in the room behind him, every piece of dormant equipment.

Instead he only said, "She's cold."

The nurse explained that the incubator was kept at an ideal temperature. She shivered because of her underdeveloped nervous system. The doctors had been careful with the amount of oxygen they gave her, in an effort to avoid blindness. But all Link could see was that the little thing was suffering, and he was sick with the idea that all she'd know of this world would be wires, lights, plastic, and pain.

The nurse said, "Now, you see her. Okay? Clean up next time you come here. Wash up. You smell bad, and it's not right. This is your daughter."

A tiny woman, not five feet tall, she scolded him with furious eyes, pointing up as he lowered his head. He nodded at her name tag—Vu Thi Tuyet—while she told him to stand up straight and look her in the face. She said, "Promise. You don't come in here again like this. Promise me, right now."

"Yes, ma'am," he said quietly. "I promise."

An hour later he called Ursula's studio apartment, then arrived with tulips from the hospital gift shop, which had come apart in the wind during his ride. He hardly recognized her at the door. Her hair had thickened and turned dark, her skin had a glazed quality, her eyes were bloodshot, and she was so expressionless that he thought she must be tranquilized. She thanked him for the flowers and led him inside, filling a pitcher with water while he sat on a box in her kitchenette. He couldn't tell if she was in the midst of packing or unpacking. In the bathroom, a wet hostess uniform hung over the shower. He asked her if she wanted to go out for something to eat. She said she wasn't ever going to eat again, suddenly puffing her cheeks like a blowfish.

She wouldn't answer any of his questions. He asked what money she was living on, and when she was silent, he said that he could get a job and pay for his end of things. He had the name of a guy in Palm Springs. Ursula asked, "Did you see her?"

Link nodded.

"Bad news?"

"No," he said. "She's tough."

Ursula started pacing and talking about how she hadn't been back for a few days: She had simply panicked at the sight of the little girl. She couldn't face it right now; she felt so guilty, so overwhelmed, she couldn't imagine going back to the hospital. Her mother and her aunt had planned to drive up next weekend to take care of her, but she had told them not to bother. She couldn't think all the way to next weekend. It was another lifetime.

Link said, "Ursula, it's not over. I promise you that. This is my daughter, and she's not going to go down without a fight."

Ursula nodded in a distracted way, moving to the window, and said, "Right, right. Because you're such a *fighter*."

Link gave her his plan: He was going to ride straight out to Palm Springs tonight, meet up with some contacts, and by tomorrow afternoon he'd have a job. He said he was ready to take care of everything— the bills, the diapers, whatever the fuck babies needed. Ursula stared at him like he was speaking another language.

The next twenty-four hours were the most frantic of his life.

By nine o'clock he found the house beside the golf course, introducing himself to a sun-baked, balding old man known as Preacher, who lived just off a sand trap on the back nine. Preacher was in the midst of a screaming rampage because someone had taken their chopper out and torn up the tenth fairway. He immediately began yelling at Link, the newest suspect. But even with his teeth bared and his eyes clouded with rage, the crazy old man seemed like a worthwhile boss. Link had never seen such energy, especially in a brother who had survived into his late fifties. From talking to Count, Link knew that Preacher had been in an engineers' battalion during the Korean War, and he apparently still had an itch to blow things to smithereens. Every few weekends, he took packs of enthusiastic Angels up into the mountains with claymores and grenades, and they would pass the afternoons blowing up tree stumps and firing at cans floating downstream.

That night, Preacher's house was packed with other Hell's Angels from around the state, all gathered for a funeral the next day: a Berdoo brother had been shot in the head when he got off his bike to fight seven street kids in the City of Industry. The group was drunk and somber now, worn out from Preacher's tirade. One man eulogized in the low-ceilinged living room, saying that the brother had gone out with dignity.

Another claimed that he would have expected a good party. To talk about business, Preacher led Link into the garage, where a claymore rested against a tire, with the inscription on the side:

Face toward enemy

Preacher didn't seem to want Link to speak. He said, "So Count called me about an hour ago and explained. You come highly recommended, and I don't think I have to tell you about the sensitive nature of our operation. The less said, the better. Count tells me you're the strong, silent type—and that's what I need. I need somebody who can take orders and keep his trap shut. Understand?"

Link nodded.

"Your little pal Hardy Stillman is running for me down in San Diego. Make sure he keeps quiet, too. He's a leaky faucet, that one. We got trials going on all over the country, and we don't need some motor mouth. Now, go back inside and have a beer. You're too fucking tense."

A little while later, Preacher came into his crowded living room clutching the neck of a beer and started musing aloud about the nature of life and death.

"We are not going to mourn old Wes!" he shouted as if to a congregation. "Not here. If you came here to feel bad, you're in the wrong place, brother. That was *his* death. His very own." Stomping back and forth across the room, he continued, "Not a day went by when he didn't know it was coming. Like all of you and like me. But he lived every day like a free man, because he didn't know what fear was. That's a life. He refused to back down, not one inch. And thirty-eight years of *real* living beats a hundred years as a slave."

Link had heard this speech; every Hell's Angel made some version of the *slave* reference at one point or another. But Preacher was such a weathered and tough-looking old buzzard that it seemed to take on new significance.

"Do not cry for this man. We're going to celebrate his life. He died like every brother should: with his boots on."

In the midst of his speech, Link met Preacher's old lady—Cherise—
a platinum blonde with a sarcastic shape to her mouth, as if she had heard
this sermon every night of her life. She had a suntan darker than her am-
ber beer, and Link couldn't help noticing how her tits stood up high and
straight under the halter top. She said, "So are you joining the cult of *personality*?" She was drunk and wavering slightly on her high-heeled
boots.

"Guess so," said Link.

"Tell me something—how noble is it to get beaten to death by
teenagers?"

"Probably how I'm going to go," said Link.

"Yeah," she said, toasting her beer in a plastic cup. "*Purple Heart.
Everybody dies with their boots on."

Link pointed down at her boots, two long red leather ones with zip-
pers up the fronts. She laughed and modeled them, standing on one
foot, then grabbing him as she lost her balance.

The next morning, Link was up early making deliveries across the
San Bernardino Valley, carting red phosphorus, ephedrine, and other pre-
cursors to warehouse laboratories and aluminum sheds out in the desert.
He listened to a few jittery cookers complain about their profit margins,
and one explained some of the chemistry in layman's terms: "Ephedrine
and red phosphorus. Think of it as a match head and a diet pill—one way
or another, it's going to blow you sky-high."

By two o'clock in the afternoon, Link had finished his errands, and he
rode in the funeral procession to the cemetery in Covina, hundreds of
Angels from all over the West Coast rumbling through the streets and at-
tracting startled onlookers from stores and apartment buildings. They
rode so tightly packed together that a single swerve might have brought
down the crowd. They swarmed through the towns, past people fleeing
out of crosswalks, cars pulling over, and cops barricading the side streets
to guard against trouble. When they lowered the brother into the ground,
Link was sober, and he felt hounded by clarity. Too many details vied for
his attention—the freeway beneath them and its streaming sound, his

daughter hooked up like a time bomb under a twenty-four-hour lamp, Ursula in her dirty apartment, and this departed biker who had lost his life in a back alley over an insult.

Preacher noticed Link and came over, patting him roughly on the back. He whispered to Link in a rush of hot breath, "We've got a hundred police around this graveyard—like anybody's going to *do* anything here." He raised one shaggy gray eyebrow, then led Link around the tombstones, saying, "Someday, son, we're going to get out from under this persecution. I'm going to build myself a free state—out in the middle of nowhere, like the first pioneers. Get away from all this bullshit stuffed down our throats. FBI, CIA, the fucking RICO statute. I want you to know that every day out there, you're a part of that goal."

Immediately following the pep talk, Link returned to the warehouses to pick up the product. Next he made the second half of his deliveries in a trail from Fontana to Costa Mesa. Just past eight, so tired and tense that he could barely grip his handlebars, he pulled up at Ursula's to give her all of his thousand-dollar cut. She let him sleep on the floor that night, and, as soon as the sun was up, he showered, scrubbed, and tied back his hair. He returned to the hospital looking like a puffy, blow-dried bear.

He stood for an hour by the incubator, watching the baby's lungs quiver. He didn't know what the numbers meant on the monitors, but he noticed that they were higher than before, and—as if all the apparatus were just a variation on a speedometer—he assumed this was a promising development. His daughter's chest looked stronger and she seemed able to move her legs in more than a startled twitch. Exuberant as he left the NICU this time, he ran around the halls and called for the nurse to tell her about his daughter's thickening legs.

For the next ten days, he alternated between deliveries for Preacher, showers at Ursula's, and nights on her floor or a bench outside the hospital. One day, when Nurse Vu Thi had just come on her shift, she told him the good news. The baby was breathing on her own. The pediatrician thought that her vision would likely be unaffected, and there was a chance that she'd have few long-term complications. She needed to put on more weight under close observation. The doctor told Link that, at twenty-nine weeks, she had been the second most premature child to survive in his time there. Link couldn't hold all the information about the nervous system and possible deafness; he only heard that his daughter had beaten all the odds.

When he reached Ursula's apartment, he was riotous with the good news. Ursula had been up all night cleaning. She said that she was going back to work, and she wouldn't need his help with the rent anymore.

"Ursula—she's going to do it. She's a tough little thing, that kid."

Ursula didn't seem to hear him. She went over to the closet to organize her clothes, then she stood in front of a mirror trying on earrings. Link hovered in the center of the dim room while she walked back and forth around him, saying something about the interview just being a "technicality," that the boss knew her well and had promised her the job.

Link said, "Ursula! I want to name her!"

Clasping an earring, she tilted her head, as if there were water in her ear. She smiled at him, sadly, like the butt of a cruel joke, and he realized that she had not even considered the possibility of her baby surviving.

"After my mother," Link said.

"What are you doing anyway?" she asked. "Where is this money even coming from?"

"Lydia Jane. You never met my mother. She died when I was about twenty-three. My father died when I was twelve. Just worked to death. Mean as hell, and he died young, and they just worked and worked until they broke in half. Never had a second of fun. Never had a nice day in their lives. My old man was the sourest, bitterest man you ever met. Beat the shit out of my mom, day and night. Tore into me, too. And all the kids hated his guts and used to plot to poison him at night. But I was his favorite, I think. And I was the only one who got upset at the funeral. Cried like a pussy. And you know what? All my brothers kicked my ass for that. Never let me live it down. Don't know where they are now, bunch of assholes. You never knew a thing about my family, I don't think. Shit, she's going to *live*, Ursula. The little girl, Lydia—Lydia's her name, and they said she was the second toughest baby they ever saw."

Ursula was rubbing her temples.

He had never thought two people could be so far away in the same small room. She looked up at him finally, her face abstracted as if she were listening to another voice in her ears, and she said, "Well, what do you know? I guess it's a miracle."

four

After waiting almost half an hour in an access parking spot behind the seafood restaurant, Link was about to step out and comb the beaches for his daughter when he saw her tall ragged figure climbing up the large rocks along the shore. She was barefoot and carried a backpack that kept sagging off her thin shoulder. He rolled down his window and waved his arm, whistling to her, but she didn't seem to remember why she was waiting. He could tell from her listless walk that she was beginning to crash; her shadow drifted toward him, wavering, as if on the deck of a ship. Her arms hung limply at her sides and the cuffs of an enormous sweatshirt drooped over her hands.

The passenger door didn't open from the outside, so Link leaned across the car to let her in as she staggered backward a few steps. She seemed confused about her own actions, and when she noticed the opened door, she gave him the finger, backtracking, and said, "Oh no, no, no. Fuck *you*, dog."

"Lydia, it's me. It's your father. Sit down right here. You're okay."

At first she made an exaggerated, childlike frown, then her eyes trailed away and she nodded, seeming to remember her phone call as if it had happened years ago. She glanced at him for just an instant, but Link could tell, from the sudden drop of her mouth, that she didn't recognize him easily. She plopped into the seat and wiped her nose on her sleeve, making the same high-pitched laugh again. Then she looked ahead through his cracked and bug-stained windshield, stewing in the long silence.

He could smell the meth in her pores—that harsh, chemical stench. She had blood on her sweatshirt sleeves, cuts on her feet, and she seemed to have no energy left in her body beyond her shivering hands and chattering jaw. However much she could comprehend of the moment, Link knew, had to do with how many days it had been since she'd slept; and from the hollow look of her bluish, pallid skin with red pimples, a sore on her neck, sweat in her hair, and chapped nostrils—she'd hit the end of a long binge and was now accelerating downhill. She sank into the seat as if she intended to live there forever. She sniffled and whispered, with a hoarse voice: "Every time somebody looks at me, it gets colder."

"I'll turn on the heat."

She jolted, as if surprised by his voice. "You can't talk to me like that. I want you to *know*, right off. I'm not going to put up with it. Ground rules." She pointed at him but seemed to have no idea who he was. "I'm not going to sit here and be treated like shit for the rest of my life. I mean it. You can't expect to treat a person like this and have them just smile, okay. Because I'm a human being—and I have *self-respect*. I have self-respect. I'm a fucking educated person and I'm not going to just sit around and have people dump on me."

"Okay, kid. Fair enough."

Her face clenched up and she cried for a moment, a passing cloudburst, and she pleaded to the windshield, "What did I ever fucking do to anybody in the world to deserve this shit? I swear to God—I didn't *do* anything."

"Nope, you didn't do anything. Let's just go on ahead and close that door."

She didn't hear him, so he walked around to her side, listening to her continue, ". . . and it was that bald Uncle Fester asshole—he was going to kill me, because I'm not stupid, and I may be a lot of things. . . ." He closed the door carefully beside her.

Back in his seat, he tried the ignition, waiting a few moments as the engine strained, finally pausing so that it didn't flood.

"I can't fucking *breathe,*" she said. "It's like the way a spider wraps up a dead bug, with this, like, Saran Wrap for sandwiches or noodles or something—*leftovers,* and you wrap it around and around, and make it look like a big ugly cocoon except everything is dead inside of it. There's no butterfly."

"Yep," said Link. "Makes sense to me."

"The butterfly's dead," she told him, with grave, childlike seriousness on her face. "It never comes out."

"That's a tough break. I'm sorry."

"And you can't do *anything* about it. Because there's no air inside. It doesn't have enough air, and so when it comes out—" She grew distracted.

Link waited for a long time, tried the ignition again. The car started, and he revved the gas to keep it running. Then he said, "Yep, a dead butterfly."

She covered her face with her hands and curled into a ball in the seat. "There's something in my throat."

Link was glad to focus on the road. She must have been twenty pounds underweight. It was incongruous to watch a girl that he thought was both so beautiful and so sick—a travesty—like seeing a Harley left mangled on the roadside. Lydia's startling blue eyes looked out from beneath swollen eyelids and dirty hair; she had speed bumps along her jaw, and the worried blemish on her neck was scratched and bleeding.

As he drove along the PCH, she twisted her head around strangely, trying to loosen her neck, and said, "It's the money, right? Everything is always the money. How much do you think all of my fingers and toes are worth?" She seemed wildly reinvigorated.

"Yeah, we're going to get the money."

"Oh no," she said through her cupped palms, drifting into another mood, moaning. "I'm so dead right now."

"We're going to get the money, kid. Off to the bank. So you can get on up to Oregon."

They flew through the tunnel in Venice, gathering speed onto the freeway eastbound. The car was fogging up with breath, and Link rolled down his window. She claimed that a group of creepy shadows had been gathered all along the beach.

"Where are we going again?" she yelled to him over the wind, pulling her hair off her face.

"Just a while longer," he said. "I promise you."

She glanced all around herself, as if she didn't remember getting into the car, and with her mouth becoming loose she said, "I don't *know* you."

There was a burning smell coming through the heater.

"No, you don't," said Link.

She was rocking to the lullaby motion of the car along the 10, drifting, and she cried until they were south of the city, passing through the interchanges and along the warehouses and train tracks. The tears were like the last drips of energy in her body, smelling chlorinated and toxic, until she was sagging to sleep against the window, lights floating past her. She murmured, "I got a gun, you know. It's loaded."

From the floor beside her, he found an oil-stained towel, and handed it to her. "Use that as a pillow."

She crumpled it up and lay against it, saying, "Mmmm, I'm not asleep."

"Yeah, just make sure that door is locked. It's got a mind of its own."

Link figured that she'd had enough juice left in her brain to remember his number or call information, and she must have made at least one rational choice while doing it. She had two parents: one who lived in a mansion, and one who couldn't afford a goddamn taco. He couldn't escape the idea that she had called him for a reason—that she knew, deep down, that he'd been in the exact same position, that he'd lived in this grim twilight of consciousness for weeks and months at a time. For a while she began to panic that she had been shot. He knew what was happening to her, he knew the last epinephrine had been wrung from her system like the drops from a wet rag; he knew that she was hooked; and when she finally closed her eyes and fell asleep in a pile against the window, he wondered what she would remember tomorrow, two days from now, whenever she woke up again—from this ride, her life, or their years of letters. It was hard for him to imagine that she'd have anything left in her head about him, just his name and a few vague pictures, hovering like the residue of a morning dream.

five

When Lydia was two years old, after a string of supervised visits, she had begun to call her father what sounded like—for some strange reason—*Barbara*. Eventually Ursula figured out the mystery and explained that it was *"barba,"* the Spanish word for beard, which the nanny had apparently taught Lydia.

From the age of six months, Lydia had been raised mostly by this nanny while living with her mother and a stepfather in a Sherman Oaks home of prissy furniture and bright plastic gewgaws for children. The nanny was a young, pleasant-faced Latina, who seemed to despise Link as if he were a homeless man off the street. She didn't appear to be particularly fond of Ursula either, whose hair and makeup were always so untouched, whose clothes were so clean that Link couldn't imagine her handling a Frisbee, let alone a child. With a stoic expression, the nanny seemed to carry out every basic function of motherhood, chasing down the toddler as she went for lamp cords and power outlets. As if overseeing the project, Ursula read guidebooks about parenting, and she was terribly concerned about how far her daughter lagged behind in speech development. Link said that her development was right on track in *Spanish*. She called most animals by their Spanish names, and, whenever she scuffed a knee or elbow, she seemed to forget English altogether and wail for her Marianna. Link asked if the girl was being raised to be Jewish like her stepfather or Mexican like the nanny, and Ursula called him a disgusting bigot.

In truth, no matter how much Marianna hated Link, he still trusted her more than he did Ursula. He hated that big stuck-up house with white rocks on the roof, a koi pond, and a terraced backyard of spiky modern sculptures that looked like obstacles for an amphibious landing; and he dreaded seeing Ursula sometimes more than he looked forward to visiting his daughter. He hated those Yorkshire terriers always riled by the canned Christmas jingle of the doorbell, and that cockatoo squawking and shitting in a pan. The bird could only say "Happy Birthday" in the shrill voice of a soused bag lady.

After every visit, Link would kick up his bike and ride away down the hillside road to drink himself numb in a bar off Ventura Boulevard. Hours later, he would show up for work with Preacher, smelling toxic. Preacher now had supply lines running all across San Gabriel and Riverside, hydroponic marijuana bred for strength along with batches of crystal meth. Link's days were a frazzled run of errands, deliveries, and the occasional shakedown. With the extra money, he bought huge presents for his daughter, and sometimes he would see faces in passing cars, laughing at the sight of him riding with a giant pink teddy bear tied to the back of his Harley.

However shaky, this pattern of monthly visits kept up until Lydia turned six. When Link gate-crashed her birthday that year, he also remembered being alarmed at his daughter's mood: She was by far the weirdest kid of the lot. She didn't appear interested in the festivities, but was fixated on some little book full of imaginary monsters she'd drawn. Link had never seen a kid act this way: She was in a trance too deep to participate in her own party. Uninterested in the cake, coaxed through opening her presents, grimacing at flashbulbs, she endured her birthday like a trip to the doctor, and Ursula grew insulted by her nonplussed reaction to each gift. But Link was proud of her: That was a *Hell's Angel* right there—a kid who didn't buy into any of this horseshit. She couldn't care less about changing a doll's diaper; and she didn't see why she needed to perform for her giddy mother, whom Link barely recognized, squealing and mincing around in a loose-knit sweater. After Ursula had scolded the kid for being so nonchalant about her extravagant soiree, Link overheard one of the mothers say that Lydia was on a new "dosage."

Link grabbed Ursula and hauled her into the kitchen, and asked her why in God's name she was putting a six-year-old on a drug without his consent. Ursula grew ferociously angry at the accusation, explaining that whenever Lydia got angry or frustrated, she held her breath until she passed out. It was a prescription for seizures. "She has the most furious temper you've ever seen, John. She changes from pink to red to purple, and then drops. The kid would rather pass out than give in."

"You called it a seizure, Ursula—and then you just described a temper tantrum. You've had more of those than any woman I know!"

A few minutes later, his daughter was sitting on his lap on the Harley while the parents took pictures and laughed. When another kid tried to climb on, Link started to get angry: He was tired of playing the clown for these parents and their snot-nosed brats. He kicked up the bike and sped off, holding Lydia in his lap as she howled and cheered with happiness, the first time she had sparked up during the whole affair. When he returned, the parents were in a frenzy. Apparently, no one thought it was safe for a man to take a small child on a Harley, without a helmet no less, and Ursula told him that she was going back to family court for a modification. Link was so angry that he stormed into the house and started breaking things. He kicked over a lamp and tried to strangle the cockatoo.

Not thirty minutes later, Link was sitting in the back of a squad car as it pulled away, watching two kids fight over his abandoned bike in the driveway. Although the initial charges of child endangerment and domestic violence were dropped, Ursula got a restraining order against him, and a judge revoked his visitation rights.

For the somber year that followed, Link was in and out of county jail on small possession charges. He didn't see his daughter. Ursula divorced the restaurateur, kept his house, and began living with an orthodontist. Link never met this newest stepfather or saw the *fancier* house they moved into on the West Side. Lydia became the greatest injustice of his life, a symbol of a systemic conspiracy against him. He knew lots of bikers with droves of kids: There were little naked babies running all around every clubhouse. He knew a brother who had six or seven illegitimate kids, and it seemed that every week even that human sperm bank was taking somebody camping, to see a shitty movie, or to play air hockey and eat corn dogs. Link resented that he had been held to a higher standard. Just because he lacked a permanent residence didn't mean, in his mind, that he was an unfit father; and just because he sold drugs didn't mean he couldn't impart some reasonable lessons about the world. After all, Ursula had put the kid on drugs to keep her from complaining. Yet somehow Link was the Antichrist.

One night in May 1990, when Link was just out of county jail on a drunk and disorderly, he met with Preacher to ask him for help in regaining visitation rights with his daughter. When he arrived, the place in Palm Springs was covered with moving boxes, and Cherise was meticulously packing up the kitchen and closets. Apparently their new desert property had finally been developed enough for them to move their operations. But they were stalled by another crisis. Preacher told him, "Good—I wanted you to be here for this anyway."

Over the course of the next few hours, his cluttered and half-packed living room filled up with visitors: the vice presidents of the San Diego and Berdoo chapters, the Angels' bondsman, and Preacher's two lawyers. The attorneys were small, silver-haired men. They had been through two long racketeering trials with Preacher, brought under the RICO statute, both resulting in hung juries; and they came into the dim, carpeted house, joking and laughing like honorary brothers.

There was bad news.

Just three days before, Hardy had been arrested at the Nevada state line with five hundred grams of meth. He was being held in Clark County jail on a hundred thousand dollars bail, and contacts in Vegas believed that Hardy was cooperating with authorities. He was giving names. They suspected that he had already signed an agreement to become a government witness in a new federal conspiracy case, and would likely try to gather information. Everyone was somber at the news, and Link moved into the kitchen to where Cherise was wrapping pots and pans with newspaper.

"I don't believe he would do something like that," she said. "He's a good boy, you know. He's just a kid."

"He doesn't have any balls, Cherise," said Link. "You could scare that kid with a rubber spider."

After the meeting, Preacher took Link aside in the dim hallway and explained the plan. The Angels' bondsman was heading up that night to bail out Hardy. "I want you to go with him."

Link stood for a long time with his back against the plaster wall, breathing heavily.

Preacher continued, "You're going to take care of this problem, and I'm going to take care of your family. Let's say twenty thousand dollars to start—and we'll work on getting you a new custody arrangement. I trust you, Link. You're tough and you keep your mouth shut. There's not enough people like you in this younger generation."

Link just nodded for a while with his mouth slanted. Finally he said, "I never did anything like this before. On this level."

"Time to graduate then, my boy. You won't have any trouble with it. He's betrayed us, and you're my guy here. Now I know you got a long history with this kid—but it's not all good. He's never been loyal to *you*."

Link shook his head.

"You honestly don't know?"

"Don't know what?"

"When your old lady was carrying your kid—maybe four months pregnant—he disappeared for about a month. Turns out he was living with her. Think about that for a second, Link. He was fucking your old lady while you were away, while she was carrying your child. Worst thing a brother can do is mess with another man's old lady. He's got no respect for anything we believe in, and he's ratting out everybody he knows."

Link was just staring ahead, frowning.

"He may be paranoid, so show up as a friend. Understand?" Preacher reached up and grabbed his shoulder, squeezing hard and shaking.

Link nodded solemnly.

"You do this for me, and I'll take care of you and your little girl. You got that as a promise."

Three days later, after the bondsman had freed Hardy to await trial, Link met his old friend outside Las Vegas to help him retrieve his impounded bike. After a gauntlet of lines and paperwork, the two rode off to the Circus Circus hotel, where they drank together for eight solid hours and lost half their money. At dawn they drank in the Stratosphere bar, Hardy talking nonstop about how he might just disappear, ride his chopper the entire length of the Western Hemisphere. Link called him an idiot, and said that there was some "jungle shit" in Panama that nobody could get through without a machete. Besides, where would he get the money?

At eleven that morning, as they were the first customers in a strip club, slumped at the edge of the stage and stuffing crumpled dollars into the G-strings of bored dancers, they talked about where they could find enough cash to get Hardy out of the country. Link had put off his assignment for so long he began to wonder if he was simply waiting for Hardy to have an accident and die on his own. If he stalled long enough, the little shit might get cirrhosis or lung cancer.

"Hey, that's real nice," Hardy said to the stripper. "Come on over here closer."

Or get himself killed in a bar.

They kept drinking, took some Benzedrine, and by dusk of that day they were reeling with delirious second winds. Link had decided that he couldn't kill the little bastard, no matter what kind of snitch he was. There was too much history, he was like an obnoxious relative. They rode across the desert, through a chaotic chain of new ideas, and, by dawn, they were drinking in a stupor at a Tex-Mex restaurant near the Grand Canyon. Link spent most of his remaining cash buying curios and T-shirts for his daughter—a Mexican bobble-head prospector and a miniature ghost town in a glass bubble of water. Hardy had a shark head on the end of a long stick, and whenever he pulled a trigger, it would bite. He kept annoying Link with it, nipping him on the beard, until Link lost his temper in the parking lot and slugged Hardy in the arm.

"What the fuck d'you go and do that for?" asked Hardy.

"You're irritating me with that thing."

They rode back into Nevada, where, once nestled into a dark casino in Mesquite, Hardy started pouting. Link bought him a whisky and told him to get over it, but Hardy called him a bully, growing enraged, saying that he was sick of how Link beat on him all the time. He began yelling and throwing chips, until security surrounded him.

Outside on the curb, Hardy began crying, while Link sat next to him, rolling a cigarette.

"Just stop that shit, man. It's embarrassing."

Hardy bawled and wiped his nose and said, "I'm *fucked.*"

Link said, "You don't think I got problems, man? I got a beautiful little daughter that I can't even see from closer than four hundred feet. I got to get into the bushes and watch her with motherfucking *binoculars* or something. Night-vision shit. Crawl around like a fucking bird watcher just to see if the little princess lost a tooth. And Ursula, don't even get me started."

"She's married to that Jewish guy," said Hardy, wiping his eyes.

"No, that was the other guy, I think."

"We ought to take him out, Link. We ought to ride back there and teach the son of a bitch something."

Hardy laid out an idea to rob Ursula's house, and it grew more macabre by the minute. They could tie up the husband and turn Ursula out in front of him. Hardy seemed more deranged than Link had ever given him credit for. He talked about torturing the bastard. Dipping him in the Jacuzzi, seeing how long he could hold his breath. Link told Hardy to calm down, breathe through his nose. But Link did briefly fantasize about the idea: a big thrill ride, a violent, looting carnival extravaganza, like getting stoned and riding Harleys through a theme park.

Hardy really wanted to ruin the husband, and he started to seem crazy, staring off into space and talking about how the guy had stolen Ursula from them; how he was a rich thief, and that he stole everything he ever had. He said that the Jews had been kicked out of every decent country in the world. This was how they infiltrated, he said. They married good Catholic girls like Ursula, and had half-breed children. He was the devil in that house—and they had to get him.

Link was exasperated with this line of reasoning, and replied, "Now don't start getting all religious and political about it, Hardy—because we don't even know the guy. And I don't even know which guy you're talking about."

"I loved her so fucking much, man."

He started crying again as he said this, and Link had the guilty sense that this poor loser had cared a lot more about Ursula than *he* ever had. But Link just said, "You keep crying like this and I'm going to have to kill you right now."

"We'll ride out there, you and me—and we'll tear the place up," said Hardy. "Torch through that house. Teach them both some respect. And when we're finished, she won't even challenge you again. Come on, Link. You let her punk you, man. She made a fool out of you. We can do this. You'll go get your daughter back. Take her someplace, don't ever look back."

Link thought for a long time, and imagined himself living out of motel rooms, town to town, trying to take care of that little girl. Seedy dives would fill up with plastic ponies, dolls and coloring books; and he could head north, across the border, eventually take up with friends in Vancouver. It wasn't any kind of life for a kid—but it couldn't be worse than the life she had now: She'd never have an ounce of freedom; she'd have her whole life written for her on the back of a cotillion program, from ballet lessons to rich prep schools, graduating from a childhood of antipanic medication to an adolescence full of vigorous cokeheads. Link pictured all the Hell's Angels' kids at campsites and clubhouses, dashing around with runny noses and stained shirts. How could God even sort out which

life was better than another? All he knew for sure was that he loved the
little girl, and that her mother was a bitch.

"All right, Hardy. We're going."

They were out of cash, so they siphoned gas and headed west, and
Hardy rode harder and faster than Link had ever seen. Somewhere just
past the state line, weaving in and out of weekend traffic at ninety, Link
began to perceive his situation more clearly in the rush of passing taillights. What the hell were they doing? Were they honestly going to ride
back to L.A. and beat up Ursula's old man, and grab his daughter and
ride off into the sunset like mechanized cowboys?

He thought of the nurse, the family court judge, and, for a while, he
even thought of his mother and how she used to berate him for his mud-
dled decision making. As a kid, he broke windows and shot pellets at the
neighbor's laundry. He liked to set fires in Dumpsters, and once he had
thrown a rock at a motorcycle cop. He broke into houses, he hot-wired
cars. It wasn't that he didn't care about the rules; he was more acutely
aware of the law than the kids who followed it. It was as if he only knew
himself in the face of some self-created danger, and he only liked himself
when he was shrugging off the consequences. He was a tough fucker,
and if you questioned him at nine years old, he'd pop you in the mouth.
There was a kind of dignity in it—a refusal to budge; and he remembered how his mother would cry, and his father would strap him with the
belt, pausing, giving him a wink, as if his punishment was less for any
crime than for simply making his mother unhappy.

He remembered how guilty he felt when his father died and he was
having such a good time with all the cousins he had never met. What a
blast it had been to have them all playing those sinister games, hiding
the retainer of one girl down under the porch, stripping off each other's
fancy clothes, playing hide-and-seek around the yard. He'd cried during
the burial, but he'd plundered the coatroom during the wake. Then Link
remembered how his mother had cried as if assaulted, so angry at all
these children who refused to share the burden, and she shouted at them
that Link's father wasn't coming back to whip them senseless. And it

seemed like the whole rest of his life had been a search for that phantom beating. He remembered it all so clearly as he rode through traffic uphill, over the desert and past the looming brush and saguaro. He didn't want to carry out this midnight plan. He tried to catch up to Hardy, who was cutting right in front of cars. Finally, when they could occupy both lanes, Link hovered alongside his partner and yelled over the growl and the gusts: "Pull over."

Hardy veered off the freeway and stopped along an empty road. Link told him, "Buddy, we're not doing this. Let's go back to Vegas and get some tail."

"*You* go back," said Hardy. "I know where she lives. You want to bitch up on me, go ahead."

Hardy sped back onto the highway, and Link couldn't believe the little bastard. He was having some kind of psychotic episode. He'd snapped. So Link went after him, trying to catch him among the cars, speeding right up next to him and throwing pennies at him across the rushing wind. Hardy was cursing from his bike, and finally pulled off the road again, up into the desert foothills, winding a long way from the freeway before stepping off beside a water relay station along the aqueduct.

Hardy said, "I've fucking had it. Right now. You and me, Link. You and me!"

"You and me what, you little shit?"

"You been fucking with me since I was seventeen years old, and I've had enough. I *love* that woman—I loved that woman since the first time I ever saw her—"

This speech embarrassed Link. In the edges of a broth-colored light, he noticed that Hardy had a long blade dangling out of his sleeve.

"Hardy—this is all bullshit. Stop this. You and I are friends, and I'm sorry I dump on you. It's just you're such a cute little cocksucker."

"You say whatever you want, Link—because I see the picture all real clear now. You're a manipulator. You've been keeping me down all my life."

"Listen, Hardy—I got to level with you about something. I was supposed to kill you about two or three days ago."

Link started to walk over, thinking he would just put his arm around the kid and calm him down, like always, but Hardy turned and stabbed him in the gut.

Crisp and jagged, the blade sunk down into his abdomen. He didn't feel pain right away, though he could tell the damage by how quickly the blood saturated his shirt and his pants; but he felt a deep and blinding surge of disgust, as if the betrayal itself had reached down deeper.

Link took off his chain belt and tried to see the wound. Hardy came at him again, lunging ahead, grunting and growling like a cornered dog that finally panics. Link whipped the chain across his face to keep him away. It broke the skin on Hardy's cheek, and the pain riled him further. He started shouting and pointing at Link and accusing him of lying. Trying to stop up the blood coming from his belt line, Link looked up and added, "I can't believe how stupid you are, Hardy. After every fucking thing I ever did for you."

"I'm going to kill you."

Link stood up with his back against the high fence along the aqueduct, lit by a distant spotlight. Hardy rushed at him and Link whipped the chain again, catching him on the hand. When Hardy flinched backward and dropped the knife, Link wrapped the chain around his fist. He called out his name, and Hardy looked right up at him. Then Link connected a punch so solidly into Hardy's temple that the kid sank right down into the dirt, holding his head around both ears. Methodically, Link dragged him away from the knife, a lumbering giant, moving slowly in the bleak light. As if by rote, a show of strength, Link stomped on his struggling hands. Concentrating more with each brutal and deliberate move, Link said, "You *see*, you dumb motherfucker. You *see* what you just did! You don't want this shit."

Hardy didn't speak, but roiled in the gravel; so Link kicked him a few more times, and shouted, "I'm dying here, you little traitor. You got me in the fucking *kidney*, I think. I'm bleeding all over." He stomped Hardy's ribs, feeling them give way like the wooden keel of an old canoe; he picked up his limp body, propped him against the fence, and busted the chain across his face. Just talking to himself and grunting, as if the procedure were now more irritating than violent, Link picked Hardy up and threw him down headfirst; then he twisted Hardy's legs, curled them upward in the air, and sat on them with all his weight, bending the kid's spine with a move called a Russian omelet. There came a loud crack, as if a sapling had broken in half. When Hardy collapsed into a lump, Link kept on kicking him and heaving him around the dirt road without a thought.

A while later, it occurred to him that Hardy hadn't moved in a long time.

Then Link sat down and felt the anger leave him as if through the open wound; the last sparks of hatred and vengeance seemed dampened by a grim feeling of worthlessness.

Twenty minutes later, Link was dizzy, dragging Hardy's dead body toward the aqueduct. He found a place where coyotes had tunneled under the fence, and he tried to pry up the rest of the wire, cutting his hands. Once he had a small, workable space, he shoved the body through to the other side, but he got stuck trying to wiggle through after it, and lay stranded, feeling the throbbing pain and blood loss. Finally, caught halfway under a crooked fence, Link passed out.

He woke with police cars around him, wire cutters clipping him free and paramedics already stripping his shirt around the gash. Someone was reading him his rights in the darkness while a few ranchers stood by.

As they placed him on a gurney and raised him back into the ambulance, Link said, "Dumb son of a bitch. Died with his boots on."

For eleven years Link kept his mouth shut.

Preacher never faced charges stemming from either Link's arrest or Hardy's death. The theory in the courtroom was that the fight was entirely over Ursula, which Link thought might as well have been the case. He was less ashamed of this as a motive. Although his defense lawyer seemed mostly concerned with developing any courtroom theory that covered Preacher, he was either so incompetent or so indifferent that he never managed to prove that Hardy had stabbed Link first. Link was in a fatalistic depression so deep that he stopped caring. When he testified on his own behalf, he convinced the jury that he was nothing more than a grave and sullen ape. He was convicted of aggravated second-degree manslaughter, and because of his previous record he was sentenced to fifteen years with the possibility of parole in eight. This was meaningless arithmetic to Link.

A year later, he killed a man at the RPC in Chino and got away with it. It felt easy now—part of living. He was without remorse for the job on the inside, because he no longer thought life was worth more than a few tough deals or bad decisions. He had heard about how long it took to fry somebody on the electric chair, how it surprised onlookers that an average man was so hard to kill. But nobody was *hard to kill*. You could have had a convict do the same job with one flick of the wrist. Life stopped being a miracle on the inside. As a prisoner, he learned to see it as a narrow path between the plans and accidents of other men. A Hell's Angel convicted of killing a brother, he was without support, and he knew that he survived only because he was lucky and quiet and—eventually—because he could make pictures under the topmost shroud of skin.

Two years later, transferred, he received his first letter from Lydia, then in the third grade. Amid a tumble of breathless descriptions of her life, from the classroom where she wasn't paying attention, to her friends, to her clothes, to her problems with her mother, she wrote, "I know that deep down you are a good person." Reading this, it was the first time that he'd been afraid in years. He desperately didn't want his little girl to discover that he was as ugly as anything she could imagine.

This correspondence over the years was his rehabilitation, for he stopped drugging on the inside, he got a job, he read, he learned his skills—not because he believed in his own redemption, but because he wanted to compose letters that wouldn't diffuse the girl's simple belief in the world. He needed to find what was worthwhile about this god-awful planet, if only to have a decent conversation with the kid someday. He wrote back to her, and she confessed things to him in sweeps of childish sentences. Four years later, when he had been reclassified and moved to Calipatria, sharing a cell with Rios, Lydia wrote him a passionate letter about how much she hated her social studies teacher. The woman humiliated her, made her stand up in the front of class every day and read her homework out loud; required her mother to sign everything she did; assigned extra projects; made her stay in for recess.

Link tossed the letter across his cell to Rios, and asked, laughing quietly, "What can we do about a Mrs. Wooten? Marlboro School for Girls."

Even under the best circumstances, prisoners live at a different speed than those on the outside, as if on a distant planet with a wider orbit. It was nearly impossible for Link to keep up with the pace at which the world changed. Eight and a half years felt like freezing into a glacier, suspended animation, only to someday step out into an uneasy future of Internet porno and two-buck-a-gallon gasoline. But it was worse for him than most convicts, because he went so long without visitors, because for so many years he'd felt excommunicated by his friends, abandoned by his family, and betrayed by Preacher. At one point, he went a stretch of two years at Calipatria without a single visit, only his daughter's inconstant letters.

Arturo Rios used to rag on him about it. Rios himself had a huge extended family, and every weekend he saw his wife and children, who came with care packages, gossip, and bribes for the COs. All over the state, during a federal racketeering case against the Mexican Mafia, guards were cracking down on privileges, but Link couldn't tell from Rios, who doled out a secret fortune each month for conjugal visits. He had fathered his two youngest kids behind bars. Whenever the older ones acted up—smoked, drank, or sassed their mother—they'd wind up in the visiting room for a lecture. Depending on the political climate with the guards, Rios would sit behind glass and dress them down on the phone, or he'd meet them in a private attorney's room and give them a thrashing with a guard's belt. He would return to the cell, turning gloomy, and Link knew that he missed the day-to-day struggles too much to be compensated by a ceremonial fatherhood. He was the kind of man who loved his children most when disciplining them.

Sometimes Link would try to strike back at Rios, saying that *of course* he had tons of visits, because he had a family of thousands like every other spic. How many junk cars did they need to get here?

Rios said that Link was just jealous because he was a big, ugly peckerwood who scared all the women away.

Link replied that Mexicans stole American jobs. Rios said that Americans stole *America*. Besides, Mexicans took jobs because white people were soft.

Link said the only place a Mex could conceivably beat a white guy was in the lighter weight divisions of boxing. He didn't want to hear about how California was *stolen,* because Mexicans stole everything that wasn't tied down.

Rios said that America couldn't function without Latino immigrants; they were the only thing that made the country float in the post-slavery era.

Rios had done too much time: Arguing with him was like getting smothered to death in a prison library. He railed on the Aryan Brotherhood, and said that anybody who worshipped European history was a fool, because the only true talent of the Anglo-Saxons was turning other races against each other. American history was an experiment in getting the poor stupid white people to defend the rich stupid white people. The middle class was nothing but a new moat around the castle, filled with managers, cops, dutiful Protestants, and a few brawling rednecks like Link.

He claimed that he respected the Hell's Angels but thought that they were suckers for still calling themselves patriots, for letting all the white-power bullshit creep in with each new wave of embittered losers. White people had never fought a fair battle once in their history; they kicked the rest of the world in the balls; sucker punched them in the dark. They had taken America with smallpox and gunpowder and wave after wave of armed, Puritan assholes, bribing and rat-fucking the Indians westward, or riding train tracks laid down by the Chinese ("And Irish!" shouted Link), and it didn't matter if you were country club or white trash, you bought into the same bullshit—that the danger bubbled up from the classes below, stirred by the newest wave from somewhere else.

Link replied that Mexicans smelled bad.

"Politics," said Rios, "life is politics," and he meant two things at once. In a high-tech prison like Calipatria, with twenty-three-hour lockdowns, where most days seemed like a progression of shadows and kited messages, conversations through the walls and the ventilation shafts, an hour grimacing at the sunlight in shackles, walking between layers of barbed wire and under towers with poised rifles, seeing only the dead gulls that had flown into the electric fences—survival was an exhausting political campaign. Maybe, Link thought, this was why so many lifers talked like they were campaigning for office. After all, a convict's descent matched, inversely, the rise of any congressman, from the college of the county lockup, wrangling over scrip and fighting for recreation, to the law school of the RPC, where a prisoner joined his party—the Aryan Brotherhood, La Eme, La Efe, the Black Gangster Disciples—and began making contacts and clawing his way up the ranks with shivs and contraband.

Link's unexpected loyalty to his cell mate, his refusal to become an informant for the guards, who were looking for ways to erode the power of La Eme—all of it had hurt his political standing with the authorities over the years. In the super-maxes like Calipatria, the corrections officers had their own gang—White Lightning—gaining numbers, and they tried to control every green light on a government snitch, every piece of gossip through the pipes, every rumble between rival cliques. The more separate Link felt from the Aryan Brotherhood, the more he became paranoid that the guards were intercepting his daughter's letters. His mail had arrived opened for a few weeks, until, one day, the flow stopped entirely.

He was therefore surprised when he had a visitor one day, and the COs were abuzz with *how she looked*. His status among them seemed to have recovered overnight as they led him to a private room and sat him down at a table across from Ursula.

It took Link a moment to recover his wits. The scent of her was like a breeze through a citrus grove, and he had not smelled anything for years but the gray soup of the prison: crop chemicals, the methane stench of cows across the irrigation trench, disinfectant, sweat, the brine of the Salton Sea. He waited with his eyes closed. She said, "I'm here because I'm at the end of my rope with Lydia."

A guard stood in the back of the room, eavesdropping. Anybody watching this meeting through the camera overhead wouldn't be able to imagine how Link had ever been with a woman like this. She didn't look touched by the years, let alone pawed by his big, ugly hands. Her hair was pulled back tightly over her head, streaked blonde; her eyes seemed bright and young; she wore a white sweater with the fuzzy texture of a seeding dandelion.

She started off talking about Lydia's medical condition—a fourteen-year-old girl on a cocktail of antidepressants. She talked about panic and rage attacks, and how many therapists and doctors Lydia had seen over the years; and she talked about her own tireless dedication to making her daughter well. Link wanted to say that the little girl had grown up on so much medication that she probably didn't know her own damned personality; but while Ursula spoke, he could see a politician's resolve not to stray from planned remarks.

She said, "So basically, Lydia has just vanished. We thought for a long time that she was living with friends, and we did everything to hunt her down. We talked to every parent. Some of them have even seen her. It's insane, John. She goes house to house, and she's got thousands of friends. . . ."

"How long has this been?"

"Well. It's been a couple of months now."

They sat in silence. Link noticed the faint puffiness beneath her down-turned mouth, angry chinks along the edges, and it looked to him like the only part of her that had aged.

So he lowered his voice and said, "Call the cops."

"Imagine that coming from *you*. We didn't want to right away, because it doesn't seem like she's moved out of her circle of friends."

"Ursula—come on. She's fourteen, friends or not—"

"Now, don't do that to me. You don't know the kind of wars I've fought with Lydia. If I called the police, and they brought her back—I promise you she'd leave the state. Whatever you do with Lydia, you get a nuclear response. That's the truth."

"So you just let her live with her friends?"

"We try to keep track of where she is. I've tried every possible thing you can imagine. She's done versions of this since she was two years old. She's got too much of you in her. You really have no idea what an ordeal it's been for me. It's like raising a bomb that's constantly going off in your face."

She took out a little packet of mints and placed one on her tongue.

"The reason I came is because I think you should understand your position in all of this. She uses you. She believes that you're a person who's never compromised in life. That has a kind of glamour to her. She doesn't see any of *this*." She looked around at the walls.

"Bring her around sometime."

"To her, we're all complete hypocrites because we've given her a comfortable life. She has this *fantasy* about you. She thinks you're the freest man in the world, all of that Angels bullshit."

He sat quietly, nodding at his bound hands.

"She may still try to write to you," she continued. She swallowed. The mint seemed to thicken her tongue. "Or contact you in some way. I know she keeps track of your information, and she saves your letters. She has these obsessive scrapbooks. Everything is so dramatic, but she doesn't know what it's like to grow up without anything—like we did. Now, I must admit to a certain amount of snooping. I've read some of your letters, and I don't think you ever did much to emphasize the mistakes you made in your life."

Link was incredulous. He looked at every wall in the room before staring back at Ursula to say: "I think they're pretty damn well *emphasized*."

At this, the meeting was over.

He thought about Ursula the first night afterward with a painfully insistent hard-on, imagining her face again, like it had been burned into his eyes by the overhead lights. He imagined grabbing her tightly bound hair and burrowing his big square fingertips down between the blonde strands, into the earthy brown underneath, holding her head, controlling it. She was surrendering, losing track of her staged speech, her eyes closed, all the muscles in that tense and pretty face loosening as he leaned across the table and stroked her with callused thumbs. And he plucked loose the buttons on that puffy sweater. Smelled the material. He undressed her and picked her up and put her on the table, unrolled stockings to the skin underneath, so pale against the tangled ink on his arms and hands; and, in his mind, she was shivering, aroused and disarmed, unable to lecture him anymore. Once he was holding her just under the ribs, and she was arching her back, she would give in to him at last and completely, hold on like he was racing a hundred miles an hour and she was afraid of falling off. His hands would feel huge around her trim waist. He would find the same skin and the same stomach and—

And when his fantasy ended abruptly, he faced the ceiling and knew he was a fool. Only the most desperate creep could have gotten himself off thinking about such an unpleasant meeting. How could any real man be so easily aroused by a family crisis and a prolonged insult?

The following day, Link wrote letters to the LAPD Missing Persons Unit and the National Runaway Switchboard. He asked Rios for advice, breaking the silence as he worked on his tattoo. Together, they concluded that there was something wrong with Ursula's tone when she discussed her daughter's chemical imbalance. What was a "rage attack" anyway? He didn't want to be ignorant, but it sounded like a fancy word for being very, very pissed off. And it seemed to him that Lydia had plenty of good reasons for it. A temper in a young lady shouldn't be a disease. After all, Ursula had once been the angriest chick in Lakeside, California.

Rios helped him put these thoughts down in a letter, even though Link complained the entire time about having to get tutoring in English from a Mexican.

He wrote to Ursula that his correspondence with his daughter was "personal and intimate" and that, no matter how desperate the situation, he would appreciate "her ongoing respect on that matter." He claimed that Lydia was a very intelligent young girl, smarter than the both of them put together, and that it did her an injustice to pawn everything off on a mental illness. He didn't believe in her "rage." He believed that she was like him, too reckless and too restless, and prone to having "a little too much fun." What was most "imperative"—was to get the girl back home and make sure that she was safe. She was fourteen and didn't have the ability to take care of herself out there. Ursula spoke about her like a "war" and a "bomb"—but she was just a little girl. He had gone to the police himself, and he hoped to have "her complete cooperation."

After much arguing, he added a line from Rios, even though he thought it was heavy-handed: "When a child runs away, she *wants* to be hunted down."

He sent it off and waited only a week.

Ursula responded with the angriest letter he had ever read. She wrote that a convicted felon had no right to accuse her of anything. He didn't know his daughter; he didn't know her volatility; and he didn't know what it took to raise a *hamster*. He had not seen the tantrums she threw over the smallest things. At fourteen, the sweet "little girl" was drinking and having sex with strangers and doing drugs and fighting like a banshee to have her way. How dare he accuse her of failing? Did he even *know* that she used to cut herself? Did he know that she had tried to commit suicide? Ursula had found her unconscious in the bathtub, having taken all of her antidepressants and her stepfather's thyroid medication; they rushed her to the hospital and pumped her stomach. And what had Lydia said upon regaining consciousness fourteen hours later? "Go to hell, Mother."

But despite all this, Ursula was the parent here, and she hurt for her in ways that Link couldn't possibly comprehend. She was sorry if, in their brief meeting, she hadn't adequately expressed her grief, that she hadn't satisfied his requirements for suffering. But she was the one who lived with this burden, every day of her life.

"After all," she concluded, "I lost my daughter. You lost a souvenir."

six

Back at the trailer after the long drive, Link carried his daughter inside and laid her down on his bed. After a brief farce of trying to sleep on his short, narrow couch, he gave up and paced most of the night in front of the monochrome glow of his old television.

He should probably have called Ursula now that Lydia was safely asleep, but he so dreaded the conversation that he chose instead to wait until his daughter had cleaned up. Who knew what Ursula would do or say? After the first six months of searching, she had stopped cooperating and acted like every letter or call was another imposition, or, even worse, his ploy to get closer to her. The ugliest moment came when he wrote to Ursula's husband asking if he would offer a reward for information. After a few weeks, they responded to his suggestion with a counter of thirty thousand dollars—by all means a solid figure, in the higher strata of rewards, but it was a slap in the face to Link. It was barely more than they had paid for Lydia's private school, probably the equivalent of her years of clarinet lessons, and it was nothing beside what they dropped on her stepbrothers and half siblings, all of them probably riding horses and boats or tinkering on grand pianos. These people gave thirty g's to charities he had never heard of, to political candidates destined to be nothing more than embarrassing bumper stickers.

Throughout that night while his daughter tossed in his bed, Link wandered in the dark, whispering responses to these years of unresolved arguments, and checking repeatedly and superstitiously on Lydia. He was like a nervous new parent hovering over an infant. He refilled the water glass beside the bed three times, listening to her gulping it down in the dark. For a while, he was alarmed by the choking cough and the way she sat up in the sheets, still unconscious, scratching furiously as if tied to an anthill; but past three o'clock, her sleep smoothed out like deep water. Around dawn, in the stale air, she shed her jeans and T-shirt, and lay face-down, arms and legs outstretched, looking like a skydiver whose chute had never opened. Her nose was stuffed. He looked in on her, staring at the tangling black hair down her pale back. She was so thin that her spine stood out like a trail of stones. Her joints were scratched, her skin looked like a thumbed gardenia.

As Link was noticing this, his daughter rolled onto her back. He averted his eyes and left the room, closing the accordion door and retreating to the front step, where he sat down and lit a cigarette. He had just witnessed a woman's body, and a woman with a lot of aggressive ideas. She had a stud in her navel, and the blue-ink tip of an ornate medieval dagger peeking out of her underwear along the inner thigh. He didn't like the idea of his daughter having any tattoo, let alone a slutty one that was poorly done. For this, he felt responsible. Besides, he knew the kinds of women with ink down there; he had carved a hundred bleeding hearts and roses, and he couldn't help observing a pattern of behavior. They were fierce and reckless pieces of ass, women whose youthful looks burned off like kindling in a bonfire, the sorts of women who showed up for the party claiming that no man could ever *handle* them, and left looking like they'd been handled half to death.

The morning was heating up as Link cleaned out his car and went through his daughter's leather satchel. He found condoms, a cigarette lighter, a glass pipe, a hundred scribbled notes to herself, and several Polaroids of smiling bleary-eyed girls. She seemed to save everything. Matchbooks, place mats, paper doilies covered with phone numbers. He found scraps of letters and Post-it notes: "I'll be back tonight—J" or "Call me—*please!* Love, Chloe." Under all this sentimental debris, he fished out a Glock 19, still loaded with half a mag. The discovery made some of his daughter's earlier ramblings seem more dangerous. Had she considered killing herself out on the beach? He hid the gun on top of his medicine cabinet until he could think of a better place.

Then he waited, watching the time.

Just past noon, Lydia rose from bed, asking where she was and only groaning to his response. She threw up, brushed her teeth with her finger, and migrated to the old couch, where she catnapped for a few more hours in front of the TV. Sniffling, she kept asking if she was in prison or rehab; then she was confounded by the fact that the TV had only five channels. Link described how the signal came through the air into the rabbit ears, and she replied: "So I went back in time."

When Link had a client at three o'clock, an old trucker from Blythe, she bummed a cigarette from him and lounged on the floor, watching. The client sat with his shirt off, tufts of white hair on his chest and a sunburned border halfway up his left arm. He wanted an eagle with an American flag in its torso, but Lydia convinced him to change the design, saying that it looked too much like the logo for a burger stand in Hollywood. Her nose was stuffy, her eyelids swollen, and she kept opening her mouth and massaging a pain in her jaw. But Link was shocked by how friendly she was to the trucker. While the tattoo machine buzzed, she listened sympathetically to his story about a sick mother. When the conversation lightened, and he began describing a long haul with a million dollars' worth of concentrated cranberry juice, Lydia laughed at all his jokes with an endearing tilt to her head. The geezer started sucking in his gut. Whenever Link glanced away from his work to see his daughter's face, he was dizzy with conflicting responses. She had a smile so wide and sincere that it made her look beautiful even during her worst hangover; but, lowering her chin and slapping at the trucker when he made crude puns, she was so inexplicably flirtatious that Link needed to suppress the urge to pick up the old man and sling him out across the highway.

By the time he had finished the tat, his daughter and the trucker acted like lifelong pals. She hugged him good-bye. Then, once he had driven off in his rig, she became morose, as if she had expended all her energy for the day. While Link sterilized his equipment, cleaned the benches and pigment bottles, he couldn't deny his jealousy that a passing stranger had so engaged his daughter. He tried to get her to eat something—Pop Tarts or sugar cereal—but she said, "I'd be healthier on just the crank."

For the rest of the daylight hours, she kept her distance from him. She talked only to herself, grumbling about the living conditions. The shower was just a dribble of lukewarm water; his coffee was only tasteless granules of instant powder ("Do I drink this or snort it?"); his records were a disheartening collection of Bob Seger albums ("Who in their right mind would listen to a beer commercial?"). By early evening, she was acting like someone who had been badly gypped in a witness relocation program.

She broke her silence at about half past five to ask him if he missed any of the comforts of jail. Then she sat outside in the twilight, listening to a radio call-in show on a transistor shaped like a Coke bottle, a long, querulous sweep of Valley girls asking advice about their STDs and unwanted pregnancies.

Link had a plan, but he figured he'd give her some space to detox first.

She came inside and scanned her old letters and the documents from Link's search, spread across the wall. She was as hushed and somber as if in a museum, until finally she plopped down onto his couch and flipped through a newsletter about missing children.

"Wow," she said. "Check this out. This one chick has been missing since 1978. She must have missing kids of her *own* by now."

When she came across the age-enhanced picture of herself, she started to laugh. But her smile gradually faded. Her eyes narrowed suspiciously—*competitively*, Link thought—until her face looked mean and hurt, as if she had just confronted a well-scrubbed twin sister who had gotten all the breaks.

"If I turn myself in, do I get this thirty grand?"

"No," said Link.

"What a rip."

Finally, she joined Link while he ate his dinner. He poured her some cereal, and after she tried a few spoonfuls, she seemed to realize her ravenous hunger and kept refilling the bowl. They faced each other across a rickety card table, crunching. Outside, the highway played the fading notes of passing trucks.

Finally she said, "Is this some kind of kidnapping?"

"Maybe."

"I don't even know where I am."

"Outside Indio."

"You know, I saw this sign once. I was driving to Las Vegas with some friends, and for this turnoff, one big sign just goes, 'Vegas,' and next to it, it says: 'Other Desert Cities.' I was like—*what* other desert cities? I mean it's fucked up that they don't even bother to list them. That's like having a sign that says, 'Everything Else.' I was all like: let's go there—I bet nobody ever goes that way."

"Did you?"

"No, we went to Vegas. And I couldn't get into anyplace because my ID sucked. I wound up spending the whole time at this water slide."

At first, Link thought her eyes were so beautiful that he had a hard time listening to her; but then they began to seem blind or crazy, so pale and glazed that she appeared to be staring into a floodlight that no one else could see.

"Anyway, I'm not staying here for much longer," she said. "I just have to keep moving."

"Yeah, Portland. I know."

"I don't have to go to *Portland*, I just have to go somewhere."

"Uh-huh."

"I'm in a lot of trouble." She took a big bite of cereal.

"You pregnant?"

She started to laugh at this, a bead of milk clinging to her bottom lip. "*No,* I'm not pregnant. Why would I have to leave town because I was pregnant?"

"I don't know."

"The scorned woman! God. That's so—medieval. No, I'm not pregnant. But I don't want to say too much: it's more like a legal issue. I shouldn't tell you; it'll put you in a bad position."

Link gave the first puff of an aborted laugh, then said, "Thanks."

"My boyfriend had this idea. We could get married so I'd never have to testify against him. You know, they can't force a wife to rat out her husband. Shrinks, doctors—they all talk now. Blah, blah—whatever you want from them. But marriage is still sacred."

"Pretty romantic."

She shoveled in a few rapid bites, then said with her mouth full, "I swear I thought he was in love with me. There were times when I looked at him and just . . ." She pantomimed cringing, as if frostbitten, hugging her own shoulders, apparently indicating some kind of writhing pleasure or indecision. "You know? If I could just get there—get to a soft spot." She rapped her knuckles on the table. "It was so close sometimes. I mean, he knew, he really, honestly *knew* that there was something different about me. He understood that. He was just really fucked up about it. He couldn't express himself without, like . . . firearms."

"And you're supposed to testify in court?"

"Oh no, no, no. No. It's all a disaster now. He's dead."

"Who?"

"My boyfriend. He got shot."

"Uh-huh."

"In the neck."

"Too bad."

"It's like—it's not even real to me yet. I just don't think it's hit me that all this is really happening." She gestured to the dim trailer all around her.

"You know, Lydia, maybe you don't have to jump town right away."

She began tapping her finger against her head, and replied, "Mmmm—

but I got lots of information. So I just got to get away from this whole situation."

"Information?"

"He was well-connected." She started rocking her head side to side as she spoke. "So there's a lot of people looking for my white ass right *now*. That's why I'm like—this is my last meal here. This bowl of fruity whatever, and then I'm out."

She held up the bowl and slurped the remaining milk from it.

"Kid? Can I say something? All my life, it was always somebody else's fault. Do you see what I'm trying to say? For thirty some years I was fighting and drinking and drugging, like everybody had it in for me. Then one day, I just sobered up and realized something: I was the asshole."

"Yeah, your higher power isn't going to do shit for me, Dad."

Staring off at the screen door, Link said, "I can get you money, but I need time."

"Don't worry about it. I'm looking around, and I know you don't have any money. You did what you could. Thank you for the cereal and the lecture—that's actually all the fathering I need."

"I got a lot of people who owe me. *Let* me help you. And you got to promise me something, too."

"Promises are totally meaningless to a person like me."

"Give me a week. Give me a week and you stay clean the whole time. If you got people looking for you, who's going to find you out here? They don't know anything about me."

"Cops are probably listening to us right now."

"No, Jesus—I'm nobody. I just piss in a cup once a month. My parole officer's got a caseload like . . ." He spread his arms out wide. "A week. You dry out. Next Saturday, if you're on your feet, kid, I'll give you everything I got in this world. Whatever it amounts to. Six shirts and a jar of peanut butter. You need to stay put for a few days, kid. Take a break from all this drama."

Lydia glanced at the fading light through the open front door, then back at her father, a queasy look on her face but no decision whatsoever in her eyes. She said, "I just ate all that shit *way* too fast."

Lydia & Jonah

part three

From the Topanga Messenger, *December 16, 2000:*

Topanga Boys Play Key Role in Murder Investigation

BY THOMAS KITTERING, *Staff Reporter*

In another twist in the ongoing investigation of the incident on Old Topanga Road, police reports reveal that several local children assisted the escape of a woman who is now considered to be a material witness and possible suspect.

After days maintaining a pact of silence, ten-year-old Joey De Salvo confessed to his family after a nightmare. His mother promptly called LAPD homicide detectives, who have since interviewed each of the boys involved. Lead detective David Holcomb refused to give specifics, but stated that two children guided a teenage girl along hiking trails through the Santa Monica Mountains.

"The children have been extremely cooperative with police thus far," states Detective Holcomb. "This has been a troubling event for the entire community, and we certainly appreciate the way that the families have rallied together and aided us throughout the week."

One of the victims of the home invasion, Martin Reynard, was reportedly a local dealer of methamphetamines. Neighborhood activists have called meetings to discuss growing drug problems within the canyon, and ways to protect our children more effectively.

"I just can't stand the idea that those kids were *playing* outside that house," said one resident mother. "That could have been any of our children. And there might be hundreds of houses out there, just like that one."

Printing from online archives, 5/1/01.

seven

Lydia first met Jonah at a little past 3 A.M. on a warm and restless night when every kid in the city seemed to be out looking for a better party.

It was the middle of July, and leftover fireworks still detonated on residential streets around kicked bottles and idling cars. In the air was a steady wash of sirens, crickets, and stereo bass, while every now and then a helicopter would circle overhead, its searchlights fragmenting through sycamore branches onto packs of loitering teens. Cops broke up a party in Mandeville Canyon before eleven, and word spread that the kegs on Kenter were a rumor. Lydia rode in the backseat of a Mustang convertible, jammed in tightly with her friends, all of them fielding cell phone calls, pledging their determination not to waste another night at the bluffs—dropping cigarettes and Hennessy bottles into the ravine.

Over the past years, these girls had been more than Lydia's friends: They had fed and harbored her; they had circulated her among guest rooms, couches, pool houses, and the four-poster beds of out-of-town parents. Lydia woke nearly every morning among a new set of volleyball trophies or glass figurines, in the shrine to a daughter gone to college or rehab, on the liniment-smelling bed of a grandparent, beneath collages of family vacations, or amid a hundred pictures of grinning strangers, brandishing ski poles or fishing rods.

Chloe, Lydia's best friend and the most righteous about protecting her, was a hardworking rich girl with the mentality of a social worker. The daughter of a movie agent and a child psychologist, she was a plump and freckled straight-A student, always blushing with excitement or outrage, who loved to sit up late, clutching her pillow and mulling over the injustices of the world. They had agreed to join the Peace Corps together, until Lydia found out that it required a college degree. But the rest of Lydia's friendships were intense and fleeting, with girls like Danielle, now riding in the front seat, who had lent her a suede skirt for the evening and threatened to call DHS if Lydia hurt it.

Beyond Danielle and Chloe, there was a network of girls, kicked out of top-tier private academies or missing credits at public schools from Beverly to Sa-Mo. Lydia was never so much a runaway as an island-hopper along the archipelago of their houses. They were privileged screwups, and Lydia was different only in that she lacked the safety net that so many of them dove into without a thought. She still carried some of her mother's eagerness to please "a better class of people," and always believed that she was an impostor, a ragged orphan swaddled in fancier clothes. She was a paradox to the other girls: She had been raised predominantly in wealthy households with rich stepfathers, but she also boasted of her *white trash* status. She even smiled when the other girls made fun of it. She talked about how her mother now wore a rock worth "ten or twenty g's," but still went ballistic if anyone left the lights on in a room.

House to house, Lydia paid her fare in stories. She could captivate her friends with sordid tales of stepfathers and boyfriends: a cokehead restaurant owner whom she and her mother fled one night near dawn; a drunken orthodontist stepfather who had groped Lydia regularly and had once dislocated her arm in a fight. One of her mother's boyfriends had been a cross-dresser with a gun collection, and Lydia had caught him one night, drunk and in a garter belt, brandishing a flintlock pistol. "The antique part's key," said Lydia. "Older that shit is, the better. Imagine that freak with, like, a teddy and a musket. Too fucking classic!" But whenever she ran out of grim or colorful yarns, she would return to her dad's saga, his criminal history and his life on the road, until she found that there was nothing better for her street credibility than a blood father in prison.

That night in mid-July, Lydia and her friends found themselves on an exhausting quest, party to party, house to house, in search of ecstasy. They lost two hours in a living room in Beverlywood, where everyone sat around in leather chairs watching two kids entranced at a PlayStation, sharing a beer bong, as a third boy made inquiring phone calls. They killed another hour at a diner on La Cienega, each girl launching into her own cell phone soliloquy, while Lydia sat quietly, listening to their overlapping voices. Danielle couldn't reach her connection; Chloe offered to steal booze from her parents; two other girls might be able to score something from a hairdresser they knew in the Palisades. Back on the road, passing the looming towers of Century City, they now seemed doomed to a night back home by the bluffs. Instead, Danielle's cell rang, and her connection referred her to someone else. She rose and faced them from the shotgun seat, blouse flapping in the wind, and announced—as the self-proclaimed savior of the night—that they could get crystal. All of the girls were holding their hair out of their faces. They voted, majority ruled, and they decided to turn around and head for Hollywood. After all, they needed to accomplish *something*.

In a parking lot just down from the Opium Den, they met Danielle's friend, who ambled to the car like a gunslinger, leaned against the door, and invited them to a get-together in the hills. The girls disagreed over this; Chloe was skeptical about any party that hadn't been mentioned in the original deal, especially because the "connection" was a sour-looking gangster wannabe sitting behind the wheel of a Chevy Impala, slapping on the door beneath him. He wanted Danielle to ride with him. She agreed, but only if one of her "niggas" came along. To silence another developing argument, Lydia volunteered with a groan.

Off again, two cars began wending northward, Lydia and Danielle in the backseat, while Chloe ran red lights trying to keep on their tail, repeatedly calling on the cell phone to scream, "This kid drives like an asshole!"

The connection's name was Tito, and it seemed fitting that on a harried night, their quest for intoxication would lead to a poser: a hundred-and-twenty-pound pseudo-thug in a wife-beater T, using Chicano slang like "foquin car, mang," bragging that he ruled the West Side, couldn't keep the bitches off him—all because he could get his hands on an eightball of stepped-on crank. He had a patchy, adolescent mustache, and a few strands of his hair were bleached and combed back. He talked for a long time about how ecstasy was bullshit—strictly for rave faggots, that he could get them two or three times as high with crystal.

Lydia said that they had both done meth, so they didn't need a lecture on pharmacology.

"Listen to her. Getting all SAT and shit."

He angled down his rearview mirror to look at her body, and Lydia put her middle finger onto her lap. On the stereo, a deep, gravelly voice rapped a list of sexual conquests.

They drove past dark alleys and the silhouettes of palm trees. As they began ascending the hills, he called back to the girls: "Listen up, yo. Y'all need to be quiet about this. I got a lot of my boys up there tonight; but my brother, he's a businessman. He don't want no product in the house."

Tito explained that both of his parents had "passed" and that his brother supported him: school, clothes, cars, *bling*, whatever shit he needed.

Danielle said, "So if he's the big businessman, why we talking to your ass?"

" 'Cause he ain't going to waste his time with two hos from the 818."

"We're not from the Valley," Danielle said.

"We'll show the utmost discretion," said Lydia, raising her chin.

"See. SAT knows what I'm talking 'bout."

"More like GED," said Danielle, bursting into laughter. Lydia pushed her down in the backseat, and they began a giggling squabble of palms and elbows.

"You are so sensitive," said Danielle, laughing. "Take your fucking Paxil."

Lydia tackled her and pinned her onto the seat, then she sat on top of her, bouncing up and down, as Danielle winced and said, "Stop, sto-ho-ho-ho-hop. Oh my God, your ass weighs a ton! Go on a diet!"

Lydia was becoming genuinely angry, and this sent Danielle into such hysterical laughter that she couldn't get out the word "Atkins." When her cell phone rang, she squirmed under Lydia to answer it, saying, "Ow, ow, *wait,* bitch. My leg just fell asleep."

Twenty minutes later, the play-wrestling match now finished, Tito was pulling up to a cast-iron gate, with Chloe tailgating him in the convertible. They ascended a long, curling driveway, crunching over acorns and brushing through the hanging whiskers of a willow tree until they reached a stone house planted into the hillside.

Immediately the driveway filled with shadows, projected in crooked stripes across a garage door.

Lydia said, "Oh, shit, does Rick James live here?"

The headlights went off and the shades clarified into men in three-quarter-length pants and white T-shirts. Their movements around the car were slow and predatory, and, as Tito stepped out, they yelled at him that the house was already full of his clowns. They scolded him like a child, and, whispering, he pleaded with them not to embarrass him in front of the ladies he had just picked up. During the long, hissing conversation by the garage door, Lydia found Chloe in the darkness on the driveway. "This is creepy," said Chloe. "I'm *so* out of here."

But the girls voted to follow Tito around a stone wall, where they were stopped by a thin man with his shirt off, long shorts clinging to his hips below bunched-up underwear. He smelled saturated with weed, his eyes red, his head shaved, gang tattoos on his scalp, and, ranging across his chest, the word "El Salvador." There was a languid, catlike quality about him, as if he had just awakened from a nap. He smiled and said, "Hold up. No weapons in here." There was little banter remaining among the girls as he frisked them one by one. Danielle tried to make a joke by pointing to his chest and asking him where he was *from,* but her voice trembled. When he searched Lydia's satchel, the others had already moved up the steps. He rifled through her phone book, condoms, cigarettes, makeup, notes and pictures, chuckling at the mess. Then he told her to put her arms out and spread her legs, and he ran his palms around her blouse and skirt.

"So which security company you work for?"

He gave a slight smile, which only affected one side of his face; and then, turning his head to the side, he pointed to the tattoo on his neck. "This one," he said, flashing gang signs on his fingers.

The patio sat in a clearing of cypresses and eucalyptus, so high up that the wind sounded like a stream above the muted city. Acorns clattered like hail onto the roof and lawn chairs. Below the scrubby hills, the shimmering flats of the West Side stretched toward the far-off darkness of the ocean, and the sky was a canopy of ambient pink. Farther down along this high perch carved into the mountainside there was a pool and a fountain in a grotto between swaying trees.

As they continued into the house, all five girls were now quiet and vaguely green, as if seasick at the first dips of open sea. The front room was completely barren—not a piece of furniture, not a picture on the wall, only a wide and glossy hardwood floor, a bay window, and a high ceiling that made their voices echo. They followed the noise and cigarette smoke down carpeted steps into a sunken game room, where a small crowd circled around a pool table. For a few wary moments, Lydia thought they might be entering a genuine gang party inside a plush safe house, but she was instead relieved to find a scene she recognized: boys in jerseys, with knit caps pulled low and whittled-down patches of chin hair; the girls clustered in tight packs, gesturing with their cigarettes. This group had little or nothing in common with the men outside. A man with a red goatee shouted, "Whoooo—Tito!" and Danielle knew a kid in a Rugby shirt from her stepbrother's all-boys academy.

But once Lydia adjusted to the smoke and clamor, she noticed that the scene also had a confused undercurrent. Like at every other party, the guys yelled and swayed with hip-hop mannerisms, but they seemed painfully aware that there were *real* thugs outside. They checked the doors and windows. They performed like nervous actors, eyes shrunken with smoke and worry.

Tito began ferrying groups of four to the bathroom, and Lydia went first with Danielle and Rugby Shirt. Tito's hands were all over Lydia, until she swatted his shoulder. Danielle didn't seem to mind as Rugby kissed under her hair, holding her from behind as she did a line. Tito put his hands on Lydia's hips and tried to kiss her while she massaged a burning nostril. His breath smelled like medicine. She laughed and said, "Let me breathe for a second."

The first rush bloomed through her, tingling in her fingertips, that seductive feeling of unimagined possibilities. But she wanted to get away from Tito, who had cruel eyes and bad skin along the edges of his flossy mustache. He was now vigorously rubbing her ass, and Lydia said, "Damn, *dog.* What do you think—a genie's going to come out?"

She retreated up the carpeted stairs as Tito called her a "tease." She ducked into a kitchen off the empty front room, a huge expanse of cabinets and counters under bright track lighting, a disaster of bottles filled with cigarettes, plates of congealed nachos, and pots of hardened noodles. Her heart beat like a stopwatch; she was trembling with restless energy. When she was a little girl she used to come downstairs into a bright, empty kitchen on nights after her mother fought loudly with her second stepfather—she would do the dishes, reorganize the refrigerator, anything to keep moving, a forced mania that kept her eyes away from the gloom at the edges of her home. She began doing the same thing in the stranger's house: She ran the sink, scrubbed the pots, cleaned the wineglasses, and sponged the counters. Rapidly, she grew familiar with the cabinets and drawers and the dishwashing machine.

While her hands were buried in the froth of the sink, a slightly older man—probably in his late twenties—wandered into the room on his cordless phone. He spoke quietly and hung along the walls, seeming unaware of his surroundings. She was certain that it was Tito's older brother, but he carried himself so humbly that she was startled. He was wearing a copper-colored dress shirt and dark slacks hemmed above his bare feet; and when he rolled his eyes, his exasperation seemed wry and sophisticated.

"Oh, Jesus—are you *serious*?" he said into the phone. "What do you want me to do? Because it's still in escrow: We can't. These people are fucking crazy. I think he's a narcissist—I think he can't even see his behavior. He thinks he's entitled to the money. No, I'm not going to twist myself up to this demented logic anymore, okay. That's a ridiculous excuse. I can't keep dealing with people like this. No, no, no—whatever. Call me later—call me if you hear any news."

He hung up and sighed, leaning against his marble counter. Lydia was washing a Teflon pan. For a long time the room was silent except for the clanking of pots and silverware. Finally he said, "I would give anything if Tito had more friends like you."

"I want your house," said Lydia. "It kicks ass."

"Yeah, if I could get the posse out of here. Nothing scares me more than white kids wearing Fubu."

"Why don't you just throw them out?"

He nodded at the floor, smiling. His mannerisms seemed to contradict each other: He delivered his joke with a spark of aggression, then glanced away bashfully at the floor. "I don't know—maybe I need a little chaos to break the routine."

"Where's the switch for the garbage disposal?"

"That panel under the sink."

She flicked the switch, waiting out a brief growl until a whirlpool formed in the standing water.

"So what happened to all of your furniture?" asked Lydia as she wiped her forehead with her wrist.

He began unloading plates from the dishwasher to give her more space. "That's sort of a liquidity problem."

"Like—a flood or something?"

"Right," he said, laughing suddenly. "A big flood of bullshit swept right through there. Washed all my furniture down the hill."

"Don't make fun of me—I don't know all your, like, Scarface Realtor words."

He was an inch or two shorter than she was, and he seemed very small and spry from the way he leaned down and covered up his smile.

He wagged a dish in the air, and said, "I like that. Scarface Realty." Then he turned sideways to pass between her and the counter, refilling a glass cabinet.

To Lydia, there seemed to be a surprising intimacy in this shared chore.

"By the way," he said. "You should be more careful. Going into a strange house and cleaning up like this. Gives people the wrong idea. Before you know it, you'll be waxing the floors."

"Oh, I am so totally going to wax your floors—*baby.*" She tilted her head back in an imitation of rapture.

He gave the first note of a laugh. "You have a thing for floors?"

"For your floors. Go look at 'em. Those are hot floors."

He shook his head and clicked his tongue. "What about bathrooms? You want to do some work there, too?"

"Depends on how dirty I feel," she said, lowering her face and speaking in an exaggerated parody of a seductress.

"Oh Jesus! I'm in trouble now." He was searching her eyes, and Lydia became momentarily insecure.

He was silent for a long time, studying her, and then he pushed the joke too far, continuing despite the lost rhythm, asking, "Can you lay tile?"

Now Lydia wasn't in the mood for this banter; he'd looked at her too closely; he'd lost the breeziness she needed.

He pressed on, "Because I'm thinking of doing some renovations in there."

Rapidly, Lydia felt a swell of irritation, and she focused on the last dishes, scrubbing as he watched her now with an eerie and detached curiosity, like a talent scout or an anthropologist.

"You're not friends with Tito, are you?" he asked.

His voice was lowered, and he spoke with a suspicion so deep that it frightened her. Her throat tightened. It was astonishing how quickly she had gone from attraction to queasiness, knocked off balance by some mean scrutiny in his eyes; and she was noticing a mechanical nature to her movements now, lathering the last dishes simply in order to have something else to focus on, feeling trapped in a ragged, horrible inertia.

Now she hated herself for having been so tacky. She wished she could rewind the moment. Finally she said, "I don't even know Tito."

He said, "Don't take this the wrong way—but I feel like we're the two most out-of-place people in the house."

"What way am I supposed to take that?"

Her heart was beating in her ears and throat, and she couldn't stand the silence as he studied her.

Neither moved, until his phone rang again. He waited three rings, then glanced at the caller ID. "I have to take this. It's nice meeting you."

A half hour later, Lydia sneaked another two lines with Danielle and Rugby. Afterward, she joined the party that had spilled out onto the patio. Alone, Lydia stood by the baluster and smelled the night air, a perfume of eucalyptus and gathering moisture. A cooling, luxurious breeze tugged through her hair, and she closed her eyes and rolled her head around in it. She recognized the dusty smell of oleanders from a house in her childhood, back when her mother was married to the orthodontist—and she had loved that house, with its two staircases, olive trees, and the quiet sound of mourning doves on hot afternoons. She would run in the sprinklers, lie in the grass. She was feeling buoyed again, free and easy in the perfect air. In fact, she loved this entire miserable city, every ugly corner of it—the whole smudge of lights below; she loved it more for being so difficult. The traffic, the gunshots—imagine what the riots must have looked like from this perch, a vigil of candle flames spreading outward from Koreatown; or the earthquake, with a sudden blackout and a distant swelling of car alarms as if from an orchestra pit. She knew there was real beauty and happiness inside the most difficult places, and she could feel better times ahead, like a warming change in the wind. This bolstered feeling couldn't just be from the drugs, because it was too overpowering, too real.

She lay down on the diving board, staring up at the flushed sky, while below she heard splashing, puffing, and horseplay in the water. "Get your friend in here, Danielle."

Everyone called for her to join them. All across the dark water, she saw indistinct figures, floating, and she couldn't identify the disembodied voices: "Marco."—"Ah, the poor bitch can't swim."—"Polo."—"She can swim, yo. Check out those tits. Fucking flotation devices."—"Ah-ha-ha-ha, whoooo!"—"In the event of a water landing . . ."—"Lydia, you loser. Come in. It's awesome."

Just then, someone grabbed Lydia from behind, hands in her armpits, and threw her into the pool. Whoever it was, he wasn't particularly strong, and, as she relaxed and dropped into the deep end, she wondered why she had surrendered so easily. As if it were a planned stunt, she let herself drift downward underwater. Her eyes adjusted to the blackness until she could see the silhouettes of trees through the wavering surface and bicycling legs spaced out above her. She smiled, broke into a loud laugh of bubbles, and followed their trail to the top.

When she came up, Danielle was in the middle of a tirade: "Because those are *my* clothes, *Tito,* you piece of shit—and that's, like, a thousand-dollar skirt. You're fucking paying for that."

Tito said that she and her bitch friends had probably done twice that much in crystal, while she retorted that she'd gotten a B-minus in calculus and could call him on his "retarded-ass drug-dealer arithmetic."

Calmly, Lydia climbed out of the pool. The soaked blouse clung to her and the skirt was heavy. She was shaking, and, when she laughed, it sounded nervous and involuntary. She ignored the ongoing argument, punctuated with splashes and squeals, as she passed through the doorway, across the floor, arms crossed over her chest.

"Hello," she called. She tracked a wet trail to the kitchen, where she wadded up paper towels beneath her feet and shuffled back over the puddles. Down a long hallway there was another series of doors, and the empty house now seemed larger and more mysterious, stretching out like an evening shadow.

Suddenly Jonah came in from the hallway, tying his robe. Lydia started laughing in staggers, and said, "I'm sorry, I'm getting your floor all wet. Your brother threw me into the pool."

"All right. Come on then."

He led her into his bedroom, where the television flickered without sound, casting light across rumpled sheets. A few strides farther, she was standing beside him in a large bathroom covered with mirrors. She saw her reflection from a dozen angles, nipples sharp, hair in mermaid tangles. Jonah went through drawers and laid out clothes on a tile counter: sweatpants, Bruins sweatshirt, and shower shoes. With his mussed hair and his fancy robe, she thought he was the most adorable person she'd ever seen, and she wanted to bite him on the ear. She wondered why he'd scared her before; he seemed so drowsy and harmless now. She was even turned on by the sleepy, salty odor of him, like a Sunday morning in the sheets.

"Okay," he said. "Change into this stuff here. I'll leave you alone."

She took off her clothes, eyeing the door, imagining him bursting back into the room; she both wanted this to happen and didn't, and her goosebumps seemed like part of a great, aroused indecisiveness, like some internal friction. She regarded herself in the mirror, her pale skin, the rolling terrain around her waist and hips; she had never before looked so sexy. She prayed this confidence wasn't just from the drugs. Jonah was displaying genuine valor by staying on the other side of that door. As she unfolded the clothes, she still pictured him rushing in on her, picking her up, sitting her on that counter or throwing her against the glass—it would be like that, she thought—on the cusp of violence, half passionate, half dangerous.

He didn't come through the door.

Holding her soaked clothes in a plastic bag, dressed as if for a workout or an illness, she returned to his bedside, where he faced the oncoming lights of the television. Speaking with a flutter in her voice, she told him that she would have the clothes laundered, pressed, and returned to him within twenty-four hours.

"Keep them," he said. "They're *sweatpants*."

She stood her ground, trying to decide if he was angry with her, or repelled by her earlier behavior. Finally she replied, "I would feel a lot better. I don't like to take things. If you want, I could mail them to you."

"What was your name again?"

"Lydia Jane Carson."

"Well, Lydia Jane Carson. Let me ask you a rude question. What the fuck are you doing here?"

She waited in the dark, hovering by the bedpost. "What do you mean?"

"I mean, I'm looking at you, and I'm seeing a smart young woman, who's got a lot going for her. But you're out wandering around in the middle of the night with a bunch of losers. So what is it? What the fuck are you looking for here, kid?"

Lydia had no idea why he seemed so angry with her, but she paused, watching, her eyes narrow and her nostrils flared, digging in for what felt like a strengthening assault.

"I need to get at least an hour of sleep. Okay? I'm not on summer vacation with the rest of you screaming fuckups. Somebody has to work and pay for this *wonderland*. And guess who that is?"

"I know."

"If it's important to your sense of honor that you return my sweatpants—"

"It is," she said.

He sighed and said, "I'll give you my cell number." He found a pen, but no paper. As he rolled around to search the drawers, Lydia noticed a small gray nine-millimeter pistol beside a box of tissues. She put out her palm for him, cupping it as if for a handout. He grabbed her wrist. His fingers were so much finer than hers. Squeezing tightly and pulling her toward him, he asked, "How old are you anyway?"

"Eighteen."

"Sure you are." Between the head and heart lines of her palm, he etched his number, pushing hard enough to hurt. "Why don't you stop hanging around with these people? I love Tito, but he's a bad seed. He's never going to be anything but a freeloader."

He finished writing his number, then closed her hand for her.

She took a deep breath that raised her shoulders. "When would be the best time for me to call you? Regarding the *clothes*?"

He was frowning, looking right through her with hard, green eyes. "Call me whenever you want, but let me give you a warning, because I *like* you. Call me because you want to talk. Don't call me for something else. Do you understand? I'm not some new connection. You come around here thinking you're going to use me for that—and I'm going to be really disappointed."

His point hit her with a gust of sudden alarm. She didn't know why she couldn't move from his line of sight, but she stood firm, breathing heavily, feeling a deep shamefulness that she had presented herself this way to him—a drug whore, a cheap skank trying to climb the hillside into his rich house. "I apologize if you got that impression."

He said, "Give me back your hand."

He took her hand in both of his, staring upward from the bed. His face softened, and he said to her, "I've been looking at you all night. And kid, you are a *disaster.* You are in so much fucking pain—you want to vanish into the dark out there. I swear to God, I *know* you. And you're better than this. You're smart and you're tough: I can see it. But you've never met a man in your life that you trusted, that you didn't fight with. You ran away from home, I heard. You're living with kids that barely know you. I know what you want, kid. I know what you *really,* honestly want, deep down—because you're just like me. I'm not talking about anything physical, nothing like that—drugs, sex, no way, nothing that easy. I'm talking about something that scares the shit out of most people—*most* people. So you call that number someday—and come back here—any time you want to know."

An hour later, with her hair still damp, Lydia sat with her girlfriends and three boys who had joined the snowballing group, all marooned together around two booths at Canter's Deli. Dawn was coming through a stained-glass skylight. The conversation drifted among objects of titillation and ridicule, until Danielle was accusing Lydia of fucking Tito's older brother. The voices in the group blended together around her: "Don't act all innocent, Lydia."—"Look at her, she's blushing."—"She's in love with that guy."—"You should be careful, though—he's like Mafia or something."

Lydia finally joined the medley to reply, "He's not in the *Mafia,* Chloe. I heard him talking on the phone about escrow."

No one knew what escrow was, but one of the boys claimed that it had to do with huge amounts of illegal money. Danielle suggested that

Lydia had overheard this phone call while she was "pulling a Lewinsky" under his desk, and Chloe hit her on the shoulder. Danielle told everyone about Chloe's eating disorder, and, while they argued over which was worse, bulimia or anorexia, a boy in a knitted cap shouted, "Jus' don't lose that ass!"

Once again, they fixated on Lydia. They argued about who had "custody" of her for the next few days, and Danielle said that she didn't understand why they had to take care of Lydia if she was going to "be all high-and-mighty about fucking that Mafia guy." Who did she think she was, anyway? Danielle was sick of this living-on-the-lam routine. She proposed an intervention: Either Lydia should return home, back to her antipanic meds and her perverted stepfather, or she should go live under a bridge with the rest of the homeless teens. Lydia promised to pay her back for the skirt.

With her eyes streaked red from chlorine, a cigarette angled upward in her fingers, Danielle smirked and replied, "I'm just questioning this whole thing. Why do we have to have a white-trash pet? I mean, there are plenty of fucking runaways. We could probably go to the bus station right now and have our pick of the litter."

Chloe said, "Danielle, you're evil."

One of the boys was laughing so hard that coffee came out of his nose.

Danielle continued, "I mean, face it, Lydia is trailer trash Barbie. Let's go down the checklist. She ran away at, what? Fourteen? She has sex for drugs. She mooches everything. And, last but not least, her biker father is in jail."

Lydia locked on Danielle's eyes. She replied, "I'm warning you. I'm not in the fucking mood right now. Say one thing about my dad. One thing, I dare you."

"I could say tons of shit about your father," she said, puffing. "Tons and tons. Like the fact that he probably raped your mother. You're the product of a *crime*."

"She was with him for almost a year."

"Yeah, that's called brainwashing, *bitch*. And you know what else I know about your father? I know that right now, as we speak, he's on his knees, taking it in the ass."

Lydia surged upward, spilling everything off the table and grabbing Danielle by the hair. Everyone leapt into the aisles and crawled into neighboring booths as dishes smashed and silverware clattered to the floor. Lydia dragged Danielle toward the hostess stand. The other girls shouted, Chloe started crying, and the manager hollered that he was calling the police. Lydia picked up a fork and pressed the tines against Danielle's cheek, and whispered, "Keep talking, bitch, and I'm going to pluck your fucking eyeballs out." Danielle screamed, and within seconds the staff was gathered around, pulling Lydia by the waist and arms as she held on to Danielle's hair.

"Get her off me!" shouted Danielle.

In a thick accent, the manager said, "The police are coming."

Lydia released her grip, fought out of the crowd, and pushed past a cook trying to contain her. The manager broke into his native tongue as she grabbed her satchel and ran for the door on clattering shower shoes. Past the parking lot and down a residential street, she trotted alone, just as the skies were turning gray and the birds were awakening in every ragged tree. After putting the shoes into her bag, she ran barefoot, hearing sirens along Fairfax. Would the police surround the deli? This excited her. It made her feel powerful and relevant, though she wasn't sure at what point a tantrum became a crime.

For a while she fluctuated between sprinting and walking, until she was just off Wilshire Boulevard. She found a phone booth beneath a decapitated palm trunk, whose shaggy leaves had probably been lopped off to prevent some epidemic of blight. It stood now like the remaining column of an ancient ruin. On its trunk was a graffiti tag, which she recognized as the same one from the bodyguard's neck. As if this coincidence unified all other events in her life, she decided that everything in this random spot related to her future. The growing light hurt her eyes; the tar pits were rich and rank nearby. She flipped through a half-gutted phone book as if scanning for a prophecy, and read, "Tile-Ceramics-Contractors & Dealers." She couldn't stop laughing. She glanced at her hand and saw Jonah's number, smudging, almost vanished from sweat. There was a quarter at the bottom of her messy satchel. She picked up the phone, started to dial, and stopped.

No, she thought. It was too soon. She might seem desperate.

For a week, Lydia tried to decipher what Jonah had told her that night. What *did* she want? He had been close to the truth: The idea of vanishing was the most exciting thing she knew, and she believed that this was the accumulation of so many moments of narrow escape in her memory. She never felt more electric and alive than when her mother had awakened her at 3 A.M. that long lost morning to escape a violent and coked-up stepfather, who had finally fallen asleep. Lydia's mother had married three men and lived with three other serious boyfriends, but often all Lydia could remember were the wild fluctuations between rage and tenderness, the shouting in the house, the broken lamps, the scrambles, the nights the police came, windows filling up with red flashing lights, radios murmuring, the bathroom door kicked off its hinges. Lydia remembered far less of her childhood than most kids—with images assembling around eight years old, and a kind of preverbal and anxious darkness spanning out before, with its own syntax of suffocating and fleeing. She knew that she hallucinated as a child: She saw toy trains crossing her beige carpet with vigorous puffs of steam. She would often see a shadow in her room with luminous, mesmerizing teeth, the way the Cheshire cat appeared piece by piece in *Alice's Adventures in Wonderland,* until there appeared a glowing pink fedora, suspended in the dark over the neon smile. Her bedspread would become the top of a mountain, and the Navajo design on her wallpaper would awaken in an animation of dancing stick figures, writhing together. She heard the train's whistle, even smelled its smokestack; she felt the room spin like a carousel and she left her body—but she didn't remember much of her real life behind those disembodied visions. There were entire houses lost in the shadows of memory, entire months and years left out, coming into the light only during the breathless moments she fled with her mother, and the loving nights they spent together in motel beds.

It was as if she grew up on the run. She remembered the flophouse by the freeway, late at night, the sobbing phone call her mother made to family outside of San Diego; and she remembered the policeman who came to file a report, giving Lydia Tic Tacs and talking to her about his own daughter, a figure skater. Her mother curled up against Lydia that night, crying, while Lydia told her, again and again, that they were far away where no one could ever find them. No one could reach them by phone, no one could see through those windows. She imagined shrinking away from her mother's arms, hiding forever, living happily in this alien terrain of carpet fibers and bathroom tile.

Was this the fear and restlessness that Jonah had seen in her? He was such an odd man, sulking, lowering his head when he joked—but watching so closely. Had he seen something in her from those distant blackouts of memory? She thought of the way that a mosquito leaves an enzyme in every bite, so that other mosquitoes, days later, can still smell the wound.

Lydia had first tried to run away at twelve, after an attempt to tell her mother about an ongoing problem with her second stepfather. Her mother had replied that the accusations were impossible: The man could never have touched her. Ursula claimed that she had been too vigilant for any such possibility, because of similar experiences in her own life. She accused Lydia of loving drama, wanting attention—and that night Lydia stewed with hatred for her mother, her stepfather, and herself. She cut her legs with a pair of sewing scissors, then crawled out of her window and walked miles down Ventura Boulevard, sleeping that night in the plastic tunnel of a children's playground. She was gone close to two days before the police found her, hungry and ragged and living in the park. She gave the cops her address, rode with them, then walked back into her living room, where her mother was hovering over a cigarette on the couch. "Do you have any idea what you just did to me?" asked Ursula. "You don't, do you?"

"Sorry for the inconvenience, Mother."

When Lydia finally ran away for good, at fourteen, she *kept* running, fleeing the parents, rules, and tensions of each new stopover. She became addicted to the rhythm of escape and arrival, the new friends that took her in with whispered complicity and the sudden fights that led to her departure, the crying phone calls and reunions. She couldn't sleep without reminding herself that everything in the room was meaningless, that it could be burned down or flooded or smashed in an earthquake—as if impermanence itself was her lullaby.

Whatever he had read in her behavior that night, after seven days of deliberating on the subject, Lydia decided finally to return to Jonah's house in the hills. It was a listless weekday when she returned from a Laundromat with his clothes, clean and folded in a shopping bag. She began making herself up for a date.

For the past few days, she had been staying with Chloe's older sister, Shannon Silverman, in an ugly slab apartment building of Russian immigrants and aspiring guitarists off Hollywood and La Brea. The black sheep of the family, Shannon was a snarky, condescending cocktail waitress, with a commercial agent and a worsening drug problem. She had appeared in two ads for hand cream and one for nasal spray. Lydia could picture her having a promising future as the pitchwoman for cold medicine, because she was always groggy and spent most of the daylight hours with an ice pack on her face.

Lydia was desperate to get out of her apartment.

Shannon was among the foulest people she had ever known. She blew her nose into paper towels and left them around the couch; she picked her toenails off and threw the crescents into the dead plants. Worst of all, she had to know more than Lydia on every conceivable topic, as if, in the five extra years she had been alive, she had done nothing but read encyclopedias. When she deduced that Lydia had a "crush" on some older man in the hills, she pummeled her with advice about everything from phone etiquette to fellatio. Because she was comfortable in strip clubs and sports bars, because she drank Pabst and could name all the Clippers, because she liked drag racing and junk food, she was convinced that she "thought exactly like a guy," as if adopting the male psyche meant little more than reading the sports page in a sleazy neighborhood.

· On the phone with Jonah, trying to keep away from Shannon's eavesdropping, Lydia described herself as "the girl who fell in the pool." He said that he *knew* who she was, then stated her full name. His life was a mess; he was in the middle of an ongoing disaster; but she could certainly come by with his clothes.

A half hour later, Lydia pulled up to the automatic gate in a taxi, holding her plastic bag. She couldn't remember ever feeling so nervous, but she told herself that this was only an errand. In her efforts to look more adult, she now appeared as if she had dressed for a job interview. She wore a silk blouse and a skirt stolen from Shannon, which she must have saved for callbacks, with muted lipstick and her hair tied up into a loose splash. The cab driver told her she smelled nice. In stiletto sandals, she walked the long winding driveway to the porch. The city was now obscured under a milky haze.

When she entered the front room, she noticed that there was now a long dining room table with only two chairs. Jonah sat at one end, stooped over and listening to his cordless phone with the cell phone beside him. All he said, over and over, was "okay," until finally he broke the pattern with "not on the phone." He wore suit pants and a white V-necked T-shirt. His hair was messy and his eyes were bloodshot. The table was littered with tissues.

She stood in the middle of the dim room, holding the bag, until he gestured for her to sit down at the other end of the table.

Finally he hung up and stared at her for a while, nodding.

It was surprising how many details Lydia had forgotten about his face: His nose was longer and sharper, his wrists were tiny, his neck slender. She had remembered him as larger and more imposing, and was surprised by what a narrow little man he was.

"I have your clothes," said Lydia.

"You're an honorable person," he said and blew his nose.

Lydia sat up straighter and said, "You didn't seem very happy on the phone—"

"I never get anything but bad news on the phone."

His cell phone rang again. Lydia laughed and said, "Even more." She waited patiently at the end of the table while he merged from one phone call to another in a schizophrenic flux between aggressive and apologetic tones. Every now and then he would glance at Lydia and put up his finger; but when she stood, he covered the mouthpiece and said, "Give me a few minutes, Lydia. I want to talk to you."

It was the most abrupt invitation she'd ever heard, sounding as if she'd done something wrong. She grew tense hovering in that near-empty front room, with dust now swimming in the afternoon light as it came through cypress trees along the hill. She whispered that she would wait outside, and she spent the next hour pacing between the railing and pool, glancing out over the thickening haze that was covering the West Side.

After a while, she wondered why she was staying here and waiting. He'd presented himself like a guru to her a week ago, and now he couldn't be bothered to hang up the phone. Plus, there was something nervous and pushy about him today, something that seemed surprisingly overwhelmed for a man of power. She hated waiting for people in general, and she especially disliked rudeness; by the time he was off the phone and coming outside, she was prepared to tell him off.

She met him head-on in the middle of the porch, wagging her head side to side and raising her finger, proclaiming, "You know what? I'm not some *maid* that comes over here with your motherfucking laundry. . . ."

But he only seemed amused by this tirade. He put his hands up in the air and said, "Shhh, shhh—I know. It's okay. It's okay." He smiled with tight lips and added, "You're so mad you're turning ghetto on me here. Come on now. Calm down." He was so unfazed by the outburst that she was confused and disarmed. She took a step backward, and he continued ahead with a stooped, goading posture, as if offering his hands to a growling dog. "Lydia. I shouldn't have made you wait—but this is my life. I wanted to talk to you. We had an interesting moment the other night, and it's been on my mind. But if I drop everything I'm doing—I've got a catastrophe on my hands. You don't want to be responsible for that, do you?" He grinned as if everything were a secret joke.

"No," she said, still breathing heavily.

"Come on now. Sit down."

He led her to a lounge chair, and he perched across from her. While she stared at the marine layer forming over the ocean in the distance, he asked her questions, rapid-fire, with the friendly but detached tone of a job interview.

He said that he had been asking around about her. He'd learned quite a bit. Why had she run away from home? He wanted to know how she lived. Did she work? Where did she stay night to night? Wasn't she exhausted? Where did she want to be in a year, in five, ten? He had the sedate tone of a therapist, and Lydia performed for him, lighting a cigarette and explaining that she could never go home, never in her life again, because everything in her mother's house was a disgusting lie. Yes, she'd been abused, hurt—but she didn't think that was her ultimate downfall. She thought it was the lying, pretending day after day that everything was fine, in pretty houses with pretty things. She said, "I just couldn't be part of that bullshit, you know—for the rest of my life." She told him about her father in prison, joking that she was actually *white trash,* an undercover redneck sponging her entire life off sugar daddies and spoiled teens.

"What's he in for?"

"My dad? Manslaughter. He's out now. He's somewhere in the desert—I looked up his number once. But I didn't have the guts to call him."

"Why not?"

"I don't know," she said, twisting her neck and massaging the top of her own shoulder. "Nervous."

"Scared he's not who you want him to be?"

"Mmmm. I guess."

"You had an image of him in your mind. He's the secret: some crazy rebel, can't be tamed—and you're scared he might just be a dumb ex-con. Right?"

She looked at him with her eyes thin. Insulted, she wondered what kind of insight or affection she'd earn for enduring such comments.

Staring away for the first time, Jonah said, "I want to help you out, Lydia. If you'll accept."

"What does that mean?"

"You're a discreet person, right? You've kept secrets your whole life."
She nodded.

"Well, I'm going to make you a business offer. Because the second I saw you, I knew the kind of person you were. And I knew that you were in trouble. If you don't want the responsibility, you turn it down flat. I won't bother you again. It'll be like we never met. You're a smart person, and I don't need to explain this to you."

She frowned and met his eyes.

"Did you drive here?" he asked.

"I took a taxi."

He smirked at this information. She demanded to know what was so funny, and he said, "You never get anything but a one-way ticket, do you?"

He wanted to show her something, and a few minutes later she was riding shotgun in his BMW as he swerved rapidly out of the mountains. The air conditioner was so cold that her skin goose pimpled and the hair rose up on her neck. He continued talking on the phone, just a headset now, until he lost reception in the canyon. He rode down Franklin, in and out of slower traffic, under the freeway and past the weeded lots and billboards near Highland. When he spoke to her, briefly and between calls, he reiterated that he understood what she felt, day to day: He knew that she was tired; he would never offer her this if he didn't feel some rare spark of recognition. "On a practical level, Lydia. But in other ways also. People need to take the good things in life when they get them."

Along Sunset, down Fairfax, he interviewed her again, this time asking about drugs. He was concerned about whether or not she could control herself.

"I just party, you know. Socially. I'm not like some junky *ho.*"

"And boyfriends? What about them?"

She smiled bashfully again. "No, I don't have a boyfriend."

"Tito?"

"Oh my God. I hope you're joking."

Just as the sun was setting, he turned onto a residential street and

pulled up across from the house. It was small, cute, and hideously suburban, with a splash of red bougainvillea blocking the barred front windows.
The timed sprinklers came on across a plot of crab grass, flanked with box-
wood hedges. Lydia took a deep breath. With its brightness, its chipper
whitewashed façade, Spanish tile roof, and flagstone walk leading to the
mesh of a security door, it looked to her like a decorative birdcage.

Jonah turned off the car and rotated to face her from his seat. He
said, "I'm going to explain the situation, and if you don't like it, we shake
hands and you walk away. Basically, half my life is normal. I have a real
estate development company. It was my father's, God bless him, and I've
expanded it every year since he died. Now, some of it—and just some—
involves being secretive. I have a very *specific* job for a set of people. I find
houses and I buy them—all through my company. I scout out a good
neighborhood. I make sure that people around it don't ask too many
questions. A good, typical Los Angeles block full of houses that turn over
quickly and people who never meet their neighbors. Ideally, I can sell the
house a year later and make a profit.

"Now, I'll pay you to live in the house. What am I paying you for? I'm
paying you to keep it clean, keep it quiet, to keep it looking normal. I'm
paying you to sit on an egg until it hatches—understand? You pretend to
go to work, you pretend to come home. You could pass for your early
twenties, so you're somebody's personal assistant; you just got out of
UCLA, and your daddy is rich and supplementing you."

"What's in the house then?"

"Listen—you don't *know* what's in the house—it's not your problem.
Even I don't always know. They're stash houses. They're like storage, or,
let's say, transfer points. This is the kind of stuff that takes a lot of organization to move, and it can't just go from point A to point B all the time.
But your job is only to live here and look like everybody else. And we've
had a lot of problems doing it the old way, with people who knew too
much. It's my ass on the line; the deeds are in my company's name—so
I'm the one who's developed this new way of doing things. You'll never
see the stuff. It'll be buried, hidden, someplace where only an extermina-
tor could find it. Our people will be in charge of everything going in and

going out, and they'll do it with workers and electricians and whatever else they need. You just stay put and enjoy."

"And if the cops come?"

"They won't. Nobody in this neighborhood ever looks out their windows. There's only one way for you to screw this up, and you won't do it."

"What way is that?"

"Well, we had some people in a house, out in the Valley. This is what I've been dealing with on the phone. They were skimming for themselves. Happens all the time. Just some tiny amount they thought they could get away with. But now the people *I* work for, they're upset. The accounting is very precise here. This isn't some kid with a big piggy bank. If we put in fifty grand—it better be there the next day. If we put in a million, two million, when it goes down to get washed, we're going to notice if there's a nickel missing. That's how people get hurt. Do I have you here?"

Lydia stared at the house.

"You treat it like a job and I'll take care of you. I've survived in this business for a long time, and I have a good feel for when things are low risk. This is an easy one, Lydia. Easy as it gets. If you really *never* know anything, then nobody can touch you. You want the grand tour?"

She took a deep breath and asked, "Why me?"

"Because you need someplace to live. And because you understand."

"You don't even know me."

"Yes, I do."

She glanced between the house and Jonah, then said, "I came over today, and I was hoping maybe you'd ask me out to a movie or something. A cup of *coffee.* Something disgustingly normal."

There was never any cup of coffee, never any movie—but the house, and her indecision about it, became a courtship of its own.

Lydia would call Jonah from Shannon's, late at night, curled up on the couch or sitting in an armchair by the window, bare feet pressed up against the glass. She would say, "It's me," and he would wait for a long time in silence.

He'd ask if she'd made her choice, and she would begin a long, airy ramble of thinking out loud: What if the police found something? What if she couldn't handle the stress? At first he would come and go on the phone, traveling back and forth through different layers of call-waiting, but as the night wore on, he would stay with her in a breathy silence, hardly speaking, now and then responding to her pauses: "You know it's just going to be up to you, Lydia. I can't decide for you. I'm not going to force you into anything that makes you uncomfortable. But I think you can do it. I think you deserve a break for once in your life."

These conversations, beginning as great, meandering bouts of hypothetical arrests and disasters, slowly gathered their own kind of gravity. Lydia would tell Jonah about her life, idle things about her friends, until the talks would turn dark, and she would analyze herself for him. "Am I telling you too much?" she'd ask. She told him about the time she tried to kill herself with pills, and said that it was because she felt dirty and broken; she remembered being overwhelmed with disgust more than sadness. She thought her way into corners; she second-guessed herself until she couldn't move. She felt ruined before she began.

"You're this beautiful, perceptive girl," said Jonah, "and the only thing standing in your *way*, Lydia, is this criticism of yourself. You're beating yourself senseless. You want some kind of punishment. Well, you can be *kind* to yourself. You deserve it as much as anybody, and I'm qualified to tell you that. I've been around in my life, Lydia, and I've never met anyone with as much on the ball. I mean that. You're so smart—and like all smart people, you've got a big burden you carry, in both arms, in front of your eyes, and you can't see around it. You've got to just put it down. Trust yourself."

When Jonah did contribute a story from his own life, it was small, matter-of-fact, and horrifying. On their third night of whispered deliberation, he said that his parents had been murdered in their kitchen when he was sixteen years old. Lydia broke into tears, apologized for going on so long about herself, and said, "God, my problems are meaningless next to that."

"Stop it," he said. "It's not like that. People have whatever past they have—and you don't compare them. It's not like it's currency or some-thing. One person's problems aren't worth more than another's. You *are* whatever you are—right at this second. Everything you did or thought in the past is over."

She had never heard anything quite so terrifying and so seductive at the same time—for she perceived in his attitude an escape route from every weight upon her; she saw in it the fantastic promise of flee-ing, again and again, of renewing herself with each day and each new crisis.

During another phone call, Lydia, still hedging about the house, drifted into a talk about love, and what she believed it was, and how she had never felt it until recently. She said that it felt like she had been in a dark and crowded room, and, out of all the whispers and shadows, someone had found her, touched her on the shoulder, seen who she was beneath her borrowed clothes and posturing. She said that she had a flutter in her chest when she heard his voice. She confessed that she now waited for the day to end so that she could have their phone call at night. She didn't want to scare him away. But she believed that they were built out of the same pain and anxiety, and that they could heal each other, little by little. People in her life tried to talk her *out* of her emotions, but Jonah just listened. He made her feel calm, and she was *never* calm, never, not under any circumstances: She had a huge, clattering pinball machine of a life. She partied and wrote and danced and shopped and did everything with a manic ferocity to stave off any feelings of loneli-ness or desperation. But he made it so that she could lie down flat on her belly on the bed, barricaded with pillows, the phone under her hair—silent. She could listen to only the wind in the earpiece; she could savor his voice like an old song; and she was aroused, more than ever in her life, by a stillness in him, a patience that seemed to her the depths of strength and power.

She gave him this speech and began to cry that she had been so lost in her life, and when she recovered with gasping breath, tears on her lips, he waited for a long time to finally say, "Do you want to come over here?"

"I don't know if I should."

"You shouldn't. Unless you want to."

"I'm just scared."

"That's okay. You should be scared."

"I'm scared of, just, how *much* there is. You know? It's so much, Jonah."

"Don't come if you don't want to."

"I *do* want to. I want to more than anything. But I don't know what's going to happen."

"Nobody ever knows what's going to happen."

"I just don't want to make a mistake. I feel like I have this weird hope—I'm serious—and I've never had it before."

"You shouldn't come. You should stay there, Lydia. We should talk again later."

"I want to come over."

"You should think some more. Make the right decision."

"I'm going to come over. I'm going to take a cab up there."

"Only if you want to."

"And Jonah. I really—I just really feel deeply about this. About everything."

"I know you do, Lydia. Just buzz in at the gate when you get here."

She paid the cabdriver during the last snaking turns along the road, then stepped out at a little past midnight into a weak drizzle. She ran up the slick driveway and saw Jonah standing in all of his clothes on the patio, the city lights around him. After a dozen strides she was in his arms, entangled in the first kisses, ranging from closed-mouth nibbles, like sips of hot water, into long, ravenous sweeps. He held her hips first, then the sides of her face, and she became acutely aware of her height, wilting downward to meet him. She put her hands onto the small of his back, and he grabbed her hair and tugged it in his fist.

She didn't recognize the smell of his breath, sour and nervous, or the smoky odor of his skin; she began to lose her sense of this man whom she'd known only on the phone. She began to wonder if he was in fact the same person whose voice she'd memorized over the past nights.

Nothing seemed real; she watched herself from a few feet away. Here she was: Lydia Jane, seventeen and on her own, sober, standing in the faint marine mist over a sprawling city, kissing a stranger. She was as lonely as ever, watching like a ghost from the side of the porch as she took his hand, nodded—then followed him into his house and his life.

eight

The day Lydia moved into the cottage, she was disappointed that Jonah didn't show up to help. Instead he sent several of his goons—Iván, the Salvadoran kid who had frisked her when she'd first come to the house; Tito, still smirking over their encounter in the bathroom; and a lurching, silent Mexican kid covered with Aztec graffiti. The three men seemed to have expected a moving van full of belongings, and they were amused by Lydia's ragged duffel and worn-out sleeping bag. For the rest of the afternoon, they sat on the wide expanse of beige carpet and snorted lines of speed off a CD case.

"Will Jonah kill me for this?"

"He'll kill you for *something*," said Iván.

He and Tito laughed, but the stout, frowning man only nodded, as if the comment were some new information to absorb.

"I haven't met *you*," Lydia finally said to him.

Iván smiled and said, "Yeah, this is Chupacabra, man. We call him that. Call him Choop."

"That's some kind of monster, right?"

"Yeah. This Yucatán Bigfoot motherfucker," said Iván. "Like half Godzilla, half King Kong. Roams around villages and eats goats and rapes the bitches."

"I knew he looked familiar," said Lydia. Iván and Tito laughed, while Choop kept his dark, unyielding eyes on her.

"He's a hit man," said Tito.

"He's a crazy fucking *vato.* You ain't never seen a dude this cold."

They were smiling, ribbing her, and Lydia said, "Really? Who has he killed?"

"Everybody," said Tito. "He killed everybody. Biggie, Tupac."

"JFK."

"Fucking *Gandhi.*"

"That shit was cold," said Iván. "Killing Gandhi like that."

"He's just crazy. You don't even want to *know,* baby. Give her the last line, man. Ladies' night."

Tito handed the CD to Lydia. She pulled back a drape of hair, snorted it up through a rolled-up bill, and rubbed her nostril. Her eyes watering, she glanced up at their three eager faces, and said, "You know I'm not fucking you guys for this."

There was a long silence, until Iván clapped his hands down onto his legs and said, "Damn. *Now* you tell us." Even Choop cracked a smile.

The three men drove off shortly after dusk, facetiously congratulating her on her new home, and leaving Lydia to wander among the empty rooms. She had expected to enjoy her newfound independence. She intended to learn something from the solitude and from each new chore, whether putting up a shower curtain or boiling water in her tin camping pot for the stove's first cup of tea. Despite having no detergent, she used the washer and drier with a feeling of sudden maturity, more in command of her life with each folded shirt; she envisioned herself repairing faucets, tending a garden, whipping up pasta salads, and carrying on sparkling conversations at dinner parties. She would grow more patient and philosophical. These empty rooms would be the stage for an overnight success story: a transient girl blooming into a sophisticated woman.

Instead, the first two nights felt like a dare in a haunted mansion. She thought that every spot on earth, whether a thousand miles away or just a few blocks, must have had its own particular sound: Here it was a fugue of tireless dogs, sirens and shrieking fan belts on a nearby boulevard, rattling wind chimes, rumbling car stereos, and the arrhythmic clanking of tires over a loose manhole cover. Mourning doves cooed at midnight, maybe confused by the ambient light. In her sleeping bag on a mildewed carpet, she lay awake and watched headlights pass through the rooms, projecting window shapes in floating paths across the walls. She spent hours giving herself a deranged pep talk as she wandered the dark rooms with a blanket draped over her: "Don't worry, don't worry. Just a Thursday night, any night. *Okay,* Carson—let's get it together. *Relax.*" But every time she was on the verge of sleep, she would wonder again about the secret buried somewhere in the house.

The next morning, Lydia called Chloe and asked her to stay over for a night or two. She needed distractions: TV, music, or late-night gossip. Instead Chloe came in her mother's car and with her father's credit card, and drove Lydia around Melrose to pick up modernist furniture and art prints. They bought Lydia a cell phone and a thousand prepaid minutes. She told Chloe that she was house-sitting for an international lawyer, and she embellished him further into a dashing adventurer who worked on human rights cases, liberating imprisoned Malaysian textile workers and enslaved Ukrainian prostitutes. Lydia was possibly in love with him.

"God," said Chloe. "Where did you meet this guy?"

"Some chat room."

On her fourth night in the house, Danielle arrived with three guys from Sa-Mo and a Persian ecstasy dealer from Beverly High. After Danielle and Lydia cried through mutual apologies, they joined the boys taking hits from a beer bong in her empty bedroom. Danielle had brought over the clarinet Lydia had left in her closet, and Lydia stood in the middle of the smoky room, stoned and laughing over the mouthpiece, playing staggered bouts of classical music. Chloe boasted that she was *awesome*

on that thing; Danielle called it the aftermath of a hopelessly nerdy childhood; and one of the boys said that she was "getting him hard."

Lydia was halfway through a rendition of *Bolero,* broken up by sweeps
of her own giggling, when the smoke alarm went off. Because she still had
no chairs, Lydia had to ride piggyback on a man's shoulders to bust it off
the ceiling, and then everyone stomped on it for good measure. At this,
Lydia announced that if the police or fire department ever came to this
house, they would all be killed, because the landlord was in the Mafia.

"I thought he was some kind of magic hippie lawyer," said Chloe,
her eyes shrunken and glazed.

"Yeah," said Lydia. "And he represents like drug lords and shit. So
everybody be incredibly fucking mellow or this clarinet goes up your
bung-hole." She broke into a fit of uncontrollable laughter, bending at
the waist, while the others called her a burnout.

Over the next several days, her friends took up the project of deco-
rating the little cottage as if it were a full-sized dollhouse. Two girls
brought kitchen utensils; Chloe seemed obsessed with hanging spider
plants wherever she could. Danielle brought beanbag chairs, and her
boyfriend (no longer in his Rugby shirt) carted over a picnic table in his
father's SUV, along with a PlayStation 2, which he rigged to an old TV
and played at deafening volume.

The population of the house grew each night. One morning, at the
end of the first week, Lydia rose from a mattress full of half-naked and
sprawled kids, fighting her way out from a tangle of arms and legs, to tip-
toe across a floor littered with twisted bodies and drooling faces. Like
crossing a river on slick rocks, she navigated the open spaces between
hands and knees and backpacks, until she reached the bathroom, to find
a sallow, fat kid going through her medicine cabinet. He wore a sweatshirt hood over his shaved head, and he looked to her like a large, doughy
child. His breathing was strained, his skin was damp and clammy, and
he had flushed red streaks on his cheeks; Lydia thought that he must have
been searching for asthma medication. He had thrown all of her perfume
and makeup into the sink. She asked, "Who are you all of a sudden?"

"I got fucking, like, acid reflux or some shit."

"You know, it's ridiculous the way you people use this house," said Lydia. "Don't throw all my shit out in the sink, okay. Please."

The kid drooped his shoulders and sighed, then began listlessly restocking the shelves.

About fifteen minutes later, Lydia saw a van pull into the driveway.

An electrician approached along the short flagstone walkway, wearing a uniform jumpsuit and carrying a toolbox. He seemed like a possible front, maybe carrying a delivery. Lydia panicked. The man was short and sturdy, with a broad and handsome Latino face and a smile with closed lips, and, when she greeted him, he was already nodding as if in the midst of a conversation. "You're the tenant?"

"Hi, hi. Listen. I have some people over. Just a *gathering*, you know. Very informal."

"The landlord wants me to check an outlet."

"Okay. Don't worry about the mess, okay. Most of it's my family. I have a humongous family."

He entered the musty front room and began nonchalantly treading around sleeping arms and bodies, disappearing into the back of the house. Lydia combed around the room, staring at the unfamiliar faces, searching for Chloe, until she realized that she had gone home. She called her, crouching down into an empty corner, and said, "I'm so fucking screwed. I need you to help me. These people have to stop coming over here, I swear to God. There's a guy in my bathroom now that I've never even seen before."

When she hung up, she began rousting the kids, one by one, by saying that the owner was coming back. The electrician never reappeared, and by the time she had forced most of the crowd outside, still climbing into their shirts and jeans, she noticed the truck was gone. Lydia worried aloud that she'd have to mow this lawn and trim these hedges or she was in deep shit—and someone in the crowd commented that she probably wasn't ready for home ownership. There were so many stragglers that it took until after one o'clock to get everyone out of the house, and the floor looked like the aftermath of a concert.

She jogged to the boulevard, where she bought carpet-cleaning foam. That afternoon she hovered over the froth on the stained carpet, scrubbing on her hands and knees, while other deliveries came and went. There was someone supposedly from the phone company, someone from the cable company, and then a knock at the door turned out to be a woman with a basket of muffins.

Lydia wiped the foam off on her jeans and shook the woman's hand, then she accepted the basket, afraid to speak. The woman said that she and her husband had seen her move in, and they were tired of living in a place where no one knew their neighbors. "You seem like a nice young girl, and we just thought . . ." Apparently, they were from somewhere in Ohio where people weren't *like this.* Lydia felt extremely hungover. The woman ranted on about her job and her family, and Lydia wondered if she'd ever go away. When the phone rang, the woman responded as if it were a timer going off on her speech; Lydia moved past the dissolving clouds of carpet foam to find the phone, newly installed in the kitchen. Cautiously she picked it up and said hello.

"This is a problem, Lydia."

"*Jonah,* God. I've been trying to get in touch with you for a week."

"You can't have so many people over there. One or two is fine, but a party is unacceptable. I heard it looks like a refugee camp over there. I trusted you."

"I know. I'm sorry—and I just kicked everybody out—"

"I'm going to come over there tonight—about eight o'clock. I want to talk about this situation."

"Okay. Eight o'clock is good. I'll make dinner."

Lydia spent the rest of the afternoon preparing. Chloe came through in a pinch, bringing a portable CD player and some Miles Davis—which she claimed was *perfect* for "older dudes." The carpet was stained and smelled heavily of chemicals, but the rest of the house was clean. Lydia wore a short summer dress, and Chloe braided her hair in the cramped bathroom.

"You look so major," said Chloe. "He's going to die for you."

"I love you so much, sweetie. If it wasn't for you, I swear to God, I'd be hanging from a meat hook right now."

By eight o'clock she had dimmed the lights, moved the table to the center of the front room and covered it with cathedral candles. With Chloe's credit card, she had bought five bottles of an Australian red wine that a man had recommended at Whole Foods, despite chuckling at her fake ID; and she was trying to cook sea bass, checking it obsessively and poking it to smithereens with a chopstick.

When Jonah arrived at half past eight, he didn't say a word. He sat quietly in the chair, moving so calmly that he hardly ruffled the candle flames. He waited while Lydia rambled about how she had "tragically fucked up the fish," how she was disgusted with herself that she hadn't been able to follow a simple recipe. Basically, she had gone wrong with the parchment paper, setting it on fire, and next she'd tried to cook the damned thing without it, until it had started to fall apart. She followed the instructions, and as far as she was concerned, Julia Child was a *bitch.*

Jonah made some quiet comment about red wine and fish, then he hardly moved; his expression was so blank that he seemed to be meditating with his eyes open.

Lydia sat down across from him, making the presentation of fish scraps and asparagus and bread and wine, despite the scorched bits of basil and the fuming smell. When she saw Jonah's posture in the chair, she finally stopped ranting.

He said, "I'm disappointed."

Lydia did everything she could to keep composed, but Jonah's composure had amplified her emotions, and she felt her mouth quivering and her throat constrict. With her eyes just beginning to water, she said, "I'm *sorry,* Jonah. I fucked up—but I cleaned the carpet all day, and I kicked everybody out, and I swear to God there's never going to be anybody in here again. They're not my friends, not most of them—they're all leeches, Jonah. They smell blood."

Out of his pocket, Jonah removed a small rectangular box, wrapped with a gold ribbon. It looked to Lydia like it might hold a bracelet, and she stared at it for a long time without moving.

"Open it," he said. "And don't overreact."

"Jonah, I don't *understand.*"

"Open it."

She untied the ribbon, pulled back the lid, and leapt off her chair. She was so horrified that she gave a sudden yelp as if she'd been slapped, and then she lingered by the doorway to the kitchen, heart rioting and hands shaking.

In the box, nestled on a thin film of cotton, there lay a severed human finger. It was pale and bloodless now, something long dead that a cat would drag to a doormat.

"Lydia, look at my face," he said. "Look at me."

On his face was the most incongruous expression—he seemed sympathetic. Fatherly. She was cringing, but he tilted his head and spoke gently: "Lydia, I live an *ugly* life. There is no glamour in it. No celebration. I want you to understand this. Sit down."

"Oh God, Jonah—that is the nastiest fucking thing I've ever seen."

"Lydia. *Listen.* Where I live—there aren't good and bad people. They don't exist. There's money and lives, and they're weighed against each other every day. If somebody wants to take a risk, they do it, and they *know* they're doing it. I'm not a petty street kid, Lydia. I don't run around in the dark selling dime bags, never thinking three hours into the future. I'm a businessman. And the people I work for aren't irrational. They aren't even bad people. They've all just entered into a pact. You come into this with everything you own, including your life; and if you don't play by the rules, then you don't live very long. My life is not some kind of rebellion. I'm not your *father,* Lydia—I'm not some stubborn wild man rejecting society. I live in an orderly universe, more than any business out there. If someone breaks the rules in a corporation, they get fired. Someone breaks the rules in *this* organization, Lydia, they get killed—and everyone knows that."

"Whose finger is that?"

He closed the lid, handed her the box, smiling for the first time. "It's yours now."

Staying alone that night, Lydia told no one. At first, she tried to plan her escape from the house. But past 2 A.M. on a sleepless night, she began a delirious apology for Jonah, thinking of his face, thinking of the unanticipated affection in his tone. He seemed to *believe* that he was helping her, that he was showing her something genuine from his own life. Yes, Lydia *had* known about the violence and brutality just beneath the surface, and it was hypocritical for her to reject him once she had finally seen it clearly. Little by little she revised her thinking, and she began to view the gift as a show of honesty and respect: He had wanted to spare her from the mistakes she was making; he had shown her the seriousness; he had given her the first real glimpse of what he endured in his life. She was beginning to know Jonah, that there was something vulnerable and caring underneath the ugliness of his profession, and so she hugged her pillow and hurt for him, cringing that he was forced to endure such brutality in his life.

Around four o'clock, she went to look at the finger again. She had tried to respond as she believed Jonah wanted, but it still seemed like more than someone else's bad decision. She told herself it was just a thing, a lost memento. There was a crescent of dirt under the nail, hair at the joint, grease in the knuckle. But she couldn't help seeing the details as part of its own history, imagining that it had belonged to a mechanic or a gardener, that he was somewhere out there tonight and could still feel it. She wondered how many things a person needed to lose—fingers, teeth, memories, or plans—before they weren't themselves any longer.

Over the months that followed, Lydia and Jonah began a pattern in which she would stay several nights a week at his house. Before each visit, there was always a great buildup on the phone, and each short stay would end in her returning to the cottage, both of them agreeing to spend time apart. They would discuss their common need for space, over the phone, until once again the calls would become heavy with longing and intimacy. To live with Jonah this way was to experience constant fleeing and returning, abandonment and reunion. Every aspect of their relationship followed this ebb and flow, intense weekends followed by excruciating, uncertain weeks alone. They didn't fight, but Jonah could become suddenly untouchable, so cold that nothing she did could convince or arouse him. He would rise in the dark and look for his ringing cell phone in his pants, refusing to answer questions. She could think of nothing she had done or said to anger him: It was as if he no longer noticed her presence. He would leave her in his plush bed, not even responding to her good-byes, as they trailed him out of the room: "Good-bye, sweetie. Good-bye, darling. Good-bye, *motherfucker.*" But, as furious as this silent treatment made her, she was becoming progressively more anxious *away* from Jonah, as if he were the only antidote to the tension he created.

Over the worsening months, she found comfort only in Jonah's crew around the house. She developed a new routine: Whenever Jonah left at night, she would find his bodyguards and party, watch TV, or play pool. Maybe because there was no real way they could make a pass at her without inspiring the boss's wrath, she found herself in a sisterly rela-tionship—with Iván, especially. Many of the jokes did go on too long. He tickled her sometimes; he and Tito once made a big show of trying to get under her robe; they stole her purse and hid it somewhere in the house; they beat her up with couch pillows, too hard to be funny anymore—but, for the most part, they seemed to like her in a childlike way.

Tito complained that she was turning into a speed freak, going through all of their drugs like an anteater, but never giving them any *game.* For a while, snorting a line or smoking ice in a glass pipe, she felt more in control of herself, confident and sexy and quick-witted. Jonah's mood swings didn't matter. The mountains of new complications were revised quickly into opportunities; the more difficult her relationship, the more she would be rewarded in the end with something wise and true.

But after only a few weeks of accelerating meth use, her reaction to the drugs began to change. The pleasant rush shrank in duration, and finally vanished altogether, leaving in its place an intense nitpicking quality, as if the world still *could* be perfect were it not for some nagging problem: the itch on her neck, her ill-fitting pants, or Tito's boring story. With more speed, this could become a mystical and insatiable curiosity, a senseless urge to see the inner workings of things, which led her to take apart radios and alarm clocks, to search through drawers on an endless treasure hunt, all the while forgetting what she was looking for. It was as if some

analytical quality had gone haywire, and she needed to take apart everything to see its tangled insides. She felt that there was a problem that
could be solved easily, so long as she could understand some secret behind
the façade; and she would wander Jonah's empty bedroom in a stupor,
plumbing through cabinets and closets, fancying herself an archaeologist,
delirious with heatstroke, piecing together a forgotten history.

One night, she completely unpacked the drawers in Jonah's bathroom. She found date books and pictures. Jonah had been with another
woman recently. She couldn't tell *how* recently because he always kept
his hair at the same length and never changed his style. He and the
woman stood together in a dark kitchen, unsmiling, their eyes scorched
red by the flash. He had matchbooks from fancy restaurants, many from
a place in Rosarito Beach. In his medicine cabinet there was Xanax, Val-
ium, Vicodin and Halcion. Beneath the drawer with extra razors, she
found more pictures, water-stained, all of which seemed to be very old
from the coloring and texture. The posing couple must have been Jonah's
parents. They stood on a glowing, overexposed beach, his father, a white
man, cooked pink, with a balding head and a grudging smile; his
mother, a trim Latina, hunching over and crossing her arms, as if she
stood in a draft that her husband couldn't feel.

Just then, she turned and saw Jonah standing in the room. She
jumped, put her hand on her heart, and tried to explain herself. He was
explosively angry and she didn't recognize him. He picked her up from
beneath her arms and threw her into the shower. He grabbed her around
the cheeks and mouth, squeezing, and he whispered through his teeth,
"These fucking drugs you're doing here, Lydia—you root around like
some kind of tweaker and you're going to fuck up every little thing I do."

She nodded and swallowed.

She had no idea how to respond except to apologize again, but, as if
she had neglected to say a magic word, he turned on the shower and
drenched her with freezing water. She rose up violently, swinging at
him and grazing his head. Jonah struck her in the shoulder, a fierce jab
that deadened her arm. She sat with her eyes closed, letting the water
pour over her hair and robe, and when he shut it off, he seemed even

angrier. "Get the fuck up! Get out of there and dry off before I break your fucking jaw."

She stepped out and dropped the robe and stood naked and shivering, and when he threw the towel at her, there was so much hatred in his face that she started to cry. He hissed at her, "*Don't* cry. I mean it. *You* fucked up, not me. You got no right to go digging around for shit on me. I'm not going to stand here and watch this performance."

She took deep breaths and calmed herself, sheathing the towel around her. He was a tiny little man with clenched fists, and she saw in the mirror that she was slouching with the wincing posture she'd once had as the tallest schoolgirl in a class picture. He was tensed and ready to strike her down. He said, "Go to bed. *Now.*"

She lay there crying with anger and heartache, until he climbed into bed beside her and began to kiss her forcefully. She was so sickened at first that she swung at him with her fist and said, "*No,* get off me, you fucking psycho."

But he continued, petting around her hair, kissing her ears and pulling open her robe, and within moments the two were crying together, and he was whispering, "I'm sorry. I'm sorry, Lydia."

Lydia said, "Why did you do that, Jonah? God, *why?*" as he hovered over her body, and kissed down her stomach, and whispered something against her skin.

"I love you," he said. "But it doesn't make it any better."

"No, *Jonah,*" she said, with a querulous voice. "Just tell me what's wrong. Tell me the truth."

That night Lydia never closed her eyes. Later, she wandered the house in the dark. She walked through the kitchen, the empty game room, and finally found Iván sitting awake on the patio. She perched down onto the bench beside him and shared his cigarette. She looked at the tattoos ranging up his neck and scalp, and asked, "What do your boys think of you being up here all the time?"

"It's business," he said. "I make money, they make money." He put his fingers together, like the tips of two guns touching. He sat still for a while, morose, and finally said, "*Lydia*. You got to get out of this, baby. You got to just *go*."

She took a drag and said, "So you heard the fight. You don't see us together like we usually are. There's something else there, there's something about him that's just—he's been seriously screwed with in his life. We got problems, but—"

"Fuck that Oprah bullshit," said Iván. "You think you going to turn that motherfucker around? That dude is *crazy*, Lydia. Crazier than you and I and Tito and all us put together. I think you want to get beat up."

"Jesus, Iván, try to exaggerate a little more."

"I ain't *even* exaggerating."

She took a deep breath, dragged on his cigarette, and handed it back to him. "I'm listening to you. But part of me just—"

"Don't give me that *part*-of-you bullshit. Part of you wants this, part of you wants that. *All* of you is fucked in the head." He dragged on his cigarette with a last flare and flicked it off into the pool. "Go back to that crack house," he said. "Get your ugly-ass clothes and all your other broken shit. And go back to that fat bitch with the freckles." He made a pistol with his hands, fired it at the city, and, from his fingertips, blew away a wisp of imaginary smoke. "Otherwise, you *want* to die. And I ain't going to waste my time feeling sorry for you."

Iván was right. But while Lydia packed up her things at the cottage over the next two days, she felt too depressed to stop the swelling tide of kids that began filling up the rooms again, arriving each night with boom boxes and glass pipes, bongs and skateboards. With all of the housewarming gifts packed into boxes, her sleeping bag rolled tight, she became swept up in the momentum of an impromptu "going-away" party, smoking ice in the bathroom and drinking peppermint schnapps. "Merry fucking Christmas!" She wandered amid the crowded rooms in a wife-beater T and low-riding jeans, clutching the bottle and waving her skinny arms. She was louder than usual, her eyes black with speed; and around midnight, she smashed the bottle onto the driveway and told the lingering crowd that she was sick of this outhouse. She was laughing and showing her teeth, and as she staggered back through the packed living room, Chloe found her and tried to hold her in place. Chloe told her that she was frightened: She had never seen Lydia so high, and there was a volatile undertone brewing at the party.

Lydia pulled away from Chloe and said, "Go save some, like, starving Bolivian kid, okay—'cause I don't fucking care anymore."

Raising her arms, pants sagging, Lydia pushed beyond her friend and watched as all the girls she'd known, from back among those privileged neighborhoods, left the party one by one, abandoning it to the louder and more aggressive young men who'd been arriving all evening like moths to a stadium light. Lydia hardly knew anyone in the house now, but she made out with a stranger by the bathroom, and smoked more speed outside beneath the avocado trees. When she began talking to the kid about her "homicidal boyfriend," he slipped away, vanishing into the crowds. She was tingling in her fingertips, she was breathing in short gasps, her heart was beating so fast that her ribs hurt.

She whispered his full name: Jonah Pincerna. The sound itself made her nostrils flare and fists clench, as if she were still under attack. Pacing in the dark, she fought against an imaginary version of him. How *dare* he put his hands on her like that. How dare he corner her and manipulate her in this squalid little house, putting her away in a cage, his pretty teenage pet. She stalked along the dark backyard, littered with bottles and cans, patches of dead lawn, the smell of a kennel, and she reenacted the fight with Jonah outside in the dark, hissing to herself, answering his barrage of insults now to herself: *Take your fucking hands off me. You're trash.* She was shivering, but—as she turned back to the house—she saw silhouettes in clusters, gesturing with bottles and the flaring tips of ciga- rettes, and she realized that this was *her* crowd now. This scene was dead, and she was going to wake up the party.

In a festive rage, Lydia wandered back into the crowd, waving her fist in the air, and said, "Let's start breaking shit, y'all!"

A few bewildered young men watched as she took the new dishes from the cabinets and smashed them onto the kitchen floor. She dug her nails into the wall, prying loose old tile, the color of dirty teeth, exposing the chalky plaster underneath. Her fingers bled. She no longer seemed enraged, but systematic, as if piece by piece disassembling a puzzle.

"How this bitch goin' tear apart her own house?" someone asked.

But as she persisted in destroying the kitchen tile, then kicking each cabinet door off its hinges, many of the other guests began to join the demolition. In the bathroom, someone shattered a mirror and tore off the toilet seat, throwing it through a window. Several boys began laughing and puncturing the walls, making karate noises with each running kick. Each broken bottle, collapsing shelf, or severed towel rack increased the energy in the house, until Lydia felt herself at the center of a surging riot. At last, it truly exploded when someone threw a trash can through the sliding glass door. Swarms of kids took the house in rapid, SWAT-team formations, beating on the walls, peeling up the carpet, uprooting plants and hurling dirty roots across the floor. The young men had insensate eyes, like sharks, and they beat on themselves and punched their arms at the open air and shouted at Lydia in passing: "Let's *go*! Let's do this!"

Every ounce of her initial frustration was overrun, and she stood paralyzed in a house full of screaming, kicking, gouging, marauding teenage boys. They smashed windows and cut their hands; they overturned the refrigerator as she stumbled backward; they pissed in the corners; they were seething with a rote destructiveness, joining a crowd, losing themselves— and soon there were several boys groping her as they moved through the kitchen, splintering the remainders of cabinet doors.

She could think of nothing now but getting out of the tornado she'd created.

She moved through the kitchen, past swells of kids—some of them looking so *young,* pillaging little boys armed with curtain rods. On the driveway she stood face-to-face with the only calm figure in the chaos. He wore a sweatshirt hood over his shaved head; he was so pale that he seemed to glow faintly under the timed streetlight. It was the awkward man she had seen in her bathroom, who seemed to hover around the edges of her catastrophic parties.

"Fleeing the scene, huh?" he said, looking away at the house. The way he smiled reminded her of the phosphorescent teeth in her childhood. Beyond him, there were neighbors gathered on their porches and lawns in the dark.

Lydia didn't respond to the man, but ran toward the boulevard. Under the motion-sensitive security lights of another house, she noticed that she was bleeding from her cracked fingernails, and that a sliver of broken glass had lodged into her shoulder. She sprinted to the corner, beside a fast-food restaurant, where she called Chloe and Danielle on her cell. Both hung up on her. She started crying in a way that seemed more like the wind had been knocked out of her, a hard strike that caved in her chest and stole her words.

She gave up trying. She wandered a few blocks farther into the residential streets until she came to a grade school penned in by high, chain-link fences. She climbed over and crossed the blacktop to where she found a playground, which looked to her in the passing headlights like a twisted apparatus of steel, strange torture devices on plains of asphalt and rubber mats. She sat on the swings for a while, rocking, then swung back and forth, feeling the rushing air and the plummeting in her stomach, until she dropped off and threw up in the sand. Then she curled up beneath the jungle gym, staring up through its bars, and lay there for hours in a sleepless delirium.

She was brought back to some clarity when children began arriving for school, playing tag and climbing on the rungs above her. Some were laughing at her, most were wary, as she rose up with tangled, sandy hair, wiping her mouth. She crossed the playground to escape the teachers who'd seen her, and she trotted back toward the boulevard, throwing up again on the curb, then searching her pockets for a cigarette while resting on a bus stop bench.

She was almost too hungover to speak. Her mouth was pasted together, her stomach quivered at each deep breath. She called Shannon, who answered the phone in a groggy voice, then cut Lydia off midway through her explanation.

"Whatever he did to you," said Shannon, "I'll kill him. Yeah, girl, get your ass over here. What you're feeling right now—I know everything there is to know about it."

So Lydia rode in the sun-heated buses to Shannon's apartment. It was an unseasonably hot day, and the streets had a torpid, sunstruck quality. Shannon buzzed her in at the ugly pink building. By the time Lydia had dragged herself across the carpet of a long, grim hallway, Shannon had read the expression on her face and put out her arms. "I *know,* sweetie."

She ushered Lydia inside and the two women didn't leave the apartment for four days. They lived as if under siege, blotting out the sun with woolen blankets, living in their pajamas in sweltering heat, foraging for ice cream and microwave pizza. They watched TV, listened to MPGs on her computer, smoked her glass pipe, and carried on long, involved conversations while shouting between rooms—Lydia in a lukewarm bath, Shannon on the couch with an ice pack. They conspired to hide Lydia forever. Shannon seemed even more eagerly conspiratorial because of the fact that her moralistic younger sister had at last shunned Lydia. Shannon had friends in Portland, Oregon. In her hoarse voice, always sounding like she had just come back from a smoky concert, she said, "They'll never find you up there: It's like a safe house. There's literally thousands of kids exactly like you up there." Lydia fantasized about joining the forest defenders, finding a glamorous new life of tree sits, anti-corporate protests, and sensitive vegan roommates.

"How twisted is that?" Lydia asked. "I had a relationship so bad that I have to go hide in a tree."

nine

A fter a week at the apartment in Hollywood, Shannon landed a commercial in Las Vegas. Lydia waited alone, avoiding every other call but Shannon's on her cell phone. One morning, she went outside for a walk, heading toward Sunset to buy cigarettes. She had been holed up for so long, living so badly, that she found herself out of breath and needed to sit down for a rest on a bus stop bench.

She didn't notice for a long time when the Chevy Impala pulled up beside her, idling. Her phone rang and it was Jonah on the caller ID display. She looked up and saw that he was calling her from the open window of the car, a few feet away.

He waved the phone at her and yelled, "Get in."

She considered running, but she felt too listless. She rose, shielding her eyes from the sun, and said, "Jonah. I was going to call you—I'm so— I just needed to get my head back together. I take total responsibility,

okay? And I promise—I'm going to raise the money to fix everything—
and I'm never going to drink or—"

"Get in the car."

She closed her eyes for a moment and took a deep breath. The
streets were bare and bright, lined with the shady alcoves of stores, none
of which could hide her for long. She looked down at the cracks along
the sidewalk and the shallow film of grime running in the gutter and
imagined that she could shrink down and shelter herself in an old can or
a milk carton. But she paced and climbed down into the backseat of the
car, covering her face and praying.

Choop was driving, and Iván sat in the backseat beside a greasy
white kid she had never seen before—introduced as Chase. They all
talked excitedly over each other, like a bunch of unruly kids off to
an amusement park, and Lydia wondered if they were driving her out
into the desert to get rid of her. "I'm serious, Jonah," she said. "I'm so
sorry."

He said, "You're hard to find, Lydia."

"I'm going to pay for everything that got broken."

"I had to search around the house, find lost cell phones, numbers. Finally found your little friend, Chloe. She thinks you've been *irresponsible*,
Lydia. She's talking about an intervention."

Lydia stared ahead, shaken by the wide grin on his face.

"Now we have some business to clean up today," Jonah continued.
"You're going to tag along, and then we're going to talk about this mess
you're in."

As they turned up Highland and merged onto the freeway, Jonah told
a story.

As a boy, he was interested in mythology—particularly Toltec mythology. He lectured everyone in the car from the 101 to the 405, while Lydia
hung her face in the air from the open window, green and panting. From
what she gathered during his lecture, the main deity was Quetzalcoatl,
who represented purity; but there was another god just beneath him in the
pantheon, named Tezcatlipoca, "a crafty motherfucker" who gave mankind
wine, music, pride, culture, *drugs*—everything colorful and dangerous.

Toltec myths weren't like the black-and-white morality of Christianity, Jonah said, because Tezcatlipoca was both good and evil simultaneously. He bestowed gifts in irresistible amounts; he made addicts; he destroyed the same people he meant to help. Jonah said, "And you see, it's complicated, because even though Quetzalcoatl was all good and all moral, he could still be controlled—because he didn't understand his *own* greed and lust. Tezcatlipoca could destroy anybody he wanted."

"What kind of religion is that, Jonah?" said Lydia. "Evil wins."

"No," he said, smiling. "There is no good and evil—there's just light and dark, order and chaos. But there's *one* kind of person he can't touch. And that's whoever can stay rational in a mess, whoever can use reason to control emotions. The only people safe from him are the people who can control their hunger. And *fear*. Get off up here."

They pulled off into Panorama City, where they turned onto a ragged residential street, stopping beside a house of unpainted stucco. A small mutt was leashed in the front yard, running in a circle and rising up onto its hind legs. As they approached the front step, Chase kicked it and the dog swung in a half circle like a tetherball. Jonah pounded on the security grate, and someone spoke to him from the shadows with the accent of a recent Mexican immigrant. "I ask everybody, sir. I do what you say. I don't know what happen."

Jonah nodded at Lydia and asked, "Sound familiar?"

The gate opened and they filed into a hot room with a revolving fan, a single lopsided couch, and a coffee table carved full of names.

"Everybody sit down," said Jonah. "We're going to resolve this *today*. We're going to figure out what went wrong here. Bennie? We're going to get the books in order. This is my friend, Lydia—she's going to be observing today."

Bennie was a middle-aged man, standing in the middle of his narrow room in just an undershirt and boxers. He had sweaty black hair stuck to his forehead, gray in the sideburns, and a mustache that hung over his top lip. He talked for a long time in clipped English about how hard he was working to solve this problem, assuring Jonah that he had done nothing wrong.

Jonah restated the dilemma, and Lydia worried that he was perform-
ing for *her* sake. He said, "We knew every dollar that went into this house,
Bennie. Listen to this, Lydia: When the money goes south, down to get
washed, we got the girls counting in the back room of the bank—because
you can't trust the machines to count it if it's wet or it's been buried. These
chicks can steal ten thousand dollars down their sleeves if you cough or
look away. So we have three people watching every girl—and they count
for *days*, Lydia—sometimes three days straight. The end gets closer, and
everybody gets nervous—but most of the time, everything you *thought*
was there, it's there. Everybody's relieved. What happened this time, Bennie? Explain it to my lady friend here."

He continued saying that he didn't *know* what had happened. Jonah
interrupted him to say, "This time there was sixty thousand dollars
missing. Sixty g's. Now, that may not seem like a lot compared to what
there was—but let me tell you something. Sixty g's is a lot of money,
Bennie. What do you think I would find if I headed down to see your
family? Where are they? Irapuato? Little side trip from Guadalajara,
right? You think they got some new shit? A fucking guesthouse, maybe?
Maybe they have room to put us up for the weekend."

Despite seeming not to understand everything in his speech, Bennie
vehemently shook his head. Lydia retreated into a corner, where she
perched on the windowsill.

Jonah said, "I want you to understand something. You're here right
now, with a chance to explain yourself, because of *me*. Do you understand
that? If you were dealing with anybody else, you'd be dead by now. But to
me—that's not a fair trade. Your life isn't worth anywhere near sixty grand.
I can't go losing this kind of money on every asshole like you. But please
understand, Bennie, I've given you chance after chance. When you fuck
with me, then it's my neck on the line. So game's over: Where's the
money?"

Bennie swallowed and said, "Okay. I tell you. Honest now."

"Good," said Jonah.

"I never take one dollar. Maybe someone. Maybe someone steals
from the house, go down and find it."

Jonah smiled, leaned back, and clapped his hands. He tilted his head and looked at the man with sympathy. "I see. Poor Bennie. You're a victim—in this terrible neighborhood. Anyone could have taken it in a place like this, right? That explains everything. I'm so sorry we scared you, Bennie. Let me ask you one little thing, though. How did you know the money was under the house?"

"I *don't* know."

"You said 'go down and find it.' How would you know it was under the house unless you went under there and looked?"

Bennie began to wave his hands rapidly at Jonah, as if he were a car about to run him down. He said, "No, no, no! *No puedo explicar en Inglés.*"

"*Explique en Español,*" said Choop—and it was the first time Lydia heard his hard, gravelly voice.

Bennie broke into Spanish and it was too fast and frantic for Lydia to translate in her head. As if awakened by the feeling of impending violence, Choop translated in staggers: "He says—that was a' example. He don't know . . . don't know it was under the house . . . just somewhere . . . just saying that was a' example."

Iván said, "This dude is *lying.*"

When Bennie stopped speaking, there was a long silence in the house, broken by the yapping dog outside. Jonah finally looked over at Lydia and said, "Do you understand now? Nobody ever steps up." He clicked his tongue, shook his head, and asked, "How many chances am I supposed to give this fucking guy?"

"Shut that rat-dog up," said Chase.

"Okay," said Jonah, sighing. "We got a lot of powerful people waiting for us to deal with this. Choop—let's get him into the kitchen. Iván, you bring the car around. Chase—are you with us for this?"

"It's why I'm here, boss," said the white kid.

Jonah said, "You watch the door for a minute. Lydia—come with me."

Bennie was surprisingly docile as Choop guided him forward and sat him down on a chair in the kitchenette.

Jonah said to Lydia, "Start looking through the drawers—you're good at things like that."

She searched for a while, through phone books and lighters and silverware, and asked, "What am I looking for?"

"Here. Hand me that Saran Wrap."

She gave him the roll and he tossed it over to Choop. "And let's find
some duct tape or something. Is there anything in there?"

"*No*," said Lydia, throwing her hands up.

Jonah said, "Wait, wait. Go back to that drawer. Yeah, those extension cords."

She held up the bundle and Jonah told her to untangle them, which
seemed to her an impossible job the way her hands were shaking. He
yelled at her that she was taking too long, and then he pulled a few cords
loose from the bundle. He and Choop tied them around the man's wrists
and the legs of the chair, trying to loop them around his ankles. The
cords weren't long enough, so Choop and Jonah had a brief argument
about how best to tie the man down. Choop seemed to think that they
could simply plug one cord into the next, but Jonah told him that was
stupid—he would pull right out of it. During this entire discussion, Bennie pleaded with Lydia, telling her he was innocent, and asking, "Will
you esplain to him? Please?"

Lydia cupped her hands over her mouth and began bending and
straightening her knees.

Eventually they had immobilized Bennie by cinching his wrists together behind his back and winding the cords around the chair. Bennie
kept his eyes on Lydia, but she couldn't look up from the sink.

"*Lydia*—relax. This was a contract."

Chase called from the door, "That fucking dog, I'm going to blow its
brains out."

Jonah nodded to Choop, who fingered the Saran Wrap but couldn't
find where the sheet began. Jonah peeled up an edge, unrolled a streak,
and began stretching it across Bennie's face. Choop took over and continued wrapping the clear plastic over the smudging nose and bulging
eyes, until Bennie's arms tensed and he began pulling loose from the
cords, his legs jolting and the chair sliding backward across the linoleum.

Jonah said, "We didn't tie him right. Let's just go thirty seconds this time, see if he remembers anything. How much is that?"

Choop gouged and stripped off the plastic wrap from Bennie's face, peeling through it like molting skin. Bennie looked frozen in a scream, his open mouth pressing up against the clear bubble, his eyes strained, twisting like a fish on dry land. Choop scraped off the last layer, and Bennie gasped and recovered his breath, sniffling, mumbling in Spanish.

"That's only thirty seconds, Bennie," Jonah said. "You got to exercise or something, man. Do some cardiovascular. That's just sad."

The white kid by the front door yelled, "Iván's bringing the car around."

Jonah dropped to one knee, cursing and securing the cords, while Choop was peeling more wrap off the edge of the roll. He began encircling Bennie's face again, this time so tightly that an immediate seal formed, fogging with breath. Bennie looked trapped under a sheet of ice. His feet wiggled and his tongue rolled out against the plastic, while Choop kept unrolling the sheets around him, thick as a cocoon, until his face was obscured under intersecting wrinkles, only one terrified eye visible through the folds.

"*Jonah*—oh my God!" Lydia was ducking away, reeling backward into the corner.

"Stay there, Lydia. If you leave this room, you're in worse trouble."

Lydia closed her eyes and heard muffled shouts and shoes scrambling on the linoleum, and the crinkling sound of the plastic condensing and settling over the man's face. Jonah suddenly grabbed her, shook her, and turned her so that she was facing Bennie. "Open your eyes. Open your eyes, Lydia—*right now.*"

"No. *Please.* Jonah, whatever you're trying to show me—I learned, okay? I learned. I'll do everything right from now on. *Please* don't kill him."

"Lydia. Open your eyes and see this—now."

She opened her eyes, and she was face-to-face with a man in his last gasping moments. Bennie's eyes landed upon her, blinking against the compressed sheets. The veins in his neck rose into lightning-shaped streaks; his skin turned red, then purple. After a few moments, the twitching arms and legs accelerated like a suffering insect's, until the eye lost focus and clouded, and a steam of breath spread around his mouth, a ghost caught in a plastic bag.

The dog whimpered in the front yard.

Lydia nearly threw up in the sink. She couldn't believe how easy it had been; and she couldn't stand the ripe garbage smell of the room any longer. The body slumped forward against the cords. Everyone inside was silent as the dog barked and the Impala hummed outside. It seemed to Lydia that she should do something, *anything,* grab the telephone or scream out a window. Instead she stood speechless, unsure if she was a hostage or an accomplice.

Jonah said, "Don't pout over there. That was the easy part. We got a long day still. All my psychos get a bonus tonight, as soon as this is cleaned up. Me—I don't get a damn thing. And I'm out sixty grand. How's that for your education, Lydia? You just went to college in one fucking day."

There followed a macabre rush of errands, the body rolled into sheets and lowered into the trunk, the house locked and sealed. On the drive away, Jonah sat pressed against Lydia, and didn't say a word except to order Choop back to his house in the hills, where he and Lydia would switch cars. Once there, the Impala sped off, presumably to dump the body in some canyon, while Jonah ordered Lydia into the front seat beside him.

"Come on. You're tired already? We just started."

He drove in silence down the hill, and she realized from the wending of the car through streets in Hollywood that he was heading back toward the cottage. It was near dusk, the sun fallen behind phone wires and billboards and the ragged tops of palm trees, when Jonah lowered the visor, which cast a shadow across his face. He spoke straight ahead at the road and the thickening traffic. "You didn't even say good-bye, Lydia."

The shock of his tone, hurt and small, completely disarmed her. She began crying, leaning against her closed window.

"Do you have any idea how pathetic this is? Do you want to kill me,

Lydia? I'm asking you straight out. Because I'd much rather you put a gun in my mouth."

"Jonah—I'll fix everything."

"I'm not talking about that," he said. "One load went out of the house a week ago, then another load went back in. The first load was cash, all of it, and it was just counted over the past two days down south. I got the news this morning: We're light."

"We're what?"

"We made an agreement, and we're both in this now. You're not like Bennie. I *do* care about you, whether you believe me or not, and I tried to teach you something. I tried to make you understand—and you didn't. But I'm not going to let your *ignorance* take me down here, Lydia. We're down almost a hundred grand in this house. Where did it go?"

"Jonah—I never saw it, I never looked. I did what you told me."

"You never did *anything* I told you, Lydia. Because you're a child, and there's only two things you know how to do: run away or throw a tantrum. The one thing I was worried about with you, Lydia—it's turned out to be true. You're *weak*. Too weak and too cowardly to stand up for anything or to be accountable. And now I don't care whether you hate me or not—I'm going to show you something. You're going to *learn* this lesson now—even if it kills you. Even if it kills me."

After a few blocks of silence, Jonah spoke in a voice as slow and calm as a hypnotist's: "We're going to come up with the money, and we're going to solve this problem. To do this, you're going to do exactly what I tell you. You're going to put in a real day's work. Or there are going to be dead teenyboppers all over this city. Do you finally understand me?"

"I always did, Jonah," she said. "I told you I did."

"Then *show* me."

Upon first arriving at the house, Lydia saw that the windows were smashed around the security bars; the door was loose and tilted against the frame. The mob had torn apart the house even more violently after she'd left. Inside there was shattered glass and bedrolls, moldering food and beer bottles; the floor looked like a homeless encampment, with tiny clouds of gnats swarming around wadded paper towels and perching on the open lid of a pizza box. Part of the kitchen wall was scorched black from a small fire, and, beyond it, the sliding glass door gaped open, shards across the linoleum floor and across the deck outside. Someone had attacked the drywall in one bathroom with either a bat or a crowbar, smashing holes into it; the metal door was missing from the fuse box, and the ceiling fan was uprooted like a flower.

As Lydia wandered the rooms, Jonah stood still in the threshold. She was ranting as she navigated the wreckage, but Jonah dismissed her promise that she could find the money. They'd never recoup the losses that way. She needed to carry out his specific orders. He explained the system of circulating money and merchandise. Whatever the load, it came from the border and needed a way station before it was divvied up and moved to distributors around the country. Los Angeles was simply the hub: So there was a massive raw tonnage of supply that sometimes needed to sit for days in limbo. The houses were mostly holding cash, waiting to be transported back south, where collusive banks would launder it. Some of the houses were currently holding shipments stalled on the way up—meant to head north or out to the Midwest. He knew a way out of this mess, a way to balance the books quickly; something he'd done before in a bind. Through his boys, he had connections to move crystal meth. They could extract bags of methamphetamine from the walls. With everyone together, they could step on the stuff in a few hours—turn a hundred pounds into two hundred pounds. Cut it with tetracycline and Epsom salts and flour. They'd undersell the competition, flood the markets—move the stuff rapidly at five grand or five-fifty a pound. But she had *put* them in this bind, and she would need to take the risks, starting with a first, tough errand. All during his speech his phone was ringing.

"When you get to the stash, it's in one-pound bricks. Get a bag and fill it up."

"Jonah, I don't even know where it is."

"You'll find it. If it's still here. I'll be back in an hour."

For a few minutes, Lydia imagined herself running toward the boulevard, vanishing onto a bus and into afternoon traffic, but the idea of an unplanned escape began to seem even more dangerous to her, as if, like a mouse tunneling into a new room, she would only leave by the same route she'd come in.

She searched everywhere in the house. She found condoms, lost wallets, cell phones, panties, contact solution, unknown toothbrushes, and fallen earrings. The toilets were clogged, the shower didn't work, the bathroom floor was soaked. There were 40s of malt liquor, wine coolers, Bacardi bottles, a residue of buds and yellow crust in the sink; there was a half-eaten ham sandwich in the refrigerator—but there was nothing Jonah described. With a flashlight, she crawled under the house, into a two-foot-high crawl space of chalky dust, cool and rank, and under a dripping portion of rotted linoleum she shined the light around the wires and the rusted conduits of pipes.

A shadow leapt and hissed at her, and Lydia dropped the flashlight.

She saw it retreat and realized it was a possum living under the bathroom. Her heart was racing so fast that she began laughing with relief.

She was just squirreling her way back toward the access panel when she heard a knock at the door above her. She lay still. The knock continued, picking up volume, sounding far away, as if she were down under a few fathoms of water. Whoever it was had a key, and she heard several distinct sets of feet move across the floor above her—an assortment of drumbeats crossing between the rooms. The voices were in Spanish and English, and someone was talking heatedly, his voice gathering in the pipes beside the bathroom. She heard a man cursing, but only the bad words had volume enough to penetrate the thick floor clearly.

She lay in the dark for a long time, then she crawled on her belly to the center point, lying under the joists, beneath the trickling pipes. She waited and breathed silently, and heard an argument trailing between rooms. Someone was rooting around in the bathroom, searching the medicine cabinet. She heard something fall, a scramble, a digging sound.

"It's here," shouted a man, his voice coming in a metallic echo. "All of it—it's still here. Fucking *cunt*. We're fine."

Were these the men that Jonah worked for? She waited and heard the men tromp back outside, their voices diminishing, long unraveling sentences finally sealed off by slamming car doors.

The sun had fallen completely past the gables by the time she climbed back out, grime in her hair and under her nails. She rushed into the house, staying close to the walls. She didn't take a single breath until she had shut herself into the bathroom. She looked down the drain; she searched the cabinets; she knocked on the walls. There was something hollow beyond them, an extra space, as in a false-bottom suitcase. One wall was rebuilt to create a pocket along the side of the house, but she didn't understand how the men had access. She opened the medicine cabinet and saw all of her things piled haphazardly inside. She cleared off the shelves, shattering perfume bottles and makeup cases into the sink, filling the room with the cloying, department-store smell that Jonah liked on her. She grabbed the back of the medicine cabinet, trying to pry it open. It was screwed into the wall. Without a screwdriver in the house, she panicked and, with her hands trembling, tried to turn the flatheads with a nail file, a penny, and finally a paring knife from the kitchen. Eventually she worked off the screws until a panel fell forward into her hands.

She couldn't reach down into the dark room beyond, so she climbed up with her knee wedged into the sink and squeezed through the open space, past the mirror still hanging open. She worked her way down onto the other side, climbing into a silo that stretched from the bathroom across the laundry room, filled with pressed walls of wrapped bricks.

Over the next frenetic hour, she threw the bags out; then she crawled back out, replaced the panel, and piled the compressed meth into her sleeping bag. She trundled it forward onto the porch, where—jolting with nerves—she dialed a taxi service and nearly cried to the dispatcher, who said it would take fifteen minutes. "I can't wait fifteen minutes. I'm late for a flight."

She dragged the bag down the steps and across the flagstone, and waited by the curb, where everyone's trash was out but hers. She realized that she was talking to herself at full volume, and she stopped and paced in long lines and snapped her fingers, until, turning off the side alley, she saw Jonah's BMW pull up across the street. He rushed out and took the sack, heaving it like a body into the backseat.

They drove through the traffic clotting around Olympic Boulevard.

Both were quiet. A streak of headlights moved across Jonah's face. Just past La Cienega, he said, "Don't relax yet. We got a long week ahead of us."

Compared to what she had been through that day, stepping on a hundred pounds of crystal meth felt like a slumber party. She stood across Jonah's dining room table from Chase, the surly dealer from the San Fernando Valley, who lectured her about everything she did. Iván and Choop moved in and out of the rooms, and they each took little bumps of speed to keep their focus over the long night. It must have been past three in the morning when they all got the giggles. Working with scales and strainers, razor blades, pestles and mortars, chopping up piles of sugar and cold medicine, mixing it to Jonah's exact specifications, Chase commented that this was a lot like being a prep cook at a shitty restaurant, and Iván said to Choop, "Why ain't'chu wearing a hairnet, motherfucker?" Everyone laughed, and it seemed to Lydia that they would have laughed at anything.

When the sun rose, two hundred tightly pressed packages lay stacked together on the new dining room table. Jonah passed through the room saying that Lydia needed to return half the load to the hiding place again, mixing them up with the pure bags. When she went first to wash her face in the master bathroom, she was distracted by her sallow reflection. The drugs and sleep deprivation were getting to her. Her pupils were so dilated that her eyes looked black and wild, like a cornered animal's, and she was getting pimples along her jawline where she had never broken out before. She tried to puzzle together the details in her mind—she had probably done twice as much crank as ever in her life; the low, steady charge, the unwavering concentration, had become its own form of inertia. She found she had been staring at herself in the mirror for a very long time, picking at spots along her neck. Twice, Jonah came into the bathroom to yell at her. She began obsessively washing her skin again, trying to scrub clean her pores. When she looked up, Jonah was standing in the doorway with an irritated tilt to his neck. He needed her to get back to the house and replace the stuff.

She panicked. She started to seize up, gasping and unable to speak, while another, more rational aspect of her was surprised by this reaction. Again, it was as if her spirit had drifted a few feet away from this stammering, hysterical body, watching a breakdown from across the room. But then, when Jonah asked her calmly if she was "too fucked up to do this right now," she woke up suddenly into her own writhing body and felt fear like a stone on her chest.

Jonah searched through his medicine cabinet, and he tried to get her to swallow some pills. Lydia flinched and pulled away from the pills and put her hands over her mouth. She recognized herself as that child who rebelled against her medication. Jonah said, "You're being a brat, Lydia," the same thing her mother had always said. He was trying to maintain his calm, trying to affect a joking tone with her, and he began tickling her as she squirmed away. She howled and giggled, screaming, "*Don't* ti-hi-hi-hi-ckleeee meeee!" But his fingers ran all across her, under her tightening arms and around her feet and between her legs, and he repeated, "Take the pills, you little brat." He tickled her so violently that she jolted away in a seizure against the wall and cabinets, and the initial giddiness gave way to something like an electric shock, with her body rioting and locking up. He kept going, throwing the pills into her open mouth and placing his hand over her lips. *"Swallow."*

She choked down the pills. He poured her a glass of water as she coughed. She drank it, caught her breath, still twitching out the last remaining voltage in her legs. She was drenched in sweat. She looked up at him across the bathroom and said, "I hate being tickled. And I fucking hate *you.*"

"Those will help you sleep. And when you get up, Lydia—you're going to be a new woman."

Jonah had put her to bed with two tablets of Halcion, and she slept until early the next evening, sprawled across the satin pillows of his bed. She woke to him petting through her hair and tracing the contours of her body. She wanted to sink into this bed and live forever against the cool underside of the pillow, but he slapped her ass and told her to get to work. It seemed that he had assumed she was awake earlier, for he was already in the middle of some speech.

". . . and keep your wits about you. All of these people are going to be nervous, really nervous about dealing with you. You're going to be the one out front. Make back every dollar you lost out of that house. I already explained, and I already set up the list. The main thing you have to do— follow the etiquette. Don't show up and get right to business. Treat everybody like they're your friend, your only client—and hang out a while. The last thing these people want is some girl coming and going in fifteen minutes. But you still have to keep all the appointments. It will take you into tomorrow night, probably."

She sat up in the bed and saw the clothes he had hung on the closet door. He wanted her to wear Adidas sweatpants and a tank top, and she asked, "Is that the uniform?"

"Look good, but not too good—okay? I don't want anybody getting the idea you've got other businesses going on the side."

At a little past six, she set off to make the deliveries, driving off in his least-practical car—a '69 Cadillac El Dorado with a rumbling boat en- gine and sleek wings. At every stoplight, there seemed to be another car- load of teenage boys hollering at her from their open windows.

Under a burnt sunset, she began her errands as if embarking on a scavenger hunt. Jonah had made her a list of stops, with the rough hours that they were expecting her, and she took deep breaths and cruised along side streets to avoid the police. She was a poor driver under the best circumstances, and had no license other than her fake ID. With a cargo that would land her possibly a life sentence in prison—that is, if one of Jonah's now spectral bosses didn't get to her first—she became phobic about making left turns along the boulevards.

Nevertheless, she made her first appointment on time. She went to the caged front door of a small cottage in Silverlake, her hands sweating, her mouth dry; and when Marcello, the first client, greeted her—she was relieved. He seemed perfectly chosen as her introduction, a gregarious and somewhat older gay man, with a mustache and a tight haircut, com- pletely at ease with himself, leading her into his clean and cozy living room. He had a massive bookshelf, and while he cut out and sampled a line, Lydia strolled along, reading the titles aloud quietly.

He said, "Don't be nervous about this—that's the main thing. Jonah explained the situation to me. He's selling this stuff so dirt cheap, people are going to be suspicious. But I know him, and it's a good deal—there's some profits here for me. Even though it's not exactly the *best* shit in the world, is it? You want a bump of this?"

She sat down and took a bump off her fingernail, sitting across the glass coffee table from him. He had piles of art books and a carved replica of a fertility goddess—one of the ancient, obese Venuses Lydia remembered from school. She smacked her lips, swallowed the chemical taste in her mouth. The man was sitting back with his legs crossed, talking in a leisurely way about how Jonah was getting on his nerves these days. "Uppity" was the word he used. Jonah used to have all kinds of spotty, ill-considered business ventures. Marcello said that he used to manage a band with Jonah, though Jonah's involvement was passive, just money. The band couldn't get along, "the lead singer was a *cunt*, forgive my language," and they had all parted ways. "But I'd be remiss if I didn't give you a teeny little warning about Jonah—he has very unreasonable expectations of people. In my experience."

"He's giving me another chance."

"Well, of course—he *loves* that. He loves to have screwups around, and he loves to forgive them—it's so godlike of him. I'm sure you have to crawl on your hands and knees, and beg him for mercy. I wouldn't be surprised if he had something of a fetish about that. Dress you up like his odalisque, have you chained naked to a rock. He'll spare you. He'll look down upon you and grant you something. It's all very Promethean. But you know what, Lydia—that's your name, right? He will cut a person off like they never existed to him. He has that ability to just *shut down.* I've seen it." He snapped his fingers as he moved his hand across his face. "You do whatever you have to do—but just know this: People who get close to him, they don't ever get away. And those bangers he pays, those *cholos* up there, he's got them brainwashed into some kind of cult. I don't know where they're from, I don't know what gang they're in—but they're his gang now. It's not just the money. He pays them well, sure. But those kids can tax drug dealers like me in *any* neighborhood, and they'll make as much. No, he promises something, and I've always wondered what it was. My advice to you: Don't trust those kids. There's something else going on there."

Versions of this same speech cropped up again throughout Lydia's errands that day. She drove all over the West Side, traversing cluttered homes and apartments, uncovering a new landscape of kitchen tables and mirrors. She heard so many points of view as she swallowed up her friendly, ceremonial lines with the dealers, so many opinions, that she began to feel it was all one giant citywide speech, delivered house to house, in stammers, with long pauses of traffic in between. In Ladera Heights, four bantering black kids sat around her on a wooden table, one with dreadlocks and his shirt off, BGF tattoos and a tear inked under his eye, urging her not to be so nervous. "You get nervous, you make me nervous, a'ight." He spoke in a forced sweetness, a kind of stagy gallantry in his tone, as if he might be tricking a less intelligent animal. She sat down in his bright kitchen, with the security cage open across the house and the sound of an argument outside. He said, "Jonah's a manipulating motherfucker, if you want my personal opinion. Acting like Al Capone up there. Nah, nah. Dude don't got his p's and q's straight How he gonna send a pretty girl down here? Dressed like that? Looking like you selling some kind of Bowflex or shit."

Just south of MacArthur Park, in an apartment building with every door opened onto a TV blasting Univision, the monologue was picked up by a thin Chicano man. "He say, I going to know you ain't no cop—because you fly; and I'm like, *no shit?* But this is Jonah, mang—he always doing this to me. Selling this shit like it's a favor."

A housewife in Redondo, twittering over the long ash on her cigarette, perched over a Formica table and said, "I mean, it terrifies me. Can I just tell you something? I think, and this is just me, this is just me, I think he's got some kind of death wish—I mean, there are people who get very, very upset about the way he undercuts the prices in this town. We have to keep it secret that we're even doing business with him. Because a pound

is going for six grand, and Jonah comes along with something at five—
even if it's not the purest—and he floods the market. People talk. I can
make my profits on this, sure—but I don't want to be around when this
starts getting ugly."

Past midnight, an aging hippie in a Venice bungalow, wearing huge,
slightly damp shorts and a Billabong T-shirt, drawled his contribution to
the other men in the room, "It's fucking sketch business practices, bra'.
Like that kid who fucking died, you know. Deke! Wake up. Who was that
kid who died? Little Filipino dude. He's fucking burnt, don't listen to
him. Anyway, this guy was Jonah's bitch, basically. Delivered shit for him.
One day they find him, L.A. River, fucking back of his head all blown out
and shit. That's why Jonah ain't here, bra'. You don't freelance in this
town. You're a brave woman. Powerpuff Girls." He reached out his fist.

"Yeah, I heard about that Filipino kid," said a skeleton-thin girl with
fuchsia hair, past 1 a.m. off Washington Avenue. "I heard that kid got
busted and he was back out. On his own, fucking like, recognizance.
Cops make you sign a contract, you know. That you have to bring down
another dealer. Buy and bust. I always heard Jonah's people just got to
him first. One of Jonah's gangster kids up there. *Boom:* see ya!"

A biker in Southgate, three punks in Orange County, a Russian off
Fairfax, and, near dawn, two whispering Korean kids on their way to
school—they each filled in portions of Jonah's history, like a tapestry of
gossip, and Lydia understood that he had done this trick many times,
scraping off the top of shipments that passed through his houses; and
she knew that there had been foot soldiers like her, who had gone face-
down into the Dumpsters, their heads blown out; and she still moved
on, checking names off her list, feeling that the mystery she was assembling, the picture she was building out of so many different points, was
simply her own death. She was locked in a slow suicide, and she kept on
as if sleepwalking, as if the ultimate goal was something already decided
in a nightmare. She did more lines as the sun came up, and she continued her errands, with no food, no water, only the manic and delirious
fuel of each deal, moving through the detached, sprawling polyglot em-
pire of Los Angeles, feeling that each section, from the undulating hills

to the ugly flats of billboards and phone wires, was the fiefdom of some dealer, and that she was a traveler, all alone, meant to watch and wait and listen.

By the following evening, she had been up for twenty-four hours, and she would now linger in apartments and houses and lose track of time. In the no-man's-land of warehouses, east of downtown, she sat in an upstairs room with an old painter who talked almost in a whisper, crushing the speed in a mortar and mixing water, soaking it in a cotton ball, and offering to shoot her up. She said no. She watched him wrap the tourniquet on his arm, plunge in the needle, and cast himself into a new, perspiring state of watchfulness. Afterward, he offered her a thousand dollars to fuck him, becoming distracted by a distant idea, his face seeming to boil from the inside. He said, "Next time—you'll say *yes*."

She had been awake for thirty-six hours without so much as a drink of water when she pulled up to the shingled house in Topanga Canyon. The man who came to the door was in his early forties, with a craggy, prematurely old face. He was wearing a loose white shirt and old patched jeans, and he sniffled and led her unceremoniously inside, to where Lydia saw the back of a young boy's head. He was on the couch, up late, watching television. She passed over a raised entry hall of Spanish tile, beyond a weighted door, into a bright kitchen, where a haggard woman sat in the breakfast nook. She could have been only in her thirties, but her face looked deflated. She made a joke, asking Lydia if she was the drug dealer or the hooker they'd ordered (she couldn't tell the difference nowadays), and she laughed with a wet rattle in her throat. Lydia gave the man the bags, and he piled them on the kitchen counter. Lydia was mortified about the little boy in the other room.

While the man abruptly prepared a line, the woman began talking to Lydia about how much Jonah had been harassing them lately. "I mean, we would rather pay the extra money for some better shit. Our clients know the difference around here. We're not a bunch of high school kids. No offense."

The man did a line, rubbed his nostril, and said, "Nope. Nope. I've had it with this. You tell Jonah this is bullshit. This stuff is so fucking stepped on I could bake a cake out of it. No. And you know what?" He was livid, and pointing his slightly dusted fingertip at her. "I'm not going to get involved with Jonah anymore. It's always some last-second panic—and he's always got a dump truck of crap he needs to get rid of. Forget it. I don't know what kind of business you people are running up there—but I got friends in high places, and I'll smear his fucking name all over this town."

"Don't yell at her, Chris. It's not her fault."

"Hold on a second," he said. He left the room and the door swung on its hinge.

The woman said, "It's just that we have a bad history with Jonah."

He returned with a tiny square of tin foil, and he poured it out into what looked like a soy sauce dish. He crushed it and went to the refrigerator. "Are we out of water? I'm not going to use fucking tap water." He found a bottle of purified water and dripped some into the powder. He tossed down the cotton ball, and sucked the solution up into a syringe.

"I'm going to show you the difference here, kid. You've been doing so much crap for so long, you don't know what this is supposed to feel like."

Lydia refused, but the man stepped over her on the chair and grabbed her exhausted arm. She pulled away, and he fixed his eyes onto hers, saying, "You're going to feel better than ever in your life. This is *relief*, kid. From everything you've just been through."

He was so aggressive that Lydia stayed still, as if he held in his hands the final and unavoidable truth about her. He tied the rubber tourniquet over her arm and slapped at her vein. Lydia was reeling; she was alarmed by how much the drugs had overwhelmed her the past two days. The woman scooted closer beside her and held Lydia's hand, and, as if Lydia were an infant, she said, "Shhh, it's okay." She sweetly petted through Lydia's hair, tucking it around her ear, and she rubbed her shoulder, as the man slid down the needle and launched the solution and sent something through Lydia's blood and spine that was like the finger of a god. She closed her eyes and tilted her head back. The woman stroked her hair, whispering, and Lydia rolled with a pleasure that was as much as her body could stand, tingling and sensitized, feeling the air in her lungs like a million charged particles; the woman was whispering in her ear, and when Lydia looked up at her, her sunken, witchlike face no longer seemed ugly, but the husk of something once beautiful and alive and lonesome, just lost to everyone on the other side of this divide. And the woman kissed her and laughed, showing bad teeth, as Lydia slid farther back on the chair, startled, feeling her heart now like it might rush out of control.

And the man said, "Tell Jonah we're not buying. Four pounds was the contract—and as far as I'm concerned, he broke it, sending this kind of bullshit over. You see the difference now."

When Lydia left the house, she was so fired up that she could barely walk. It was an odd paradox: There was so much vigor behind each motion, each breath, each second that passed, that she no longer wanted to move.

This ecstatic feeling faded by the time she reached the apartment in the West Valley, sinking back into a raw and hungry feeling like the world was an unsolvable riddle. She drove up into the sprawling complex through Canoga Park, and she stepped out and moved toward the next address on her list, a far building beside the freeway and a tall sound barrier. When she saw the kid on his front stoop, she jumped backward.

He was heavy, in large, drooping pants; his thick cheeks were covered with sparse facial hair, and he had shaved his head down to the lumpy gray skin. He approached with his head down, loafing along.

He had been to the cottage in Culver City—several times. He was the man who had gone through her medicine cabinet, who had been mysteriously lurking around parties. She watched him approach across a walkway and toward the parking lot, and she was astounded that he showed no sign of recognition. Was this the person who had stolen the money? He must have recognized her, and as he accelerated his pace toward her, Lydia panicked. She saw him adjust something in the low waistband of his clownish pants. A gun, maybe?

Before he could reach her across the poorly lit cluster of cars, Lydia leapt back into the El Dorado and drove away, screeching out of the lot as he called and trotted after her. Her heart was racing, and she believed that she had—at last—found the thief.

But during the long drive back to Jonah's, some new paranoia grabbed hold of her as she began to wonder why Jonah would *know* this cretin, and why he had put him on Lydia's list of deliveries. He was the last man of the night, last on a long list, and she had been waiting to meet him in a dark, isolated parking lot beside the heavy white noise of passing cars. Did Jonah know this man? Did he do business with him? It seemed an insane coincidence, and she was determined not to let her mind race ahead of her.

She was no longer just shivering but flinching, having a hard time keeping the wheel straight. She was paranoid, of course. She hadn't slept, the drugs were taking their toll. Keep your eyes open long enough and everything is part of a vast conspiracy. But she couldn't overlook what seemed so clear, no matter how deeply she still wanted to believe in Jonah. No, no, repeat the arrangement: She'd made a mistake and she was taking responsibility. She was running errands, making back the cash. But what if she hadn't made any mistake at all? She remembered that after Jonah put her back to bed with tranquilizers that night, he'd sent someone else to replace the packages—and he hadn't even *asked* her where they'd been hidden. Lydia had the delirious sense that she had been put in that house long ago for this very reason: to make some visible mistake, to make secret deliveries, steal money or drugs out of stash houses, and maybe, never to be heard from again. Was Jonah using these tenants to steal from his own superiors? Was it possible that what Jonah had seen in Lydia, all those months ago, was a talent for vanishing without a trace?

ten

At the end of their second day together, Link drove his daughter back to the city, where she told him that her belongings were ferreted away in a Hollywood apartment. At dusk, they were heading west past the hundreds of windmills outside Palm Springs, just silhouettes now against a last hazy trail of light. Lydia was in a stupor of withdrawal, sagging against the closed windows, then jolting upright whenever he changed lanes. Just east of downtown, she started to regain some energy, chewing a stick of bubble gum from her backpack. She played with the radio, and announced, "You're on empty."

"I'm always on empty. The gauge is broke."

"Then how do you know when you're going to run out of gas?"

"I got a sense for it."

"You're like the horse whisperer."

She found a screeching hip-hop station, and listened to some mixture of heavy metal and rap, which she claimed that he should appreciate because it had guitars in it. Link thought it sounded like a bunch of screaming morons fucking up their parents' record players. He turned it off and they rode in silence, until he asked her what she wanted to be when she grew up.

First she riffed off the lyrics from some rap, and he thought she was going to describe her ambitions to be a groupie: She had a way of acting silly instead of responding to him. But suddenly she calmed down and told him in a gloomy voice that she had once wanted to be a linguist or an archaeologist, whoever those people were who studied the history of languages and figured out migration trails. She had once had a book that explained the etymologies of every word, and it had been her favorite thing to read in the bathtub, although she had been distracted by the histories of the dirty words. That was all she could remember now. She told him that the "c-word" came from the Latin word for wedge, and later on: "It was the name of this street where all the hos hung out in Oxford: *Gropecuntlane.*"

She told him that "bastard" came from a French phrase, *fils de bast,* which meant something like "packsaddle son," and that she was his packsaddle *daughter.*

The first written example of the f-word was in the 1200s: "John Le Fucker."

"Get out of here," said Link.

"I swear to God. *Fock* meant, like, dick in Old Swedish. And there's all kinds of words like 'fick,' and 'fack,' and everything, all the way back to the cavemen—so it was seriously all over. But the first time anybody saw it in English, in writing anyway, it was this guy, a nickname or something. John Le Fucker."

By the time they had passed downtown, onto the Hollywood Freeway, she was saying wistfully that she had probably missed her chance for that kind of "hard-core academia," and that now, if she ever got to Portland, she was going to be a tree sitter.

"You go up there and you just sit in this tree house made out of ropes, so that the logging companies can't cut it down without killing you. It's really beautiful, when you think about it." She said that there were whole species of rare molds and fungi that lived in old-growth forests, and the only way to protect them from extinction was to have dedicated kids up there. She figured it was a good opportunity to make herself useful, fugitive or otherwise.

"You're going to sit in a tree to save some kind of *mold*?"

"You just asked me what I wanted to do. That's the current plan, if I can get up there. I mean, at least I'll be doing something meaningful for once in my selfish, miserable life."

"Sit in a tree and get high?"

"They have rules, I think—that you have to be sober."

"Like hell they do. Nobody would do it who wasn't fucked up."

"What are you then? Some kind of right-wing freak? Were you one of those Hell's Angels who beat up hippies all the time?"

"I'm just not real worried about a tree."

"Well, pretty soon we might not have any more."

"Sounds like a tragedy."

"The death of an entire ecosystem. *Yeah,* it is. Total destruction of the planet."

"I'm crying already."

Through thickening traffic, exiting beside the hills and empty lots near the Hollywood Bowl, she led him to the apartment building, a giant stucco slab just off La Brea, where the early-bird hookers were already working their corners in latex skirts, strutting between palm trees and the gated entrances to underground garages. The building was a faded mustard color, rising tall amid the groves. Lydia tried to buzz in beside a row of drooping birds of paradise, but there was no one home. When a listless Russian kid opened the door, Lydia said, "*Spasibe.*" He smiled with crooked teeth and replied, "Whatever," in a thick accent.

The elevator was broken, so they took the stairs to the sixth floor. Lydia said that she didn't have a key, so they were screwed if her friend Shannon was still in Vegas.

When Lydia knocked on the apartment door, it came unlatched by itself. She looked back at her father, eyes wide, and said, "That's not good."

"She's probably home."

"No, no, no," said Lydia. "People lock their doors here. This isn't *Seinfeld.*"

Her father pushed past her into the apartment, where he saw that the place had been torn apart.

Lydia tiptoed around him, moving into the center of the disaster. The floor was covered with CDs and broken cases, the smashed and gutted wiring of a stereo system, fragments of mugs and plates, uprooted plants, and the remains of a shattered glass table. Someone had pissed on the couch. An aquarium had been dropped, transparent rocks piled among kitty litter and torn papers, and, in the debris, a few exotic fish lay motionless with bulging eyes. The room smelled like a bucket of chum. Hissing and traumatized, the cat still roamed around overturned bookshelves and smashed computer chairs.

While Lydia sifted through the wreckage, Link checked the lock: the wood around it was splintered; someone had bluntly pried open the door with a crowbar.

Lydia started packing a duffel with the frantic pace of a looter. She searched a table beside the phone, where cards had been plucked from a Rolodex, flipping through ripped-up address books and notebooks, whispering to herself. She found what looked to be a giant scrapbook. "They read my diary, I think." In a drawer, she found a pastel-colored cell phone and said, *"Yes."*

She dialed the phone and moved back into the bedroom. Buried under a mess of pillows and overturned kitchen stools, another phone began ringing. Lydia shouted, "Can you get that?" Link hunted for the ring around drifting feathers and album sleeves, finally digging up a pink phone. He put his ear to it without speaking, and then he heard his daughter's voice in the receiver: *"Daddy?* So good to hear your voice. What are you doing?"

"I'm in the living room."

"Wow, that's great. I'm in the bedroom."

"Maybe you shouldn't use your cell phone."

"Okay, I'll be right there."

She came out of the doorway with another armful of clothes, and she threw the cell phone to him across the room. Link said, "Why don't you quit fucking around and tell me who did this?"

"Did what?" asked Lydia, standing with her legs spread over the drifting remains of a stabbed pillow. "I'm just really, really messy." She snorted, not quite following through with a laugh; and then she seemed to get lost in some autistic daydream. "Toothbrush!"

For a while, he could hear her digging through the bathroom, moving a broken shower door. Link waited beside the kitchenette, watching thick droplets of something ooze down from the refrigerator door. On the counter lay a black case. Carefully, he opened it to reveal a grimy clarinet, sullied with breath and fingerprints, but seeming almost like a living thing with its rows of valves and latches. Lydia had been in the bathroom too long. The sink ran, the toilet flushed. She emerged with rejuvenated pink coloring in her cheeks, nodding at the trash around her as if for an argument she had already heard. "So—we're out of here. All my camping supplies, my scrapbook, my—oh, nice work! You found the clarinet."

"You play this thing?"

"Yeah, you deadhead. I wrote you like a thousand letters about it. My mother was seriously boot camp about it. You want to hear me play something?"

Link was chewing his lips and beard, so angry at the suspicion that she might have taken a bump in the other room, but he sat down and closed his eyes, figuring it would be better not to confront her while she was high—the little c-word, the foulmouthed linguist. He took a deep breath and said, "Make it short."

She took the clarinet and perched on the edge of the couch. She readied her fingers, curling them up into a long row like the legs of an overturned centipede, and she placed her lips over the reed.

He listened to the song. Her fingers rose and fell, and she bobbed her head around to the melody, eyes focused downward and faintly crossed. Link watched the varying pucker of her mouth, and noticed how it was the same shape as when she exhaled cigarette smoke. When she finished, she smiled and looked eager for approval. He studied the cracked rosy streaks on her face, her dilated pupils, and the sweat on her forehead.

"Pretty," he said.

She told him it was Ravel. She spoke so rapidly now that he could hardly keep up. Apparently, she had once done a recital of Benny Goodman, but had botched it so badly that her mother had taken it as a personal attack; she was okay at classical, but she "sucked dick" at jazz. She could play the piano also, but never well enough, because she had these big, awful fingertips, thick and bulbous and not at all feminine. They weren't suited to musical endeavors. Her mother hadn't thought of the possibility, but had assumed that Lydia would grow up "prissy and cute and dainty" like she was. Instead, she had sprouted into a "gigantic buffoon" with the hands of a bear; and, though she believed that she might have had musical talent in her *mind,* or in her heart, or soul, or wherever real music was conceived, she was born with the wrong hands to deliver it.

"We should go," said Link.

In the car for the next hour, she alternated between manic stories and attempts to play the clarinet while Link swerved through traffic. She wanted to play "Name That Tune" with him, and she was delighted with herself whenever she performed some classic rock flourish as if redone by skittish fairies.

Meanwhile, Link was watching a suspicious white car in the rearview mirror, which matched his speed and lane changes for at least thirty miles. Lydia played Deep Purple and Steppenwolf; she played Led Zeppelin and Jefferson Airplane. Her giddiness lasted all the way to the train yards and factories in Fontana; and when the sprawl of incorporated cities gave way to hills and horse ranches, she asked if he had known Grace Slick? No. Jerry Garcia? No. Sonny Barger? "Sure, met him back when he got out of Folsom for a while in seventy-seven." Did he ever go to any of Ken Kesey's parties?

"Where did you learn all this shit?" asked Link.

"I had an English class where we read *The Electric Kool-Aid Acid Test* and *Zen and the Art of Motorcycle Maintenance,* and then I did this extra-credit report on outlaw biker clubs, because you were a one-percenter."

Scanning the headlights behind him, Link noticed how, whether he braked or accelerated, the white car maintained the same skilled distance. Link had the sense it was a cop, maybe from a stakeout around the building.

"What kind of teacher would let you do that?"

"Oh, he wanted me, this guy. He was all like—*we're going to work hand in hand; you're so talented, but so unfocused.* Yeah, right. I know where he wanted me to focus."

She started playing a Police song on the clarinet, the one about the teacher and the underaged girl, while Link glanced at the mirror and noticed that the white car was closing the gap now, possibly trying to get a better look at his plates.

"That's what all that tuition was for?"

"Don't get preachy in your old age," said Lydia, frolicking into his shoulder, in a way that seemed suddenly too kittenish. She hovered against him, her hair smelling like the shampoo from his lousy shower. "I know your whole story."

"Yeah, what's that?"

She rotated so that her back rested against the dark passenger window, and she put her bare feet onto his lap, wiggling her toes. The lights of the last little cities, like afterthoughts, rolled past her shadow. She said, "I'm serious. My mother must have told stories about you more than anything else. How you guys rode all over, and you were this psycho bar brawler. Couldn't keep out of a fight. If anybody looked at her twice, you beat the hell out of him. Is that true?"

"No."

"She would tell that shit at dinner parties. Everybody was all: Wow, that woman really lived it up; she's got a wild side. That's what everybody would say. But you know what? She was a lousy lay. A CPR dummy."

"That's no way to talk about your mother, kid."

"Yeah, but I know. For a fact. You want to know how I know?"

"Not really."

"You're not even one little bit curious?"

"No."

He looked up and saw a patrol car now surging along the slow lane, flanking them. Link's hands were sweating, and he tried to calculate in his head how many parole violations he had made in the last twenty-four hours by hiding this girl and her nine-millimeter handgun, whatever she had done, her duffel probably full of broken evidence.

She rolled her head back against the closed window, lights soaring past her darkened face, and she said, "I know because every guy she was ever with—well, not every guy, but practically every guy—a pretty significant percentage, I would say—"

Link slowed the car and eased into a pocket behind the white car, which decelerated rapidly with flaring taillights. The patrol car pulled around and passed him on the left side, and Link wondered why they were stalling.

"—all her boyfriends, husbands, you name it, sooner or later, they would make some kind of move on *me*. What does that tell you?"

Link suddenly lost track of the two cars.

Lydia wiggled her toes on his lap.

"Are you shitting me?"

"No," she said. "Honestly. I'd say pretty much every guy in her life tried something on me, at some point or another. Except you." She cleared hair from her face. "Of course, you never really had that *opportunity*."

Link responded to this as if she had come up on him with a knife. He grabbed her bare feet and threw them off, then he jerked the car into the emergency lane. The white car didn't stop in time, and, as if avoiding a confrontation too early, it pulled off the freeway at the exit about two hundred yards ahead. Stopped under a bluish streetlight, Lydia's face looked glossy with sweat. She had a huge, tickled smile, as if she were winning a game of tag.

Link said, "Stop it."

"Stop what?"

"This bullshit. Stop it. Right now."

"What bullshit?"

"It's not cute—it's disgusting."

"I'm sorry I disgust you."

"Number one, don't talk that way about your mother. She's got her problems like anybody else, but I don't want to listen to your bullshit theory about her."

"Like you even *know* her."

"Second thing—you tell me some motherfuckers put their hands on you, you better give me names and addresses, because I will hunt them down and smash their fucking teeth in. You don't tell me that shit like it's funny. It's not. I'm going to firebomb their houses. You hear me? I will turn fucking serial killer right here in this car."

At this, the smile left her face.

He continued, "And don't you dare play me like some kind of punk. You got at least a gram of speed in you right now, and you're talking to me like I'm just another asshole. I'm not. I'm your asshole *father.* I held you in my hand, one goddamn hand, when you were no bigger than a Twinkie. You got to be out of your mind talking to me like you just did. If you can't treat me with some respect, then we got a big problem on our hands."

She replied, "That's just what I figured. *Respect.* Of course. You have all my undying respect, dearest Father." She spoke as if dictating a letter to him in prison, then she made a robotic pivot in her seat to face the road ahead. He draped his hands over the wheel; she braced hers against the glove compartment.

"Anyway," he said, "it's good we stopped. Some John Le Fucker was trailing us home."

When Link made it back to the trailer with his daughter, at a little past midnight, he was confident that he had lost the white car in the San Gabriel Valley. While Lydia watched the black-and-white TV, Link searched for his sponsor's new cell phone number, cursing his poor memory. He wrote it in marker across the back of a flier, which he taped beside the phone. Whispering, so that Lydia couldn't eavesdrop, he told Kirby that he was inches away from giving up and getting shit-faced for good. He might not even drive to the liquor store; he could just get a straw and drink the antifreeze out of his radiator. Kirby gave him a speech, every phrase of which Link had heard before, like lyrics in a hit country-western song; but when he was finished, Link thanked him and grabbed a Dr Pepper. He sat outside on his steps in the cold wash of desert air, listening to laughter from a talk show inside.

From far down the highway, a car approached. It passed and swung suddenly into a U-turn through the gravel along the road. It hovered with the engine rumbling and a stereo reverberating through closed windows— a late-sixties Chevy Impala convertible. The sound died, the headlights faded, and the car became a silhouette near the one pale streetlight.

Four shadows rose out of the opening doors.

Link had seen this kind of swagger practically every day of his life; he had learned the nuances of it like the grammar of a primitive language. The rolling of the shoulders, the dangling of the arms. Before he could see their faces, he knew that two of them were dangerous, one of them was questionable, and one was a punk. He knew that they had guns in their waistbands from their altered strides and the way their shirts hung unevenly.

They emerged out of the dimness and into the outskirts of his porch light. Two wore three-quarter-length pants with tube socks pulled high and Eighteenth Street symbols emblazoned across their arms and necks. One of them had a giant tat that read "El Salvador," which looked scratched in by a homemade gun. Some of the tattoos on the thicker, shorter *cholo* showed that he was CLCS (Columbia L'il Cycos), a clique near MacArthur Park. He also had a brand on his fist that read "Kanpol," which Link knew meant "southerner" in Nahuatl, the Aztec language.

"Can I help you gentlemen?" Link asked.

They didn't answer until they had formed a semicircle around him. The third was a long-haired white kid wearing an L.A. Kings jersey, with the Brotherhood shamrock on his forearm. This was interesting: If this kid was working with the others, then he was likely NLR, a Nazi Lowrider, a newer prison and street gang, an enforcement arm of the Aryan Brotherhood that collaborated sometimes, secretly, with Chicano gangs.

The fourth kid seemed like a prospect, scrawny and loud, with a fuzzy little mustache and peroxide in his hair. He had definitely never done time, and he looked too anxious to prove himself. He was sniffling and groaning, as if sick with a head cold, yet he spoke first: "Yeah, man. We want *tattoos.*"

"I'm not open."

"The sign says 'Or by appointment,' so we want an appointment."

"Come back tomorrow."

"Nah, man. Not tomorrow," said El Salvador. "Right now. I want some shit on my arm. Like a big skull or something."

"Or a heart with a girl's name in it," said the prospect.

"Yeah," agreed NLR. "On my dick." He grabbed himself, and the young prospect broke into such laughter that he needed to take large twisting steps around the gravel to restore his poker face.

"Go home," said Link.

"We got money," said NLR. "That's bad business, turning us away."

"Yeah, don't judge us by our looks," said El Salvador. "Judge us for who we are on the inside."

"Our money is good."

"I'm not judging you," said Link. "I'm closed. I'm going to bed in a minute."

The prospect said, "What if I said I wanted this bitch's name on my stomach, yo?" He pulled up his shirt and showed his thin torso, free of ink, a Glock nestled diagonally into his loose pants, matching the one in Link's bathroom. "Lydia Jane," he said. "L-I-D . . . some shit like that."

"Not today."

"And her picture under it."

El Salvador said, "Pretty white bitch with black hair."

Link stood with a groan. From the top step, a few feet higher than all of them, he saluted and said, "Come back tomorrow with a picture. I'll make a stencil."

"You don't need a picture, old dude."

Link stepped back inside and closed the door. Lydia had been watching through the blinds, perched on the couch in the monochromatic light of the TV.

"Friends of the deceased?"

"Uh-huh," she said, squinting.

Link hooked his finger into the blinds over her head. One of the kids tore the mesh on the screen door and shouted that he wouldn't go home without a tat, and the others kicked up dust in the parking lot. The youngest seemed to control the mood: When he grew frustrated and slapped on the aluminum wall, shouting for them to come outside, the others began kicking the trailer, shaking it on its foundation.

"Knock it down, man," shouted someone. "It's a piece of shit."

They began throwing handfuls of gravel, which clattered like hail across the roof and windows.

"What do they want?" asked Link.

She licked her lips and said, "I guess—*me*."

Link grunted. Glancing back through the window, he said, "These guys are the real thing, Lydia. What were you doing out there?"

"I told you," she said, shaking her head and furrowing her eyebrows. "Dad—seriously. I don't even know what to do."

"No shit."

The gravel was chipping against the windows and one boy was leaping into the wall. The trailer rocked, another cloudburst of gravel fell, and one of them circled around the brush in back, knocking on windows and hollering, *"Lydia.* Come on out, baby. It's your boys. Let's party, bitch."

Link opened the front door and the youngest kid hustled back toward him again from the far end of the trailer.

"What do you want with her?"

"We want to talk to her, mang."

"Why?"

The boy sniffled, tried to mimic respect, but there was the fleeting expression of lustful hatred on his face, a smile with teeth bared, and Link recognized it immediately from his years on the inside—the snarl of a fresh convict with a need to assert himself. Link could feel something in the kid's expectant posture. He understood that these four meant if not to kill his daughter, then to make a brutal statement with her—in the backseat of a car or an abandoned shack.

"We want her side of the story, dog," said the Salvadoran. "Some shit happened back in the city yesterday—and we want to talk to her about it."

"What are you, the citizen police? What the fuck do you care?"

The Salvadoran kid said: "Easy, old dude. We don't need to have no trouble with you. It's just business we got wit' her."

The young boy with the gravel in his hand was angrier than the rest now. He stirred up the dust around him and yelled, "Yeah, motherfucker! It's not personal shit—it's *business!*"

"Stop throwing that shit at my trailer or I'm going to stuff it down your throat."

"Fuck you, old man," said the youngest, raising his shirt to show the handle of his gun.

"Get off my property. Now. Or I'm calling the cops."

"You ain't calling the cops—because you on parole, motherfucker. And she's on the lam."

"Yo, biker dude!" said the white kid. "Where's your property line, man? Here?" He tiptoed along an imaginary line, then shuffled up a cloud. "Or here? Fuck, man—come down and show me."

Link stepped back into the trailer and shut the door, and the kid yelled, "Don't fucking turn your back on me!"

Lydia had moved to the kitchen window in order to watch, and when Link saw her in the broken stripes of light he said to her, "Better get down lower."

She dropped beside the kitchen cabinets just as there came a loud blast and a single gunshot piercing through the aluminum door with a ricochet. Smoke steamed off the edges of the coarse peephole into a thin streak of light, and the room smelled like burning metal.

Link moved along the narrow hall in the darkness, muttering. As he began digging through cabinet drawers over Lydia's head, another shot fired and shattered the living room window.

Link picked up a carving knife.

Lydia said in a whisper, "I have a gun."

"I know," said Link. "And I'm going to get blamed for this."

He moved across the narrow hall to the bedroom as another bullet punctured the wall and rang across the trailer.

"This is a goddamn cluster fuck," said Link. "I'm going back to the joint. They're going to nail me on this bullshit. I guarantee."

He found the gun in the bathroom. He loped like an ogre back into the main room, where the boys were butting the walls and scooting the trailer faintly back on its blocks. "Straight question, Lydia. What happens to you when the cops get here?"

"Dad. I can't. I'm so fucking dead."

"You're telling me what I think you are?"

"I fucked up so bad."

He sighed and turned in the darkness, and, when he saw arms scrambling up through the shattered living room window, reaching forward to grab the arm of the couch, Link lurched forward and stabbed the carving knife straight through the anonymous hand. Someone screamed as the blade penetrated all the way into the wooden frame, so that the kid hovered for a moment before the knife came loose. "That's it," shouted Link. "I'm going back down. Fuck! With my luck, that's aggravated assault right there. Return to Custody."

Someone was still shouting and groaning below; the kids had been riled into a frenzy by the sight of blood. A sudden barrage of shots came through the windows and walls, ripping through particleboard and plucking off letters and pictures. Link crawled back to his daughter under spraying chips of glass and flying thumbtacks. She was huddled in the corner between the refrigerator and the paneling. He touched her on the head, then he rose up, cleared glass and tangled blinds from the kitchen window and pulled back the slide on the Glock. "Just forget it now," he said. "Firearm. Aiding and abetting, harboring a fugitive—they're going to bury me in San Quentin."

The white kid wandered back toward the car, clutching his bleeding hand, and Link fired a shot, intentionally missing but throwing up a splash of dust beside his foot. The others ran back to cover him.

"It's all a third strike now! Attempted murder, failure to report a crime," said Link. "Tack that on. Might as well go all the way—might as well take out the fucking president."

"Dad, they're going to kill us."

Another flurry of shots tore through the walls, and one round struck the top of the kitchen faucet, spraying water upward like a geyser. Link moved to the corner and aimed the gun. "I fucking *hope* somebody hits me," he said. "I'm not dying in the pen because you fell in with the wrong crowd." He waited as the kids backtracked to the street. "And you better be damned happy the cops are so far away from this row of shit boxes."

"Dad, I'm really scared."

He closed one eye and braced the gun. "Which means somebody is either going to die or *hitch up*." Then he pulled the trigger—and the window of the distant Chevy exploded and rained glass onto the street.

The four kids retreated to the car. When he saw them opening doors and the trunk, he cheered and shouted, "That's right, you chickenshit motherfuckers! That's right! Why don't you come on back and gimme a little *beso negro*, you fucking *maricón*."

The one clutching his hand stepped onto the street and broke into a fit, scraping his voice and choking on his words: "Fuck you! Fucking ink-slinging dick-sucking piece of motherfucking—"

And Link yelled over the top, "*Chupame la polla!* You're such cute little punks. . . ."

Out of his mind with rage, the prospect jumped up and down and threw his arms around, shouting an indecipherable run of profanity; but just then, as Link believed they were giving up, he caught a glimpse of El Salvador handing out assault rifles from the trunk. They had an arsenal. They climbed back into the car and placed a jacket over the broken window. Headlights awakened. Link saw the shadows of rifle barrels. The engine rumbled like an idling boat, then shifted into gear.

"Lydia," he said, "you need to do what I say."

"Okay."

"Get in the bathtub. *Now*."

She scrambled across the room in darkness, just as the car spun its res into a hard U-turn and began crunching across the gravel.

Link fired his last shot as he saw it approaching, arms and heads and barrels hanging out the windows. Then he dropped his gun and began rushing ahead, wincing, feeling as if he were moving in slow motion across the rooms. "They're coming huge, Lydia! Make room for me."

He rolled into the bathtub, thudding on top of her just as the walls and the windows and the air lit up with crossing fireworks. They banged their arms and hips against the cramped porcelain, wrestling together and trying to find space as a horizontal storm came through the aluminum and ripped cabinet doors off their hinges, shattered mugs and mirrors, rang off pipes, burst through louver slats and tore through the bathroom tile, raining chips across their faces. The mirror exploded into slivers; the light fixtures burst; pigment bottles splashed across the living room; and the fire alarm in the bedroom rang as it was struck. They nestled their heads down together, and Link could smell her nervous breath and chemical sweat; they twisted sideways as the bullets seemed to gather and accelerate into a sideways torrent, until at last they found an interlaced formation in the tub, a contorted embrace, Lydia's face pressed against the inner curve of his neck, where he could feel the warm puffs of her scared breath; and he draped his heavy leg over her side like a shield as the shots kept coming, loud as helicopter blades, tearing the shower curtain like a tattered pirate's sail, chewing up his machines and benches and photographs, whistling and skipping off the porcelain turret, until at last there was a sudden, silent pause.

He could feel the jolting contractions in his daughter's rib cage. He held her and said, with a touch of rowdy laughter in his voice, "Just hang on, kid—they're almost out of bullets."

The car moved with the ascending note of reverse gear, then spun the tires in the gravel. Link felt her body tighten in his arms, and he was overcome with the single-minded desire to hold her still as he closed his eyes and savored the twisted embrace, thinking *this is the same little baby* as the car accelerated toward them, rising in volume; and he whispered, "This is it." The car smashed head-on into the side of the trailer, caving in the bedroom wall and throwing everything into chaos as they tilted upward off the blocks. With the deep scraping sound of yanked screws and burning bolts the trailer tipped sideways, and Lydia began to scream as at the first downturn of a roller coaster, as the last light flickered out, and autoclaves, needles, pillows, sheets, and broken glass flew across the air, jangling together. They were thrown against the shower-head and into a corner where the curving ceiling met the tile as the trailer slid down a gradual incline, uprooting yucca and skunk weed, until it finally settled in the desert sand.

Everything was still.

They listened as the Impala sped away, fleeing a nearby car alarm that had gone off in the distance.

Lydia was panting and they sat up together in the dark.

As if in the first lull after an earthquake, Lydia whispered, "Is that gas?"

"Yeah, the water heater. We'll shut it off. I don't know where your buddies went—they might just be off to reload."

The next ten minutes passed like a dream. There was the steady sound of barking dogs and the shadows of neighbors standing on the road in the distance. Link waited for a siren, but it never came. He found the gas meter and shut off the valve, then, back in the shipwreck, he gathered Lydia's bags and some of his own clothes. When he emerged into the parking lot again, his daughter was pacing through the piles of spent shell casings, trembling, slapping her hands onto her thighs. The sky was flooded with stars. Then she sat with him in the car, and Link realized that whatever meager life he had scraped together out here, with ink and needles—it was gone. The shadow of his trailer looked like nothing more than an old accident on the side of the road.

He turned the ignition and the car just sputtered.

"Don't do this to me."

Lydia sat stiffly in the shotgun seat, looking at him with huge, startled eyes.

He tried again, and the engine just strained and stammered.

"Not now—you fucking piece of shit!"

He tried a third time and the scrape deepened with each repetitive drone, but the car wouldn't start as he flooded the carburetor and slapped the steering wheel and yelled, "Perfect! That's fucking perfect. Whatever I fucking do—I got the worst luck in the world. God hates me."

From her quiet gasp he could tell that his daughter was crying.

"If we sit here long enough an asteroid is going to fall on us."

He waited for the rich smell of gasoline to diminish, then he cranked the ignition again, bobbing his head to each rhythmic stutter, saying, "Come on, come on, you stupid little bitch, you little whiny piece of *shit*, wake up! Wake up!"

"I'm sorry, Dad. I can't believe what's happening."

He punched the dashboard and the knob fell off the radio. "What the fuck do I have to do?"

"Dad," she said, breaking into sobs. "I'm so *sorry*."

"Goddamn it, I'm going to rip your fucking valves out!" He beat on the dashboard, then took a deep wheezing breath and tried again, listening to the strangled sound of the engine, until he threw his arms up and fell back in his seat.

When he turned to his daughter, he saw her face streaked with tears that looked silver in the faint light. Her mouth was bent down into a pleading expression and her eyes were full of disgrace and longing. "I'm so *so-ho-ho-horry*," she cried, a chugging sound in her lungs. "I did this to you. I'm sorry."

He reached across the car and, with his rough thumb, wiped a thin stripe of water from her cheek. After he had watched her for a long time, he said quietly, "As soon as you're all cried out, kid, we're going to need a push."

Link & Lydia

part four

STATE OF CALIFORNIA

PAROLE VIOLATION REPORT

NAME: John P. Link   Case Number: C-101-651
DATE OF BIRTH: 4/11/49
OFFENSE: Aggravated Manslaughter B
SENTENCE: 15 years
PAROLE DATE: 3/1/1998   EXPIRATION DATE: 3/1/2004
SUPERVISION TYPE: Mandatory

I REQUEST AN ARREST WARRANT BE ISSUED
I ARRESTED THE INDIVIDUAL WITHOUT A WARRANT ON _____
DUE TO EXIGENT CIRCUMSTANCES

BASED ON THE FOLLOWING VIOLATIONS AND MY KNOWLEDGE OF
THE INDIVIDUAL, IT IS MY OPINION THAT THE PAROLEE:
  (a.) Is a likely danger to the public.
  (b) Is likely to flee.
  (c.) committed a crime in my presence.

CHARGES:
  (A.) Possession of an unlicensed firearm by a felon
  (B) Aiding and abetting a fugitive
  (C) Failure to report a felony
  D. Resisting Arrest

Submitted by:
Probation/ Parole Officer II

A.R.T., 4/10/01.

eleven

J ust before sunrise, the Nova ran out of gas.

Link and Lydia pushed it along a flat dirt road that stretched between palm groves. The radio played a hip-hop station that echoed in the emptiness, until Link yelled at her that it would wear down the battery and wake up the town.

She crawled inside and turned off the ignition as he pushed the car ahead into an Indian reservation. It was a dark and dusty settlement amid wind-battered date palms, where houses were made of cinder blocks, the fences made of severed doors, and the chain-link gates of a schoolyard were clotted with migrating trash. In the purplish light, a few roosters and dogs were already awake. Link stopped the car beside a pickup truck and took out a piece of severed garden hose from the clutter in the back-seat. He told Lydia, "Put two bucks under his windshield wiper."

He fed the hose into the pickup's tank and began sucking on the other end.

Lydia watched this procedure for a few moments as he tried to create a vacuum in the hose, then she said, "Wow, you must have been really popular in jail."

He flinched back from a surge of gasoline, and, as he coughed, he fed the hose into his own tank. Rising up quickly, he spat and wiped his tongue on his sleeve, looking in the darkness like a giant boy throwing a fit over a spoonful of castor oil.

"I have some gum," said Lydia.

"Fuck," he said, shaking his head rapidly. "You made me swallow that shit, kid—anything I eat now is going to taste like a carburetor."

"Are you mad at me?"

"Yes." He stooped down and spit repeatedly at the ground, big raindrops diminishing into damp puffs of air. "Some screaming Indian is going to come out of that house."

"Is he going to scalp us?"

"Just get in the car."

An hour later, in the first weak light along the mineral-colored mountains and the Salton Sea, Lydia was painting her toenails with her feet propped against the dashboard. As Link drove south on a paved two-lane highway, he still periodically wiped his tongue with a napkin. There was the distinct smell of fumes coming from his breath and beard. Outside, the wind had picked up past dawn, and the sea was a ragged stretch of white streaks and metallic blue. Plumes of salt swirled over the highway and dust obscured the horizons. Just beyond her toes, Lydia saw two fighter jets making practice maneuvers, darting off as fast as hummingbirds toward the mountains. After gesturing to them, her father told her that, just to the east, there was an aerial bombardment range.

"I used to run away like this with Mom all the time," said Lydia.

She had never seen anyplace quite so burnt-out and desolate. Every now and then they passed the torched remains of a solitary house or a stripped-down car frame in the desert. The one town along this stretch was a stubborn encampment of trailers in the shadow of a high protective sand berm, and beyond it there didn't seem to be much but the sparse traffic of graffiti-covered freight trains.

Lydia asked, "Where are we going anyway?"

"Down to the slabs. Guy down there owes me some money."

They stopped at a gas station in Niland. Lydia stayed in the front seat and watched her father at a pay phone, struggling a few times to remember some phone number before finally reaching someone. When he spoke, he had an expression on his face that she hadn't seen before, a look of shame and dread; and she tried to read his lips as he shuffled his feet and grew exasperated, saying something like, "That doesn't *help*." He must have been talking to his sponsor, because when he returned to the car he seemed to have a grim new resolve.

They headed the last few miles into the desert toward Slab City, past a strip of plywooded windows and the portico of a long-abandoned government building, across several sets of train tracks and along a wide empty patch of desert now glittering with broken glass in the emergent sunlight. The "city" turned out to be a postapocalyptic trailer park, huddled under a dust storm on some of the driest topsoil in America. They entered the settlement past a huge monument, a mound of brightly painted adobe—pink flowers and colored waterfalls and crucifixes. There was a chintzy, childlike look to the sculpture, as if it were the world's biggest grade school art project. A giant heart in the center read, "Say Jesus I'm a Sinner, Please come upon my body and into my heart."

Lydia said, "Come upon my body? Nasty."

Past a makeshift commercial district at the entrance, where trailers sold handmade windmills and flags, they drove among huge wooden signs criticizing the government with misspellings and tortured syntax. Link waited for a few dogs to leave the middle of the road, then continued on to where the pavement fractured and the dirt roads began. There were dozens of families living in the sunken campsites around greasewood trees and creosote bushes. All along the road people sat motionless in their cars, moored to nettle bushes by flapping laundry lines, looking as if they had stalled and decided to stay. Link told her that the place was still "free," built on unwanted and unnoticed government land, using slabs left behind when a military base pulled up stakes decades ago. Now it was a seasonal town without any official services, a new frontier of squatters, libertarians and dropouts. A painted sign be-side a wall of stacked tires indicated that a library existed somewhere up a sandy hill of cholla; another sign pointed the way to a mechanic, hid-den somewhere in an assemblage of rusted station wagons.

They passed a silver trailer covered with bullet holes, graffiti painted onto the side: "By by, no more drugs, go somerls."

"Some kind of dyslexic vigilantes," said Lydia.

Finally Link pulled up to a clearing of bushes and mesquite, where dozens of Harleys stood in varying stages of reassembly. The trailer was more kept up than its neighbors, with a bright sunset painted onto its side and a majestic desert more colorful than the grim real one beyond it. An American flag stretched out in the wind.

Lydia stayed in the passenger seat while her father shambled out and stretched his legs. Her eyes and teeth hurt; her bones were sore; her neck itched. This was that zombielike hour she hated, when, though all the last chemical charge was gone from her system, she was still too fueled and nervous to crash.

Link knocked on the trailer door, shouting "Dagget," and there emerged a man so emblazoned with tattoos that it took Lydia a moment to realize that he was naked. In fact, with the man's intersecting murals of skulls and chain mail, a mixture of unfurling vines, blades, and flames (as if his legs were a jungle in the midst of deforestation), the menagerie of different pictures crammed beside tribal designs, he didn't seem capa-ble of being naked—rather, a small crooked penis looked stranded on an island of red pubic hair. Lydia broke into laughter. The man pointed at some untouched spot on his back and Link squinted and nodded with the detached expression of a doctor.

Link was waving for her to join them. As the man climbed into a pair of shorts that had been drying on the spikes of a yucca tree, she ap-proached barefoot, her toenails just dry. The man stood still, facing away, as Link gave her a tour of the colored-in landscape of his body. Most of it seemed to be the usual agglomeration of heavy metal imagery, bones and battle-axes, as if the man were composed of Silly Putty that had been raked for twenty years across concert posters. But in a clearing beside his

shoulder blade there sat a silhouette of an old man on a spindly horse—
an elaborate stick figure, with a spear and shield, and beyond him, on a
scribbled donkey, there was the thick shadow of his companion, riding
along in a desert covered with small, stylized windmills.

Lydia said, "Don Quixote?"

"Kid's got an education under all that mess," said Link. "Yeah—
Picasso."

"That's awesome, Dad. You did that?"

"I had some people want to put that in a magazine. But they couldn't
find this motherfucker for the photo shoot."

"That ain't my job," said Dagget, staring off in the other direction. "I
ain't some kind of male model."

"Damn right you're not," said Link.

The two men moved away from her across the plot, discussing another installment of the money he owed, and Lydia deduced that he was
a veteran waiting for a check. She stood still, feeling a residue of sadness
from the picture. Maybe her father wouldn't blame her for the damage to
his equipment, but she nevertheless was crippled with guilt. She needed
a drink or a joint. She called ahead, "Dad—I need to go for a little walk."

"What kind of walk?" he yelled back across the bikes.

"A *morning* walk."

"Lydia—I can't watch you twenty-four hours a day."

"You want me to squat down and piss right here?"

"No, no—go find a bush. I'm just saying, don't wander off. There's
snakes."

"Snakes. Okay, if I see one, I'll scream."

She scaled a sandy hill, and, once on top, her clothes and hair came
briefly alive with wind. On the other side, she found a secluded spot
among brush and ocotillo, looking like plants at the sandy bottom of a
fish tank. The air smelled like sage and cooking earth. She was squatting
and peeing in the bushes when she saw dust devils swarming up in the
distance, two dirt bikes spinning doughnuts on the flats. As the riders
saw her in the undergrowth and began approaching, she reeled up her
panties and jeans and rapidly kicked dirt over the evidence.

They rode all the way to her and sat on their growling dirt bikes, two teenage boys with sunburned faces and dirty nails. One had teeth that seemed too large for his mouth, like some kind of prehistoric fish; the other was shy and stared at her from behind strands of his long hair.

She played along with their questions. What was her name? What was she doing here? Did she want to go for a ride? And she answered as she drew figures in the dust with her toes. They were full of boasts, but they also began an immediate defense of their neighborhood. People from the towns, down in Calipatria, they may have looked down on them, but they didn't understand. They could ride their bikes wherever they wanted; there weren't any laws; no curfews; no living for somebody else. It struck Lydia as a paranoid, home-school pledge of allegiance.

She asked if they partied.

They moved a few feet away and deliberated, hissing at each other, until they wheeled their bikes back up to her and announced that they *did,* and that they could get some good weed from a kid named Trent, but that they needed to be quiet about it, since most people around the slabs were old and just did "Viagra and shit like that."

The one with the funny teeth offered her a ride on the back of his bike, and she slipped on behind him. Ten minutes later, it seemed that all of them had forgotten their goal to get high. The two boys were emboldened by how loud and enthusiastic Lydia became on the back of the bike, whooping and cheering and screaming at each jolt and dash between trailers and under laundry lines. Lydia felt reenergized by the gritty wind. They stormed through the desert village on a rutted dirt trail. She laughed at his wheelies, and she waved to people in their cars, and she squealed as they leapt over ridges and splashed through flocks of sand grouses.

As they cut toward the mountains and approached the Nova, she saw her father standing in the middle of the road like a matador. They swerved past him, and she thought for a moment that he might try to grab her off the bike. She shouted, "I'll be right back! Don't *woooo-rrrrr-yyyy.*"

Both boys raced along the dirt road to a plot at the farthest edge of the settlement, where the mountains loomed just ahead and the desert

unrolled for miles toward the wind-streaked sea. There, a few other boys
lived in a cluster of camouflage tents and canopies between two pickup
trucks. In a perimeter around them, shattered bottles sat on the rocks
and rusted gas cans dangled from cottonwoods. Every tree trunk was
punctured heavily, as if attacked by woodpeckers, and the chassis of one
truck was filled with rusted holes. Even the rocks looked chipped and
scuffed by months of itinerant target practice. Three shirtless kids roamed
around in loose jeans.

At the entrance of one tent there hung a Nazi flag, and the sight of it
froze Lydia as if it were a snake. The boys talked in clusters, angling their
heads in a way that was too conspiratorial, and soon one kid was digging
through his duffel in a truck. He came up with a baggie of green buds
and a beer, which he opened against the door handle. He gave it to Lydia. The hanging tin cans clanked together in the wind.

This wasn't a very good scene, but while Lydia stood with a chilled
beer in her hand, warming in the mid-morning air, she marveled at her
ability to find drugs, like a bushman could find water. She asked if they
had speed, and one boy, becoming aggressive, told her that crank was all
over the place. There were probably fifty meth labs down there by the
waterfront. The whole place was a meth lab, practically. "Not in the slabs,
but down there. *Yeah*, I can get speed—why didn't you fucking say so?"

She told him the bag of chronic would be fine. She had some money,
but the mere act of reaching for her pockets caused halting noises from
all of them. "Whoa, whoa—you don't need to worry about the money,
baby. Just hang out."

"No—I think I'd rather pay. It's just more—" She started to laugh,
stooping over and standing up straight: She had almost said *kosher*.
"What do you think? A twenty sack?"

"That's a dime."

"That's not a dime. It's not even a nickel."

"It's a dime. I just weighed it."

"Hang out and party with us," said another. "What's the matter—
you think we're scary? Trent, man, tell her we're not scary. We're just
having a good time, dog."

She continued to say no, and she could feel how some of the others, lingering in the background, were growing frustrated. She tried first to say she was buying the bag for someone else; then she claimed she was an epileptic, and that she couldn't smoke without her medication nearby. She sometimes went into seizures. Standing on a rock behind her, a kid said, "Fine with me. Just jump on and take a ride."

"Shut the fuck up, Wigs!"

From far down the road there came the sound of crackling tires on gravel. Lydia pocketed the bag as the boys moved out of the light, and when the Nova pulled up to the campsite, she was standing by herself with a beer.

When Link stepped out, he was so angry that he failed to notice her relief at seeing him. Approaching, he said, "What am I going to do with you?" He grabbed her by the arm and shook her like a sapling, spilling the beer everywhere as he dragged her back to the car. Through his teeth he said, "You stand right there." She licked the foam out of the light hairs on her forearm.

He walked back uphill; her father seemed to grow angrier with each step, as if insulted by the defiant postures and sarcastic faces of the boys.

"Dad! Can we just go, please?" She hung against the car and swigged the remaining froth of beer. "They didn't do anything. We were just talking." Link was pointing vehemently into the chest of a young man when suddenly a skinny kid pointed a gun at him, which seemed only to aggravate him further. Link wrested the gun away from him and then, as the boy fled, kicked him in the seat of his pants.

Soon he was hunting down these slender kids like calves in a rodeo. He threw another boy into the dirt, and, when he grabbed the kid with the funny teeth, he gave him a violent wedgie. Lydia started to laugh and covered her mouth. Moving in and out of the shadows, her father made the remaining kids sit down in the dirt, and he paced among them, giving threats like a drill sergeant. He knew how to handle boys so much better than a daughter. Lydia reached through the open window of the car and honked the horn repeatedly.

Her father paced over, stepping between her and the sun. He became an imposing shadow, thick arms cocked at his side as if for a duel. He said, "Twice now, two times, you lied to me. Get in the car."

He stood for a while, then, suddenly, he kicked a dent into the driver-side door. "Get in the car," he snapped.

"No."

He stalked to the back end, and with his steel-toed boot stomped the taillight into red fragments in the dirt.

"See if I fucking care," said Lydia. "It's *your* car, not mine. Stupid caveman."

Link seemed to forget her, becoming distracted by a deep-seated bitterness toward the car itself, and in a bloodlust he kicked off the back fender, broke the other taillight, elbowed through the window, and began butting his shoulder into the rocking Nova as if he wanted to overturn it.

Horrified at the thought that he might strand them in this right-wing libertarian outpost, Lydia climbed into the passenger seat and folded her arms over her chest. "You're very adult, very *mature*—I'm so glad I found you so you could help me through this. You have so much perspective, Dad! And that's what I really needed right now."

An hour later, she took a break from criticizing him to fill an ice bucket for his swelling foot and elbow. She returned to their shared motel room and sat on her separate queen-sized bed. The blinds were drawn and the room was colored by stripes of hot afternoon daylight and the faint television, playing a live broadcast of a freeway pursuit in Los Angeles. Link was lounging on the bed in all of his clothes, only his boots off, a ripe, musty smell coming from his socks. She handed him the bucket of ice and said, "It would serve you right if you broke your foot. I was just about to get into the car—and do you listen? No. You're just like every other idiot—just wanting to break shit. Stomp on people's sandcastles. You never fucking, like, communicate. Never. All those letters I wrote you, and you would never answer—you would just send a drawing, like a pony or a rainbow. Like I'm a *girl*, and all I can understand are ponies and fucking rainbows."

He tilted the bucket and nestled his big dirty toes into the ice. "What do I have to do to get you to shut up?"

"You'd have to understand who I am, as a human being."

"Oh," he said. "Is that all?"

"And relate to me on some other level than *do this, do that.*" She moved into the bathroom and began washing her face. "Senseless fucking violence," she said. "I hate that. I hate people who think fear is the same thing as respect. I'm afraid of roaches, that doesn't mean I respect them."

"I sure as shit do," said her father.

She scrubbed her face, then, staring at herself in the mirror, realized how exhausted she was. She took a deep breath that relaxed her shoulders, and when she returned to the room, her father looked to be drowsing in the heat. He said, "Are you still yelling at me, or can I go to sleep now?"

"I'm not yelling at you. I'm yelling at the situation."

"You got the worst instincts for people," he said. His voice sounded low and soft, as if he were on the cusp of sleep. Trucks and cars were washing past outside, and a housekeeper was knocking on distant doors. "You remind me of those chicks that get hitched to assholes on death row."

"You're the one who brought me there. I just got on for a ride."

"You know, I broke parole," he said, closing his eyes. "The second I didn't report a crime."

"I know that."

"And my trailer. My shop. All my shit. That was my sandcastle, kid."

"I know, Dad. And I don't know how to make that up to you."

"Must not seem like much to a kid from your neck of the woods."

"I didn't ask to stay with you, Dad. This was your plan. If you think I'm responsible for all of that, then that's fine. I'll go, and I'll send you a check to reimburse you."

"Go to sleep, Lydia."

She sat Indian-legged on her bed and took out the clarinet, and readied herself to play it as if facing a cobra in a basket. Then her father began to snore loudly, and she put it down on the bed, and watched him, his mouth open and his face stunned, as if sleep had sneaked up from behind and sucker punched him.

She knew she should try to rest also, but she needed something to help her out of the jittery restlessness. So she bought a soda from a vending machine and drained it into the sink, then made a pipe by poking holes into the dented aluminum with a nail file. Then she tried to come down by smoking a bud while sitting in the bathtub under the open transom. She ran the fan and brushed her teeth, then she lay down on her bed across from her sonorous father. But still she couldn't sleep.

She felt so guilty about him losing his shop and his equipment that she began whispering a hypothetical response. He was the one who wanted her to submit to a week in some kind of monitored custody, like a mystical transition period he had learned in twelve-step programs. She couldn't overlook his clumsy efforts at authority. He seemed to be trying to enforce someone else's ideas of right and wrong, as if he were now working for an inflexible new boss. Maybe it was his newfound god, the god of AA meetings. The same god that prisoners found at the last possible moment and football players always pointed to from the end zone: that chintzy, unyielding deity honored with roadside crosses and adobe monuments and crucifixes hanging from rearview mirrors. There was nothing more depressing to Lydia than this kind of last-ditch religion, because it made her imagine a heaven that was filled with drifters and dogmatic lunatics. The afterlife would look something like a giant Greyhound terminal, flocked with prisoners and panhandlers. If there truly was a heaven, she didn't imagine a man like her father could be much more than an undocumented worker there. There were probably whole droves of penitent murderers who just cleaned the pearly gates with toothbrushes.

She was ashamed of how she'd disrupted his life, but also disappointed: The man seemed devoid of philosophy. She feared that it was the same disillusionment Jonah had once described: He was no rebel, he was simply a tired and slow-witted old man. She had expected him to *know* something. But if it weren't for the tattoo he had shown her that morning, she might have figured that he had no internal life at all. Even still, pictures aren't thoughts. She had heard about rhesus monkeys that, in tightly monitored experiments, had learned to draw portraits with alarming skill. She couldn't assume that the replication of a Picasso in any way signified intelligence. Rather it seemed that the man had faced death, violence, darkness, and evil, and survived it all by doodling. Maybe this was why he seemed so childlike at times. This sort of escapist behavior must have been the opposite of wisdom.

She suddenly felt very lonely and afraid, and she realized that she had been fading in and out of a delirious partial sleep for the past several hours. The dark window disoriented her. Her father was sprawled on the bed under a stripe of headlights moving counterclockwise around the walls.

As she rose from the bed and moved into the narrow bathroom, she could think of nothing else but to make up her face, as if for a party. She traced her eyes with a pencil, and blended two shades of lipstick, and tried to get her hair to do something, anything, in the stale, dry air. When she was assembled—not right, not perfect, but at that exasperated point in which she needed to leave the mirror to avoid wallowing in flaws— she left the room, walked past the pool, and waited in the lobby.

There was no one there except the clerk. She couldn't see him, but heard typing in a bright room behind the desk. She sat on the couch and found the TV remote. For a long time she surfed through channels and ate butterscotch candies from a dish.

She was hardly paying attention to the news when her own picture came up onto the screen.

The police were searching for information about a missing girl wanted for her possible connection to multiple homicides; a warrant had been issued for her as a material witness. Lydia leaned forward, transfixed. It was her eighth-grade school picture, when her hair was lighter and only shoulder-length, and her cheeks were rounder, and she'd had a zit on her chin that her mother had asked to have airbrushed. There she was on TV, a virginal Lydia, with a smile that looked like a polite response to a corny joke. The story went on for a good two or three minutes longer, about how she was traveling with her father, a convicted felon. They showed mug shots of him in front of a lined background, his long hair drooping, the crown of his stooped head reaching between the 75" and 76" markers, his beard darker, his nose swollen and cut at the bridge from a recent fight or accident.

The news moved on to another story about an *E. coli* outbreak at a fast-food chain, but Lydia stopped watching and covered her face. She started to laugh into her cupped hands, her body growing tense and expectant, as if she were in a plane just before its wheels left the ground, and when she could no longer contain herself she leapt up and started shouting, "Oh my God! I'm a fucking celebrity!"

The clerk came out of the filing room, frowning.

She said, "Shit, shit, change the channel. Find the other channel."

She grabbed the remote and flipped to a neighboring local channel, then squealed and broke into laughter. "That is so *crazy*!"

The clerk twisted his head and marveled at the image on the screen, shifting his eyes back and forth to Lydia. She moved back to the check-in counter across from him, catching her breath. Abruptly, she became still. "God, that's a terrible picture, though. Do I look like that?"

"Must have been taken a while ago," said the clerk. He was a tall, extremely pale man with reddish hair and a long, sharp nose. He seemed groggy, as if he had fallen asleep in the back room.

"Try three years ago," said Lydia.

"You look good." He glanced at her, then back at the screen. "Hard to say if you look better or worse." The same picture of her father came up, and the clerk asked, "Who's that?"

"My dad."

"Did he kidnap you or something?"

"I guess."

"You don't look like him at all."

She looked at the clerk and stretched her palm across her face. "I do across the cheekbones," she said. "You can't tell because he's a fucking wookie."

The clerk took the remote off the counter and flipped around other news channels, shaking his head. "Looks like it's just local."

"You don't know that. Try *Headline News.*"

He found a story about a blizzard gripping Denver.

"Snow," said Lydia. "How is that news? Cold shit fell from the sky today. Amazing."

The clerk had a determined look on his face as he kept searching through channels, into the higher numbers where pitchwomen grinned on shopping channels, preachers wagged their fingers, and country-western singers danced in the backs of trucks and horse trailers.

"It'll be national," said Lydia. "Trust me. It'll be all over the news."

"What makes you think so?"

"Because I got star power. *Baby.* I'll be on *Nightline.*"

"No way."

"Or, like, when it's all over—I'll go cry to Montel Williams. He'll hug me and get all fucking misty, and, oh shit, I'll be a national treasure, dog. Like that chick they pulled out of a well."

"You're crazy," he said.

She was laughing, thrilled with the fantasy, until a car passed on the highway outside and the room suddenly seemed bright and visible to everyone, like a glass display case. "Yeah, maybe not."

"You should come in here for a second," he said. "Come back here with me. I want to show you something."

Lydia searched his face. He was turning pink, smoldering, but she saw in his rumpled clothes and sleepy face that he was curious, stoned, hated his job, and probably related more easily with those in trouble than those in charge. He led her into a cramped filing room and closed the door behind them. "I'm going to get in so much trouble for this," he said. "But I just got to show you." From beside the fax machine, he picked up two curling pieces of paper and handed them to her.

Her picture and her father's, the same ones from the news—they had probably been sent to every motel, gas station, and diner along the highway. The information below was far more extensive than on the news. It warned local proprietors not to confront them; they were to call authorities immediately.

The clerk said, "You don't look like any kind of murderer."

The word hit Lydia suddenly, hard and cold. She stared at the clerk for a moment, and finally replied stiffly, "Thank you. Neither do you."

twelve

A t a little before midnight, Link woke to the sound of a car engine idling at a gas station across the street. It was only a late-night traveler, but the booming radio had merged with the last residue of his nightmares, seeming like rhythmic kicks and battering rams on the motel door. In the dream, he had been cutting his daughter's braided hair with a kitchen knife, claiming that he needed a souvenir. Now, he was completely awake and confused by the mix of sympathy and anger he had felt while sawing through the hair. He needed to lay still for a moment and reaffirm his simple goals: Keep Lydia safe, keep her clean. His plans need not be complicated. The girl would learn some balance. He assumed this was the way that a father taught a child, by running alongside her, as if holding a bicycle, until she found her own center of gravity. But if his daughter didn't trust him, she would pull away too soon, and drive herself straight into the ground.

Awake but drowsing, Link wished he had some perfect crystallized advice for Lydia—like the words of a magic spell—that would soothe her and set her off on a better route; but he worried that anything he told her would sound hollow coming from a man like him. After all, he represented everything in the world that he wanted her to avoid, and he worried that he might only be a good father by convincing her to reject him. Kirby had said on the phone that he should help her find the Lord, but to Link, God only presided as an even higher authority figure with a grudge against him. Link tried. Yet, as a Christian, he was like someone hedging his bet; and if he couldn't fool God, he probably couldn't fool a teenage girl either. She knew him already. She saw that he was shipwrecked. She was already beginning to despise it like some disease in her own bloodlines. And he didn't think he could live without at least the fantasy of her affection. It seemed a punishment worse than going down for the rest of his life.

And then it occurred to Link that maybe a man could do everything wrong and still, somehow, be a good father in the end. All he needed was to give her faith in a *direction*. There were so many different ways to go in the world, a kid like Lydia might just spin in circles for the rest of her life. Maybe a good parent just centered the kid and shoved her forward, as in some game of pin-the-tail-on-the-donkey, set her off blindfolded toward a spot across the room, and prayed that she didn't bump into a lamp. Maybe it didn't take wisdom or goodness, but just a little nerve. A scared parent would cling to the kid and never make the final push; an indifferent one would let them wander seasick around the room; and one like Link's father would probably just spin the kid around until he dropped. The idea inspired him. It meant that a good father needed only to perceive something beyond himself, out in the distance, past the horizon. And through all the paralytic remorse of his own life, on its decline toward a heaven he'd scrapped together out of clichés and apologies, maybe he could just push his crazy daughter toward the light, and watch her carry on, outlive and outlast him.

He was starting to doze back to sleep when he realized that Lydia wasn't in the room. This sudden jolt came at nearly the same instant that the phone began to ring, an old-fashioned bell, which he couldn't locate in the dark. When he finally pawed the receiver, he accidentally answered, "Missing Link Tattoos."

"You have to come downstairs," said Lydia. "It's the craziest thing ever."

"What is?"

"I'm down in the lobby. We have a serious problem, but it's hilarious. You have to come down here. I left a bunch of stuff in the bathroom—so don't leave that. It probably has DNA on it."

"DNA?"

"Just grab as much as you can and come down to the lobby. Oh, and don't turn on the lights. There's a good chance we're being watched. Come the back way, by the pool, so no one sees you. And Dad? Check the lobby. Make sure it's clear. I'm so on top of this. You are going to be so fucking impressed with me."

He peeked through the blinds at the parking lot, and—rather than police—Link saw a white Ford Taurus sitting at the gas station next door, headlights on, radio turned down. This was a coincidence, certainly— every rental car in America looked like this; but he didn't like the way the car sat and idled.

A few minutes later, Link pushed his way into the lobby with their bags and a pile of dirty clothes. His daughter grabbed the duffel and quickly ushered him into a back room, where a teenage clerk sat on a swivel chair, looking like a steamy chat-room pervert. Lydia was flushed and fluttery, and the room smelled like cigarettes, grass, and gum.

He shut the door, sealing them in with the ripe air.

"Lydia, what the hell is this?"

Lydia plopped down on the floor and lit another cigarette, exhaling out of the corner of her mouth like an outlaw. She dripped ash into a soda can. "Did you get the stuff in the bathroom?"

"*Yes*, I got the stuff in the bathroom," said Link.

"Good," she said. "Because the cops are coming. Sooner or later. They may be here now." She handed him two faxes from the table above her, showing their pictures and descriptions, suspected whereabouts, instructions for contacting the police.

Link rolled up the two papers and pointed them at the clerk. "And so this little cocksucker called the cops?"

"No, Dad! God! He's with us. He's helping us. Jesus, you're such an asshole."

"It's all right," said the clerk. "I got thick skin."

"Is that the way you act? You call somebody a cocksucker when they try to help you?"

To avoid her righteous face, Link unrolled the papers and read them again.

The clerk said, "I just came on at ten. Those were already there, and I think, knowing the day guy—"

"It's always the day guy," said Lydia. "The day guy always fucks the night guy."

They all sat cramped into the tiny room, as if trapped in a cargo elevator, and deliberated about their best options. Link barely spoke. He felt mired in some meandering teenage jam session, in which everything was a stoned philosophy to be explored, and the more everyone analyzed the situation, the less chance there was of doing anything. They had the nonchalance of kids arguing about whether to go to the beach or the movies. When he suggested they get the hell out of the motel, both Lydia and the clerk hissed at him, explaining that there was already a stakeout. They seemed too media-savvy for their own good. They were predicting police behavior based on what seemed to Link a giant montage of bad TV shows, and they were trying to impress each other with their obscure knowledge. The clerk knew that police needed a search warrant for a motel room, and that it sometimes took hours, but that they would keep watch on the room while the papers were processed. Lydia told him that this factual tidbit was "crucial," and then asked Link if he agreed.

"Let's go already," said Link. "I'm leaving."

"They have the license of the car, Dad. How far are we going to get in that piece of shit, anyway?"

"You'd have to steal a car," said the clerk. "Can he hot-wire cars?"

"Dad? Can you hot-wire a car?"

"Do we have to take this creep with us?"

"He's just helping us. Relax. Besides, I'm sure there's already a stake-out."

Looking between his blushing daughter and this lurching geek, Link realized what it was that so terrified him about the girl's flirtatiousness. Every man has a woman in his mind who represents *the best-looking honey he could possibly get*. Lydia was genuinely pretty, but oily and quirky enough, weird and unwashed enough, to be that girl for practically every toothless wino or hard-up sex fiend along the road. She was a beauty with bad skin. A knockout in dirty laundry. Every loser's lucky day.

It was just past one in the morning when they heard a car in the parking lot, footsteps along the sidewalk, and the bell triggered by the front door. The kids were right: It was two cops.

The clerk welcomed them to the Paradise Motel, then had a conversation with them at the desk while Link and Lydia sat quietly on the floor. She lit a cigarette for Link by placing the tip of it against hers. He was bothered by her expression: She was more proud of herself for being right than she was concerned about their safety. When she began to whisper, he put his hand over her mouth. When he removed it, she moved up close to his ear and told him that he smelled like gasoline.

There were two cops, with similar monotone voices. They'd received an anonymous call a few minutes ago, from the gas station across the street: Link glanced immediately at his daughter, and she looked back with quizzical eyes. Link could only figure that the call had something to do with the white car outside: an undercover cop, a private investigator hired by Ursula, an off-duty parole officer—God only knew. Maybe it was one of the lunatics who worked for Lydia's dead boyfriend, wanting to flush them out of the motel any way they could, and using the cops to do it.

The clerk gave them the room number and told them that he hadn't seen any activity. Only four rooms were occupied, and everyone had been asleep since his shift began. No new check-ins. He gave them a map, and with the usual rehearsed tone of speaking to customers, he described the location of the room. The cops asked about the back exit through the courtyard, around the pool and the vending machines. He told them the back gate was always locked; there was no way out through the courtyard.

The bell rang on the front door, and the cops passed the window again. Outside there was only the sound of an engine, a police radio, and a slamming door. The clerk crept back into the room. He held a key in the air, but first Link only noticed how badly his hand was shaking.

"This is the master key. I just gave one to them, and I'm giving you the other. You're surrounded, so I don't think you can just run. And I'm basically shitting in my pants right now. Take the key. Every room is empty except three, ten, and fifteen. They won't see you if you take the inside stairs. You'll come out on the second floor—along the catwalk. Just find a room and hide. Okay? I never saw you; you never saw me."

Lydia rose and took the key. She said, "You're the nicest person I never met."

Trundling their bags, they moved along the desk, up the back stairs, along the walkway over the pool, where the moon was now wavering in the deep end. They slipped into an upstairs room, and while Lydia eased shut the door, Link paced to the window to survey the parking lot. The white car had left the gas station, but now there was a squad car idling at the entrance to the motel, with two other unmarked cars sitting along-side it.

He whispered, "Shit," then stepped back as a flashlight moved across the ground.

"Better stay away from the window," said Lydia.

Link sat down on the edge of the bed, and she plopped onto the carpet beneath him. For a long time they were as still and quiet as fishermen, until Link exhaled and lowered himself onto the floor across from her. Lydia's back was pressed against the eggshell-colored wall, and Link's touched the bed frame as they faced each other in the dark. Lydia offered him a butterscotch candy. For a long time the candies rattled against their teeth.

"Dad?" she whispered in the dark. "What's county jail like?"

"Different for men and women. I sort of liked it in my day. You can fight, play cards. Prison *sucks*, but county is sort of like summer camp."

"Do they protect people? I mean, like, if somebody is after me— would they make sure I was okay?"

"There's protective custody, but . . . Lydia, you got to talk to me about this."

"It's okay," she said. "They won't search all the rooms."

They heard the raid on their former room: knocks, warnings, the door opening with the master key, followed by a stampede of boots. The voices grew softer, the footsteps slowed and stopped.

"That's probably it," said Lydia. "Right?"

Link put his finger to his lips.

The police broke into their car next, talking to each other, complaining about the mess as casually as car wash employees. They threw out trash, papers, fast-food cups and Dr Pepper cans while the police radio murmured a litany of street names and unit numbers.

Link whispered, "You lit up with that stupid kid, didn't you?"

"I didn't light up with anybody."

"Stop lying. I'm not a moron."

They paused, listening to the knocking on a door beneath them. The police announced themselves, unlocked the door, and fanned out across a new room. Lydia understood that this meant they were continuing, room to room, and her amused expression was suddenly gone. She said, "We're so fucked."

"Why do you have to get stoned with a guy like that?"

"I didn't. Besides, alcohol is twice as damaging as weed."

"I don't want to start a fucking—*ballot initiative*. You just can't go get high with every stranger you meet. It's stupid."

"I'm so stupid I saved both our fat asses."

"Does my fat ass look saved?"

For some reason, Lydia thought this was hysterical, and she struggled to contain a bad case of the giggles as the police search migrated to the next room, moving southward along their side of the motel. Lydia fell onto her side and held her breath, then busted out so loud that Link had to put his hand over her mouth.

She pulled back, wheezing, and said, "I'm okay, I'm okay," as if trying to stifle a giant sneeze.

She sat up straight, removed the two faxed pages from her back pocket, and began smoothing them out on the floor. She said, "I'm going to keep these for my scrapbook."

The police searched another room, accelerating the procedure. Link wondered why the cops assumed that they were still hiding in the building. Had the clerk broken under pressure? They listened to the rumble of footsteps beneath them, the repeating pattern of knocks, the rattling keys, shouting, heavy shoes dispersing across narrow rooms—again and again, as if they were a team running staggered plays during a long practice.

The anxiety made her slaphappy. She squeaked with suppressed laughter and said, "Oh my *God*, I'm so sad. I'm going to have some prison matron with a shaved head and, like, Popeye forearms. Like the *mother* I never had."

"Don't get ahead of yourself here."

In a room below there was a burst of hollering, kicked furniture, and broken glass, followed by dozens of Spanish voices in a commotion that spilled into the parking lot. Suddenly the motel was surrounded by people, all of them hollering at each other.

There followed a faint knocking on their door: three beats, a pause, and another two. Link said, "Lydia, try to answer me one serious question. If you get pinched—say you go into protective custody—do you think these guys will get to you?"

She said, "Dad? I won't last five minutes."

"Okay," he said. "*I'm* not going back either. For anything."

He pried the metal bar off the towel rack and held it like a club. "Stay there," he told her. "This is going to get ugly."

The knocking continued on the door, and Link moved slowly along the wall. He was prepared to bludgeon the skull of the first cop that crossed the threshold, and, with luck, he hoped that a fallen body might clog up the passageway long enough for him to grab a weapon; but his

plan only advanced far enough for him to hope that some brutal new opportunity might present itself in the chaos. He had lost his share of fights
in his life, always outnumbered like this. He turned to his daughter and
said, "It's been good seeing you, kid."

"Yeah, Dad. Same."

Just then, on the other side of the door, a voice said, "*Lydia.* You guys
in there? Answer if you're in this one."

Through the peephole, Link glimpsed the clerk trying to hide
against the rough stucco wall. As he opened the door, the kid whispered
into the widening crease, "You got to come *now.*"

When Link saw how fast his daughter picked up their bags and
rushed out onto the catwalk beside him, he experienced what must have
been fatherly pride. No, this wasn't a clarinet recital, a spotless report
card, or a victory for the track team; but, as he struggled to keep up with
her, down the stairs, through the lobby, and out a service door, he
thought that there couldn't be any talent in the world more valuable than
being able to move so quickly in the dark. After a short sprint across
an empty section of the parking lot, they rounded the adjacent gas station,
where a nervous crowd of men had gathered beside an idling pickup
truck. The clerk explained in a rush that the cops had stumbled upon a
room housing thirty or more illegal aliens, a coyote's drop spot, a hub for
human trafficking, and that the entire area was now a mess of immigrants fleeing in different directions. He helped them up into the bed of
the truck, where they found space among sacks, tools, and the legs of
other men.

The clerk said, "It's cool. I know these guys in the front. Just keep
your heads down." As the truck began to roll away, he walked alongside
them, and Lydia leaned down and kissed him dramatically on the
mouth. He waved his hat; she blew him kisses; and Link said, "Jesus
Christ, it's fucking *Casablanca.*"

Passing the motel parking lot, they saw immigrants being cuffed,
facedown on the concrete, and soon they were rolling past the men who
had escaped, walking and running in packs along the highway. They
rode in a wind thickening with harvest dust.

The sky was just changing texture. As they continued onward, they could begin to distinguish the stoic faces of migrant workers along the other side of the pickup bed: three men, two older and one young, all seeming unfazed by their own near miss, expressions stern under their flicking strands of hair.

The light clarified the hills on the horizon, then became strong enough to show features in the landscape and distinct faces, as if sculpting everything from shadows. They were heading up into the date palm groves, circling to the other side of the Salton Sea. There were seagulls awake now and wheeling in the gray sky. The men watched Link and his daughter, distantly, as if they were nothing more than figures on the horizon. The air gusted past, broken by the cab in front of them, where two white men gestured in an adamant conversation, rolling down their windows every now and then to spit or toss flaring cigarettes onto the road.

Link sighed and said, "Going on two years out of the joint and I'm back in a truck full of Mexicans. Where's the halfway house?"

As the light strengthened and uncovered everyone in sharp detail, face-to-face in the truck amid the tools and sacks, Lydia introduced herself in clumsy Spanish. She gave them her wide, pretty smile, and she said, *"Él es mi padre, pero no le gusta hablar."*

One of the men nodded faintly.

Link was grumbling, and, in response to his discomfort, Lydia said, *"No le gusta nadie. Sólo motos. Y tambien, a él no le gustan Mejicanos."*

Link could understand what she'd told them: He didn't like Mexicans, only motorcycles. One of the men smiled at this, and he made a strange show of tipping an invisible hat to Lydia.

Link said, "If you think I don't speak any Spanish, you're nuts."

"I don't know how to say Aryan in Spanish, though. *No se preocupen. Él es un oso grande, pero no es peligroso."* Something about him being a big *bear*.

The men were laughing, smiling at her and nodding their heads in amusement at her heavily accented Spanish—for some reason she sounded even more like an American mall rat in a foreign language. Her voice was an octave higher, as if it carried with it a permanent apology.

"Before you start organizing some kind of fucking union here, why don't you just be glad we're out of there?"

"I don't want these guys to think I'm rude because you're a white supremacist."

"Oh Jesus. I'm sure they all love you, Lydia."

"What do you have against them anyway?"

"Nothing. I just don't like people coming up here, taking my job."

"Did you used to pick oranges for a living?"

"I'm sure some American did."

"No, no. Not true. No American ever did. In fact, no *white* person has ever picked a piece of fruit off a tree, unless you count *Eve*."

"So I'm a fucking racist then? You're the one saying Eve was white. Where the fuck was the Garden of Eden—Norway?"

She started laughing hysterically, throwing her head back. "That's awesome, Dad. You're right. Eve was an Australopithecus."

"I think you're getting your beliefs a little screwed up."

She leaned forward and said to the men, heads bobbing, all smiling faintly now at the scene in front of them, *"No se parece, pero mi padre no es tan mal. Es un buén niño Católico. Cree que a Jesus nos ama a los todos."* He wasn't so bad, a good Catholic boy; Jesus loves us all.

The men grew solemn, nodded at Link, and crossed themselves in the wind.

thirteen

J ust past dawn, after hitching a ride, Link and Lydia were riding southbound out of the citrus groves in the cab of a sixteen-wheeler with a trucker who looked as if he hadn't slept in months. He had a snug bed behind the front seats, with a neatly tucked yellow blanket and a good luck teddy bear, old and ratty and held together with duct tape. After Lydia dozed off momentarily against her window, the trucker offered her use of the bed. She crawled back and curled up on top of the blanket, scattering hair over her face to block out the light.

The CB murmured between Link and the trucker, a more energetic and urgent conversation than Link was used to hearing so early in the morning. Link had nothing to say to the man behind the wheel, who was chewing a wad of tobacco and spitting in a coffee can at his feet. At one point, the man smirked, leaned toward Link, and asked, "Where'd you find her?"

The question startled Link. He looked angrily back at the trucker and replied, "In the fucking delivery room."

The man swallowed a pinch of chew and looked away, turning a greenish pale, and finally added, "Didn't see the family resemblance right away."

Link faced toward the morning skies and the wheeling seagulls. Silent for many miles, he grew steadily more curious about the gossip brewing on the CB. He had listened to his own radio for so long in lieu of television, preferring its sleepy rhythms, that he could immediately recognize this altered and urgent tone.

It had begun with a warning about a rare backup on highway 111, which was a desolate road along the eastern edge of the Salton Sea. Another trucker had explained that CHP was setting up roadblocks on both sides of Niland, searching every car. It sounded to Link from the description as if he and Lydia had already passed outside these parameters, but he nevertheless was concerned, and assumed that another roadblock might be waiting farther south before Interstate 8.

Little by little, he began to understand that something else had happened last night while he and his daughter were holed up in the motel room. Truckers were referring to a murder in the desert near Slab City, arguing about the details. One man was livid, claiming that illegal immigrants had killed a white kid, suggesting that the mangled body had been found along a well-known route for smugglers and coyotes. Link asked the trucker if he could change over to channel 3, the frequency used by the campers and squatters Link knew around the settlement.

Link intended only to call Dagget for information, but he emerged into a conversation about the same murder, this time with a dozen disembodied voices speaking with far more sadness and alarm. Link keyed in, asking for Dagget. A woman answered him, saying that Dagget had gone off to San Diego yesterday, trying to clear up a problem with the Veterans Bureau. "And it's lucky he did," said the woman. "I think whoever it was came here looking for *him*."

Link hadn't heard the news, and several intersecting voices began retelling the story. At a little past midnight, a white car had driven into

Slab City, wandering plot to plot for some time with the headlights off. They had stopped at Dagget's trailer, possibly because of the bikes, and when they were unable to find him, they smashed his work, vandalized his trailer, and moved farther toward the hills.

"There's been trouble with those kids out on the southeastern edge," said a woman. Apparently they had been dealing small amounts of weed for the past few months underneath the radar, avoiding the scrutiny of Slab City's own volunteer security forces. One of the kids, a twenty-year-old named Trent Rucker, with a shaved head and neo-Nazi tattoos, had willingly stepped into the white car in order to make a deal. Whatever happened next was anyone's guess, but, just past sunrise, two younger boys on dirt bikes had come across his mangled body in the desert, a frenzy of crows and seagulls around it.

What shook the residents of Slab City so deeply was not merely that a young drug dealer had been murdered, though they took it upon themselves to keep this element out of their frontier town, but that the job had been so savage. The killers had apparently stolen tires from the makeshift walls along the dirt roads; they doused them in gasoline, set them on fire, and threw them over the boy's head and neck. He had burned to death trying to free himself. At dawn, there had still been a sickening cloud of rubber smoke hovering over the campsites.

Link thanked the woman for telling him and told her to stay tough.

The trucker said, "Some sick fucks out there."

Lydia woke up and climbed back into the front seat, rubbing the corners of her mouth. She faced the wind and shook the hair off her face, then studied the passing desert with squinting, stoic eyes. Link thought for the first time that she was tied up in something far more complicated than he had expected. The murder sounded professional to Link, meant to leave evidence as a warning, to start rumors, create a reputation, spread fear and respect; and it seemed more expert and calculated than the sloppy, trigger-happy bravado he'd witnessed up at his trailer. Who were these people, and how were they so close behind?

Lydia noticed some changed expression on his face, and she asked, "What?"

"It's okay—we're getting off up ahead. I'll tell you later."

"Was I farting in my sleep or something?"

"No, kid, I don't believe so," said Link. "You're off the hook on that one at least."

The truck let them off on the outskirts of El Centro—a hub at the southern edge of the Imperial Valley, a few miles north of Mexico, stranded halfway between entry points into Tijuana and Mexicali. A city of immigrants and old cars, it had always seemed to Link like disputed territory. Most of the storefront signs were hand-painted in Spanish; cramped cement row houses hung flags of colorful laundry; radios blasted festive accordions. It lacked only the tourist traps and diesel smell of towns on the other side.

Almost ten years ago, Preacher had disappeared somewhere into those distant foothills, hidden beyond the haze, fifty miles, maybe a hundred miles out into the obscure air. After surviving two trials on federal conspiracy and racketeering charges under the RICO statute, Preacher had sold the house in Palm Springs and bought up a sweep of barren acreage, desert canyons and abandoned military hangars along the edges of the bombardment range, with the idea that he could start over, build a libertarian utopia of die-hard bikers and useless land. When Link was out on bond, taking his last deep breath before going to trial, he'd sold his chopper to Preacher to help with legal expenses, making the deal in a bar somewhere on the eastern edge of this town. Because he had never betrayed Preacher, never said a word to prosecutors or accepted a plea bargain, Link believed that he deserved more than help.

In a phone booth, he hunted for the address of an old biker bar he knew, while Lydia shuffled down the aisles of a supermarket, buying pretzels, licorice, and soda for breakfast.

Just past ten o'clock, they found the dive, the only surviving segment of a boarded-up stucco strip mall. Four bikes sat outside against the curb. Link asked Lydia to wait outside, but she refused, arguing that *he* needed to be chaperoned as much as she did. So they stepped together into the dark, damp, windowless room, past a screaming jukebox. Three drowsy men looked up from the bar, first ogling Lydia, then sizing up Link.

The bartender was a huge, doughy man with a Fu Manchu mustache and a hoop through his pierced septum. While dipping glasses into a basin of suds, he asked Lydia for ID, and she began digging through her satchel.

Link said, "Hey man, I'm looking for a guy named Tom Harris— people used to call him Preacher. I wonder if he still comes around here."

When Lydia handed the bartender her ID, he clicked his tongue, then showed it to the men along the bar, one of whom laughed with weak sputters and coughs, as if his beer had gone down the wrong pipe.

"Ever hear of him?"

"Maybe. What do you want from him?"

"I got old business with him."

The bartender shook his head and dipped another glass into sudsy water. At the far end of the bar, a very old man had Lydia's ID, and he was attempting to make a joke about confiscating it, but his mouth was so caved in and his words so mashed that Link couldn't understand a word he said. The others laughed, maybe to support the old fool's sudden gust of clowning energy as he stood and feinted at leaving with the card. Whatever joke he intended, he kept doing it over and over again until no one paid attention. Then he flung the ID back across the bar and gave a dismissive wave of his arm.

"Just give her a glass of water anyway," said Link. "He lived in the foothills last time I heard."

"Nobody's doing any business around here, buddy. Not right now."

Lydia downed her ice water in ten accelerating gulps, and the men watched her throat move like it was a burlesque show. Link told her to stay where he could see her, and he rushed to a pay phone across the room, where he needed to close his eyes and calm himself enough to remember his sponsor's number. Kirby answered and immediately offered to come and get him. Kirby was pushy and desperate, as if he could see the bar and the rows of whisky under a single slanted light; and he pleaded with Link to give him an address where he could come and help.

But, in a lull between jukebox songs, Link became distracted by the way Lydia was talking to the old drunks across the bar. There was no such thing as unwelcome attention to this girl. She laughed, raised her chin, rocked back on the stool; she wiggled her hips and rose up straighter like a charmed snake; and she said something in response with a giddy quaver in her voice.

"Kirby," said Link, "I want you to be careful, buddy. I may be in some deep shit down here, and somehow, these motherfuckers know where we're going. Only thing I can think of, maybe somebody went through my shop, found business files or something."

"Okay, John," said Kirby, sounding beleaguered on the other end. "But listen, you got to trust me. You got to ask me for help here, and be straight with me. You trying to get this kid across the border or what?"

"I don't know yet, man. I'm looking for a guy down here who owes me. Old lunatic I told you about—Preacher Harris."

"And you think he's going to be a help, after all you been through with that."

"I got no choice, Kirby. Listen, I got to go. This little girl is like a cat in heat, and she's already got a crowd around her. I'll call you again, man."

When he returned, Lydia had a napkin with writing on it, and she crumpled it up and stuffed it into her bra under the tank top. Link sat down beside her and asked for a cup of coffee. She was eating the remainder of her pretzels, and she chewed for a while in silence. He could feel how she kept looking up to study his profile, and finally she asked, "Do you want to hear a joke I know about a Hell's Angel?"

"Is it funny?"

"No."

"All right. Let's hear it."

With a pretzel still in her mouth, she said, "So there's this flea, okay. Spent his whole life living on dogs, having an easy life, and one day, he jumps into the mustache of a Hell's Angel. An hour later, he's getting thrown around by the wind. He's hanging on for his life. He's freezing to death at night, and he's getting punched by big fists, and he's getting battered by hail and rain and dust all day. So this flea's like: 'I'm getting out of this guy's mustache. This sucks.' They get to a bar, and the flea jumps out, and, first chance he gets, he goes right up a woman's skirt. Gets between her legs and says—'Now that's more like it.' And he's so tired, he just settles in and goes to sleep."

Everyone else in the bar was listening.

"A couple of hours later," she said, "the flea wakes up, and he's getting pelted by wind and rain and dust again, he's going a hundred miles an hour—and he says, 'Oh no—I'm back in the Hell's Angel's mustache!' "

All around the bar, the men were clapping and laughing, harder than Link believed was natural; but he only watched his daughter's face blush. She looked up at him finally with a tight smile on her mouth and said, "We need to talk about something. Seriously."

She grabbed his forearm and led him to a booth between the juke-box and a dartboard, and she moved with such patronizing seriousness that Link expected her to break the news to him about some feminine product she needed to buy. The jukebox hit on a random Allman Broth-ers song, and Lydia leaned across the table and yelled the speech into his ear. "Listen, all night and all morning I've been thinking about this, okay—so just hear me out. I have a workable plan here. Now, I know it's a crime not to report a crime. Right? And I know you've been harbor ing me, whatever that means. And I know you don't have visitation rights and any of that other stuff—so there are some parole violations. But, re-ally, other than that—what have you done wrong? Nothing."

"Kid, it doesn't work like that. You help somebody get away with something, and that's a serious crime."

"But, see, you could pretend that you didn't *know*. You could say that I just showed up and we just hung out for a couple of days. Like, father-daughter shit."

Link just stared at her for a while.

"My point is, you could go back. You might not *have* to do any more time, and you could even cooperate with the cops—because I'm going to be long gone. I figure from here—I just head west to Otay, and slip across the border. Nobody ever sees me again. I speak Spanish. You heard me. I'm like fluent almost."

He waited a long time, then replied, "You're just so goddamn *bubbly* sometimes, ain't you?"

"What do you mean?"

"I mean—what the fuck are you talking about? A pretty little white chick with no money in her pocket, wandering all by herself in Mexico. That's a hell of a plan, Lydia."

"You don't think I can take care of myself?"

"Not even in *this* dump here—let alone in Guadalajara or some big turd factory down there. I don't think you could get across the border. And then if you did, you'd be turning tricks by the end of the week."

"That's like the most insulting thing anybody has ever said to me."

"Well, how else are you going to make any money?"

"I could go down to Guatemala where they have those schools. And I could teach English to little kids."

"You don't hardly *speak* English. What are you going to teach them— jokes about eating pussy? The history of dirty words? You dropped out of high school."

"Oh, and people down there are going to ask for a *diploma*. Yeah, right."

"They sure as shit ain't going to hire a weird drifter off the street."

"So that's what I am to you, huh. I'm a *weird drifter*. I have no abilities or skills whatsoever? I'm just a complete loser."

"Why don't you settle down and be realistic. You screwed up *bad*, and you need to get your head out of the clouds."

"I can do millions of things, Dad. I'm not useless, okay. Just because you don't know me—just because you can't fucking *read*, doesn't mean I don't have any, like, marketable skills."

"Fine. Tell me what you can do. Tell me what you think somebody is going to pay you for."

"I speak Spanish."

"Other than that. About a billion people speak Spanish—so you ain't on the cutting edge there."

"I'm a good artist. I have a good eye for design, and stuff like that."

"Well, there you go. We're all dying for more of those people."

She took a deep, flustered breath and said, "I'm smart."

"No, you're not."

She was so angry she had to look away at a neon clock on the wall.

Link added, "Besides, being smart isn't a *skill*. It's just some shit that annoys everybody else."

"Oh my God," she said. "You're such a—"

"Look at this, Lydia. You're already panicked. You're going to cry right here. How the hell you going to sell yourself out there in the big bad world if you can't even tell *me* what you're good for?"

"Fuck you," she shouted. "I can play the clarinet."

"And I'm sure there's an opening with the Tijuana symphony."

"Running—middle-distance—I was on the track team in tenth grade and I almost went to city in the eight-hundred. Have you ever run eight hundred meters?"

"I never ran eight meters."

"I know a lot about politics—and activism. You know, political science. How corporations screw people, and how messed up things are with the World Bank and third world debt."

"So you're good at complaining."

"I'm friendly. I'm a nice person. I'm motherfucking *personable*. People enjoy my company when they're not asshole biker ex-con cocksuckers who have absolutely no reason to live."

"Uh-huh. So what job is that?"

She threw her hands up and slapped them down onto the table. "I don't know. Retail? I give up, Dad." Tears were welling up in her eyes, and her bottom lip was twitching. "I'm completely useless. Nice fucking inspiration, great work. So you just go home to your tattoos of goblins and genies and shit. And just leave me here to do whatever—give hand jobs for a living."

She started crying violently in the booth, pressing her hands to her face. Link reached across the booth to touch her arm and she flinched away from him.

"I was trying to say it was a bad plan. I wasn't trying to say you were useless."

Into her cupped palms, she said, "Why are you still here? Just go away. I don't want to look at you anymore."

He waited as she tried to recover herself. Her suffering only seemed to intensify, and she was moaning and throwing her head back as if every new thought cut her more deeply than the last. She said, "I'm a *fucking murderer*."

"All right," said Link, nervously scanning the men at the bar. They were all watching, sitting forward on their stools now as if mustering energy for a fight.

"I'm not going to make it, am I?" she said. "This is never going to go away. This fucking feeling is never going to go away."

"No," he said. "Probably not."

"And they're going to torture me, Dad."

"Shhhh, these guys are itching for trouble over here."

She cleared the hair from her face, and her eyes were a brighter shade of blue, as if rinsed by a passing storm. She said, "Dad? Will you kill me?"

He turned to her suddenly, frowning. "Lydia, sweetheart. Settle down."

"I mean it. When they get close to me—the cops or these guys—and they're going to—will you just kill me? Please."

"No," he said. "No, you idiot. What kind of stupid idea is that? Look, kid, we can't think about next year or the year after that. We're not there yet. Understand? We got to go one day, one hour, one minute at a time. We got to get enough cash to stay afloat, hide you for a little while. You need to get cleaned up. Get the cobwebs out of your head. Sleep, eat better. You can't make a plan while you're running full-speed. I'm an old loser, I agree, but I know about having the shit fall on you. And I'm here, and I'm committed, and I'm trying my ass off not to go over there and down a bottle of Jack Daniel's. You say you can't turn yourself in for this—and I *believe* you. After what I saw from those punks up at my shop, and what I heard today, I think you may be right. But people get caught because they're stupid. And I'm not going to let you be *this* stupid."

"I'm sorry I ruined your life."

"I didn't have anything left to ruin, kid. I'm having the motherfuck-ing time of my life. I haven't had this much fun since I was fifteen and I stole a car and tried to drive to Miami Beach. This is a party to a dirtbag like me. So shut up and let me try to help you. I know a crazy old man who used to have a lot of money, and he lives somewhere out in the mid-dle of nowhere around here. So if we can find him—"

Lydia pulled the napkin out from her bra, unfolded it, and handed it to him. It was a map drawn in crooked intersecting lines, with smudged handwriting that gave directions to Preacher's ranch up in the hills.

Link shook his head, started laughing, and said, "There's one thing you got, kid. One definite skill. You *do* know how to charm the devil."

fourteen

Following the bleeding crisscross of lines on the napkin map, hitching rides on trucks and horse trailers, eastward toward the mountains and down dirt roads, Link and Lydia arrived at the gate of a vast ranch in the foothills. They were sunburned and exhausted. It was the hour when their shadows slanted far ahead of them along the path. There was no sign or marking on the wooden gate. The ranch burrowed into a canyon between scrubby hills, sprawling across acres of brush and greasewood trees that lived along the shallow path of a dried-up stream. Link and Lydia descended the road, past bottles and broken glass along the creek bed, and, farther along, circles of scorched rocks, oil drums, and lawn furniture sunken into the silt and pebbles, as if a party had been wiped out suddenly by a flash flood. Once they had hiked completely into the shadows, they passed a breeding ground for flies.

They began uphill, swatting at the air, through a clearing and into a break of slanted afternoon light. A gathering of shanties, teepees, and lean-tos surrounded a steel-and-concrete hangar, which towered over the scrap houses like an altar. Her father told her that this land had also once belonged to the military, and it seemed that a hamlet had formed over a few generations of squatting. One ring, farther back, was of small adobe houses with open windows and blankets over the doors; and another, closer to the hangar, was of shingled boxes with trapdoor windows. As they neared the center, a few chickens scampering across their trail, Lydia saw a woman on a lounge chair, sunbathing in a bikini, with reflectors under her chin. Her body was so tanned and leathery that Lydia was startled when she opened her eyes. The woman said, "Back by popular demand."

She had sunken cheeks, and her mouth didn't seem to sit right on her face—maybe from a bad toothache or a long history of sarcasm. When she stood, she was a skeleton except for her garishly fake breasts, which seemed to Lydia like a curse—two young and perfect boulders that this gaunt body was forced to forever trundle uphill. She shielded her eyes from the sun and continued, "It's the missing Link. I'm speechless. Can't believe they ever let you out."

"Cherise, this is my daughter. Lydia."

The woman placed her hands on Lydia's shoulders, peered into her eyes, and said, "Wow. It was just yesterday, wasn't it? Well, go on inside and say hello to the dinosaur. Don't get lost in there."

They moved into a front section of the hangar, the size of a mechanic's garage, with bikes under a tarp and a vast collection of military souvenirs, ranging from antique flintlock rifles mounted on the walls to entire tables full of fragmentation grenades, field mines, fuses, and trip wires. Crossing the floor were bunching arteries of extension cords, leading into a hallway made from unfinished drywall. Beyond this entry area, the other three-quarters of the hangar had been broken into cubicles by makeshift walls and cork partitions. Link and Lydia followed the sound of typing on a computer, passing under hanging Indian beads and tapestries, until they finally emerged into an office. At a steel desk with an impressive arrangement of computer equipment there sat the oldest-looking man that Lydia had ever seen. His shaggy eyebrows drooped like hoarfrost, and the white stubble of his beard grew out over a permanent sunburn. He perched at his high-tech console, rapt at the computer screen, reflections of text scrolling up his narrow glasses.

"I expected you a couple years ago," he said, without looking away from the screen. "Hold on—I need to finish my thought."

He typed only a few more letters, then stood, formally shaking her father's hand. As if her father had never been away at all, Preacher immediately began explaining that he administered his own Web site for military collectibles, and that he had recently begun "blogging." It had increased traffic at his site threefold, though he faced the constant threat of losing his domain, particularly because of the advice about grow rooms and hydroponic marijuana.

Lydia thought there was a mad-scientist quality to him, since he hardly seemed to notice the people he addressed, so long as they were willing to walk with him along his vast laboratory of experiments. He gave them the tour of his indoor village, slot to slot through the fabricated walls and alleys, until the structure seemed to Lydia like a maze within a giant pinball machine. He had a giant aluminum shed in the back that he described as his security vault. He had a room filled with uniforms from a dozen wars: brownshirts, Napoleonic epaulettes, ANZAC fatigues, a Confederate officer's coat, an RAF jumpsuit. There didn't seem to be much distinction made between eras or ideologies. The Nazis hung alongside the Vietcong; World War I boots propped up a musket. The clutter was so complete that Lydia imagined this room as the backstage wardrobe for the entire history of human conflict.

Her father interrupted to say, "I want to talk to you about our old deal."

The old man was either growing deaf or had selective hearing, for he led them onward to his arsenal room, where he spent a long time detailing all of the unexploded ordnance he had from six different wars and police actions. He became suddenly grandfatherly and asked Link if he remembered the trips out to the Mojave. Before Link could answer, he told stories about dropping grenades down rabbit holes and setting up trip wires that they detonated with remote-controlled cars. He was a man in his heavily armed dotage, and because there was something so nervous and unfulfilled about him, Lydia began to view him as if he too were an antique booby trap that had never exploded.

Link finally stopped walking alongside him and called ahead through a hallway of particleboard: "I want her back, Preacher. And I want to talk about the money."

"Which money is that?"

"Don't pretend like you don't remember—you senile son of a bitch. Because I kept my mouth shut for a long time."

Preacher returned and put his hand affectionately on her father's shoulder, and with an abstraction in his eyes as if he couldn't focus on anything closer than the horizon, he said, "Yes, you did. You were always the quiet one."

"I don't ask you for anything more than what you owe me."

Preacher stared at Lydia inquisitively, a souvenir from a war he couldn't recall. He kept his eyes on her while he spoke to her father: "Business isn't so good at the moment, brother. Let me go through the books, see what I can do. The boys will come by later, you can catch up. Just relax, have a good time. You're welcome to stay here long as you like. But, you got to understand, I can't just scrape up money the way I used to. I used to be able to find twenty thousand lying around the house— but it's not like that nowadays. Some of my contacts got busted up in Orange County, and that was the Alamo, John. That was the last holdout. The golden days are over. Ninety-three. In ninety-three, we lost. You were lucky you missed it."

Two hours later, Lydia sat outside with her father on vinyl chairs as dusk came over the bare hills. Just past sundown, choppers began rumbling up the dirt road. They were giant machines, and the men who rose off them, with heavy earthbound bodies in leather vests, seemed to have a tough time readjusting to the ground. In the last light, she watched her father's reunion amid opening beers and throttling bikes. The men were either obese or rail thin, as if some had absorbed the years and others had been eroded by them. The women were loud and brassy and had surprisingly goofy laughs. When some danced around a portable tape deck, Lydia had a hard time believing that anyone could be threatening with such a poor sense of rhythm.

Her father roamed around greeting the bikes before he found their owners. Some men were wildly enthusiastic about seeing him again; they hit his shoulders and chest in a way that, to Lydia, seemed too hard to be friendly. One man, with shiny fake teeth, long gray hair, and a tattoo of a dragon eating its own tail, shouted, "This motherfucker had the stomach of a monster. He could drink for two weeks straight and still walk a straight line. Look at yourself, old man!"

What surprised Lydia was that her father was so reserved—almost bashful—during these loud exchanges. He nodded and recited their names quietly: Count, Sheila, Cask, McCoy. He seemed to abandon himself to a gauntlet of violent greetings as they tackled him and pounded on him; and, the longer he stayed quiet, the more he loomed as a silent, mysterious shadow. The sight of this made Lydia feel tender toward him, for he endured the play fighting and facetious headlocks, even though he was irritated and sober; and she saw him as a large, tired dog who allowed a rowdy gang of children to leap onto his back and pull on his ears.

He introduced Lydia as his daughter, and everyone howled and talked over each other. She heard stories about herself as a baby. Someone had bought diapers for her when Link had planned to kidnap her from her bedroom window, and someone else had joined Link and Lydia at a Baskin-Robbins. "You had that green kind of ice cream—like turtle shit!" Lydia didn't remember any of these moments, and she had a funny sense that she had once known her father in another life, somewhere in the long blackout before the age of eight. The man with the dragon tattoo described how everyone had expected her to die as an infant, and Lydia replied that she knew this story. Her mother talked about it as if it were the great trial of her life. But Lydia hadn't known that her father was there.

Her father kept pacing back and forth from the hangar, checking on her. She asked him if she could have a beer. In a grumpy voice, he said, "Can I?"

"Can you?" asked Lydia.

"If you have one," he said. "The dam breaks and I'm having fifty."

"That's a lot of pressure, Dad. Thanks a lot."

All of his old friends booed and hissed at him, calling him a sellout, but Lydia stayed sober, fearing what she might unleash.

After someone threw a grenade down in the creek bed, Preacher roamed around shouting at the dark figures. The party resumed with more deadhead guitar riffs from the tape player, and soon there were bonfires casting up sparks along the silt. A group of men played horseshoes in the dark, tripping and snickering. There were a surprising number of children running around, crawling in a tree, wrestling in the bushes. One of them was thrilled at the project of throwing old furniture into the rising flames.

For a long time this seemed to Lydia like a happy band of middle-aged people, with only a few sulking younger men in the packs moving with lowered heads and a more foreboding motion in their shoulders. They revved their engines and shouted everything they said, as if their masculinity were measured in decibels. It was clear to Lydia that these were violent men, all of whom had done time, but they seemed easy and relaxed on this forgotten plot of land, and she stopped feeling nervous. As they became drunk, they talked to her a bit more, joking that she was lucky to have a pretty mother—because her father was "ugly as a warthog." She said that she thought her father was cute, and they all laughed up at the sky.

But her easy feeling ended when Preacher came wandering back to her to begin a story in a pushy, stentorian voice. He told her that he knew everything there was to know about her, and that she couldn't fool him by laughing, smiling, and acting friendly.

She shrugged at this, completely baffled by the hostility.

Someone was playing a guitar in the distance, and the smell of a skunk reached her in the breeze. Preacher said, "You kids have so much bullshit in your lives, you don't recognize real freedom when you see it."

Lydia had no idea why he'd decided to attack her all of a sudden, but she nodded politely, as if she agreed with his comment.

With the slowed pace of a schoolteacher, he explained that this was a party full of "survivors," and that this ugly patch of desert would remain long after the rest of the country had destroyed itself. He talked for a while about the end of the society, telling her that it was much closer than anyone in her generation realized: They were all too spoiled and preoccupied to see it. It seemed to Lydia that he had taken the usual Hell's Angels philosophy, a basic rebellion against society, and married it to several different apocalyptic theories. He went on and on with a speech, gathering a crowd of bemused onlookers. He said he was the last true outlaw in America; everyone else had given up or gone soft. America had a way of buying out the subversives, turning them into fashion trends. "It happened with the Angels in the sixties and seventies, and it's happening with that fucking *rap* music now." With a trace of spittle on his lips, he said that the corporations packaged and sold revolutionary poses to little suburban princesses like her.

The old man seemed to have so much invested in the end of the world, Lydia noticed a manic frustration that it hadn't yet happened. She figured that doomsday prophets were the world's most tedious salesmen, since they needed to contend with every new day. The others around Preacher nodded occasionally, as if listening to a radio program in the distance. Their respect for him seemed worn-out, based on a memory. Lydia desperately wanted to escape, and she watched the others at the party, drifting away, back to their jobs and their lives. One man was an Amoco mechanic, another had said that he managed a go-cart track.

As the store managers and foremen headed off on their choppers, Preacher told her that her eyes were opening and she would never be the same again. Just by coming here, she had finally stepped out of the fantasy of her everyday life.

"Thank you," said Lydia. "I'm going to go find my father."

Stifling a laugh, she ran back to the hangar.

There, on the wide-open floor, her father was polishing his old chopped Harley. She waited by the door, and he didn't see her. He had a can of compressed air, and he was spraying out dust from around

a v-shaped engine, then kneeling down with a rag and gumming out
dirt. From thirty feet away, she could feel his quiet concentration, more
intense than when she had seen him tattooing. Something about her
father was so solitary, like a boy happy to play by himself in his room.
After all the proselytizing outside, she thought for the first time that
her father had a secret and silent wisdom about him.

She didn't interrupt. She walked across the floor and sat down by
the far wall. When he saw her, the purposeful look on his face didn't
change. He said, "How are you holding up out there with those mani-
acs?"

"I think I was supposed to prove some kind of point to the crypt
master."

"That's what crank does to your brain. That ought to scare some
sense into you."

He sprayed something onto the tailpipe and began working it with
a rag.

"Old guy's got a lot of followers."

"Yeah, you start young," said her father. "Make sure everybody gets
dumber every year with you. You all go down together."

"Are you dumber than you used to be?"

He waited a long time and said, "I think I was so dumb when I
started, I didn't have anywhere to fall."

She laughed at this, echoing in the warehouse, and he looked surprised by her tickled response. He sat down on the floor across from her,
draping the rag over his jeans. "I couldn't get in touch with the sponsor
tonight. His cell phone died on him, I guess."

"Are you okay?"

"Yeah, I'm keeping busy. But I called information, called a neighbor—woman I did a tattoo on a little while back."

"Your girlfriend?"

"Stop that shit. No. I asked her about my trailer. Police cordoned it
off, but a few nights ago, she saw some kids going through it, past the
tape. Digging around. These kids—they might have gone through my

business files. My addresses. Personal ones too. So we should call everybody, soon as we can. That means your mother too. These guys are going
to go way past tearing up your little friend's apartment back there in
Hollywood."

Lydia nodded solemnly at the ground, then, after a long pause, asked
only, "So is that creep going to sell your bike back to you?"

"He owes me more than that, kid. I'm not going to talk to him about
it right now."

"No, not right now. I wouldn't."

"You did a nice job out there, Lydia. You're clear in the eyes, you
know. You've been drying out a little these past days. It's hard to know
somebody when they're wired up like a bomb all the time."

"What is the war this guy talks about losing all the time? Ninety-
three, all of that?"

"Well, that's when the ride ended, I guess."

"How so?"

"Well, ask around out there, they'll tell you the government allied
with the Mexican side of the fence, sent our business down south. This
shit that you do, that you see everywhere—in every neighborhood—it
wasn't like that when we controlled it. I'm not saying we were better
people. We were a bunch of assholes. But we didn't push. We treated it
like a crop, and we tended to it and were patient with it. We sold it in
small loads, kept the prices high. We didn't go to high schools and grade
schools. That's not morality: It's just economics. Then, in ninety-three, it
all changed."

"What? NAFTA?"

"Sort of. Same year—I was on the inside—but a couple of government branches got together and made it impossible to get ephedrine in
this country. Or red phosphorus, or any other chemicals. I don't know if it
was a conspiracy, but the Mexican cartels just picked up the trade right
away. They had all the supply lines, and they didn't even need to worry
about the Colombians anymore. So you had these assholes from Guadalajara and Tijuana taking over our business. They could get shipments of

pure ephedrine straight from China. And when the DEA got down on China, they could get sugar mills in Burma to start making the shit from molasses. They got boatloads of every chemical they needed, and they made speed in super-labs—ten, twenty, fifty times bigger than any stupid biker ever had. Hundreds of peasants cooking the shit for nothing. That's just a classic business strategy. They could outproduce a guy like Preacher, and they flooded the market. They got kids hooked; they had connections opening up in the Midwest, everywhere. Brought the price down to nothing. You couldn't *cook* enough speed to make any real money nowadays. You couldn't do it. The guys they nailed up in Orange County, they were working with the cartels and the assistant DA, because you need labs like NASA now, and you need intelligence like a small country. It's not like you can just buy a crate of cold medicine and split off the pseudoephedrine. What little I know about chemistry, it'd take a truckload of chloroform. I heard some of that shit outside just now: This motherfucker ain't waiting for the end of the world, Lydia— the world already ended. These guys are bitter, because legal or illegal, they feel like Uncle Sam took a good old American drug and handed it over to somebody else."

"You feel like that?"

"*Fuck no.* We were drug dealers. Boo-hoo. Who the fuck is crying?"

"So onto the tattoo needle. Right?"

"Doing American flags," he said.

"Land of the free," said Lydia.

"Yeah, kid. Love it or leave it."

The party was dying down outside with a last flurry of cherry bombs and throttling engines, and as each new wave of choppers trailed down the hills, the crowd thinned until distinct laughs and voices could be heard in the driveway. In an alcove in the hangar, Link had made his daughter a bed on the floor from the pillows off a couch. She curled up and clutched her sweatshirt between her knees. For hours Link kept guard over her as she faded in and out of sleep.

Link picked up a few coils of her hair and studied them in his palms, black and rich. Outside, the last choppers roared and ground away down the dirt road while Link worried that the sound would wake his daughter. She only flinched, as if from a bad dream. He watched her hands unfold. If she could sleep at least three or four hours, he thought her system would begin to recover its natural rhythm, and he was determined to keep a vigil over her. But he grew drowsy, and closed his eyes, and saw, like a flickering home movie, images of fistfights and unraveling roads. He imagined himself beating her little boyfriend to death with a hammer, until he fell asleep.

He awakened with something poking his ear.

The light through the high transoms was a washed-out gray, and he could hear echoing sparrows that had gotten into the hangar. Link glanced up and saw Cherise, dressed in a dirty terry-cloth bathrobe. She nudged a shotgun against the side of his head, a motion less aggressive than curious, as if she were jabbing some roadside animal to check if it were still alive. Link shoved the barrel off his temple and said, "What's wrong with you?"

She told him to wake up his daughter.

Link shook Lydia gently by the shoulder and said, "Kiddo   we got to get up. Come on, rise and shine."

Lydia twitched away from him and rolled flat onto the ground. Cherise began tossing Lydia's hair aside with the end of the shotgun. When Link pushed it away, she said, "I'm serious, Link. This is a loaded firearm, and I *will* shoot. The past is the past."

He grabbed Lydia by both shoulders and shook her up and down against the pillows, but still she didn't respond. She smelled vinegary with sleep, and her face was creased by the edge of the pillow. "You need to get up, Lydia. It's some kind of kidnapping thing."

She groaned loudly, rolled to the side, wiping drool from her mouth. "Fuck," she said. "Tell them to do it *later*."

Cherise shot up into the steel rafters, scattering birds across the vaulted ceiling. Lydia sat up and scraped the corners of her eyes. When she yawned and stretched her arms upright, Cherise cocked the gun and

pointed it at her, dropping the spent casing onto the floor beside the pillows. "God, stop," said Lydia. "I'm up already."

Link said, "You can't wake people out of a dead sleep with this
shit—"

"Let's go. Let's move into the office. Preacher's working out the details."

Cherise led them down the patchwork corridor, through the hanging
sheets and the beads, into the office cubicle, where Preacher sat at a
computer with his shirt off and a pen gripped in his teeth. The printer
ground out color pages, and amid a clutter of wires and a .38 revolver, a
curl of paper unrolled slowly from the fax machine. When Lydia plopped
onto the couch across the room, Cherise gestured with the shotgun and
said, "Don't let her fall asleep again."

In the clutter of papers, Link saw pictures of Lydia, and then he saw
a poster fall out of the stack onto the floor—complete with the age-
enhanced picture and the offer of a thirty-thousand-dollar reward.

A sparrow landed on the partition, then flew back into the girders
above.

Link said, "You try this bullshit, I'm going to put your head through
that computer."

"A lot's changed," said Preacher. "I appreciate your loyalty, Link—I
truly do. But I can't let opportunities slide by anymore."

"You're going to be pulling glass out of your teeth."

Preacher wagged the revolver while he continued typing with one
hand. "Let's be civil about this, Link. We're not going to turn you in;
we're just going to follow the letter of the law here. Now thirty grand,
that'll fill up some holes around here. She goes home to her gold-digging
mommy, you hit the road. Status quo."

Cherise ordered Link to sit down, but he picked up the chair and
hurled it across the cubicle to where it smashed into a panel of drywall
and tumbled onto the floor. Preacher said, "That's great, Link. Very professional. Cherise—what are they even doing in here? Let's lock them up
someplace until we can get organized. All right?"

With her face down in the couch, Lydia said, "You can't call the cops."

"I'm going to beat you to death with that fucking keyboard," said Link. "Then I'm going to burn this place down."

"Cherise is going to lock you two up. We need to figure out how to get this girl to the police in one piece, keep it all at a safe distance from here."

Lydia sat up, cleared the hair from her face, and said, "If you turn us in, the cops will bust you for the shit you do out here."

"*You* are just a snot-nosed kid," said Preacher, suddenly furious. "Don't presume to motherfucking tell me how to run a business. I was running the Coachella Valley before you were an itch in your daddy's sack. I'm seventy-one years old, and I've been in a crisis my whole life. I am a fucking survivor, little girl. Korean War, Tenth Engineers Combat battalion. Third Infantry. Dug up enough mines to blow up the moon. So don't presume to tell me *anything*. Cherise! Get them out of here before I lose my patience."

As Cherise waved them out with the shotgun, Link turned and said, "You keep talking like that, senile motherfucker." He shuffled ahead, down a dark hallway with Lydia, talking to himself, the gun jogging his back. "See how much you got to say with a screwdriver in your skull. Dumb fucking redneck—probably got shrapnel in him from the *Civil War*, don't mean he's going to fuck with me. Damn musket-firing motherfucker. I'm going to beat him to death, Cherise—then I'm coming for you. I'm going to kill you with his dentures. They're going to find you in a ditch with a bite out of your ass."

Cherise forced them all the way across the unfinished corridor to a long aluminum shed in the back, where she undid a padlock and shoved them inside.

It was the grow room. For a moment, Link and Lydia stood quietly and regarded the long aisles of six-foot cannabis plants, rising upward like a jungle from the hydroponic network of PVC tubes and buckets. All around the arrangement there were thermostats and humidistats, and above stretched panels of fluorescent lights. Lydia paced around the stalks with a hushed awe, like a tourist amid the sequoias, until finally she said, "We need to call your sponsor again."

But Link was so angry that he hardly registered his surroundings. He kicked repeatedly on the aluminum door until it began to dent in the center and bend off the frame. He lowered his shoulder and smashed into it, rocking the entire shed, and then he punched it for a while until his knuckles bled. "Open the fucking door, Cherise."

"Link, I'm scared of you right now," she shouted from the other side. "And I got a loaded shotgun. You get away from that door."

He kept stomping the aluminum, mangling it further and increasing the daylight around the padlock; and Cherise shouted, "You twist it any more and I'll never be able to get the lock off. I'm going to shoot right through the wall, Link. Unless you stop. I can't be responsible."

Link reached around the space at the edge of the door, and she shouted, "I'm going to shoot your hand off! I mean it. Don't you grab at me!"

Lydia touched him on the back. Link had grown so deliriously enraged that he had forgotten her, but the moment he saw her large, pleading eyes, he stopped fighting the door. Lydia took his hand and looked at the bleeding fingertips. She said, "Shhh, Dad. Stop, okay. *Stop.*"

Cherise kept warning him on the other side while his daughter studied a swollen knuckle. Then Lydia whispered, "Look around, okay? You don't need to beat down the door—this woman is an idiot. She put us in here with the entire crop."

This occurred to Link just as she said it, and he cursed himself for always missing obvious solutions when he was angry.

Lydia said, "They want thirty g's—there's a lot more than that in here."

Link stooped down to the open space beside the door, and said, "Cherise? Let us out of here, or I'm yanking up every fucking plant."

Cherise called to Preacher, and in a few moments both of them were outside the crooked door, arguing in whispers. Link pulled off one of the PVC pipes for a weapon, holding it like a bat as the circulating water

began to pour out onto the corrugated floor. It was saturated with nutri-
ents and fertilizer, and the smell made his eyes water. Preacher was talking calmly, as if to a man with a bomb strapped to him, telling Link that
he was letting him out, but that he needed to push the key into the lock
at a tough angle. The key scraped. Holding the pipe like a spear, Link
paced to the door and thrust it through the bent space, hearing Preacher
wince on the other side.

"Dad! They're trying to let us out."

Preacher yelled, "You just hit me in the shoulder, you son of a bitch.
We're not getting you out of there unless you cut that out."

Link told Lydia to hide among the plants, then he waited silently as
he heard them fiddling and finally turning the key. When the padlock
was removed, he kicked the door open. The edge struck Preacher in the
face, and he stumbled backward. Link scrambled back into the long shed
and started ripping up plants and throwing them toward the entrance,
huge heavy stalks with tangles of wet roots.

Cherise and Preacher splashed into the room, into the shallow
runoff, with their guns cocked. Preacher was talking, on the verge of
tears, saying that they had to get rid of Link because he was too volatile;
and as Link slipped and crawled forward under the PVC garden, Cherise
got the barrel of the shotgun against Link's neck "That's it, I got him."

Lydia came forward with her hands up, and she and Link moved
out of the grow room, soaked with pungent water. The four began down
the hallway, through the Indian bead curtains, Preacher guarding Link,
Cherise with her gun on Lydia.

They stopped before the last doorway, covered by a paisley sheet.
Preacher gestured for Lydia and Cherise to move ahead through the narrow space. Lydia passed first, and then, as Cherise followed, Link ripped
down the sheet over the top of her. Lydia reacted quickly, escaping across
the open portion of the hangar. While Cherise struggled to get the sheet
off of her, batting at it like a swarm of flies, Link grabbed the old man
from behind and pilloried his arms, reaching his hands around to the
back of his head and working him into a full nelson. He pushed his head
down hard and Preacher struggled to breathe.

"Drop the gun, old man, or I break your fucking neck."

The revolver dropped onto the floor. Untangled, Cherise pointed the shotgun at them, but her eyes were wide with shock.

Link backed away, moving the old man around as easily as a scarecrow, and he said, "All I got to do is lean into him, Cherise—and his spine breaks. I can feel his vertebrae right now, like little Rice Krispies. Drop the gun."

"You hurt him and you're going to die," she said.

"So what?"

"And then I'll go outside and find your little girl."

"She's long gone. Probably already hitched a ride."

"I'll shoot you right around him."

Link moved back farther along the drywall. "Try that, Cherise. Good idea. With a shotgun."

Preacher could hardly get enough air to speak, but he tried to whisper something. Link lifted him up and made him dance like a limp marionette, showing her how easily he could move him as a shield. With his face raised slightly, Preacher said, "Put the barrel on his head. Back him into a corner."

"Oh, that's a great idea!" said Link. "Get it right up into my face, baby. In fact, wait—here, I'll open my mouth. Go ahead."

Link had moved all the way back into a corner in the twisting hallway, and as Cherise pushed the barrel forward, Link opened his mouth and nibbled at it like a fish. She was trembling and wiping her nose as she moved forward.

Link said, "Uh-oh, I heard something pop in his back. You okay, Preach? Yeah, he's still okay. I thought I broke his spine there."

Cherise maneuvered the barrel past Preacher's down-turned head and planted it on Link's temple. When her mouth straightened out, he could tell that she was about to fire. He rotated and threw Preacher against the barrel. Her aim was knocked off and she blasted into the drywall, throwing dust and powder outward into a splash.

Link let go of the old man, grabbed the gun, and wrested it away from Cherise; then he rushed out of the cloud and found the revolver, saying, "This is the saddest fucking shakedown I ever saw." In the office, he rifled through the desk, finding a drawer full of money stacked neatly. "I'm sick that I ever worked for such amateurs." He stuffed bills into his jeans pockets, and when they were overflowing, he turned onto the next drawers and searched through papers.

"Where are the keys?" he yelled.

Preacher came sullenly into the room, rubbing his neck, while Cherise sat solemnly with her back against the drywall. "Link, let's calm down and talk about this. You have to understand my dilemma here. Try to put yourself in my shoes. You know I still love you, you were the best foot soldier I ever had."

Link put the gun down, picked up the computer monitor, and threw it at him across the room. The glass shattered and the keyboard and mouse dragged around it. "Where are my keys?"

"Second drawer in the file cabinet behind you."

Lydia was outside hiding in the trees and brush along the dried riverbed when she heard a loud series of blasts. She rose up out of the yellow grass as her father shot out of the hangar on his bike and wound down-hill toward her. She was already running toward him by the time he called, and she leapt onto the back. He kicked into gear and she grabbed on to him around his broad torso, leaning with him into the turns. They burst out past the open wooden gate in a swirl of dust and wind, moving onto the paved road and accelerating eastward toward washed-out skies.

The landscape trailed away on all sides as her hair flapped over her face. She leaned back and felt some of the anxiety trail off in the rushing air. The chopper was a monstrous thing; she had never been on anything like it—the firing decibels and the climbing speed and the way the road seemed to grind beneath them like a belt of sandpaper. The air was full of grit, the seat was hot, and they rode so fast that she felt as if she were sliding in a low orbit along the ground. Her father smelled like gunpow-der and fertilizer, and his hair flapped in streamers around her. Lydia leaned down into the windward spot behind his back, resting her head against him and feeling the engine through the hollow of his chest, trembling like a struck bell.

They stopped at a gas station near the Arizona border.

His skin was raw from the wind. He wiped his dirty hair from his face, then said to her, as the tank filled, "We need to change the program here. We got a lot of people on our trail."

In the mini-mart, he bought groceries while she waited on the curb. He gave her a bag of potato chips and a root beer, then he tilted the bag to show her the scissors, soap, shaving cream, and razors. "Be *careful*," she said. Close to twenty minutes later, when he emerged from the bathroom, he had completely shaved off his beard and given himself a crooked, short haircut. Lydia sat gaping. Aside from the one arm with a sleeve of tattoos and his crusty jeans and T-shirt, he looked like any middle-aged man. She recognized his face. He had the same breadth and fleshiness across the cheeks as she did, the same weak chin under an improbably wide mouth, the same high, almost Indian cheekbones. His skin was pale and tainted gray against black eyes and lashes that seemed longer now.

Lydia held a swig of root beer in her mouth, and, from her spot seated on the curb, began running her legs in place. She burst out laughing, throwing her head back and wailing at the sky.

"Shut up," he said.

She abandoned herself completely to the laughter, falling down onto the sidewalk and howling at the stucco overhang of the roof, then rolling over and covering her face. Root beer came out of her nose.

"Yeah?" he said. "Well, you're next, you moron."

She lay on her back, sighing and recovering her breath, saying, "I can't even look at you without laughing."

"Just keep going. I'm going to cut your hair like a middle-aged lesbian."

Her chest seized again, and the wheeze intensified into another bout of now-painful hysterics, and she got onto her hands and knees and gasped for air. "Oh my God, I think I just ruptured my spleen."

An hour later they were safely ensconced in a motel room in Yuma,

Arizona, prepaid and signed into the register under fake names. Lydia stood in front of the mirror, fretting at her new short splash of black hair. Link had bought her blonde and red dyes, and she had been arguing that her hair was too thick for this kind of coloring. Scattered across the counter in front of her were crumpled papers and debris from her pockets, the napkin map to Preacher's hideaway, the faxed bulletins sent to the motel, which she was attempting to smooth out under the weight of soap packets and tissue boxes for inclusion in her scrapbook. Link interrupted their discussion to call his sponsor, complaining that all his friends were turncoats and that his daughter was driving him crazy. After Link had described his ordeal at the ranch, he asked Kirby to look up all of the meetings in Yuma.

There was something concerned and curious in his voice. He frowned and asked Kirby if he was feeling all right, and listened for a while to some outburst on the other end of the line. Lydia worried that the sponsor was having a breakdown, and that he might drag Link down with him. Link became calm on the phone, explaining that everything was all right, and that Kirby hadn't *disappointed* him at all, that people made mistakes, that life was brutal. He was sorry that he had put Kirby through so much. "No," said Link. "I don't want to talk about the ranch out there—it didn't go well. No, Kirby—I said we're not there anymore. We left some stuff there, maybe I'll go back. I just need you to look up a meeting down here for my daughter. Kirby? Kirby, focus, man. Kirby, you got to call *your* sponsor, buddy."

When he hung up the phone, he simply stared ahead with his mouth open. Continuing their earlier conversation, Lydia said, "To get my hair blonde, you would have to use a nuclear weapon. I'm not going bald for this. I think I'd actually rather die than damage my hair the way you're asking me to."

On the bed, Link put a damp washcloth over his face. "I don't want to argue anymore, Lydia. You need to look as different as you can."

"Well, most of that is fashion sensibilities. We have to get new clothes anyway, and we're not going back *there* just for our stuff."

"I'm going back. Tonight."

"No, Dad. No, you're not."

"Yes, I am."

Through the mirror, she could see his boots facing upward on the flowery comforter.

"Dad—that's stupid."

"I'm going back for your clarinet."

"Why would you do that?"

"And all of your things—your letters and your stupid bag full of Kleenex and matchbooks. And your cell phone."

"We can't use the cell anyway. The cops could probably, like, trace it or something."

"Lydia, if anybody gets ahold of your phone, they'll have every number you called in the past two weeks. Do you understand me?"

"Just leave it. *Please*. Just let it go. I think you're going back to get that creepy old man, and—"

"There's a lot more to this than you know here, Lydia."

"Dad, take the washcloth off your face and look at me."

"I'm just going to get the evidence you left, and then I'm going to hurt them really bad."

"Okay, listen. For me. I'm asking you not to. I absolutely put my foot down on this. You're not going back there."

"Those people betrayed me in more ways than you can count. They betrayed a code of honor. I'm going to get organized, and then give them a first-class beating."

"For *me*. I'm asking you not to."

"For *you*, I'll go back and put ten pounds of claymores in his ass."

"Why aren't you listening to me?" she suddenly shouted at him. "I'm asking you nicely. I asked you ten times."

"Because it's not your decision," he said from under the washcloth.

"Are my feelings just completely meaningless to you?"

"You don't know anything. You're just a kid. I got pants older than you."

"And that doesn't mean they should be making the decisions."

"Say whatever you want, kid. You're not my mother."

His response so riled Lydia that she couldn't think straight any longer. She picked up the box of blonde hair dye and threw it at him across the room, and then, when it glanced off him, she threw the TV clicker. She threw the phone, and then she pulled out the drawers and hit him with the Gideon's Bible, which tumbled off him across the room and fluttered like a bird into the corner. "You fucking *asshole!*" He was laughing at everything she tossed at him, and this incensed her further, until she moved into the bathroom and came back out throwing soap and toilet paper rolls that unraveled across the room. When the floor was littered with streamers, she stormed over and began pounding her fists onto his big shoulders and chest. This didn't particularly trouble him; but when she tried to hit his face, he grabbed her wrists, cinched them together in his fat hands, and held her still. "That's enough. Cut it out."

"You're going to go and get *killed* now, because you can't let anything go."

All of her emotions seemed to have bottlenecked into her stuffy nose.

"*You* can't let anything go," he said.

"If you go back there and burn that place down, I'm going to kill myself."

"Fine," he said, letting go of her wrists. "If you kill yourself, I'll kill myself. And I'll take a bunch of innocent people down with me."

"You think I'm joking, but I've tried to kill myself, Dad. I've *tried* before."

"Whoo-wee. I've tried lots of times."

"I took all of my stepfather's pills when I was twelve."

"Oh, pills are bullshit. People take pills when they want somebody to find them."

She screamed at the top of her lungs and fled into the bathroom.

He waited, then called, "Great, Lydia. *Great.* Now they're going to think we're making some kind of snuff film in here."

She rushed out again, shouting, "I tried to hang myself when I was ten years old!"

"That's crap. You wouldn't know how to tie a noose."

"Don't you even understand how miserable I am?"

"Sure, I do. Congratulations."

"Ten years old."

"I knew a ten-year-old kid who killed his whole family with a rock."

"Every time I start to think maybe you're not so bad—"

"Come here, dummy."

"No."

"Come here. I want you to feel something. You have to. It's impor-tant, goddamn it. Come here and feel this."

He rubbed a spot on his head and knocked on it with his fist.

Finally she paced over to him and let him guide her fingers onto a patch underneath his hair. She felt something hard and smooth like the panel to a fuse box, and she squealed, leaping backward. "Oh my *God*, what is that?"

"I drove my motorcycle off a cliff on the PCH and split my head open. I meant to do it, I think. Fell down into the rocks—and they *still* saved me. That's a steel plate in my head. And look at this."

"I don't want to. You're a fucking cyborg."

"This is where I tried to cut my veins open in prison. With a razor I smuggled in. They sewed me up, I lived just fine—and then I almost died of hepatitis. Two months in the prison hospital watching soap operas and game shows. Two months of porridge and Bob Barker. I said, 'I don't need to die now. I'm already in hell.' "

"You win," she said.

"If you wanted to die, you should have said so a long time ago. What are we going to all this trouble for?"

"I don't want to die."

"If you do, let's go do it. Let's quit fucking around here. Go out with a party. We'll get a can of floor stripper and rent a movie."

"I don't want to *die*."

"Good. You shouldn't. You're a young kid."

Lydia sank down onto the floor, staring at the brown threads in the carpet. She said, "I don't want you to burn down that ranch. That's what I'm trying to say. It would make me very upset."

"All right. I promise—no pyromania. If you do something for me. I'm still going to ride back, I'm going to go in armed—I'm going to get our stuff out, and I won't break a bone—if you do something for me. I want you to go someplace—the only safe place I can think of. Just go and listen. Sit down, have some coffee. Introduce yourself. Talk all about your problems. But don't get too specific."

fifteen

Before Lydia's first AA meeting, at a private home in Yuma, she convinced her father to let her ride his bike in first gear around an empty parking lot beside the Pentecostal church. Link told her she was going to kill herself, but after she begged him, he agreed to let her try, with a worried smirk on his face. A restored 1956 Shovel-head chopper with a suicide shift—he told her that not even experienced riders could handle its power.

He kick-started it and left the bike rumbling in neutral. As Lydia climbed on, she gave a nervous howl and started laughing.

Link said, "Oh boy, are you going to die. *And* wreck my bike. Okay, okay—squeeze the clutch with your left hand—right there. All the way down, dummy!"

They yelled to each other over the engine.

"Holy shit," she said. "Okay, I'm ready. I'm going to kick ass!"

"Now put your left foot there on the gear shifter. Right here."

"You put your left foot in, you put your left foot out—"

"Hey, if you don't concentrate—"

"And you shake it all about."

"—you're picking gravel out of your face."

"Okay! Okay! What do I do now?"

"Kick it down into first."

She clicked down on the gear changer, keeping her left hand pinched on the clutch lever.

He said, "You're a crazy chick, Lydia. I mean that. Now, moment of truth. Give a little tiny throttle with your right hand while you ease up on that clutch—slow. Real slow."

She hiccuped ahead, screaming at the top of her lungs, straightening out the bike, and she moved forward so slowly that she could barely keep her balance. As the Harley rolled ahead, she kept squealing until she broke into wild laughter. Link ran alongside her, trying to keep the bike upright as she drifted a drunken path across the lot, then began accelerating toward the parking blocks and a retaining wall.

"Stop!" he shouted.

The panic on his face sent her into more hysterics, until she looked up and saw herself approaching the wall at a trotting pace, and said, "I'm going to hit something!"

"Grab the clutch and hit the brake. Your right foot! Your right foot!"

She stopped abruptly against the parking blocks, and Link, racing forward, leaned all his weight into the bike to keep it upright before dropping the kickstand. He couldn't breathe. Lydia had never seen him look so terrified, but she was erupting with enthusiasm. She leapt off the seat and ran in wide circles on the parking lot, shouting, "That was awesome! Did you see me? I was so fucking sexy on that thing."

"Yeah, you were a natural, kid."

"Oh my God. Can I try to get into second gear?"

"No."

A few minutes later, after he had soared off through traffic, Lydia sat on a foldout chair in the low-ceilinged living room of a woman's home. On a coffee table there were peppermint candies, and on the wood-paneled walls there were star-shaped clocks and windmills made of sand dollars. After the group recited a speech together—". . . the strength to accept what I cannot change, and the wisdom to know the difference . . ."—a woman in large secretarial glasses read something from a book, and each person was supposed to comment, as the room filled rapidly with smoke. Lydia introduced herself, and she was greeted warmly by a room of stoic-looking women, many of whom tried to tell optimistic stories. One woman was happy that she could now keep her pets alive. Another woman spoke for a long time about her husband and children, her testimony so saturated with apology and self-loathing that people watched her speak as if witnessing an execution. But other women seemed to have a weathered and comic sense of absurdity, and they used their cigarettes to pause and mull ideas, speaking with shrugs, and wistfully telling tales about backing their cars through garage walls or waking up in bedrooms they didn't recognize with men as ugly as wolverines. Survival alone was an accomplishment. Surviving yourself was a career.

Lydia suspected that most of these women were probably not much older than her mother—but some looked ancient. Their voices were raspy, throats made of smoke and weak coffee, and their laughs turned quickly into coughs. Lydia got the impression that they all knew each other well, as if they had been in this room, in this exact semicircular formation—like a Tupperware party for felons and fugitives—since they were young. One woman said that she trusted this group, "Because you people got me into this mess." It was a beleaguered camaraderie at best, but Lydia found herself swayed by it. They could have been patronizing to a young kid, but they were motherly in a way she had never experienced. They seemed to accept her by virtue of the fact that she was in trouble like they had been, and they respected her for coming, as if by sitting quietly she had given them added resolve.

Lydia had passed initially, but soon she wanted to talk. She told them that the only reason she was here was because her father had forced her. She had been sober for almost two days altogether, after sneaking bumps of crystal, smoking buds and drinking. She was craving speed badly; it felt like a thirst for salt. She didn't remember ever feeling this hungry for anything else—and a woman told her that it would never go away entirely, especially not if she'd started on the needle. She'd have to learn to accept these cravings, let them wash over her, view them as emotions as chronic as loneliness or heartbreak.

It was just over a week since the man in Topanga had slapped her on the inside of the elbow, found the vein—since she had met Cully by the freeway sound barrier in the middle of the night. She started to cry, sitting by herself, stooped and contained: She was thinking of the strange pact with Jonah, which she had never understood; and she was filled with shame and heartbreak. In his old El Dorado, she had returned to Jonah that night, higher than she'd ever been in her life, believing that she would see on his face some indication that he loved her, that her discoveries that night were simply part of a chemical-induced paranoia. She had opened the gate herself, tiptoed into his room, and found him going through paperwork in his closet. He jumped when he saw her; she was a ghost in his doorway. As she told him about the dealer in Topanga who had refused to pay, Jonah recovered a phony expression and told her, "Beautiful work, Lydia."

Lydia was not sure why she was breaking down now, in front of these women, but she told them it was because she was tired of watching her life unfold like an unavoidable car accident. What she wanted to say was that murder truly was a marriage: Over and over, she saw herself pulling that trigger; she saw Jonah sagging down against the stairs. And she couldn't escape the feeling that he was waiting for her. There was a shadow now that she'd never outrun.

Everyone rose for the end of the meeting, said the final recitation, hugged and said good-bye, and Lydia waited in the middle of the empty room. The owner of the house asked if she was all right. She nodded at the floor and asked, "Can I just wait on the porch for my dad?"

A few miles away from the turnoff to Preacher's ranch in the foothills, Link pulled to the roadside to study a twist of smoke blowing in an eastward slant. It could have been from a bonfire of excess garbage and weeds, but Link's attention was drawn to it because it was so black against the dingy white sky.

When he turned up the hill, he smelled heavy clouds of rubber and chemicals. The wind had strengthened all day, and a mixture of sand and smoke now formed a low haze over the shacks. Link stepped off his bike and walked to a clearing beyond the hangar, where he saw the ground littered with bottles, tire tracks, and shell casings. The adobe walls of old huts were freckled with bullet holes, the desert was pocked with detonation holes from Preacher's old munitions; and beside Link, a fire still smoldered with a blackened tangle of chair legs, steel furniture, and tires. Some papers blew freely, partly charred—pictures of Lydia, posters and fliers.

He circled around the pile. On the other side he came upon a human arm reaching out from underneath the flames, blackened but not yet devoured.

The fire was flapping and ruffling in the wind, between snarls of mesquite as kindling, popping with resin and casting up sparks. As Link stepped closer, he saw that the body was Cherise, her features and hair scorched away from her face, and only the bloody, darkened sheath of a damp robe remaining around smoldering bones. Higher up on the stack, Preacher had been burned on top of the tires, and his remains looked like brittle chicken bones, steaming and reeking of iron and hair. One hand was still intact upon a broken table, fingernails looking as if they were alive and grappling.

All around this fire there were bottles and footprints ground into the light dirt, and Link could tell that the murderers had paced in circles, drinking and watching. It had been a party. They had made no effort to rush away or cover their tracks.

He put his hand over his mouth when the winds shifted. The smoke had a ripe human smell. He was surprised that anything in this life could still scare him, but as he looked at this twist of wreckage and bodies, a cluttered sacrifice, he understood that he was just a common brawler, incapable of anything close to this display. Gangs didn't do this—kids from barrios needed to be prodded by the Mexican Mafia just to stop and get out of their cars. Preacher's charred head tipped back as if his throat had been cut open first—a Colombian necktie—and Link knew that there weren't many people willing to kill with their hands anymore. Maybe they had intended to keep Cherise alive. From the way she was haphazardly thrown into the mess, sprawled like a murderous afterthought, Link thought she had panicked trying to defend her old man.

By the books, this was a cartel assassination. If it wasn't the Tijuana cartel or Guadalajara, it was someone who had studied them and followed the recipe. But how had they found this place? How had they managed to get so close onto Lydia's trail?

He kept his wits and climbed back onto his bike, and ten minutes later he pulled up to a gas station, where he made a collect call. The voice on the other end sounded slightly out of breath. The automated operator asked if she would accept the call, and there was a long pause, until she clearly articulated: "Yes."

Link said, "Ursula."

She didn't respond.

He said, "I've got her, she's safe. Everything is okay, but listen to me."

She only caught her breath in the receiver. She had been exercising maybe, or running up the stairs.

"Listen real good. Get your family together, and get out of that house. Drive up the coast, don't tell anybody where. Lydia is in some serious shit, and it's much deeper than I thought."

"John, the police have been all around here. They're looking for you."

"I know. But you either need to go to them for protection, or you need to get out of there. I mean it. I know you don't want to talk to me, but just listen. She had some boyfriend, and I thought he was just another punk. But he was into some serious shit. I don't *know* how they keep coming up with so much information, but they do. They might have my files from the shop, and if they do, *you're* in them. And these people will come after you. They'll come after anything Lydia cares about."

Ursula didn't speak for a while, and then she asked, "What makes you think my daughter cares about me, John?"

"Ursula—get over the insults for a second and just get to a safe place. I can take care of Lydia. Will you just do that for me?"

"She was involved in a murder, John. You have to go to the police; this isn't a game anymore. They're going to catch her, and they're going to catch you."

He looked out at the dust blowing in giant plumes off the road, the lumpy horizon of obscured hills, swaths of colorless sky and salty earth, and he said, "They'll catch *me*. But I'm going to give the kid a push in the right direction."

An hour later, pulling to the curb across the street, he reached the Craftsman-style house in Yuma where Lydia's AA meeting had just let out. When Lydia saw him from the front porch and rose up with her satchel, running with such animation across the dried-out lawn, her loose sweatshirt sleeves unrolling over her hands, her long arms and clumsy legs—such a big and goofy kid, her face coloring with relief upon seeing him—Link realized that he had never loved anything or anyone so much in his life until now.

For decades he had lived it up with nothing to live for, had tried to kill himself without a cause worth dying for; and during the thirty-some-odd strides his daughter made down the cement steps and across the empty street, he was convinced that he would endure any suffering or make any sacrifice to put things right again. He felt neither sadness nor hope, but all the weight of his own history, as if every highway he'd raced down, every day he'd squandered, every bad idea he'd chased down a dead-end road, in one single, swelling moment, could finally have a purpose.

sixteen

"What I can't get straight," said Link, sitting across from his daughter in the booth of a chain restaurant, "is how they're so close behind you, whoever these guys are."

"Maybe Preacher called the cops," she said. "Maybe they have moles in the police department? I mean, what you say about that kid up at the slabs, the way they did that—that's got to be Jonah's bosses, right? They're probably connected all over the place."

"I don't know, Lydia."

To the waitresses and diners, they must have now seemed like any average father and daughter, sitting in the far corner, facing the cloverleaf exits off the interstate. Lydia had gone shopping. Her hair was short but stylishly ruffled, and she wore overalls with a white blouse beneath. Link wore a button-up workshirt and stiff new jeans. On the booth beside them were Lydia's ideas of disguises: shopping bags, new suits, and dresses in the shrouds of transparent wrappers.

Lydia was shaken by the news about the ranch, and she tried to tell her father everything she remembered about Jonah. Frankly, she didn't *know* who he had worked for—he had never told her, and she had begun to get the impression that they were capable of anything.

"But he was a Realtor?" asked Link.

"No, no—he wasn't a Realtor. He developed, like, canyon properties and things like that. And he was a slumlord. And he had this other business, on the side, where he found stash houses. They'd store money and drugs in these houses, and he'd take, like, a percentage, I guess. Problem is—he was taking more than that."

As they drank coffee and shared a slice of key lime pie, Link drew a sketch of Lydia on the back of the place mat. He asked her what Jonah was taking, and she told him everything she knew up until the night before the deliveries.

"I got back to his place that night," said Lydia to her father, her elbows on the restaurant table, "and he looked up at me with just—total shock. That was his confession to me right there. I wasn't supposed to make it. I could tell by the look on his face."

"If I had this kid in front of me right now," said Link.

"Then he tried to cover it up. He asked me if I'd made the delivery to this guy Cully, the last on the list, and I told him that I'd gotten so tired, and that the place was so dark that I chickened out. He smiled, told me what a great job I did. I was still in that mode, Dad—like Jonah was everything to me now, even if I loathed him. I had to please him, I had to say the right thing. So I talked to him about the house in Topanga, told him about the problems there. I told him they'd broken the contract; I said they were threatening to tell the other suppliers what he was doing, maybe his bosses. There was still this part of me that thought I could show him I was strong enough. The only way I thought I could survive was by convincing Jonah that I deserved to.

"He wasn't mad at all; he didn't even seem worried—and I just knew I'd had it. He was talking to me so sweetly, like he was trying to trick me into a corner. And he said we'd head back the next day, shake down the people who'd insulted us in Topanga. I just knew that was it:

I wasn't going to get away. That kid in Canoga Park, he'd been coming to the house all along. He'd been there, he'd drifted in and out. The next day, when we were all driving to Topanga, he just came along, this dude *Cully*—as if Jonah was saying, *I know—you figured me out.* And I just played along until the last possible second, thinking I deserved it. Thinking it was all I could do."

Her father leaned back in the booth, staring out the window and tapping the fork out on the table. Finally Link said, "So he was skimming out of all his houses? He'd send this kid in to steal, or somebody else, pass the blame onto the tenant."

She said, "Yeah. He'd do some version of that, go to some tenant, give them this whole story about how they were finished because something was missing from the house. Then he'd use them to steal more out of the house—like I did. Cut the stuff, sell it cheap. Then he'd cut the person loose, kill them, leave them someplace—pretend that the tenant had been skimming off the top. After all, they were just drifters. Illegal aliens, runaways. Idiots like me. He found people that wouldn't go to the cops, and people he thought he could control and people who would believe him. He just put them in the middle, right between him and the money. Turned them into these go-betweens."

"And he had you pegged from the beginning?"

Her mouth dropped at the edges and her eyes dampened, but she contained herself by staring out the window at the flow of cars under a steady, dirty wind. "I guess so."

"Now why would his bosses come after you? It seems like they'd go after his people: They were the ones running the scam. You know where all the other houses are?"

"I think Jonah gave me a chance to prove myself. That day. I think if I'd shot this woman like he wanted me to—"

"Lydia—you got the mindset of a battered housewife, and it scares the shit out of me."

"I don't know what to think anymore. I know he lied to me, the whole time, but I just don't know what's wrong with me."

"Lydia, listen to me here." The waitress approached and slapped the check onto the table. Link waited until she had gone again, and said, "We have one thing to think about, and that's getting you away from these people. But to do that, I got to figure out exactly who this is on our trail. Is it his guys? Is it somebody he worked for? Do they have some kind of connection with those cops that got right on us the other night? There's a lot we don't know. So I'm going to do some research of my own. Talk to a guy I know, back over in Calipatria."

She blew her nose into a napkin, then asked, "Can you get back in there?"

"There's not a CO there that'll recognize me like this. I don't recognize myself. I'm going to call my sponsor and get him to FedEx his driver's license down here. Few days ago, he promised to help, any way he could. Let's hope he's sober again. He had a little slip—the stress of *my* goddamn life, I think."

He handed her the drawing he had worked on throughout her speech, shaded and done with a light touch—and Lydia was surprised by how calm and courageous he had made her face. She folded it up, slipped it into her backpack, and said, "They'll have to kill me to get this one."

A little past eleven o'clock the next day, Link picked up Kirby's package from FedEx and dropped his daughter off at the crowded mall beside it, watching her as he idled against the curb. The place was already teeming with Christmas shoppers, and Lydia had assured him that she could stay safely immersed in crowds. The movies would begin in an hour, and she would snuggle into the seat of the most populated theater. She would leave her cell phone on, and Link would give only a quick call when he was back, so that nothing could be traced or triangulated, by either the police or Jonah's bosses. He left her his sponsor's number to call in case they were separated. She chuckled as she programmed it into her phone, and she seemed to like this new role of calming a worried parent.

A few minutes later, Link was racing westbound on I-8 back toward the 111 turnoff for Calipatria, wearing an olive-colored suit she had bought for him with their windfall from Preacher's desk. The jacket

inflated with the wind, and Link felt emboldened and alive to be accelerating like this again, in a deafening pocket of noise, with the air
stinging his cheeks.

By a little after noon, he was moving along the stretch of farm road,
past the cow pastures, scaring up flocks of seagulls that had been sitting
on the road. The Salton Sea smelled thick and pungent as he turned and
passed through the gates into the massive, sterile city that sat alone on a
patchwork of farms and irrigation trenches. He made it through clear-
ance, the metal detectors and the search batons, frisked by a CO who
knew him but didn't recognize him; and a half hour later he was sitting
in the private meeting room, impressed that Rios still had access to it.

Rios was led into the room in his jumpsuit and shackles. He wasn't
taking care of himself. His usually shaved head was grown out into a
lumpy, fuzzy mix of black and gray, and his mustache drooped long over
his mouth. He had new memorial tattoos, which were poorly done—not
half as precise as Link's work. Link felt a pang of jealousy and wanted to
kill whatever asshole had done such sloppy work at the trunk of his
neck; but before he could get too worked up, Rios sat down across from
him and stared ahead, with no recognition whatsoever on his face.

He said, "What's this all about?"

"Conjugal visit," said Link "Kiss me."

Rios smiled hugely, trying to stifle a laugh. He asked the guard to
give them a second alone, and the kid complied. Then Rios squirmed
around on his chair across the table, doing everything he could to contain himself. Finally he just busted out laughing, prompting Link to
laugh just as hard back at him. The two men howled at each other, face-
to-face across the table, until the sound became like an aggressive barking. Rios started to recover, sighing and saying, "Shi-hi-hi-t, man," and
then he sat up straight and said, stone-faced, "You look like my lawyer."

They both broke into a new paroxysm of laughter, and Rios fell onto
the table, and when he finally recovered from the second bout, his body
looked tired and his eyes were wet. "Damn, man—you're an *ugly* dude.
Grow the beard back, please."

"All right, enough already. I need your help."

He pointed to the tie and said, "Wait—don't tell me. You need help *tying* that?"

"Shut up already. It's not funny anymore."

"It's funny, man. This shit is funny *forever*."

"Listen, listen. You remember my daughter?"

His face straightened out, and he cleared his throat and said, "Yeah, of course."

"She's alive, but—she got into some serious trouble with some guys, and I need you to help me sort this shit out."

While the final aftershocks of laughter played out, Link told him everything he knew from Lydia, and he was encouraged when Rios began nodding along as if he recognized the name—Jonah Pincerna—and parts of the story. He was a patient listener, and he wasn't one of those people who nodded to be polite. When Link finished debriefing him, he asked, "Anything ring a bell?"

"Well, Pincerna. First of all, homes—he ain't Chicano, so don't put that shit on me. That's a Greek name or something. But from what you say, I think I know who he is—he sounds like a junior."

"What's that?"

"One of those rich punks the Tijuana cartel started using, mid-nineties or so. Fucking mess. Biggest mistake of the AFO, man—and we had problems with it too. I mean, we just had a cease-fire on the streets. And we had a green light in here on anybody that still did drive-bys, because I don't want no fucking little kids getting capped. But then these rich putos from both sides of the border, they come in trying to prove some shit. Doing everything too fucking loud."

"But go back—go back—they get brought on board—"

"Basically it's like this. The cartel has a nightclub in Tijuana. You know, like Tijuana and San Diego used to be like one big town. So now it's getting harder to get back and forth. There's kids with Tijuana connections—lots of money, you know. They belong to the country club and they go to the nice restaurants: It's a really small town for the people with money. Some of these kids, they basically grow up on the other side. They go to big Catholic schools in San Diego or up north or wherever. Like Saint

Augustine. They're rich—nobody notices when they're driving bigger cars. They got all kinds of connections down south; and they blend in up in the States. They were perfect for a while. Educated. Greedy. Bored as shit. So the AFO started recruiting these kids out of this nightclub. They'd use them to do all sorts of jobs—some of them just organizing things in various cities; laundering, maybe; some of them would do hits. But they're crazy. Everything they know is from the movies, man. They took out a judge in Tijuana, some of these rich kids: They shot him twenty-something times in front of his house, and then they ran over him about ten more time with a'SUV."

"My daughter would say the worst part is the SUV."

"We don't *do* shit like that. It's bad business. You want to stay on top—you got to do it like Cali—quiet, *cabrón*. With honor. These kids are loud and they're sloppy."

"Okay, so these juniors—they would have jobs for the AFO?"

"Right. This guy Jonah you talk about—his family already had a business. Right? And he took that over, and he did this angle for them with the stash houses—probably working for the cell head in Los Angeles. If that's what he was doing, then he wasn't a big deal in the organization. But I guess he *wanted* to be."

"What would he have to do with the CLCS? Those are your kids, and I saw some of those tats on his guys—"

"He's paying for some muscle. I mean, they're around. Those kids will do work for money. They usually tax for us, man, but we can't control everybody. It's bad business. The Red Steps and the Logan Heights kids have been doing this AFO shit for years; and it's moving up north now—that's a problem. You can always find some muscle in *dieciocho*. There's fifty, sixty thousand people under that *bandera*, man—that's a small country. If he pays, if he's good to his people—he'll find somebody. And maybe they're loyal. Maybe they're your problem."

"But this kid, Jonah—he's dead. Would they be loyal enough to keep working when the money stopped?"

"I don't know. Maybe they're trying to position, you know—take over his business."

"Now—yesterday, I go back to check on some stuff out in the desert, just east of here—some old Angels, AB ties, couple of old grass breeders. They were torched. Burned on tires—that kind of thing. And it was meant for us. So if this guy was just somewhere, mid-level, this Jonah kid—what the fuck are these people doing? What do they care about my daughter?"

Rios nodded and thought for a minute. "Listen—I don't think anybody is going to give a shit that this kid went down. I think somebody was going to have to kill him sooner or later anyway, if he had some side business going. But if they're coming after your daughter—she must have something."

"She doesn't."

"Does she know where some shipment is? Where it's going? Where it's hidden? Something like that. Maybe she don't even *know* what she knows. Maybe one of those houses has got all kinds of information in it—like some insurance policy for the kid. This is money, John. These guys aren't staying after her for anything else."

"Yeah, okay." Link thought for a minute, and said, "She might know something."

"The thing about these juniors—they're unpredictable, because they don't fucking know how to do this shit right. They ain't never done any time. They don't understand the politics, man. They don't know how to fight—not for real. Not up close. They don't know shit but what they seen in video games, and they make mistakes that *veteranos* like you and me just don't make."

Time was running down, and Link nodded at the ground. He asked for Arturo's gut response: Was the AFO on his trail, or just Jonah's remaining clique? Rios said, "I can't tell you for sure, man. Either way, if they want her, they'll get to her. And she won't be safe anywhere. Unless you change her, hide her—she's got to be a good girl. She's got to stay in the daylight, stay clean, that's the only way to get away from these people. But this kid, Jonah: He's *lucky* to be dead. He was going to get hurt worse than you could imagine. She put that motherfucker out of his misery, if what you say is true. You don't steal from these people. You just don't. They took out a whole family in Ensenada. Forty-something people shot and laid out in the street. He was the one with all the secrets to protect. If I had to *bet*, I'd say it's somebody close to him that's on you now. A business partner. They're the ones with everything to lose."

Link swatted Rios on the shoulder.

"But one more thing, *cabrón*. This kid—I know something else about him. A rumor. Did his family get killed?"

Link settled back into his chair. "I don't know."

"I think so. His father, man—he was DEA in San Diego. Big time, really fucking crooked. Married this good-looking woman from a big family down in Tijuana. Tore up his kids—fucking animal."

"No shit?" said Link.

"So anyway, the rumor goes—Jonah, he was always at this night-club. He was going to school up north or some shit, coming home every weekend. One day, one of the brothers in the AFO gives him the pitch: has the kid in a car, asks him if he's got any enemies. This is how they invite these kids in. The kids say, yeah, some dude that fucked my girl or said something to me. Couple of enforcers mess the guy up—maybe kill him. Then you owe the organization, and you go to work. So what I hear: Some guys from the AFO ask this kid the question, and Jonah says something like, 'If I'm going to work for you, I need to clean up my own house.' "

"They killed his old man?"

"*And* his mother," said Rios. "He asked them to. He took his little brother, never went back south."

The CO returned to the room and stood by the door with his loop of keys.

Link stood and said, "Arturo, my man, I owe you another one."

"You don't owe me shit, man. Get out of here. Go take care of your kid."

seventeen

E arlier that morning, after Lydia had watched her father ride away down the busy side streets, she blended in with schoolgirls and shopping families, moving under displays of tinsel and giant Christmas trees beside the front doors. There was something disconcerting about the ashen desert sky, the sandstorms on the horizon, and these Norwegian pines bound up for sale along the walk. Once she was inside, amid canned music and echoing voices, she felt as if it were Christmas on the moon. She had a pocketful of money, and she played and shopped, tried on lipsticks and perfumes. She bought presents for her friends, feeling wistful that she might never see them again. Laughing and causing a confused look from the saleslady, she bought her father a tie with little motorcycles on it. When the saleslady finally asked her what was so funny, Lydia sounded almost as if she were going to cry. She said, "It's just so horrifying."

"Isn't it?" said the saleslady. "Do you want it gift wrapped?"

She bought him a watch and some gloves, from which she assumed he would lop off the fingers, and then she saw a bracelet that she knew Chloe would love, and she bought it, figuring she could send it to her anonymously from the road. Store to store, kiosk to kiosk, she killed a few hours, and by one o'clock she was ensconced in a narrow cineplex movie theater during the first scenes of a holiday blockbuster. When her cell phone began ringing, shadows in the audience began to hiss at her. She leaned into the aisle and answered in a lowered voice, "Hold on, I'm pissing everybody off." There was a party on the screen, a loud conversation over music, and Lydia couldn't hear. She put her finger into her ear and trotted toward the exit, gathering her shopping bags. Once beyond the padded door, she heard damp exhales, strained, as if someone were breathing through a straw.

A voice said, "How's the movie?"

Lydia stopped and stayed in the middle of the long, dim corridor. The voice was deliberate, but mutilated, the words delivered with an altered, half-swallowed wind.

"Disappointing?"

Lydia scanned the hall. To one end were bright bathrooms and rows of doors, sealed like submarine hatches, the sounds of muted violins and helicopter blades escaping.

He said, "You didn't expect me, I guess."

For a moment, Lydia thought it was a joke meant to frighten her, but, as he spoke with restraint, hostility, and the trademark condescension—she knew it was too good to be an imitation.

She said, "*Jonah*, please," quickening her pace along the red carpet and trying to find someone, anyone to hover alongside. "How did you—okay, okay. So you heard the movie?" she said. "You just heard a movie."

"Right," he said. "Good for you. Maybe I'm sitting at home, right? Nothing for you to worry about out there. In Yuma. At the Southgate Mall."

She pushed out through the glass doors into the main vaulted structure, where children's voices echoed from a village of candy canes and reindeer below. She avoided the escalator to stay along the second floor, passing into the food court, where there was a lunch crowd, hundreds of voices clamoring in the cove of white tile.

Jonah said, "What did you do to your hair, Lydia? It looks terrible."

She rotated in a slow circle with the phone pressed to her ear, trying to spot him somewhere in the crowds. Lines were forming around every stall and cash register, from drums of simmering fry grease to the bins of precooked Szechuan, and Lydia drifted among them, as if trying to hide herself in a giant, grazing herd. Quietly she said, "Nobody is ever going to hear from me, Jonah. I'm no threat to you."

"That's unbelievable. You have no idea what I've been through be-cause of you. You'll see in a minute. I'll show you. We had three under-ground doctors, and they grafted skin from all over my body. That's a sick feeling, to have bites out of my thighs and my calves—so my neck could be patched up. Wedges taken out of me, like I'm eating myself to stay alive."

Lydia moved farther into the court, traversing the pizza lines to stand beside a revolving slab of lamb. She was flanked on both sides by teenage boys.

Jonah said, "Don't try to leave. We've got guys all around you right now. And if you think I can't see you in there—let me tell you something: You've got the most distinctive walk in this mall."

He hung up the phone and Lydia moved to a table of teenage girls with teased and sculpted hair. They were dressed gangsta-style, with brown lipstick and heavy eyeliner, and, when Lydia hung beside them, they glanced up at her with knee-jerk offense. Lydia said, "Can I ask you for help with something? There's a guy here that's harassing me, and I wonder if you could do me a favor?"

The girls ignored her first, then began making fun of her, until one of them waved theatrically and said, "Bye."

Putting down her bags, Lydia sat and waited at the end of a crowded lunch table, among children and families, a mother scolding a little boy with ketchup on his hands, and, farther down, two old women hovering silently over giant buckets of soda. Along the aisles, a pack of animated boys moved toward Lydia, one of them carrying a skateboard by its rim and another with his hair glued upward into a splash. From twenty yards,

Lydia had considered them dangerous, but once they surrounded her she saw their spotted complexions and heard quavering adolescent voices and felt more comfortable, as if hidden in a landscape she knew better than anywhere else. They pelted her with aggressive comments and asked what she was doing all alone. Did she have a boyfriend? Did she party?

"I need you guys to do me a favor," she said.

"Anything, baby. I'm your man," said a boy with headgear and braces.

"There's this guy stalking me. Okay? And he's got friends with him. And he may have something to threaten me with—something that makes me have to leave with him. I'm going to give you a cell phone number—do any of you have a cell phone?"

They all began pulling phones and pagers from the pockets of their baggy pants.

"Okay, good," said Lydia. "Punch in this number. It's a guy named Kirby—and I want you to do something. If anybody tries to get me out of this mall—anybody—I want you to call this number and describe what happened. Tell him who I'm with, where I'm going. Describe whatever you see. If you see me get into a car outside, give this guy the license plate. Any information, okay? I'm going to try to stay right here, but I have no idea what these people are going to do."

"You want us to get the cops?"

"Not yet. But if they get me out of here, if it gets to that point—then, yeah. Call the cops."

"Just hang with us," said the smallest boy. "We'll protect you."

"Thank you," she said, smiling. Her phone began to ring again, and she answered it while the kids were still boasting that they could handle the situation. On the other end, Jonah said, "Get rid of the Little Rascals— or they're going to turn out like those little dealers out at Slab City."

Lydia covered the receiver and said, "He says you guys have to go. Please. And please just stay someplace where you can see me."

Now they seemed to assume that she was blowing them off or playing a prank, and they talked with sweeping cocky gestures, saying that she was tripping, until Lydia rose her voice sharply and said, "*Now*. Let's go. I'm not playing."

They responded with the sighing, listless compliance of teenage boys, and for a few brief seconds, as she held the phone and watched them trail away, she thought it was the first time in her life that anyone behaved as if she had some authority. This glimmer of triumph quickly evaporated as she saw Chase and Cully approaching along the support columns.

From out of the crowd, Choop slipped into the plastic bucket seat beside her and began wiping spots of ketchup off the table. He didn't greet her. Chase sat down across from her with a dusty wrapping of old gauze around his right hand, and Cully lingered between the edge of the table and a trash can. Lydia took a deep breath and exhaled down against her collarbone. They sat in silence for a few minutes, no one acknowledging her, until Jonah worked his way through the crowd and sank into the unsteady seat across from her.

Heavy bandages and plastic wrappers covered the lower right corner of his neck, from just above his collarbone to below his windpipe, with gauze that looked dusty and ragged. From the glassy look in his eyes, Lydia could tell he was taking huge amounts of painkillers, and this altered his voice into the deliberate, overenunciated pace of a lecturing drunk. No matter how many back-alley doctors had sewn and patched up his neck, Lydia thought it was only by sheer luck that he could have survived, the combination of a cheap 9 mm range bullet and an amateur shot that missed his arteries by a fraction of an inch. She was sorry for him as he struggled to speak in his usual businesslike tone.

He said, "I can't think of any worse hell than a mall the week before Christmas." His breathing was strained; he took a napkin and wiped his mouth.

Cully said, "They're not doing well, man. Retail is way down."

"You get anything for me, Lydia?"

On the lunch table, Jonah began unpacking her shopping bags and tearing through the wrapped presents, the tie for her father, the bracelets in small blue boxes, a hand-painted belt, and a new, empty scrapbook. Lydia watched his face closely as he tore through each gift, and, with his eyes fixed and determined, he seemed to be little more than a cruel and impulsive child. Then he looked up, smiling as if he were very pleased at the mess he'd made. He held up the tacky bracelet, twirling it around his finger, and said, "This is what you were all along, wasn't it? Just a cheap little mall rat."

Lydia glanced beyond him to see if the skaters were watching still, but she couldn't find them anywhere; they had spread off into the crowds around the portcullis door of an arcade.

"What are you looking at? Somebody's going to help you over there? Look at me," said Jonah. "Listen close. You're going to be calm, and we're going to walk out of here."

"I got somebody watching. He's going to call the police as soon as I go."

Cully said, "Go ahead and call the cops, *bitch*. We'll get to you. Protective custody or not. Just hire some crack ho to cut you open in county."

Jonah said, "We have some insurance. We've got somebody you know."

She searched his eyes and said, "Bullshit, my dad would kill you or himself—I don't believe you."

She recognized just the faintest twitch of indecision in his eyes, and she knew that he didn't have her father; so she sat up straight and smiled.

Choop had a gun buried in his sleeve, and Chase now held one up against the bottom of the table as well, cursing because his hand had scraped over stalactites of old gum. Jonah said, "You're going to get up, and walk calmly—"

Lydia ran. She climbed onto the table and vaulted to the next, leaping platform to platform over drinks and cafeteria trays, dodging through spaces in the crowd, regaining her balance each time with tiny steps. When she landed on the floor off the last table, she sprinted past the music stand and arcade and rounded a bend into the anchor department store, clambering down an escalator and into the silent, brightly lit display of bedroom and dinette sets.

Across the wide floor there was a small log cabin, raised on blocks, showing a rustic theme of tartan blankets and kerosene lamps, taxidermy and hunting trophies. Lydia crawled inside of it and scrambled behind a tinsel-covered Christmas tree, between phony presents stapled to the ground and a woodstove fire made from ruffling orange cellophane. She heard people moving toward the display, then her phone rang again. She switched it to the vibrating mode.

Someone had moved right into the entrance of the cabin display, and Lydia prepared to escape out the window behind her onto the queen-sized beds. But it was a saleswoman. She cleared back the branches of the tree and said, "Young lady—no. No. You can't play in here like this. Let's go."

"Ma'am, *please*. I'm in so much trouble."

"No, no. This isn't the place for this. Let's get up. I'm going to call security."

"Call security," said Lydia. "*Please*. Call them and tell them I'm going to die."

The woman rushed to the cash register, and, from far away, Lydia heard her describe the situation: "We've got a girl up here who's *on something*. Can you please come right now?"

Twenty yards past her, traversing through aisles of cookware, his warped reflection in the copper pans, Chase was moving slowly while reading the screen of his cell phone. Lydia figured that they were sending text messages to each other to coordinate their search. She fled from her hiding place.

Choop was already behind her, approaching.

She dashed across the floor, mounted a shelf covered with evergreen and Christmas bulbs, and ran along it, leaping off beside the escalator to shamble downhill. When her path was blocked by a woman encumbered with shopping bags, she climbed onto the middle divider and slid the rest of the way down, jarring her tailbone on a metal bump, finally landing on a floor of mannequins decked out in gangsta clothes.

She traversed the aisles, back to the main body of the mall, where she realized how organized Jonah's crew had been. After spotting Tito, who had obviously been watching from a distance earlier, at the base of the far escalators, she saw Cully and Jonah hovering for an ambush around the exits.

She could think of nothing but getting security to haul her out of here—maybe to a back room where they would threaten to call her parents.

So she ran ahead and knocked bracelets off the racks of a kiosk, pushing through the browsers, and moving to a central, sunken area of blue and white tile, where she stepped into the fountain and stood in ankle-deep water, turning in circles as a crowd gathered to watch. "Security!" she shouted. "Help me! *Please*. Somebody!"

The shoppers, many of whom were lined up with children for a visit with a mall Santa, began trailing backward away from her, and the more she cried for help, the more mothers guarded their kids. The rubberneckers hung far away around plants and store thresholds, until her desperation seemed to have created the largest open space in the mall.

Out of the perimeter of the crowd came a man with his head down, wearing a ball cap and a store uniform, and he swiftly stomped through the shallow water and grabbed her. He was calling to everyone that it was all right; it was not until she had walked a dozen steps with him toward the exits that she realized it was Iván. He whispered, "Walk with me or this is going to get even uglier."

"You're my friend," she said as he worked a gun into her side. Lydia turned and began screaming, but he picked her up and carried her, kicking and fighting, through a panel of fire doors into the parking garage.

From farther down the ramp, Tito yelled that security was coming, released finally from an orchestrated distraction across the mall. They needed to move fast. They were frantic as they tried to force her into a white rental car. She fought and splayed her legs until Tito came up behind, sniffled with a heavy cold, and shouted, "Fuck this." As four men held her writhing arms and legs, Tito punched straight down through her face, stunning her. They threw her collapsed body into the backseat. She felt blood coming from her nose and she covered her face as if she expected a boot heel or another fist.

In seconds they were screeching out of the garage, and from her spot in the back, collapsed against Chase's knees, she saw Choop hand an envelope to the parking lot attendant from the driver's window. Jonah leaned across and said, "There's the rest of your tip. Remember—you didn't see shit." There was another car pulling through behind them, and in the confusion of whipping turns and accelerations, the landscape from her view was only passing phone wires and empty sky.

She heard no sirens. She saw a few red streetlights, and she felt only a series of right turns throwing her head into the door. There was a gusting rise of speed as they merged onto the interstate. Her cheek was swelling. From her crumpled position on the floor she saw cirrus clouds and signs passing overhead that indicated they were heading west. The men were calm, talking about directions. Jonah made a call to the trailing car, asking if they had all the tools. Time stretched out and slowed, and Lydia started to cry.

She looked through tears at the sand-swept horizon, whispering, "Please, Jonah, please." She whispered *please* a hundred times, and finally added, "I'll go away. I'll go away forever."

"I know you will," said Jonah.

A cell phone was ringing incessantly and no one could find it.

Jonah checked his, listened for Choop's, and put his ear toward Lydia. He started to laugh finally and said, "The fucking sponsor."

Jonah opened the glove compartment and dug through papers and notes. He found the phone, answered, and listened for a moment. "Who is this? I know. Who are *you*?"

He hung up and shook his head. Then he twisted around to look at Lydia, and he said, "Somebody just called to tell me my *own* license plate number. Friend of yours?"

Lydia stared up at him with her mouth open.

He said, "You don't think my people can go through a crime scene and find a few names and addresses? Your dad's been calling this AA piece of shit for days now. We had him the whole time—got his address out of the wrecked trailer."

Chase laughed and said, "Tell her."

"This dude was like a cult member," said Jonah. "Wouldn't talk, wouldn't say a thing—going on and on about his *code*. Lost three toes and his kneecap before he started talking, and then Chase had the idea: Get him fucked up. You ever see an ex-alkie take shots with a gun to his head? He looked like he was killing his own son. And then, you know what? He got a little too moralistic for me—I lost my temper. I've been under a lot of stress, Lydia, and I just vented on him a little bit. He didn't last long."

Jonah leaned all the way back into the space between seats to talk to her again, twisting, as if he could coil around the seat. Her phone buzzed against her leg. Jonah said, "This shit out here—these alkali flats—it's all full of bodies anyway. All the smuggling routes. You got vultures and rats and coyotes, a whole little ecosystem feeding off of dead people who tried to sneak across the border. You're not the top of the food chain out here, Lydia. You're just blood and water and bones. But I'll tell you something: That asshole friend of your father's was lucky. It may not be a Christian burial, but I'm sure he'll be at the next AA meeting in heaven. You? You got a long afternoon still ahead of you."

Kirby's phone began ringing again, and they all laughed. Jonah answered, still giving a labored chuckle that sounded more wincing than amused. "Good, it's you. The old redneck," he said. "I'm your new *sponsor*. Here's some advice: Drink up."

eighteen

When Link returned to the mall that afternoon, there was a patrol car idling in front of the main entrance, where an officer was talking to a saleswoman, along with four boys as they fidgeted on their skateboards. Link asked what had happened. At first, he was alarmed that the cop addressed him so courteously, believing it must be a bad sign. But then he remembered his own uniform—the monkey suit, the clean-shaven face, and the tie around his throat—and he marveled at the effect. From his tone, the officer seemed to have already spent a long time piecing together a story. A girl had leapt into the fountain and made a scene, high on something, until her friends calmed her down and carried her out of the mall. He didn't believe it to be much more significant than that.

When Link asked how he knew they were her friends, the officer said that numerous witnesses had seen them together in the food court.

Calmly, Link told the cop that the girl had been abducted. The police needed to get a description of the car and put out an APB.

The officer stared at him for a while with his mouth open, but then radioed to another unit in the parking garage, from where a muffled voice responded that the attendant hadn't seen anything out of the ordinary. The teenage boys had agreed with Link, claiming that she was trying to get away from "some stalker dude," but, as they skateboarded in circles and hit each other, they seemed the least credible witnesses in the mall.

"If you're not going to deal with this," Link said to the officer, "then get back on the radio and find somebody who will."

"Sir? We're looking into that possibility. We're talking to everyone who saw anything. Did you know this girl?"

Link didn't answer, and it was amazing how long the cop went without losing his patience. He was a young kid himself, with his hat off and a touch of sunburn under his crew cut, and he had slow, trusting eyes that craved procedure. Link finally shook his head and walked away, accelerating through the glass doors.

He was light-headed and his fingertips were tingling, but he avoided drawing any conclusions. If this was a disaster, he couldn't look at it yet. The air inside the mall was artificially cool and crisp, like another climate, and all around him the steel railings and shining glass looked as sterile as a hospital. He turned into a clothing store, where a few shoppers roamed amid the aisles, and he rushed to the front counter. Taking the phone from beside the cash register, he tried to call Lydia's cell, then began dialing Kirby's number, knowing but refusing to formulate the thought. When the salesgirl came to protest, he simply put his finger to his lips and said, "My wife just had a baby."

The phone rang through until a strange voice answered. While looking up past the track lights and a steel staircase to a window striped with clouds, Link knew they had found Kirby, and the thought filled him with such anger and disgust he felt as if he'd just emerged from a long, violent blackout. He steadied himself against the counter and watched the salesgirl mouth the word, "Congratulations."

The man on the line told him to start drinking again. His voice was crushed and airless, as if he were speaking between coughs. Jonah asked, "You're not going to say anything about your friend, huh? You figure I'm just the answering service."

The salesgirl gestured that it was okay for him to continue, then drifted away toward a customer. Link waited and said, "You're going to pay worse than you know, motherfucker. Now just tell me where my daughter's at."

"The old biker," said the voice. "I've heard a lot of stories about you."

There were a few shoppers milling around the counter, so Link picked up the phone and moved a few paces away, as far as the cord would reach. He stopped beside a ladder that rested against a high wall of shelved jeans. "You're the guy I want, right?" the voice asked. "Is this you?"

"Yeah, I'm the guy. Nice work." The reception was spotty, and Link could hear rushing air and other murmuring voices. He thought he heard Lydia call him from the background.

"I want to talk to her," said Link. "Put her on the phone."

"No, I don't think that's going to happen."

Never before had Link experienced the kind of hatred he felt for this voice on the phone, not in prison, not in the hospital, not for murders or betrayals: His mouth went dry and his eyeballs stung; his palms dampened and his skin bristled. The intensity of the feeling muddied his thoughts, and for a while he could only listen to the kid's strained breathing.

The salesgirl was folding sweatshirts behind Link, so he moved forward, putting his head down into a cubicle of jeans, and whispered, "I'm going to say it real straight to you here, kid. You're a businessman. You're a smart guy. I think you're going to know a good deal when you hear one."

"Oh, Jesus," he said, exasperated. "Here comes the pitch."

"I'm going to make you a trade. You come back and get me, and you let her go. Just listen, don't hang up. I'm going to tell you why this is the right thing to do—from your standpoint."

"Enlighten me."

"I know twice as much as Lydia does. I know all about your business—and I know exactly who to talk to over your head. I know the houses from Culver City to Valencia, man, and I figure you skimmed—what?—about a hundred or two off every load. I won't go to the cops, buddy; I'll go to the shot callers. I'll get in touch with the cell heads, L.A. and Orange County; and if I have to, I can talk to the AFO directly. I'm not a big man here, but I did a lot of time and made some friends over the years, and I got people who can get me through the door. They'll be real interested in solving this problem."

There was a windy pause on the line, until finally he said, "Don't threaten me with something like that, old man. I know my situation better than you do. Besides, we just killed your daughter about fifteen minutes ago. She's already dead."

"No, you didn't," said Link. "If you did, then it's easy: We're both dead men. I got no fear of dying, kid, and I hope you're the same. You better hope you can trust those idiots around you, because they're going to have to stay loyal for years. And while you run out of money, there'll be a good bounty on your head. And let me tell you something: You might stay alive for a month or so, but wherever you go on earth, these people are going to find you. *I'll* find you. I'll offer my services for free. You can do it like that, or you come back and get me. Clean up the mess now, while you still can."

"You know what? I'm amazed. After everything your daughter hoped about you, you really are just another stupid biker. Do you honestly think I'd fall for this shit?"

"It's a simple trade. You tell me where you want me to be. I'll meet you anyplace out there in the desert—so long as we can make a deal. Then you take me and you let her go. You set up the meeting place, you control the situation. How could I do anything but follow my word?"

"And why would you trust me? I could just kill both of you."

"I don't trust you, but I'll tell you why you're not going to do that. Because this is personal with Lydia. You don't want to kill her; you want to hurt her. You want her to suffer for what she did. I know you, man. I know all about you. You want her to see what you see. You want that kid to *get it*—and it sounds like that's all you ever wanted from the beginning. And you know what? Killing her won't do a damn thing. You'll be angrier afterward; you'll feel worse than before. No, you make her watch me go down. Whatever you meant for her, you go ahead and do it to me. Mark my words—she walks away and she's no danger to you. She'll remember, and that's how the professionals do it. They let one person get away, so they can build the legend. You make her carry this for the rest of her life. Watching her father die. You know what that's like, kid. Right?"

"What the fuck are you talking about now?"

"Like I said, I know who to talk to."

Through the crackling reception, Link could hear Jonah talking to someone else in the car, then he said into the receiver, "If I gave you a meeting place—it would be just *you*. If you tried to bring anybody, or do anything unexpected . . ."

"Of course."

The manager was approaching Link across the store, trying to get him off the phone. The salesgirl interrupted, and Link could hear her excitement as she retold the story about his wife in delivery. Link glimpsed the manager's face, however, and saw that he was far more skeptical. He stopped beside a table of military fatigues and said, "Sir, we don't allow this phone to be used by customers under any circumstances. . . ."

Jonah said, "Give me a number where I can call you back. We're going to find a place to meet."

Link looked down at the phone, then at the manager, and asked, "What's the number here? It's an emergency."

"Sir, this is not a public phone. There's a pay phone by the restrooms."

"Is it a boy or a girl?" asked the salesgirl, drifting away down an aisle.

"A girl," said Link. He pulled out a wad of cash from his pocket, a few hundreds along with a mess of tens and twenties, and he stuffed them into the shirt pocket of the manager, who looked down, flabbergasted. "I don't have any cigars," said Link. "So buy yourself a pack of Cubans. Now what's the fucking *number*?"

The Impala and the white rental car drove past the sand dunes and headed northeast along a dimming horizon, following a highway so desolate that

there were soon no longer any ranch fences to block the migrating tumbleweed. Lydia sat upright now, her wrists duct-taped together and her
hands in a praying formation, staring out the window with a detached, exhausted feeling, as if she were watching television without sound. She had
been crying for close to an hour, intermittently pleading or cursing, until
she had overheard the conversation between Jonah and her father and for-
tified herself with the idea of an extra hour or two of waiting. That time
seemed to stretch out for miles, and she found herself fixated almost hyp-
notically on shadows and formations of clouds.

On the alkali flats, the two cars turned off the highway and drove
over the crusty desert toward dark mountains in the distance. For what
must have been twenty minutes, the rental car bounced and rocked over
the rough ground, faintly uphill across the badlands, over cracked and
sloping earth that looked like a hatching eggshell. Twice the car's wheels
got stuck in trenches, but each time Choop was able to free them by re-
versing and pulling forward again.

They slowed on a stretch of flat ground, the wheels grinding like
pestles and stopping. A few hundred yards farther the ascent became
steeper, into hills of flaking shale and carved sandstone. The wind was
picking up, blowing dust across the windshield and obscuring the horizon with an auburn haze. The Impala idled just a few feet away, with its
front fender mangled and its headlight smashed. Jonah tried to call Tito
on his cell phone, but there was no longer any reception. He gestured for
Tito to roll down his window while he did the same. Leaning out, his
sculpted hair swarming out of place, Jonah hollered, "We're not going to
be able to call out here—so let's figure this out."

The six men gathered between the cars for a conference, each
squinting and grimacing into the stinging wind. Jonah's white shirt had
come untucked, inflating like a sail off his thin shoulders. He had a gun
nestled in his belt. The others gathered into a circle around him, close
enough to hear his voice over the bigger gusts, but Iván soon wandered
away toward the drainage gullies beside the car, watching his feet like a
dejected child. Choop stared away at the mountains; Tito stopped listening to sit on the hood of the Impala and pout. Lydia had not seen this

sullen behavior before. Rather than confront his brother or Iván, Jonah spoke with still more force to Chase and Cully, who nodded along. They were worn out and frayed and short with each other. It looked as if they had been on a long expedition together, filled with mishaps, and Jonah had the shrill, exasperated quality of an overwhelmed guide.

As they hollered over the wind, Lydia could hear some of the plan. Jonah wanted to draw her father to this spot in the desert, elevated enough that they could watch his approach off the highway. Then they would escort Link and Lydia to another isolated place to assure that he hadn't planned an ambush. Someone would have to drive a few miles south to where there was still cell phone reception, and relay the directions to him: "Give him the mile marker."

Next, Jonah wanted someone to wait in the Impala at the highway's edge in order to make sure that no one came along behind Link.

Lounging on the hood with his eyes closed, Tito yelled that this part of the plan was pure bullshit. Jonah grew so angry that he needed to walk a circle around the cars to calm himself.

Rolling up his sleeves, Jonah paced back to Tito. His voice was buried in the wind, but Tito was speaking loudly enough for Lydia to hear him. "Because we're going to take him to another spot, right? So if one person is waiting out there, then what are you going to do—tie him to the fucking roof, dude? There's not going to be enough room in that shit car."

"I know that, Tito! Jesus. So three of you—you, Iván, and Cully—you ride down to the highway, wait for us—"

"I'm not going with fucking Cully, dude. I'll shoot his fat fucking head off, I swear to God."

Cully said, "Fuck you, you whiny little bitch."

Jonah was so livid that he pulled out his gun, walked a few steps away, and fired twice out into the empty desert.

After pacing listlessly around the desert, kicking rocks, Iván returned to the outskirts of the discussion with Tito. He sighed and rolled his head around as Jonah stomped back, waving the gun at him.

Lydia yelled through her closed window that she had to pee, and Cully made an exaggerated crying face to her.

Iván stood directly beside Lydia's window now, motionless except for his flapping V-necked shirt. "*What* are we doing?" he asked, not seeming so much mutinous but defiant in the way of a student who refuses to pay attention. Jonah was now gesturing with the gun, reiterating his plan, emphasizing her father might have bikers waiting to surround them. "So wait down there. Then you follow us back down to the dunes, and we take care of them there."

Iván shook his head at the ground. His stubbornness had an odd, introverted quality, as if he were too ashamed to face anyone. Something had sickened him deeply over the past few days and he was a different person, all of the swagger gone. "Nah, man," he said. "I don't want to be like that."

It was the most unthreatening Lydia had ever seen Iván. All of the posturing was gone, and he seemed to hang in the air, draped with loose laundry, flapping in a stiff wind. This made it even more astonishing when Jonah lifted his pistol and shot him through the leg. Iván fell down and writhed in the dirt. As if firing were not an act of violence but dismissal, Jonah immediately turned away and began clarifying the instructions to the others. Choop lunged down and began dragging Iván to the Impala, while Chase and Cully quickly backed up Jonah by drawing their guns. Tito was shouting furiously, but he quieted down when Jonah put his gun on him. "Anybody think they're going to get out of this shit without me, they're dead fucking wrong. Now do your job, and do as you're told. *Now.*"

Choop lifted Iván into the backseat of the Impala with tenderness, then returned to his job, undaunted, nodding at Jonah's order to drive the rental car. Cully took Iván's gun, duct-taped his hands and ankles, then joined the rest in the idling white car, while Chase hollered from outside that he would make sure Tito didn't try anything stupid. Somehow, after this series of tantrums, they seemed to regain their focus. All of the bitterness between them terrified Lydia, as if even in the worst situations a person still longed for *someone* clearly in charge.

Tito gunned the engine of the Impala and fishtailed downhill with spinning tires, an automotive display of anger. The car shrank against the murky horizon until it was no more than a moving cloud of dust.

The remaining three waited with Lydia in the rental car to stay out of the gritty wind. Under the visor mirror, Jonah tried to fish out a piece of sand in his eye. The car was silent except for the whistling of air through the unsealed windows. Lydia rested her head against the glass and gave a slight humming sound.

"Don't you start in on me now," said Jonah. "I got even less patience for you."

"I didn't say anything."

There was a long silence. Beside her, Cully had taken off his shoes to pour out a few small rocks, and the car filled up with the rank smell of his feet. Lydia asked, "Does the radio work?"

"No, the radio doesn't work."

"Maybe AM radio works."

"We're not listening to the radio."

After another long silence, Lydia asked, "What are you going to do to my dad?"

Jonah twisted around to look at her, and she saw that some of the discolored gauze and bandages on his neck had accumulated more grit and dust from outside, like air filters. As if he had been rehearsing the line in his head, he told her, "You did this to yourself, Lydia. I didn't make this happen to you. You need to understand that."

Cully had been going through Lydia's purse to occupy himself, and he began unwrapping pieces of gum. She asked if she could have a piece, and he said, "Open your mouth."

"Jonah—tell him to give me a piece. I haven't eaten anything all day."

"I'm going to give it to you, bitch—just open your mouth."

She opened her lips and Cully tried to pitch the square of bubble gum into her mouth, laughing as it bounced off her chin and onto the floor. "Wait, wait—let me go again."

"Not now. It's got shit all over it."

Cully brushed off the fuzz from the floor mat, then began taking aim again. "Come on. Open."

"No."

"Then you don't get any."

"Just fucking give it to her, Cully! Jesus Christ."

She opened her mouth faintly, and Cully slapped the gum between her teeth, palming her face for a moment. His hand smelled like wet cardboard. She called him an asshole and he made a fake whimpering sound.

For ten minutes on the dashboard clock, the car was silent except for Lydia's chewing; but soon Cully began whispering to her, trying to slide the barrel of the gun between her crossed legs. Jonah watched in his mirror and didn't seem to care, and this made Lydia's eyes well up with frustration. Jonah grew angry at the sight of more tears, and he said, "Why don't you accept some fucking responsibility for once in your life. You want to see this?" He peeled back the bandages on his neck to reveal a messy patchwork of sutures and grafted skin, a seam as deep as Frankenstein's. "You did that. As far as I'm concerned, whatever happens now is fair game."

Choop pointed to something in the distance, and each of them stared ahead at a moving smudge of sand and dust, looking like a wind devil traversing the scrub.

"Fuck, he's early," said Jonah.

They each stepped out of the car and Lydia was ordered down onto her knees. Cully held his gun against the back of her head, hitting her with the barrel.

The wind had grown so strong that portions of the earth seemed to be shedding into the air. The last thin topsoil formed a spindrift along the ground. Already the light was obscure, the sun falling and turning red in the mineral haze.

When her father was visible as a speck in the distance, casting a wake of sand and debris, she could already hear the engine, sounding like an angrier and deeper wind approaching. Then the bike slowly became visible, a dim shape in the murky air, and her father was soon distinct, with a tie waving like a streamer behind him.

He stopped the bike about two hundred yards downhill, idling.

"What is this motherfucker doing?" asked Cully.

Her father stepped off the bike with his hands in the air, his clothes gusting.

"Let's go!" shouted Cully.

"Hold on," said Jonah. "He's just showing us he's not carrying."

Her father took off his jacket and waved it beneath him like a matador, then he draped it over the handlebars.

"Okay, keep going!" shouted Jonah, gesturing at his own clothes.

The jacket nearly blew away, so Link wadded it up and secured it under the kickstand. Then he loosened his tie and carefully unbuttoned his white shirt, knotting the sleeves around the handhold. He took off his tie and threaded it through the spokes. He stood up again and turned around, stripped to his undershirt, pulling out the pockets of his suit pants to show that they were empty.

"The shoes!" shouted Jonah, lifting his own and slapping them.

Link waved that he understood. He stooped down beside the bike, taking a long time to untie one of the laces, then he placed his shoes and socks against the back tire.

He walked gingerly ahead now on bare feet, hands in the air, until he was close enough that Lydia could see his heavy breathing. Jonah said, "Keep the gun on Lydia—he might still have something."

Lydia could see her father's eyes now. He was just a few feet down the road when Choop met him and frisked his pants. Lydia could read nothing on his face—no fear or plans or anger. He seemed to be in a trance.

Choop nodded that he was okay, and Jonah called down, "Let's hurry up and get them both in the car. We're going someplace else, old man. Bet you didn't think of that."

They cramped together into the backseat with Lydia flattened against the window. Cully managed to squeeze into the back alongside them, keeping his gun tight on Link. Jonah sat in the front seat, guarding Lydia; Choop drove slowly ahead down the dirt path, his gun resting on the dashboard.

As Choop steered along the drainage route between rocks and brush, Jonah began to fiddle with his cell phone. Cully peeled a strip of duct tape with his teeth while he still held the gun in one hand. Lydia had expected her father to put up a fight before getting into this cramped car, but he offered his wrists for Cully to bind, as stoic as a prisoner after last rites. As the car stopped, he put his lips against the crown of Lydia's head and whispered, "Hey, kid."

Strung with his remaining clothes, the chopper stood in the middle of the only clean pathway onto the smooth expanse of desert. Choop stepped out of the car to move it. Jonah's gun was in his lap, his head down beside the dashboard as he fussed with the antenna of his phone, all the while mumbling, "Whatever shit you try, old man—I figured it out already."

The seat belt reminder rang steadily.

Lydia saw what she thought was a gesture to her, a flicker of his index finger, pointing to the ground. He nudged his elbow into her side.

Lydia's mind was working as quickly as it would in an accident. She understood. In the corner of her eye she saw Choop grab the handlebars and lift the kickstand off the bundled jacket. She threw herself down against the passenger seat. Choop's motion pulled a trip wire, which detonated one of Preacher's claymores into a sudden splash of dirt and blood against the windshield, hurtling debris from the motorcycle like shrapnel around the car. The blast was so sudden that Cully and Jonah were thrown into a moment of confusion. The windows shattered; the air bags deployed with a gunshot sound, and the engine shut down. The burning remnants of the bike's fuel tank caught fire and cast tumbling sparks across the desert.

From her curled position, Lydia could tell that Jonah had been struck hard by the passenger-side air bag. Her father had gone straight for Cully's gun, and both men were holding it now, wrestling to keep it aimed away. At the same time, Link kicked the passenger seat just above Lydia's head, collapsing it forward. As the gun discharged, deafening Lydia, Jonah panicked and scrambled out of the car.

But her father stayed calm, almost robotic, maneuvering the pistol as Cully repeatedly hit the trigger, cutting through the remaining windows like cracked ice, puncturing the visor, the roof, and the headrests. So loud and so close, each shot seemed less like a noise than a blow to the ears. Her father dropped his leg over her, as if to shield her from the random barrage. While with one hand he pinned the gun against the edge of the driver's seat, he reeled something up from the back of his throat and slashed it across Cully's face: a razor, buried in an eraser, tied to a wisdom tooth by a string. It was a brutal prison trick that forced Cully to drop the gun and grab his bleeding eye.

But Cully realized his mistake, and, as the gun fell to the floor mat, they both grappled for it, until a shot fired and the ceiling was sprayed red.

The blood washed across the seats and over the floors; it was in Lydia's hair, syrupy thick; and, as if she had been submerged entirely in cold water, she didn't breathe or move—not until she heard her father groan, "Ah, fuck," scooping blood from his eye sockets. She realized that the bullet had gone straight up through Cully's chin.

Another series of shots came from outside.

Link opened the door and Cully's body fell partway out onto the ground, his legs still hooked over the seat.

Jonah was now stalking around the car, firing through the broken windows. Lydia caught a glimpse of him and saw how badly he was cut from the glass of the windshield. Holding his neck, he was bleeding heavily, and Lydia thought that his stitches must have pulled open in the fray. But he was firing wildly as he retreated behind a tall bluff.

Link slashed the razor through the duct tape on Lydia's hands. He was out of breath. When he tried to climb into the driver's seat past the deflating bags, he winced and grabbed at his side, falling backward again. So Lydia crawled behind the wheel and restarted the car. The wind was blowing sand and smoke through the broken windshield, and she tried to wipe the blood from her face and eyes where it stuck to her lashes.

Far downhill, she saw the Impala churning toward them. She said, "They're coming back, Dad—there's three more in the other car."

"Turn us around," he said.

She shifted into reverse and rode them uphill. Cully dragged for a few yards before dropping out the open door and rolling beneath the tires. Lydia said with her voice quivering, "*Uh,* my God, that is so fucking wrong."

Jonah emerged out of hiding and fired two shots, one shrieking through the aluminum of the passenger door, sounding like a zipper. As

Lydia craned her head around to face the path behind her, she saw her father pulling up his shirt, breathing with jolts in his chest and shoulders. She couldn't tell if the blood on his shirt was Cully's or his own. He sagged onto his side and dropped the magazine from the pistol: "What kind of gun is this thing?"

"It's a Luger or a Ruger or something," shouted Lydia. "Did he have a full mag?"

"Just about."

"Then they went shopping," she said, over the ascendant sound of reverse gear. "That means they're loaded down there."

"You got to go to a gun show for shit like this," he said quietly. "That fucking hollow-tip shit your boyfriend is firing through here—fancy motherfucker. I see why you liked him."

He examined his stomach above the belt line, where the skin looked scorched with gunpowder. Blood pooled and ran over his pants, and each time he touched the spot with his fist, there was more smeared across his fingers.

"Dad? Don't even fucking tell me you're hit."

"Keep driving."

She turned around and began accelerating over rough terrain, away from the Impala, which looked in the rearview like a tornado stirring up debris. The car bounced over ruts and trenches and sheared rocks, and at times Lydia could barely keep traction across loose shale.

Her father peered out the back window, grimacing, and said, "Your boyfriend just got in the other car."

"Stop calling him that!"

Lydia ground uphill on a wind-stripped patch of rough ground, the tires losing grip and the car swiveling, turning diagonally against the slope, until the path flattened out again. The Impala was now gaining on them along a separate route, firing from a distance.

When a shot tore through the frame beside the door, Link said, "What the fuck are they firing back there?"

After bucking over a rough stretch, Lydia found a smoother run toward the mountains and began accelerating across miles of open badlands. She could hear nothing now but the drone of the engine and something stuck under the grille, knocking rhythmically beneath them. The wind blasted into her eyes. She smelled fire and blood and dust. The light faded and became so flat that it was hard to see the dips and gouges in the desert. Headlights didn't help. It was that hour when the sky becomes the more discernible landscape, from the last lit edges of clouds to the sharp silhouettes of the mountains. Her father was suffering terribly in the backseat, his lips clenched, his arm pressed across his waist. Lydia narrowed her eyes, feeling a painful love for him that now seemed more penetrating than the fear that had bound her all afternoon. "If I could get around these guys, Dad—I'll get back to the highway—"

"I don't even know where the highway is," he said, sounding as if his lungs were full of smoke. "Hey, the bullet went right through me, kid. I just found it in the seat."

The car glanced violently off a sharp rock, and, with a sound like another gunshot, the left tire blew out. Lydia pushed hard on the accelerator and continued worming forward on the flat, but she soon came to a wide crater, stretching out across the sloped desert. She ripped off the deflated airbag and pounded on the wheel.

Ahead of them, the ground rapidly descended into shadows, down loose rocks and chipped shale into a deep, barren valley. The slope was far too steep for a car, but it looked as if a person could navigate it, riding downhill on the seat of his pants, a hundred yards or more along an unstable cliffside into the depression, which looked as if it might be the softened remains of an old detonation site. Farther down in the dimness, the crater stretched out and blurred into years of accumulated rockslides, a rough ladder of loose scree to the base of the first coal-colored foothills and the mountains beyond.

The Chevy Impala was coming right for them, throwing up a wake of dust. Its headlights flashed on. Lydia waited in a windless pocket just beneath the barricade of hills.

Her father had also been studying the slope for a few silent moments. Finally he said, "Lydia—listen to me. I'm pretty bad. This is more than a souvenir this time. Get out and start climbing down that hillside.

You got a couple minutes and I can hold these guys off you. Then you follow that crevice there, right into the mountains. Head due west, follow the last light. And keep your eyes open—"

"Dad, stop it."

"Because that's the Naval Testing Range in there—and there's going to be bombs and ordnance all over the ground. You go right through, kid, watch every step, and you're going to come out the other side of this."

"I'm not listening to you."

"And when you get out—I want you to figure out a way to get in touch with a guy in Calipatria. His name is Arturo Rios Tehada, prisoner number C-77105. Remember that number. Say it over and over. Come on. C-77105, C-77105."

"No, Dad," she said, chewing hard on her gum.

"You tell him what happened and he'll try to help you. Are you listening to me?"

The car was rising to meet them, now just a dark shape against the lit skies.

"Why are you such a pessimist, Dad?"

"That's not pessimism. That's getting you out of here. That's the most optimistic I ever been in my life. I'm ordering you, Lydia, right now: Get out and—"

"No!"

"I don't have time to argue with you!"

"Then don't argue."

"Lydia, you stubborn fucking brat—get out of the car."

"Fuck you if you think I'm leaving you here."

"I'm going to count to motherfucking *three,* and if your bony ass isn't sliding down that hill . . ." He winced, the pain of his shouting cutting through him. He held his ribs.

The Impala was right beside them now, and it drifted slowly, like a predator circling a wounded animal.

"I can still hold 'em off," said Link. *"One . . ."*

"Dad, I just told you I'm not leaving."

"Two."

"Count to a million if you want to. If you think I'm getting out of this car without you—"

"Two and a half!"

"—then you don't know me. All this time, and you never even knew me."

He stared at her across the car in the last light. Behind her the Impala gunned its engine. It was battered and filled with tumbleweed in the grille, but it sank lower on the hydraulics, as if ready to prowl slowly ahead. Link was staring into her eyes, and he must have seen something he recognized, because he nodded and handed her the gun. "All right, baby—nice to meet you. Hold them off as long as you can."

There were rifle barrels now emerging from the windows of the Impala, and Chase, his long hair in silhouette, rose up against the convertible roof to steady his gun. Lydia stared at the butt of Cully's pistol as her father offered it.

"Fuck that," she said. "Grab a seat belt."

She turned the wheel and spun the tires, heading for the ledge, focusing on a path where the eroded rim had already given out in a partial landslide. As soon as Link realized what she was trying to do, he started to laugh, until it became a wincing cough. She hit the edge and the car dropped, accelerating into the fall, jolting downhill on shifting earth and a growing rockslide. Chips of shale and sandstone gave way and bounced all around, and the dirt and dust rose up into a full avalanche around the windows. Finally the angle sharpened and Lydia regained control over the buried wheels, steering and attempting to point downhill on a plummeting trail over twisted roots and dislodging rocks.

"Keep straight," said Link, holding on, yelling over the hailstorm against the car. "We turn sideways, we're rolling."

Lydia blew a bubble and snapped it down. She flew back and forth against the wheel. At one point the car dropped so hard onto its front tires she thought they were about to flip end over end, but she came off the landing, skipping diagonally, and regaining some tiny bit of control by accelerating and turning back into the landslide.

"Don't brake," said her father.

All four tires were blown and shredded now, and she was spinning the rims, trying to control the car like a sled in the growing force of earth. But suddenly the ground sank entirely, a whole portion of the slope giving way, and the car tipped onto its side and rolled, crushing the roof against their heads. The collapsing hillside swallowed them, so that instead of tumbling they slid downhill as dirt rushed through the windows until—at last—they came to rest, buried in rocks and dust.

"Dad?"

"I'm here," he said from the backseat, kicking aside stones.

"Oh my God, that was awesome! Do you believe that? We just took half the mountain down with us."

"Calm down. We need to dig out of here."

Within moments, she was digging in the twilight around the overturned car, keeping her eye on the Impala high above them. She could see the deep groove where they had torn down the hillside, a geologic sampling from the shale to the pinkish granite below, and it now looked even more difficult for anyone to follow them in the diminished light and down the shaky aftermath of the landslide. The shadows along the ridge were pacing back and forth like sentries on a high wall.

For a few minutes, Lydia was thrilled with herself for making the plunge, but this feeling evaporated as soon as she began helping her father out the open window. She realized from the tension in his body and the awkwardness of his movements that he was hurt worse than she had thought. He was shivering. Lydia wasn't strong enough to lift him, only to help him crawl backward onto the silt at the bottom of the ravine.

Someone above fired a shot that sparked off the axle of the overturned car.

Link couldn't stand, and he resisted her arms, seeming angry at first, until she understood that it was only a sharp reaction to the pain. She took the gun from him and fired back at the ridge. The shadows moved back behind the car. Far above, Jonah was moving with dizzy, injured paces, and she wondered if one of the random shots in the car hadn't grazed him earlier.

Then Lydia helped her father to his feet, and supported much of his

weight as he limped ahead along the softening ground. He had been hit
in the stomach, and he couldn't straighten his legs. Lydia needed to plant
her feet and fight with all her weight to keep him upright.

Finally they found a barricade of sticks and logs, piled together from
the runoff of some distant storm. Her father was gasping for air, sweating through his clothes. Lydia smelled the wound on him now, sweet and
metallic. As she rested him against the thicket, he said, "In about . . . ten
minutes," coughing and grimacing, "it'll be too dark for them to see us.
Then we got to head deeper in. Are they coming down?"

"I don't know," she said, peeking out at the cliff. "One or two of
them might. I know all four won't. Jonah looks hurt."

"Oh, shit," he said. "I could sure use a fucking drink. What are the
odds of me getting another sponsor now?"

Lydia covered her face, sniffed hard, and broke into a deep, emo-
tional laughter. She tried to control herself, and the sound, wailing and
stricken, was almost like tears. "You are such an *asshole*," she said.

"Well, he was a good man. I don't give a fuck about heaven, 'cept for
guys like that."

Lydia turned somber now, breathing hard and steady, and she whispered, "I got my cell phone, Dad. As soon as it's dark, we could get up on
top of one of those hills and get you help. I swear to God—"

"Come on, kid. There's no reception for miles."

For a long time, Tito stood on the ridge, howling like a wolf and firing off rounds. Lydia glanced around the rocks and saw that the Chevy's
headlights were now on, and the car was backing away from the edge.
Maybe Jonah was hurt badly enough that they were pulling away; but
she worried that they would regroup and come from another direction.
She told her father that they were pulling back, and he said, "They're
driving right into an ambush."

"Dad?"

"Crazy old buddy of mine, Count, if he timed it right. He was going
to call in an accident right there at the mile marker. A Harley smashed
into a rental car. That's practically sacrilegious, but he promised me and I
trust him. He just said, *Good to have you back, old man*."

They were quiet for a while, listening for sounds along the rocks. Windless and clear, the night turned cold. They heard nothing. The world reduced to a plot of sandy earth and the starlight above. Link was shivering and Lydia tried to warm him by nuzzling close, but it was too painful and he jerked away. At this, Lydia began to cry quietly, mostly from fear. In the darkness she felt him place his hand onto her hair, working through it, his coarse thumb against her forehead. He grabbed her roughly but tenderly by the back of the neck, as if picking up a kitten, and he said, "Hey. Don't spend one second of your life regretting this, kid. I wasn't anything but dirt until you came along. You stay alive, you stay tough. Promise. Because I never knew a thing until right now. You saved *more* than my life, kid. And you better damn well remember that—or you never knew me either."

nineteen

Lydia didn't sleep that night, down beneath the cover on the streambed—but rather she kept the gun in her lap and listened for any sound. Sometime after the moon rose, she saw flashes of light along the hills, which were followed by deep, seismic blasts. Dark fighter jets cut overhead, and fireworks thudded around the Chocolate Mountains in flurries, until it was silent again.

Her father was barely strong enough to speak, but he wasn't asleep either. At one point he whispered, "Bunker busters."

His mouth was parched, and she promised him that she would find water as soon as the sun rose. The air was close to freezing, but the sand was still warm, having retained some heat from the lost sun. So Lydia piled it over her father's arms and legs, burying him like a child playing at the beach.

He said, "Good girl."

He fell asleep for a while, breathing with a rattle in his chest.

This was the first time that Lydia was hopeful, believing that if the wound sealed itself, he might be able to rise in the morning and climb with her out of the ravine. But this strand of optimism frightened her, as if she had suddenly realized there was farther to fall. She leaned over him, smelling blood and fever, touching his damp hair as if he were an infant.

A while later, she heard rocks clattering down the slope. It had been so still that each sound was now amplified: a cracking stick, a rockslide, light footsteps and panting. She pulled back the slide on the gun. Was it Chase or Tito? It sounded like a large group.

Then she heard an unearthly warbling noise, like some hatching brood of hungry animals, and she realized that it was a pack of coyotes in the darkness. Their barks were high-pitched, like nothing she had expected. They were sniffing aggressively around the sticks and branches, and one of them began rooting through the sand piles around her father. They smelled blood. Lydia rose to her feet and shooed them away, but they kept assembling under the stark moonlight—strange, skulking animals, ratty and half starved. When she fired the gun into the air, they scattered, yelping and hiccupping to each other.

She knelt beside her father and saw that he was still breathing. She touched his forehead and was alarmed by how terribly hot and damp he was in the cold air. She could see the ghost of his breath, faintly luminous in the moonlight. Lying down, she rested against him, wiggling her shoulders, and this time he didn't flinch in pain.

She was so thirsty and hungry that her insides felt scraped and hollow.

She dozed, and when she woke a few hours later she could feel that the sand packed around her father had turned cold. Shocked by the change, she scrambled a few feet away and in the pale light she looked back at him. "No, Dad. *Come on.*"

For a long time she rocked, with her face in her cupped hands, afraid to look at him. When the light returned, tracing the mountaintops and coloring a few blurred jet trails overhead, she sat down beside him.

He had been awake when he died. Now he stared up at the sky, eyes glassy and lighter than she remembered, sand and dried blood on the new gray stubble forming on his cheeks, his lips hovering in a shape as if he were about to whistle. He was buried in shallow sand, over his suit pants, across his bare arms, which were faintly outstretched as if for the beginning of a snow angel.

Lydia felt numb and was unable to cry. She knew that she couldn't get him out of this ravine, but she couldn't stand the idea of leaving him this way. She loathed those coyotes, filthy and savage, and thought of them now as if they had been evil spirits. All that morning before the first clear light, she dug in the sand of the arroyo, cracking her fingers and bleeding from under the nails. She was still digging when the sun rose high overhead and roasted down onto her bare neck. She checked the ridge above and saw that the Impala had gone, and she returned and continued gouging up handfuls of silt, beginning to feel faint moisture below. Deeper still, there was a puddle forming. She cupped it and drank the water, her mouth full of sand.

She dug for hours that afternoon, and finally buried her father, choking as she covered him with silt and earth. Afterward, she marked the spot with black rocks, hoping that she could find it someday, return and reclaim him, put him properly into the ground. She didn't know if he was a real Christian; she didn't know if he would care. But she thought now that there was a reason for doing what was supposed to be done—every grave, she thought, was a barricade against the wilderness, against this chaos and solitude. Her throat was burning and her eyes stung, and she lay down on the soft ground, baking in the heat.

She tried to imagine what he would say to her now: He would yell at her; he would tell her to get moving. So she rose and struggled toward the back of the chasm, climbing up scree and loose granite, holding on to roots and weeds, and finally emerging onto the broken, undulating terrain that led into the Chocolate Mountains.

It was slow going. Dehydrated and sunburned, she struggled ahead in the slanted light to where the shade was cold and dry. The land was a vast cracked stretch of gray and pink mountains and she traversed it uphill into the first dim canyons. At her feet, like her father had said, she saw steel and shrapnel, the torn casings of bombs, the scattered debris of crushed mountains.

She climbed a narrow ridge along a mountain, and when she reached the top, she was demoralized by the view: She had gone the wrong way. The landscape unfolded in all directions, nothing but carved channels through foothills and juts of striped peaks, spanning out like rough seas. She continued downhill in the shade, dizzy, with a ghostlike feeling of disconnection. She began to feel far away from her shambling feet, watching the elongating arrow of her shadow down the rocks.

When night came, it was frigid cold. She woke several times from a delirious sleep, feeling as if someone had touched or sniffed her. The air was stinging. She heard animals or footsteps, thousands of yards away, projected to her in the motionless air.

The next morning she woke and was too weak to stand. Her head throbbed, her eyelids were swollen, her mouth was pasted shut. The light was painful on her pupils, and she worried that she had burned them and blinded herself. She was still trembling from exposure to the cold, and she lay on the rocks for a long time, gathering heat like a reptile. She felt like crying, but no tears came; and when she sat up, she began dry heaving, pulling up nothing but acid and bile. She was being yanked inside out. She rose and tried to walk farther, hoping to find some road or feature in the distance. But there was more gravity holding her in place than impelling her forward. Her legs were stiff; her knees locked; she grew so frustrated that she lay down on a patch of dust beneath the hard sun.

She made a circle in the sand and waited inside it, pretending that it was the entire world and that she'd never have to leave. The sun cooked down on her, and she tasted blood from her cracked lips. She had been hurt in her life, here and there, but now something had overpowered her, and she was surrendering to the grief, allowing it to grab her and flatten her to the ground. It had sapped every thought of tomorrow or the world beyond these mountains; it was drying her out and turning her bones to chalk. She was desolate, and she hated herself like a traitor.

She would not ask to be saved or forgiven, but decided that she deserved to die in this circle, punished, bled from under her nails. She would suffer because she had believed only in suffering; she would hurt because she had craved it like the truth. What had she done wrong, why was she dying? Her skin was peeling under the sun, her mouth was coarse with thirst; but her mind needed a reason. She couldn't find any clear ideas, but she raced across her fractured memory, knowing only that she had expected something more here in the emptiness, an epiphany—something beautiful and strange, some tiny kernel of truth like the slivers of quartz that formed around the impact sites of meteors or detonations. A diamond condensed out of millennia of pressure; a pearl grown from filtered poison—everything prized was the by-product of destruction; and Lydia had believed that true agony should leave something denser than these sore bones, something heavy and holy. But her father was gone, and she lay in the dust, not fifteen miles away. There was nothing in this. Pain was as common as the dirt. And as she held her own body and fell asleep, she missed her father, and said out loud, "I'm sorry, Dad."

The night came, frost over a sunburn, and her muscles were rioting at the change. She began to sweat out her last water, passing through a brutal fever and tasting blood and salt on her lips. She closed her eyes and saw herself as a small girl, riding along the gusting air with her father, then playing in a trimmed backyard among the oleander hedges, alone beneath a hazy sky. Oleanders were poisonous, she knew—and she had been tempted to chew on them. She wasn't sure if she had done this or not. She saw her mother sitting in a dim bedroom, watching old movies on television, still in her pajamas in the late afternoon, and for some reason this image terrified her. *It's so easy to lose everything,* she whispered to herself, as she faced the sky. She was speaking to the open air, and she began to use Spanish. She said, *"Ayúdame, ayúdame,"* and she was speaking to Marianna, and she was nothing but a lonely little girl who was afraid of leaving another house at midnight. *"Tengo sed,* Marianna."

There was a woman above her, framed by starlight.

Lydia watched the figure, a distant hallucination, but then she was startled to feel real hands, warm and damp, pressing against her face. There were men speaking in Spanish in the darkness all around her, chattering, calling over each other.

"*¿Está muerta?*"

"*No,*" said the woman above her. "*Y habla español.*"

Someone asked something from farther down the path, and the woman responded sternly, "*No. Americana. Una gringuita.*"

The woman continued petting through her hair, and someone lifted Lydia's head and propped it up with a blanket. She felt water pushed against her lips, and she heard an argument, each voice coming from different elevations along the dark path. Lydia began to awaken, feeling the cool foreign stream of liquid down her throat. She coughed and gagged. She could tell now in the collection of shadows that they were immigrants, moving along a coyote trail between checkpoints. Someone in the group was angry, but the others silenced him. When Lydia couldn't hold down the water, the woman wet her fingertips and placed them in Lydia's mouth, and she gripped them and drank the moisture like a suckling child.

"Drink," said the woman. "Okay."

Lydia closed her eyes in the crowd of passing legs, scraping trousers.

When she sat up, it was morning. She thought for a moment that the episode had been a dream—but beside her sat two bottles of water and a small plastic bag weighing down a map that fluttered in the wind. She took the water, drank. She cried violently. In the bag there were raisins, peanuts, and a handful of crackers. She cried and said thank you to the thin air; and she thought that it would take a solid lifetime to pay back the kindness. She drank more swallows of water, then she placed the cracker on her tongue, feeling it dissolve like a wafer.

Finally she stood and faced the horizon, and figured that anyone deserved a miracle, as long as they still had the capacity to recognize it. No, she thought, as she treaded downhill—no reward, no flash of light, no glittering epiphany: Just carry on, for the lives behind us and the lives beyond. And she felt tough and hopeful for a moment, figuring there might be only some thirty thousand paces from here to an inland sea, and each one she could imagine as a lifetime. "Straight ahead, straight ahead." And as she walked, she nearly sang to herself over the renewed rhythm of her footsteps, "I see, I see, I see." She repeated it until it was only a sound, evolving: "I see, *sí, sí,* C-77, C-77105. Calipatria. Calipatria. Cali-*patria.*"

Lydia & Ursula
epilogue

twenty

T he intercepted California DOC memorandum read as follows:

On February 16, 2001, Corrections Officers in Corcoran
State Penitentiary reported the death of Jonah Pincerna, who
was awaiting trial on charges of drug trafficking and murder.
Pincerna had been arrested on weapons charges two months
earlier in the deserts of Southeastern California, after an
anonymous call about a hit-and-run accident along an unmarked ranch road. He was transferred in January from the
County Facility in San Diego.

The execution-style hit on Pincerna indicated a retaliation
from cartel members, possibly for an agreement to testify
against his suppliers. But, weeks after the assassination, members of a prison gang were heard bragging about the murder.

Officials now believe that the murder may have been

ordered by high-ranking members of the Mexican Mafia ("Eme"), possibly as part of an ongoing dispute with the AFO. A shot caller in La Eme, currently serving a life sentence at the Calipatria State Facility, was questioned in connection. He refused to cooperate.

At the bottom of the page, someone had scribbled this note:

Dear L,

It's taken care of. Here's more for your scrapbook. Keep your head up now, stay tough, stay clean, and don't let me ever hear of any trouble again, or I'll whip your ass myself. Make your old man proud. He was an ignorant redneck in a lot of ways, but in my book he was okay.

A.R.T.
Calipatria.

Ursula handed Lydia the manila envelope, across the table, as they met for lunch on the patio of a seaside restaurant. She explained that she had no idea why it had been addressed "care of Ursula Carson." Because the opening was torn and retaped, Lydia could tell that her mother had read through the contents—an investigation report on the killings in Topanga, her father's parole report, the Department of Corrections memorandum about Jonah's death—but Lydia refused to explain.

Ursula said, "I was so startled to get your call, Lydia. I thought I'd never hear from you again—and I just rushed out of the house. Hardly had a chance to get ready."

Lydia only wanted her mother to know that she was safe. She explained that she rarely came back to Southern California, but that she'd like to make it a habit of meeting now and then. All the while she spoke, she noticed how her mother was staring at her new short hair, cut into crisp shards, as if looking for an answer in Lydia's changed appearance. Over the past six months, Lydia had gained back all of her weight. Her mother seemed to view this critically, commenting, "You look healthier than when you *left*."

Lydia wouldn't allow herself to be provoked. She told her mother that she was still angry sometimes, but that she was finding better ways to express it than tearing up houses, cutting herself or throwing tantrums. She only said that she'd had a difficult six months, but that she was recovering, learning to take care of herself, staying clean, and living up north with new plans. Her future was a tangible thing to her now. She explained to her mother that she had stopped reacting to day-to-day crises, because she had an image of herself far ahead, grown and wise. She stayed calm and worked hard in order to someday meet that mature woman.

Lydia watched a seagull perched beside the table, coveting her French fries, when her mother reached over and adjusted a strand of Lydia's hair. "Are you cutting your own hair now?"

Lydia didn't answer this, instead waiting for her mother to continue. She listened as Ursula talked about Chloe's divorcing parents, and Lydia's stepfather, who was being promoted in his firm in Century City; she described her volunteer work with an organization that was trying to stop worldwide abuse of women. Lydia nodded, listening distractedly while she watched her mother's stiff posture and lavish hand gestures. She felt as if she'd never before looked closely at the woman. Ursula was talking as if Lydia were a stranger, pulling away further with each grandiose comment about her busy days in a house beyond those shady hills overhead, through the canyons, past the bluffs.

All at once, Lydia felt intensely lonely. She grieved for her father, and fantasized about driving down into the desert again to find the rusted scraps of his Harley. Maybe she'd put them back together and learn to ride that thing. Like this, piece by piece, maybe she'd learn to endure the quiet melancholy of her new life. Ursula kept on about the bridal shower of a woman Lydia barely knew, then how she planned to remodel her living room, until Lydia couldn't stand the tone of the conversation: Her mother was so chipper that she seemed delusional.

As a dozen seagulls now gathered around the table, waiting for a chance to lunge ahead and raid the plates, Ursula had moved on to

describe her troubles with a contractor. Whatever years of disappoint-
ment and drama in her life, they seemed to have accumulated only into
this desperation to appear untouched. Lydia hurt for her, but couldn't
speak over the flow of words. Her mother's face was youthful, so pre-
served that no one could have ever guessed at her struggles. She had
been run down, left, beaten, and scared—and yet those memories were
buried under a thick layer of gossip and plans. Lydia wanted to look
down the well of her mother's pupils and see all of those moments in
which they fled together; and she wished that she could have held that
terrified woman one last time.

But, as Ursula picked up a glass of Chardonnay that caught the fading light, Lydia could tell from her tight mouth and her shifting eyes that
the façade was a religion now, and no amount of anger or shouting or
kicking would bring it down. So Lydia reached across the table, over the
bread and water and wine, and touched her mother on the corner of her
mouth, slightly smudging her lipstick. Ursula flinched as if a snake had
sprung at her; but Lydia softened her face and tilted her head, and said,
"*Mom*, it's okay. We're going to be fine."

As Lydia stood, scaring off the seagulls, who lifted up on the breeze
and slanted off over the beach, she put her hand on her mother's shoulder, felt it tighten, and said, "Someday you'll *know* me, Mom. And I'm
getting better. It's raining every day where I live—but I'm dry. I've got
new friends, a new place, and all my little dreams. Dad would have been
happy. Because I'm no punk and I'm no pushover. Every day I wake up
and say here's another chance, kid: Here's another chance to pay him
back. I don't need anybody to tell me who I am anymore, Mom. I'm a
real tough girl nowadays."

Lydia grabbed the check, threw a wad of small bills down for her
share, then glanced up at her mother's frightened eyes. Ursula seemed to
think she was listening to the speech of a madwoman, and this made her
glance away at the glare off the sea, to where three children were playing
in the tide, throwing a stick to a dog.

"In fact," said Lydia, squinting into the light, "I'm the toughest bitch
you ever saw."

WITHDRAWN MAR 2005